Aaron Hill has it all—athletic good looks and the many privileges of a star quarterback. His Sundays are spent playing NFL football in front of a televised audience of millions. But Aaron's about to receive an unexpected handoff, one that will give him a whole new view of his self-centered life.

Derrick Anderson is a family man who volunteers his time with foster kids while sustaining a long career as a pro football player. But now he's looking for a miracle. He must act as team mentor while still striving for the one thing that matters most this season—keeping a promise he made years ago.

Megan Gunn works two jobs and spends her spare time helping at the youth center. Much of what she does, she does for the one boy for whom she is everything—a foster child whose dying mother left him in Megan's care. Now she wants to adopt him, but one obstacle stands in the way. Her foster son, Cory, is convinced that 49ers quarterback Aaron Hill is his father.

Two men and the game they love. A woman with a heart for the lonely and lost, and a boy who believes the impossible. Thrown together in a season of self-discovery, they're about to learn lessons in character and grace, love and sacrifice.

Because in the end, life isn't defined by what takes place on the first day of the week, but by how we live it between Sundays.

Other Life-Changing Fiction™ by Karen Kingsbury

September 11 Series

Beyond Tuesday Morning
One Tuesday Morning

Stand-Alone Titles

Oceans Apart
Even Now
Ever After
Where Yesterday Lives
When Joy Came to Stay
On Every Side
Divine

Cody Gunner Series

A Thousand Tomorrows
Just Beyond the Clouds

Redemption Series

Redemption
Remember
Return
Rejoice
Reunion

Firstborn Series

Fame
Forgiven
Found
Family
Forever

Sunrise Series

Sunrise
Summer
Someday (spring 2008)

Red Gloves Series

Gideon's Gift
Maggie's Miracle
Sarah's Song
Hannah's Hope

Forever Faithful Series

Waiting for Morning
Moment of Weakness
Halfway to Forever

Women of Faith Fiction Series

A Time to Dance
A Time to Embrace

Children's Titles

Let Me Hold You Longer
Let's Go on a Mommy Date
(spring 2008)

Miracle Collections

A Treasury of Christmas Miracles
A Treasury of Miracles for Women
A Treasury of Miracles for Teens
A Treasury of Miracles for Friends
A Treasury of Adoption Miracles

Gift Books

Stay Close Little Girl
Be Safe Little Boy

www.KarenKingsbury.com

KAREN
KINGSBURY

BETWEEN
SUNDAYS

ZONDERVAN.com/
AUTHORTRACKER
follow your favorite authors

We want to hear from you. Please send your comments about this book to us in care of zreview@zondervan.com. Thank you.

ZONDERVAN®

Between Sundays
Copyright © 2007 by Karen Kingsbury

This title is also available as a Zondervan ebook product.
Visit www.zondervan.com/ebooks for more information.

This title is also available as a Zondervan audio product.
Visit www.zondervan.com/audiopages for more information.

Requests for information should be addressed to:

Zondervan, *Grand Rapids, Michigan* 49530

ISBN-10: 0-310-28093-1
ISBN-13: 978-0-310-28093-4

International Trade Paper Edition

Interior design by Michelle Espinoza

Printed in the United States of America

07 08 09 10 11 12 • 23 22 21 20 19 18 17 16 15 14 13 12 11 10 9 8 7 6 5 4 3 2

Dedication

To Donald, my Prince Charming...

I smile as I write those words because of our recent trip to Ohio. I would take the stage at my speaking events and say, "So, this probably isn't a good time to mention that I'm a Michigan fan." When the boos died down, I would hurry and tell them, "But my husband's a huge Ohio State guy." After the hearty applause, I would say, "See ... he really is Prince Charming!"

We made great memories with the kids, and Kim and Keith, and we gained thousands of new friends. But here's the thing: you really are my Prince Charming, Donald. I mean it. I love you more with every passing day, understanding as we settle into these middle years that time is not a guarantee. Today is a gift, and tomorrow uncertain. And so I treasure these beautiful, loving days, looking forward to our intimate moments in a quiet walk or laughing over something only we would understand. The ride is breathtakingly beautiful, my love. I pray it lasts far into our twilight years. Until then, I'll enjoy not always knowing where I end and you begin. I love you always and forever.

To Kelsey, my precious daughter...

You are eighteen now, a young woman, and my heart soars with joy when I see all that you are, all you've become. We prayed that through the teenage years you would stay true to who you are, to that promise of purity you made when you were thirteen, once upon a yesterday on a bench overlooking a sunlit river. But I never dreamed you'd so fully hold true to that promise. You look forward to that far-off day, when you can share with your future husband the gift you've saved for him alone. But in the meantime, you trust God that laughter and friendship and dancing and singing and spending time with your family is enough. More than enough. Honey, you grow more beautiful every day—inside and out. And always I treasure the way you talk to me, telling me your hopes and dreams and everything in between. I can almost sense the plans God has for you, the very good plans. I pray you keep holding onto His hand as He walks you toward them. I love you, sweetheart.

To Tyler, my lasting song ...

So many wonderful things are happening in your life right now, things we once only dreamed about. You're the Cat in the Hat in *Seussical*, but not once have I seen you act arrogant about the fact. Worried, yes. Something that makes me smile, because I know ... I know you'll be the absolute best ever at that part when the show opens later this month. I'm proud of you, Ty, at the young man you're becoming. I'm proud of your talent and your compassion for people, and your place in our family.

But two things will stand out when I look back on this time. The way my heart melts when you sing "Proud of Your Boy," and the earnest look in your eyes when you told me last week that maybe ... just maybe, you'd want to be a teacher like your dad. A drama teacher, of course. Giving kids the skills to be successful on stage. You're fourteen and six-foot-two, Ty, no longer my little boy. But even as I see the future in your eyes, I'll treasure my memories of all the stages of your life. However your dreams unfold, I'll be in the front row to watch it happen. Hold onto Jesus, Ty. I love you.

To Sean, my happy sunshine ...

Today you came home from school, eyes sparkling, and you told me you'd tied the school record for the high jump at track practice. The fact that your mark didn't count because it wasn't in a meet didn't dim your enthusiasm even a little. I was struck, as you recounted your jump, how much the story symbolized everything about you, Sean. You're so happy, so optimistic. You have a way of bringing smiles into our family, even in the most mundane moments. I pray that God will use your positive spirit to always make a difference in the lives around you. You're a precious gift, son. Keep smiling, and keep seeking God's best for your life. Make sure the bar's set high—not only at track practice. I love you, honey.

To Josh, my tender-hearted perfectionist ...

Watching you work on your social studies project today, I saw again what always amazes me about you. Your work is so careful, so detailed, it would almost seem you'd traced pictures straight from the textbook. I couldn't turn in the work you do if I took all week. And yet—even with track and soccer and homeschool tests—you still take the time to seek perfection. Along with that, there are bound to be struggles. Times when you need to understand again that the gifts and talents you bear are God's, not yours. And times when you must learn that perfection isn't possible for us, only for God. Even so, my heart almost bursts with pride over the young man you're becoming. You have an unlimited future ahead of you, Josh. I'll be cheering on the sidelines always. Keep God first in your life, and who knows … one day maybe you and Alex Smith will be teammates. I love you always.

To EJ, my chosen one …

We had a family meeting the other night, one of those talk sessions you kids sometimes tease us about. The subject was a reminder that sitting around the dinner table each night are the very best friends you'll ever have. Your sister and brothers. And also that everyone needs to pitch in more. We talked about giving a hundred percent, because some day far too soon, when all you kids are grown and in families of your own, you'll need to give a hundred percent always. That's what love looks like. In the days that followed our family talk, Dad and I were thrilled to see you truly stepped up your efforts at helping out. We'd see you standing at the sink, washing dishes and singing a happy song, and you'd grin at us. "A hundred percent!" you'd say. EJ, I pray that you hold onto that very small lesson always. You're a wonderful boy, son, a child with such potential. Every day, every season, just give a hundred percent, okay? Because God has great plans for you, and we want to be the first to congratulate you as you work to discover those. Thanks for giving your heart, EJ. I love you so.

To Austin, my miracle boy …

I was editing this book when you came into my writing room yesterday and smiled at me. "You're the most beautiful mom in the whole world," you said. "I really mean it." Then you plopped down on the sofa beside me and put your arm around my shoulders. "I think I'll cuddle with you here all day." I smiled, "Okay … you can watch me edit." And then—here's how I know you're getting older—you jumped up and giggled. "No, Mom. Just kidding. I have schoolwork to do." You kissed me and patted my cheek, and then you were off.

But in the storage room of my heart, I had a memory I'll hold onto forever, sweet son. That, and the one from this afternoon. You're taking voice lessons, and this week your song is from Casting Crowns—"Who Am I." When the teacher was gone, you came upstairs with Dad, and from the other side of my writing room door, I heard Dad start to play his guitar. I stopped editing for a moment and stared out at the forest beyond my window, holding tight to the precious sound. You're my youngest, my last, Austin. I'm holding onto every moment, for sure. Thanks for giving me so many wonderful reasons to treasure today. I thank God for you, Austin, for the miracle of your life. I love you, Aus.

And to God Almighty, the Author of Life, who has—for now—blessed me with these.

ACKNOWLEDGMENTS

A book of this magnitude does not come together without help from many, many people. And so, here I humbly take a few minutes to thank the family and friends who partnered with me to bring you *Between Sundays*.

First, a special thanks to my dear friends at Zondervan Publishing. Without a doubt, in the world of Christian publishing, the team at Zondervan understands best my dedication to writing Life-Changing Fiction™. They are completely committed to getting these books to you, and to praying along with me that somewhere between the first and last pages, people will find their lives changed by the power of story. I am blessed beyond words to work with you. Thank you to Sue Brower, my truest supporter. And to Leslie Peterson, my editor on this project. You pushed me and challenged me, Leslie. I need so much more of that. Let's work together again soon!

Also, thanks to my amazing agent, Rick Christian, president of Alive Communications. Rick, you've always believed only the best for me. When we talk about the highest possible goals, you see them as doable, reachable. You are a brilliant manager of my career, and I thank God for you. But even with all you do for my ministry of writing, I cherish most your prayers. The fact that you and your wonderful wife, Debbie, are praying for my family and me keeps me confident every morning that God will continue to breathe life into the stories in my heart. I could never find the words to truly thank you.

A special thank you to my husband, who puts up with me on deadline and doesn't mind driving through Taco Bell after a baseball game if I've been editing all day. This crazy wild ride wouldn't be possible without you, Donald. Your love keeps me writing, your prayers keep me believing that God has a plan in this ministry of fiction. And thanks for your help with the guestbook entries on my website. I look forward to that time every night when you read through them, sharing them with me and releasing them to the public, praying for the prayer requests. Thank you, honey.

And thanks to all my kids who pull together, bringing me iced green tea and understanding about my sometimes crazy schedule. I love that you know you're still first, before any deadline.

Thank you also to my parents, Anne and Ted Kingsbury, and to my sisters, Tricia, Sue, and Lynne. Mom, you are amazing as my assistant—working day and night sorting through the mail from my reader friends. I can picture you and Dad sitting there in your family room, while you interrupt his paper or news show every few minutes. "Wait, Ted ... listen to this one!" I love that you and Dad still get tears in your eyes—the way I do—when you hear that another life has been touched, a heart healed through what God's doing with fiction. Amazing.

Tricia, you are the best executive assistant I could ever hope to have. I treasure your loyalty and honesty, the way you include me on every decision and exciting website change. My website has been a different place since you stepped in, and along the way, the readers have so much more. Please know that I pray for God's blessings on you always, for your dedication to helping me in this season of writing. And aren't we having such a good time too? God works all things to the good!

Sue, I believe you should've been a counselor! From your home far from mine, you get batches of reader letters every day, and you diligently answer them using God's wisdom and His Word. When readers get a response from "Karen's sister Susan," I hope they know how carefully you've prayed for them, and for the response you give. Thank you for truly loving what you do, Sue. You're gifted with people, and I'm blessed to have you aboard.

Thanks also to my forever friends and family, the ones who have stood by loyal and true through the years. Worldly success does strange things to people who watch it happen, even though that success is transient and pretend. I always say there'll be no autograph lines in heaven, so this is only about helping people see a little brighter glimpse of God and making friends along the way. Thank you for not seeing me or us differently, and for your love and laughter. You know who you are!

A very special thanks to San Francisco 49ers quarterback Alex Smith, who helped me research an inside look at the NFL and at the country's foster care system. Thanks for writing a foreword for *Between Sundays*, Alex. Our children's books are going to be a lot of fun over the next few years. And one of these days, we'll have to see that fox-trot we're not telling anyone about.

And the greatest thanks to God. The gift is Yours. I pray I might use it for years to come, in a way that will bring You honor and glory.

FOREVER IN FICTION™

A special thanks to Candace Rathbun, who won Forever in Fiction™ at the San Ramon Valley Christian Academy auction in Northern California. Candace chose to honor her daughter, Paige Judith Rathbun, by naming her Forever in Fiction™.

Paige Rathbun is nine and loves bringing sunshine to the lives of her family, including her older sister Katie, and her younger brother, John. Paige has blue eyes, blonde hair, and a contagious smile. She loves Disneyland, swimming, playing with dolls, and spending time with the people she loves. She wishes her four cousins still lived next door.

In addition, Paige loves to sing in her church choir and she prays for anyone with a need. Everyone who knows Paige, knows she's a hugger. And while she's passing out hugs, she's also likely to pass out her toys or books, anything someone else takes a liking to. Her huge heart is part of what makes her special.

When her family rescued a golden retriever last year, Paige took him under her care. They named him Shakespeare, and he and Paige have become best buddies. Paige asks a lot of questions, but only because she's intelligent and knows there's an answer.

In *Between Sundays*, Paige Rathbun's character is the niece of the 49ers head coach, Chuck Cameron. During a season when Chuck's career is on the line, Paige makes weekly phone calls to her uncle, encouraging him, and helping him keep his focus on Jesus. Because that's the sort of thing Paige would do in real life.

Candace, I pray your daughter Paige is honored by your gift, and by her placement in *Between Sundays*, and that you will always see a bit of Paige when you read her name in this novel, where she will be Forever in Fiction™.

For those of you who are not familiar with Forever in Fiction™, it is my way of involving you, the readers, in my stories, while raising money for charities. To date, this item has raised more than $100,000 at charity auctions across the country. If you are interested in having a Forever in Fiction™ package donated to your auction, contact my assistant, Tricia Kingsbury, at Kingsburydesk@aol.com. Please write *Forever in Fiction* in the subject line. Please note that I am only able to donate a limited number of these each year. For that reason, I have set a fairly high minimum bid on this package. That way the maximum funds are raised for charities.

Note to the Reader

While set against a very real backdrop, the characters in *Between Sundays* are completely fictional. There is absolutely no resemblance between 49ers quarterback Alex Smith and the fictitious Aaron Hill, nor is there any resemblance between any of the characters in *Between Sundays* and any real professional football player.

As with any novel, I have taken poetic license in some areas of research, in an effort to create not only believable football players, but relatable characters. I was very careful in my NFL research, but it would be impossible to be completely accurate in my depiction of professional football.

That said, any inconsistencies between this novel and the real-life world of the NFL are entirely mine.

Foreword by Alex Smith,
San Francisco 49ers Quarterback

As an NFL quarterback, I spend my Sundays during football season calling plays, reading defenses, and avoiding sacks. All of this takes place in front of a national television audience and eighty thousand screaming fans. However, my Sundays were not always spent this way, nor were my days in between. That is why my time spent "between Sundays" is so important to me.

Back in San Diego, California, where I grew up, Sundays were spent with family. Sundays were "game time." Sundays were times spent talking and laughing and being together. We were able to create a supportive team and that team did not rest during the week. Team Smith consisted of my mom and dad, my older brother Josh, and my sisters Abbey and MacKenzie. I would not be where I am today if it were not for the love and support of my family and the invaluable time we spent together, caring for one another.

My family always believed in the importance of love and encouragement, the necessity of an education, and the value of reading. As a reader, I've seen the power of story. Sometimes a story is the only way to touch the heart of a person, to help them see the truth through something that isn't true at all. That's the case here. Though *Between Sundays* tells an entirely fictitious story, it is set against the backdrop of a very real problem facing our country today—the problem with our foster care system.

I chose foster care as the focus for my Alex Smith Foundation because most foster children do not have what I have. My "team" structure, my upbringing, and my family life, is the antithesis of what most foster children have. More important, my family's love and support did not end when I turned eighteen. Foster children are taken from their homes and families for reasons of neglect, abuse, and abandonment; and on their eighteenth birthdays, they are abandoned again by the state.

Less than half of foster kids in our nation graduate from high school. Within a year of leaving the system at eighteen years old, a third end up homeless and another quarter end up incarcerated. College is out of reach for most of these youth. Recent studies indicate that just 7 to 13 percent enroll in college, compared with 62 percent of high school graduates nationally. Less than 2 percent of former foster youth who begin college complete a bachelor's degree. This is compared with 27 percent of the general population. We as a society are failing these children, and, sadly, their stories and struggles go unnoticed today. These children deserve a better opportunity at life. They deserve a chance for a successful adulthood, and they cannot get that on their own. Which of us — alone and poor at the age of eighteen — would be able to succeed?

Giving these foster youth a chance at life, a chance for success, is so much more important to me than improving my passing rating, scoring touchdowns, and wins and losses. I play a game on Sunday for a living, and I have a great team to support me on and off the field. These kids don't play a game for a living. Their game is survival and they need and deserve all the support they can get.

We all need support. Whether that support comes from running backs, receivers, linemen, coaches or parents, siblings, teachers, or mentors, we all have a responsibility to work together. As a quarterback, I know this firsthand. I would be nothing if it were not for the players around me. Likewise, I would not be where I am today if it were not for the love and support I received from my family and friends off the field.

I appreciate Karen Kingsbury for allowing me to share my story, and I appreciate her willingness to expose the positive side of a professional athlete's life between games. But most important, I appreciate the opportunity to create awareness for my foundation and to increase support for foster children everywhere.

It's not what we do in front of eighty thousand people on Sundays that defines who we are. Just as we are not defined by what we do on Sundays in church. It's what we do and how we live Monday through Saturday, when no one is watching, that defines our legacy. It's more than a game, it's life, and we all have a chance to make a difference as we live our lives between Sundays.

For more information about my foundation, you can go to AlexSmith Foundation.org.

See you there!

Alex Smith

Prologue

September 2005

The ache in Amy Briggs's chest hurt worse than before, and every breath came with a frightening wheeze. A wheeze no cough could loose. Not that she had the strength. She'd taken ibuprofen an hour ago, but still her fever raged. It made the air in their boxy apartment feel hot and stuffy, and it blurred her vision. She tried to sit up, but her body was too tired.

Cough syrup, that's what she needed. Cough syrup to break up whatever was suffocating her. She stared at the rickety table next to the worn-out sofa. The bottle of Robitussin lay on its side, empty, next to a stack of bunched up tissues and a half-empty box of Kleenex.

"Cory ... " Her voice barely lifted above the sound of the TV. "Can you get me ... some water?"

Her little boy was six, mesmerized by a special on the San Francisco 49ers. He jumped up. "Yes, Mommy." He stopped near her face, and his eyebrows lowered. "Are you better?"

She struggled for her next breath, but even so, she forced a smile. "A little." The lie was all she could manage. Cory couldn't help her. If things grew worse, she could call Megan, her friend and coworker at the diner. Megan could take her to the hospital if her cough got bad enough.

Her eyes closed and the sounds of the announcer dimmed in the background. Days like this, the battle was almost more than she could bear. Being a single mother to Cory, wondering where next week's food was coming from. Especially now that she was sick. Three missed shifts this week and she wasn't any better. A week without pay would mean she'd be bargaining with the superintendent at the end of the month.

"Mommy ..."

Amy opened her eyes, but it was a struggle. She nodded to the table. "Set it there, okay?"

He held the table so it wouldn't wobble, and waited until the glass was steady. "Need anything else?"

"Yeah." She took his hand in hers and met his eyes. "I need you ... just you, Cory." She tried to fill her lungs, but failed. A series of coughs came from deep inside her, and she turned away.

"Your skin's really hot." He touched his fingers to her forehead. "Maybe you should go to the doctor."

Maybe, she thought. But she was too tired to move. "After my nap, baby ... all right?"

He wrinkled his blond brow. "You sure?"

"Yes." She coughed into the pillow. "You watch your team."

For a heartbeat, Cory seemed torn. He looked at the TV and then back at her. "Feel better."

"I will, baby." She inhaled, but it sounded like she was underwater. "I love you."

"Love you too." He still looked worried, but he turned and moved a few feet closer to the TV, then he dropped down cross-legged and stared at the screen.

At his 49ers.

Since Cory was born she'd made the team her single obsession, even moving to San Francisco so that her son might have the chance he deserved, the one she prayed for every day.

The chance to know his father.

Of course, there were other reasons for leaving Los Angeles, reasons that had nothing to do with Cory or football. Those suffocating, terrifying minutes in the dark bushes that lined the campus parking lot that night had changed everything. Even if she hadn't told anyone then, or now.

A thousand bricks lay stacked across her chest. She had to sit up, had to find a way out from under the pressure. With her elbows, she used all her energy and slid up onto the arm of the sofa. A burst of oxygen filled her airways, and suddenly there was sweet relief.

She felt herself relax and again the sounds around her grew dim. She was falling, drifting into sleep. In the background, the announcer was saying something about Aaron Hill and how this was going to be his best year yet. *Aaron Hill ... the one everyone's watching*, the voice said. Or maybe it wasn't the announcer talking at all, but her heart.

Aaron Hill ...

Her heart slipped into a rapid, pounding rhythm and she tried to push herself up again on the sofa arm. This time, there was no relief. She felt hotter than before, her lungs heavy with fluid. She wanted to cough, needed to find a clear breath. But there was none.

"Mommy …" Cory's voice held an increasing sense of alarm. He stood over her and ran his little boy fingers along her forehead. "You look sicker."

"I'm … I'm okay." She had to be. Cory didn't have anyone in all the world but her. "I'll tell you … if I feel worse."

He frowned, nervous and frightened. Slowly he turned back to the TV, to the special still on. The 49ers. Ready for another season. Amy tried to focus, tried to listen to the announcer, but panic pulsated through her veins. Why couldn't she breathe? What was happening to her?

Strange voices filled her head. Voices from the TV. Or from Cory. She wasn't sure.

" … Aaron Hill … the quarterback to beat."

" … maybe the best year ever … a team desperate for a championship and …"

Amy rolled onto her side. She sucked in a breath, but she couldn't tell if any air entered her lungs. She needed to call Megan. Her friend would find her a ride to the hospital. Amy clenched her teeth and dragged back the smallest bit of air. *Relax*, she told herself. *Everything's going to be okay.*

A siren sounded in the distance, loud and louder, and after a minute Amy realized the sound wasn't coming from out on the streets. It was coming from her throat, her chest.

"Mommy, I'm calling Megan." Her boy was standing near her again, his breath soft on her face.

She tried to open her eyes, but the effort was more than she could make. Instead, she moved her lips and forced just enough air through her lips so he could hear her. "Please … call her."

Spots appeared before her eyes and danced in tight circles. The sounds around her blurred more, and time froze. *Aaron, you should be here …* She wanted to breathe, but the sound scared her. If it weren't for Cory, she would've moved on, as far from San Francisco as possible. But Aaron and Cory belonged together.

And this was the year.

Right, God …? Please, God …

I am with you, daughter ... and I am with your child, now and always.

Peace filled Amy's heart. *Good, Lord. Thank you.* One benefit of leaving her parents' house six years ago was this—she'd found a friendship with God. Not the critical, narrow-minded God of her mother's world. But a God who had sent His Son to open the gates of heaven for her, a God whose Word was alive with hope and promise and direction for her future.

Cory's future.

"Wake up, Mommy." His little hand was on her head again. "Don't go to sleep."

I won't, baby ... Mommy's okay. Jesus is here with us.

She said the words, but she wasn't sure they made it past her lips. The sounds around her faded a little more, and even the whistling coming from her lungs didn't seem as loud.

Amy wasn't sure if she slept or fell into a dream, but suddenly around her there was a burst of motion. Someone picked her up and she was on a long bed, moving fast, faster down a hallway. And she was in a car and there were sirens again but this time they weren't coming only from her throat but from everywhere, all around her, and she was moving on the bed again and a little boy was crying.

Cory! Cory was crying, and she had a sudden burst of energy. Her eyes opened and there he was, right beside her.

"Mommy, don't go to sleep ... please." His eyes were red and damp and scared.

She brought his fingers to her lips and kissed them. "I'm okay, baby. Keep praying."

"I am." His breaths were fast and uneven, his features overtaken with fear. "Don't leave me! I need you!"

"You're okay." She pressed his fingers against her cheek. She wanted to do as he asked, but she was so tired. Her eyes blinked twice, three times. Then they closed. "I ... love you." Her words were the softest whisper, and the darkness settled in around her again, a darkness thicker and more complete than any she'd ever known.

Something was pulling at her. Something or someone, and suddenly she couldn't fight it a moment longer. She let go, let herself be drawn in, and the feeling was wonderful. But as she did, as she moved toward whatever was calling her, she was seized with alarm.

Cory!

She had more to tell him, more to say. Her son needed her. Who would care for him if she wasn't there? The pull was stronger than before, and instead of the darkness, she was surrounded by a warm glow, a living light that was unlike any she'd ever known. With everything in her, she understood that her future was here, in the light.

But, God ... what about Cory?

At that instant, sound and sight returned to her world and she could see Megan, her arm around Cory, comforting him, and a knowing filled her. Megan would take care of Cory. And one day, she would hold her son again and he would understand that God kept His promises. This was the waiting room, all of earth. The real adventure was on the other side. The adventure she was going to take. Cory would be okay, just like she'd told him.

There was something else Amy was sure about, more sure than ever before. Almost as if God Himself were making the future suddenly clear. Her son would always have Megan, but very soon he would have someone else too.

Cory would have his father.

ONE

Two Years Later

Sometimes Cory Briggs took the long way home, pedaling as fast as he could so Megan wouldn't worry about him. Because Megan said eight-year-old boys should come straight home from soccer practice, especially on late afternoons. San Francisco was the sort of city where it was best if you were in by dark.

But that early August day, Cory did it again. He slipped his backpack onto his shoulders, left the soccer field at McKinley Elementary, and rode his bike up the hill and a few blocks out of the way, to Duboce Park. He would make up time on the downhill, so he stopped just outside the fenced-in play area and stared.

Shadows made it hard to see the bench, the one where he and his mom used to sit. But Cory shaded his eyes with his hand and squinted, and suddenly there it was. The same bench, same brown wooden slats, same way it looked back when he was a first grader, back when they came here every afternoon. He didn't blink, didn't break the lock he had on the bench, and after a minute he could hear her again, her happy voice telling him everything would be okay.

"God has good plans for us, Cory." She would kiss his cheek and smile at him. But her eyes weren't always happy, even when she smiled. "We'll find our way out together."

He remembered her still. He blinked now because he didn't want to cry. A bit of wind blew against his back, and Cory squinted against the tears. The day was hot, but already the bay breeze was cooling it off, which meant it was time to go. He climbed back up onto his seat and looked at the bench one more time. His mom was buried in Oakland somewhere. Megan took him once in a while, but Oakland was far away. When he needed to see her one more time, when he wanted to hear her voice, he came here.

Duboce Park.

"Take good care of her, God," he whispered. Then without another look back, he set off along the sidewalk pedaling hard as he could, turning down Delores to Seventeenth, and the third story apartment where he and Megan lived.

Cory knew the streets between his school and his apartment. He even knew the way to Monster Park, where the 49ers played. But Megan would never let him ride his bike all the way to the stadium. That was okay. It was enough just knowing it was close. Because once a year he and the kids from his neighborhood entered a drawing for tickets to a game, and this year ... this year he was going to win.

He focused on the ride. He knew which alleys to stay away from, and which areas had gang members standing around. He took the streets with the least traffic lights, because that was smarter. He had to stop for only three before he reached their building, jumped off his bike, and walked it through the doorway.

Bikes were allowed in the elevator if they fit, and his did. At the third floor he stepped off and already he could hear it. The sound of happiness. Laughing and loud voices coming from the Florentinos' apartment. He walked past two doors and stopped. The smell of spaghetti and garlic bread slipped beneath the door and filled the hallway. Sometimes, when Megan had to work late, he would knock on the Florentinos' door and they'd invite him in for dinner.

They had seven kids, but Mrs. Florentino said she always had an extra plate.

Cory raised his hand to knock, because Megan might not be home yet. Then he remembered. She'd made a Crock-Pot dinner this morning because she got paid first of the month. He walked his bike to the end of the hall to No. 312. The newspaper was there, opened, and a little scattered. The Florentinos got the paper every day, and after they read it, they set it outside his and Megan's door. Megan might deliver the paper, but that didn't mean she could take a copy free. That's what she said.

So instead, Mrs. Florentino brought over hers, and that way Cory could read about the 49ers. Especially now, in the preseason.

He used his key and walked into their apartment. Then he set down his backpack and the paper, walked across the room, and opened the front window. Nothing but alleys and winos below, but Cory loved having it open. A little bit of summer came in with the breeze.

Oreo, the cat, rubbed against his ankle.

"Hi, boy." Cory bent down and rubbed his fur. He was black and white with a lot of gray around the whiskers. Some days he was Cory's best friend. Cory straightened and looked around. The apartment was small, but it was clean. Megan liked clean. And almost every day she left a snack for him. Cory went to the table, and there on a napkin, were two chocolate chip cookies and an empty glass.

"So you'll remember to drink your milk," Megan always told him.

At the other end of the table was the Scrabble box. Each day was a different game. Sometimes Yahtzee or a deck of cards or Memory. But Scrabble was their favorite. They'd eat dinner first and then they'd play a game before homework. Megan was nice that way. Plus, the TV only got four channels clear. So board games were good.

Cory poured himself a glass of milk and sat at the table. The cookies weren't warm, of course, but they tasted like smooth vanilla and Hershey bars. Because that's how Megan made them. Which was nice because Megan didn't have much time. Early mornings, before he was awake, she delivered the *Chronicle*, and after that, she worked all day at Bob's Diner downtown. Two jobs because she said that's what it took to keep food on the table.

There was the sound of a key in the door and then it opened.

"Cory!" Megan stepped inside. She had a grocery bag in her hands and her cheeks were red, the way they got when she walked fast. She held up the bag. "Fudge brownie ice cream."

"The best!" Cory stood and ran to her and hugged her tight. When he'd first come to live with Megan, he didn't like to hug her because she wasn't his mom. But she was his mom's friend. And after two years, hugging her was almost as good as it used to feel to hug his mom. Plus, Megan liked the 49ers. So that made her and the apartment feel like home. Especially during football season.

Cory took the grocery bag. "Thanks." He grinned at her. "The Crock-Pot smells good."

"Not as good as Mrs. Florentino's dinner, but …" She grinned. "It's the best we can do."

"Yep."

He helped put the ice cream in the freezer, and he held the door shut extra long because it didn't stay closed that good.

"Salad?" He opened the fridge and looked at her.

"Of course." She lifted the lid on the Crock-Pot. "Always salad."

He took out the head of lettuce and a worn-out knife from the drawer. If he had money of his own, he'd buy Megan some new knives. Forks too. And maybe a warmer sweater for the days she had to walk fast after dark.

They worked together, and Cory smiled to himself. It felt nice having Megan there. When they were sitting at the table eating the Crock-Pot dinner, Cory watched her a couple times when she wasn't looking. She was pretty, and she loved him like he was her own. That's what she said. And maybe she could keep him for good if the court hearings went okay. So far Megan said it was nothing but red tape and the runaround.

Whatever that meant.

Megan put her fork down. "I talked to the social worker again." A half smile lifted her lips. "I told her I want to adopt you, Cory."

He finished chewing a bite of potato. "What'd she say?"

"She said"—Megan raised one eyebrow and looked straight at him—"you told her the same thing. About having a dad."

Cory shrugged. "Yeah." He studied the pieces of meat still on his plate. Then he looked into her eyes. "Everyone has a dad."

She gave him a look that said no-funny-business-mister. "You know what I mean." A sad breath came from her. "If you tell her your dad's in the picture, we'll need his signature. I can't adopt you until he says so."

"Right." Cory checked his dinner again. He poked his fork around and pushed the carrots to one side. "If we get his signature … I can meet him."

Megan waited for a second. Then she breathed long and loud and looked at her plate. "Let's talk about something else."

They talked about soccer practice and the other guys on the team and about her work at the restaurant, because she had a rich guy come in today, a big baldy, who left her a twenty-dollar tip.

"That's why the ice cream!" Cory raised his fork in the air.

"Exactly."

After dinner, they played Scrabble, but Cory couldn't think about big words. Some turns he couldn't think about any words at all. He wanted to read the newspaper, the sports section. Because the 49ers were getting ready for the season and he didn't want to miss a single story.

Megan won with the word *zebras*, and Cory hugged her. "Good job." He took a few steps back. "I'm gonna read the paper."

"How about the dishes first?" Megan had dark hair, and she tossed it over her shoulder when she stood up. It was easy to think of her as older, sort of his mom's age. Maybe twenty-nine or thirty. But she was twenty-five. Megan said that wasn't exactly young and that she had an old soul.

The two of them washed dishes, him scrubbing the plates and Megan rinsing. When they were finally done, he grabbed the paper and ran it to the couch. He was halfway through the sports section when he saw it. The headline read, "Derrick Anderson Hosts Pizza Party at Youth Center."

Cory raced through the short story. It talked about how Derrick Anderson loved foster kids, and that he was having a pizza party on Friday night at the youth center. All foster kids and their parents were invited.

"No way!" Cory shouted. "Megan, look at this!"

She was washing off the counter and made a little laugh. "Must be big. Read it to me."

"It is big!" He read her the story, every line, and then he let the paper fall to the floor and he ran to her. "Please, Megan. I could meet Derrick Anderson! He's the backup quarterback for the 49ers, the famous one who used to play for the Bears. Remember him?"

"The whole world knows Derrick Anderson." She did a sad sort of smile. "Well, they used to know him. Back in his prime."

"What?" Cory jumped around. "He's still *in* his prime, Megan! He's thirty-nine, and he's still one of the best quarterbacks in the league." He jumped some more. "I can't believe we can meet him." He stopped, his eyes wide. "We can, right? Can we? Please, Megan?"

Her eyes twinkled. "Are you kidding?" She messed her fingers through his hair. "That's the best Friday night offer I've had for a year, at least."

"Did you know about this, the pizza night?" Cory blinked at her. Megan volunteered at the youth center three times a week. She should've heard about this long before the newspaper.

Her eyes danced. "I had an idea. But I wanted to be sure before I told you. The 49ers' front office set it up. I guess the team wants to do whatever it can for the city. With all the talk about building a new stadium thirty miles south in Santa Clara."

"Yeah." Cory didn't like thinking about a new stadium. The 49ers had played at the same place since 1971. They were the best pro sports franchise in the state. Anyone knew that. Plus, Megan said if the mayor convinced the 49ers to stay in the city, they were going to build a bunch of new houses and stuff. Cory and Megan would have to move for sure. He blinked and tried to forget about the whole stadium thing. "Besides, Derrick's doing the pizza party for a different reason."

"Oh, really?" Megan gave him a half smile.

"Yeah, because he likes foster kids. And that's all."

Megan tilted her head, and her eyes said she was done teasing. "I think you're right."

"So"—he felt his heart dance around inside him—"We're going?"

A laugh came from Megan. "Definitely."

He grinned and held out his hand, official-like. "Okay, then. It's a date."

"Date." She shook his fingers, and then she laughed and went back to wiping the counter.

Cory picked up the paper again and stacked it on the sofa. Friday was only four days away. Which meant it wasn't too soon to do what he'd done a hundred times before. He ran to his room, pulled a box out from beneath the bunk bed, and grabbed a piece of paper and a pencil. He took out a dictionary to use for his table, and he started to write.

Every other time he'd done this, he never actually gave the letter away. Because when his mom was alive, she told him he couldn't just send it off without knowing where it would go, or if it would even be opened. So usually, he wrote the letter and threw it away. Or tucked it into his box, or his backpack. In case he ever ran into the guy at the park or something.

But this . . . this was the most exciting thing to ever happen, because Derrick Anderson could deliver his letter, Cory was sure. And maybe these were the good plans from God his mother had always told him about.

Cory thought for a long time. He would write the best letter yet, stick it in the nicest envelope, and write across the front. So Derrick would know who to give it to. And Derrick would do it, because he loved foster kids. The *Chronicle* said so. And the letter was for one of Derrick's teammates, one of the most famous football players in the country. A man Cory prayed every night he might someday meet.

The man was quarterback Aaron Hill, but Cory didn't want to meet him because he was the city's favorite football player. He wanted to meet him for a different reason.

Because Aaron Hill was his dad.

TWO

Megan couldn't go five minutes without Cory asking her about the time or how long it was until they left or some other question about the pizza party. Now it was five-thirty, almost time to leave, and Megan was in the bathroom running a brush through her hair. In the other room, Cory was talking to himself, going on about how this was the big day, the time of his life, the chance he'd been waiting for.

A smile tugged at Megan's lips. Cory's excitement was refreshing, and it gave both of them a reason to look forward to the night. But Megan worried about the boy too, about the letter he'd written for Aaron Hill.

Megan stared at the mirror. "You hear that boy out there, right, God?" She kept her conversation quiet, the way she always did when she talked to God. Cory's mother may have been a churchgoer, but Megan wasn't—she didn't trust organized religion. But from the time she'd been out on her own, God had been her closest friend. She held her breath. *Please, God ... don't disappoint him.*

"Almost ready?" Cory popped into the doorway. His eyes were wide, his smile so big, his freckles stretched ear to ear.

"Almost." She set the brush down and studied her look. She didn't wear much makeup, and tonight was no exception. She dabbed on fresh lipstick and tossed her hair. Then she turned to Cory. "Okay ... let's go."

"Yay!" He wore his best 49ers T-shirt, a 49ers baseball cap, and blue jeans. He grinned at her. "Do I look like their number-one fan?"

She tugged at the bill of his hat. "Definitely." Something bulky stuck out from his back pocket and she raised her eyebrow at it. "The letter?"

"Yes." His voice was practically trembling with anticipation. "Derrick'll get it to him, I know it."

Megan didn't want to dim the boy's enthusiasm, but she had to keep him grounded in case he never had a moment alone with the veteran quarterback. "You know, Cory, he might be too busy. It'll be packed tonight."

He grinned, unfazed. "I only need a few minutes."

"Hmmm." Megan walked past him into the kitchen and found her bag on the counter. The center had called on every volunteer to help with tonight's event. "You might only get a few seconds."

Cory thought about that for a heartbeat. "Perfect! That's just enough time to give him the letter and ask him to get it to Aaron."

Megan opened her mouth to say something about Cory having too vivid an imagination and setting himself up for heartbreak, but she changed her mind. There were a dozen ways Cory could get hurt or disappointed by the end of the night. The whole idea of a letter for Aaron Hill telling the star player that he was Cory's dad was crazy in the first place. If Aaron Hill was Cory's father, Amy would've said something about it. Megan and Amy talked about everything. The two were together all the time. And though they were both 49ers fans, the subject of Aaron in connection with Cory never once came up.

The notion was nothing but a little boy's fantasy. Megan could understand that much. There was no father in his life, so Cory had dreamed up a Hollywood movie scenario, the idea that his favorite quarterback was also his dad. But every time Megan tried to correct him, Cory was adamant. Lately she'd stopped trying to convince him. Life would take care of that all too soon.

This was the biggest thing to happen to Cory all year, maybe ever. "Okay." She smiled at him. "Let's go."

They took the stairs, since the elevator was being repaired. Once they were on the street, Cory ran a little ahead, turned around, and waited for her to catch up. "You think he'll be bigger in person?"

"Derrick Anderson?"

"Yeah. He's six-two, but I mean"—he patted one of his shoulders—"bigger because of his muscles."

She stifled a laugh. "I'm sure he'll be big."

Cory walked backward, so he could see her. "Yesterday's paper said Derrick wants more foster kids at the games."

"I saw that. I'm glad he's thinking about it." The sidewalk was busy, full of people getting off work and loosely assembled groups sharing cigarettes and swapping stories outside the row of shops that made up their street. Megan took gentle hold of the boy's shoulder and turned him forward. "You're going to back into someone."

The party was at the Mission Youth Center on Market Street, an eight-block walk uphill from their apartment. They had twenty minutes, and Megan wanted to be there a little early—so they could get a seat close to where Derrick would be set up. Cory wasn't the only one who wanted a few minutes with Derrick Anderson.

Megan had her own reasons for wanting to meet the man. Ever since he arrived in San Francisco, he'd been passionate about foster kids. In that way, they had much in common. Foster kids were everything to her, and reform in the system was something she dreamed about.

But she was lacking everything it took to make a difference—time, money, and influence. Everything Derrick Anderson had in reserve.

Megan took long strides and thought about her life, the difference she wanted to make for kids like Cory. It was something she dreamed about in the predawn hours when she walked her fifteen-block route delivering the *Chronicle*, something that played over in her mind between serving plates of scrambled eggs and club sandwiches at Bob's Diner.

Most of all, she thought about her vision for foster care during the three days a week she volunteered at the center. The state had no money for the program, so the center was kept open largely by volunteers and donations from private citizens. Megan was an after-school coordinator, and in her spare time—at night after Cory was in bed—she worked on a grant proposal, one the director hoped to present to the state legislature.

Cory skipped ahead and then stopped himself and waited for her. "Two more streets!"

Megan pushed herself, the way she always did when she walked the steeper hills. No money for a gym, and no time for an exercise hour, but Megan did more walking in a day than most people did all month. She pressed on, picturing the kids who would be at the party today. Most of the foster kids who hung out at the center were fourteen, fifteen, even sixteen. A few were nearly eighteen.

Which meant that in a few months, on their birthdays, government services for those kids would suddenly stop. A shiver ran down Megan's arms. The kids could feel the deadline coming, and most of them were talking about it. Turn eighteen, and then what? Megan felt the familiar pain in her heart. She'd been there once herself, not that long ago. The answer for many of them lay in the statistics. Half ended up unemployed, a third became homeless, and one in four wound up in jail or prison.

"We're here!" Cory practically shook, he was so anxious to get inside.

The door was propped open and a chorus of voices spilled out onto the street. Megan stayed behind Cory as they walked inside. Already the place was packed. Many of the faces were familiar, kids who spent more time at the youth center than at their foster homes and group homes. Derrick Anderson had brought out every foster child in the city.

Megan peered at Cory. "Kinda crowded."

"Not too much." He stood on his tiptoes and stared past the milling people into the double gymnasium. "Do you see him, huh? Is he in there?"

"Let's get closer." Megan took hold of his hand and moved through the crowd. They should've come an hour ago. She reached the doorway and scanned the front of the room. It was still quarter to six, so Derrick might not be here yet.

"There he is!" Cory released her hand and ran toward the front of the room.

She saw the quarterback at the same time. He was near the front corner, and already a line of kids stood waiting for a chance to meet him. Cory was right; he was bigger in person. His dark brown skin stood in contrast to his white polo shirt, and even from this far away, the guy's warmth shone from his eyes. Megan worked her way closer, between the cafeteria tables that had been set up across the gym floor. She found an open spot at a table three rows from the front.

The atmosphere was frenzied, foster kids packing the place as if this single event was every birthday and Christmas rolled into one. She placed her elbows on the table and leaned into them. The line of mostly boys formed a thick crowd around the veteran player, and a string of volunteers worked to straighten them into a single line. Across the room, another batch of workers came through the side doors, each carrying a stack of pizzas. Pauline's Pizza had given them half off, and Derrick Anderson picked up the rest of the tab.

A few tables over, a little girl sat with an older woman. Both of them looked lost, overwhelmed by the chaos. The girl had dark hair and blue eyes, and a wistfulness about her that made her seem far older than her young age. Something haunting and familiar shone in the girl's eyes, and it took a few minutes to realize what it was. The girl looked like Megan, the way Megan had looked at that age.

The sounds around her faded as Megan was drawn back in time, back to the days when she came to this same youth center, attended the same community pizza parties.

"Your mother isn't stable," Megan's social worker had told her just before they took her from her downtown apartment and placed her in the first foster home.

Megan didn't need anyone to tell her that. She'd taken care of her mother from the time she was five years old, back when she first realized how troubled the woman was. Her mom was a crack addict and a binge drinker. She loved Megan with all her heart and always promised she'd find treatment. Once in a while she did, but only for a season. Megan spent her life in and out of foster homes.

At least until she turned eighteen. That year, she was released from foster care and returned to her mother. Megan had the highest grade point average in her graduating class, and for a year she managed to care for her mother and carry a full load of university classes. But her mother's health deteriorated the summer before her sophomore year, and Megan had no choice but to drop out.

By the time her mom died at the end of the next year, Megan had the paper route and the job at the diner, and college was little more than a distant dream.

Megan blinked and searched the line of kids until she found Cory, not far from the front. Amy would've loved this, a chance for Cory to meet a player from his favorite team. Megan squinted against the glare of the past. Hard to believe two years had passed since her death.

Cory looked over his shoulder and gave her a nervous grin. Her heart responded, the way it always did around the boy. What would've happened to him if she hadn't taken him in? His grandparents in Southern California were both dead, and he had no father in the picture. An image of Aaron Hill filled her head. No realistic father, anyway.

During her long talks with God, Megan concluded she'd been placed square in Amy's life for the sole purpose of taking care of Cory. Who else in Amy's world would've understood foster care the way she did? That was one of the reasons she wanted to adopt Cory—as soon as possible.

She blew at a wisp of her bangs. Maybe Cory's letter really would make it all the way to Aaron Hill, and maybe he'd get a message back to the boy that, well, he simply wasn't the boy's father. Cory believed it with all of his heart, so the truth was bound to hurt. But at least then he'd stop telling the social worker that he knew who his dad was, and in time, the adoption would go through and they'd both be happier.

Megan took a long breath. The smell of warm cheese and pepperoni was making her hungry. But she couldn't eat, couldn't move or blink or do anything but watch the line of kids and the big, strapping quarterback at the front. This was the first step toward the moment of truth.

Cory was next in line.

⚊

Finally Cory could hear Derrick Anderson's voice.

Because he was only four more kids away from his turn.

Cory put his hand over his heart like when they said the Pledge of Allegiance before a game. It was pounding hard, right close to his shirt. He swallowed and stared at his old tennis shoes. Derrick would give Aaron the letter, right? He would do that sort of thing because he was a nice guy. Otherwise he wouldn't be here having pizza with a bunch of foster kids.

They moved up another spot and he could hear Derrick laughing, the same sort of laugh he sometimes had when he was on TV and the news people talked to him. "Well, I don't know about that," he told the kid at the front of the line. "I'm there for Aaron, certainly. But I can't say I want his job."

Derrick Anderson didn't need anyone's job. He could retire now and be in the Hall of Fame in no time. That's what Megan said, and it was true. Derrick already had two Super Bowl rings, and that was more than Aaron Hill. Derrick was steady and dependable, year after year. The newspapers always wrote that about him. Aaron was flashy with a lot of big touchdown passes. Plus, he had good looks and a lot of endorsement deals. That's what they said about Aaron Hill.

Cory felt the letter in his back pocket, and his heart beat even faster. Maybe since he was closer now, he should take it out and have it ready. So he wouldn't waste any time once he got to the front. He reached back, but then he changed his mind. Better to keep it in his pocket where it was safe.

The letter wasn't super long, but it had all the stuff Cory wanted to say, like how his mom always told Cory that Aaron was his dad, and how they moved to San Francisco so they could be close to him and so that Cory could meet him one day, and how this might be the year because he never was able to get a letter to Aaron until now. The letter had Cory's phone number, plus some other good stuff at the end, but Cory couldn't think of the exact words right now.

He swallowed again. The nervous feeling in his stomach was worse than before any soccer game. Plus, the line wasn't moving very fast, and he was shorter than most of the guys in front, so he had to keep leaning sideways and trying to see exactly what was happening to make it take so long. Maybe some of the kids were filling out their raffle ticket for the prize basket. All the guys were talking about it. Five ticket packages with two seats each were being given out tonight. The best gift ever. Cory had already filled his out, and he wrinkled the slip of paper up a little in his hands so maybe Derrick would feel his more than the others, and Cory's name would get picked.

The line shuffled a few feet closer. Two more kids, that was all. Cory gave a little wave to Megan, because she was watching him. She didn't like it that he was giving Derrick a letter. She didn't say so, but Cory could tell. He smiled at her and looked back at his shoes. Then he tried a trick to make the time go faster. He thought about his last soccer practice, and the drills, and he pretended in his mind that he was going around the cones and dribbling the ball and passing it to the other guys on the team.

And then, just like that, it was his turn.

Derrick smiled at him. "Hey, partner, how's it going?"

His throat was dry, but he licked his lips and stepped forward. "Good." He stuck out his hand, proper like the way his soccer coach did when he met one of the other coaches before a game. "I'm Cory Briggs."

"Hi, Cory." Derrick shook his hand. Up close, his face looked a little bit like Michael Jordan's. He had a friendly smile and nice eyes and a smooth voice. "I like a young man who can look me in the eyes and give a proper handshake."

The rumbling in his stomach settled down. "Megan says you're the best quarterback who's ever played the game." Cory waited a few extra seconds before letting go of Derrick's hand.

"Megan?" He looked behind Cory, and his eyebrows bunched together, confused.

Cory giggled, because Derrick seemed like a guy who laughed easy. He pointed at Megan sitting three tables away. "Over there. She's my foster mom."

"Oh." Derrick waved at Megan, and then he took a photograph from a stack and signed it to Cory. "Here you go."

All of a sudden, Cory felt panic because maybe Derrick was going to tell him goodbye, and that it was the next kid's turn. But he put his hands on his knees and looked right into Cory's eyes. "You play football, Cory?"

"I want to." Cory felt his shoulders sink a little. "I play soccer. Megan says football has to wait." He didn't stay discouraged for long. "I'm gonna be a running back in high school."

"Running back's a tough position." Derrick sized him up. "I think you'll be a good one."

His words made Cory feel twelve or thirteen, instead of eight. He stood super tall, and then in a flash, he remembered the letter. "Oh." He twisted around and pulled the envelope from his back pocket. For a second he stared at it. The name Aaron Hill was across the front. *God, please … let Aaron get this.* He felt a little shy all of a sudden, and embarrassed because maybe he should've brought a letter for Derrick too. He bit the inside of his cheek and gave Derrick a worried look. "Can I ask a favor?"

Derrick put his hand on Cory's shoulder. "Sure, partner." His smile looked real, like it came from inside his heart. "What's the favor?"

"This." He held the letter out to Derrick. "It's a letter for Aaron Hill."

Derrick took the envelope and looked at the front. "Aaron Hill … yep, it says so right there." He gave Cory a look, the sort of look a dad might give a son. Because Cory had seen it when the dads talked to the other guys on his soccer team. That kind of look. "Is Aaron your favorite player?"

Cory wanted to say no, Aaron wasn't his favorite player. He was his dad. But Megan said that was the sort of detail that Aaron had to find out before any of his teammates did. So Cory shrugged one shoulder. "Kind of." He rushed on. "Course, you're one of my favorites too." He gave a nervous laugh. "I liked you before I liked Aaron, and that's the truth. 'Cause I've been watching football since I could walk."

Derrick did one of those grown-up kinds of laughs. Then he held out his hand again, and Cory shook it. "Tell you what. I'll make sure Aaron gets it." He leaned in a few inches closer. "Promise."

Everything inside Cory lit up all at once. "Really?"

"Really." Derrick tapped the envelope on his knee, and then slid it into his own back pocket. "I'll give it to him tomorrow at practice."

"Okay." Cory licked his lips again. "Thanks, Derrick. I mean it a lot. You're the best."

Derrick nodded toward Megan. "I think she's saving you a seat."

"Yeah." Cory looked at her and waved again. "She's good about that."

"Get yourself some pizza and maybe you'll win the tickets. We'll pick the winners in about half an hour."

"Okay." Cory was going to shake Derrick's hand a third time, but he changed his mind. Too much of that sort of stuff bugged people. So he took a step back and pointed to his letter in Derrick's pocket. "Tomorrow?"

"Yep." Derrick gave his pocket a few light pats. "Soon as I see him."

A few kids in line were saying hurry up, and that Cory was taking too long. He took a step backward. "Thanks again."

Derrick winked at him, and then just like that, the meeting was over. Cory walked back toward the table where Megan was but he didn't remember taking even one step. And he didn't want pizza either. All he wanted was to sit there and watch Derrick and imagine that sometime tomorrow he would take the very same envelope that held Cory's letter and hand it over to Aaron Hill.

The whole event was a dream come true.

"That looked like it went well." Megan gave him a hopeful smile when he reached her. "He took the letter, at least."

"Yeah." Cory's voice was full of victory, the way it was after he scored the winning goal in the first soccer scrimmage a few weeks ago. "He said he'll give it to Aaron tomorrow at practice."

Megan told him to get some pizza, and even though he wasn't hungry, he obeyed because maybe he'd be hungry later. Plus, he had to find something to do to make the time go faster between now and the drawing for the preseason game tickets. This was his best chance ever to see the 49ers play in person.

Cory kept his eyes on Derrick, even when he was eating his sausage pizza. Finally, the director of the youth center stood on a platform and tapped her microphone. It made a loud sound and she backed up a few inches. "Okay, kids, settle down."

The kids weren't that good at settling down, not usually anyway. But today everyone settled very fast because the director was going to tell them about the tickets. Derrick came over to her, and another lady gave him a big basket of names.

"Now boys and girls, you know there's only five sets of preseason game tickets available tonight. But Derrick brought lots of water bottles and 49ers T-shirts and bumper stickers. So after I draw the winning names, stay quiet. You still might win something."

Cory crossed the fingers on both hands, and then, just for a little extra help, he crossed his hands and set them on the table next to his empty pizza plate. *Come on, Derrick ... pick me. You gotta pick me.* That would be perfect because then he could meet Aaron, and by then Aaron would've read the letter and they could get right down to business and talk about how Aaron was his dad.

Derrick swished his hand around in the basket and pulled out a slip of paper. It looked wrinkly as he handed it to the director.

This is it! Cory held his breath.

"The winner is ... Tommy James."

All the air in Cory's lungs came out. Now how would he ever get a chance to go to a game and meet Aaron Hill? Across the room, a big kid jumped out of his seat and shoved his fists straight into the air. He hooted a few times as he ran to the front of the room. Someone took a picture of him and Derrick, and then Derrick gave him a package.

Four more times Derrick picked a name, and four more times it wasn't Cory's.

When all the excitement calmed down, the director handed the microphone to Derrick. "I know there's a bunch more of you kids out there who'd like to see a game at Monster Stadium."

The kids clapped and cheered.

"So, here's the good news. I'll have a pizza party like this every Thursday or Friday night through the preseason — depending on whether the 49ers are home or away. And each time we'll give away five pairs of tickets and a bunch of other stuff."

Cory's heart felt light again. If Derrick gave away five sets of tickets at every pizza party, one of them was bound to go to him and Megan. It had to.

Of course, there was one other way they could make it to a 49ers game this year. Derrick could give the letter to Aaron at practice tomorrow, and Aaron could read it, and he could be glad that he had a little boy named Cory living just a few miles from the stadium. And he could call Cory up and invite him and Megan to a game. Then he could ask if Cory wanted to come down to the locker room afterward so they could hang out. And that, Cory told himself as they left the youth center that night with nothing from the prize table, would be even better than a water bottle or a T-shirt or even preseason game tickets.

Because that's what a dad would do.

THREE

Derrick walked out onto the field at the Santa Clara practice facility fifteen minutes before any other player. Today would be light, since the past week was one of the hardest so far. Derrick headed to the warm-up track and planted his feet, shoulder width apart. He put his hands on his hips and leaned to the right for ten seconds, then to the left. Stretching took longer than it used to, his bones and muscles and tendons holding tight to the memory of a hundred NFL games.

He drew in a long breath and stared at the place where the brown rolling hills met the sheer blue sky just beyond the field. This was it. His last chance at a game he'd loved since he was in kindergarten. He could feel the finality as surely as he felt the constant ache in his throwing arm. After a standout career and a dozen playoff wins, after two Super Bowls and the roar of the crowd one touchdown pass after another, the whole glorious ride was about to come to an end.

He squinted toward the afternoon sun. *God, show me how ...*

Another deep breath and he started to jog. He took the first lap slow, just fast enough to get the blood flowing through his body. Retirement would be nice, no question. His wife, Denae, had all sorts of plans for him and their three young teenage kids. Trips to Hawaii and Mexico and a cruise to Alaska. And of course, coaching. Two of the three were boys and Derrick rarely saw them without a football. He would coach them as long as the local high school allowed it.

Derrick had a pretty good hunch they would.

But all that could wait. Here, now, he had just one goal that mattered, one that had consumed him since he took his place with the 49ers. He had to help this team reach the big game, had to win one more Super Bowl. He'd made a promise, after all. If Derrick wanted to be remembered for one thing when he hung up his helmet, it was for being a promise keeper.

Fans of Derrick Anderson never had to worry about opening the pages of the sports section and finding his name linked with drugs or drunken behavior or police activity. He might not be flashy like Aaron Hill, but he was dependable. God alone had given him the ability to play, and when he went out, he would do so with the sort of tribute his God deserved.

If he could only figure out exactly what that tribute was.

He rounded the first lap and picked up his pace. The run was easy, second nature. With every lap he felt his body waking up, falling into a familiar rhythm and quickness that he would need if he was going to make a difference this season. And he would, because God had told him so. Derrick's only question was how that would happen.

Near the entrance to the facility, a few other players were arriving. But Derrick kept his focus. This season was going to be special, maybe the most special of all. There was the foster program, of course. The city was inundated with foster kids, most of whom had no plan outside their eighteenth birthday. Derrick wanted to change that. The pizza parties were only the beginning. He wanted to pass on his love for foster kids to the other players. Get the whole team to embrace the city's parentless kids.

That wasn't all the next four or five months were about. Coach Chuck Cameron's job was on the line, for one thing. He'd taken the team to the playoffs four of the last seven years. But he hadn't won a conference championship, and he hadn't made it past the first round in five years. This year, once again, the best thing going for the team was Aaron Hill, the top-ranked quarterback in the league, but the 49ers were weak at the line and two of their top receivers had undergone surgery in the off-season. No one expected them to break records this year. Grumbling was coming toward the coach loud and clear from the front office. Win it this year, or pack up and leave. The owners expected a new stadium in five years—whether it was in Santa Clara or at Monster Park. They wanted a championship team long before that.

Coach Cameron wasn't the main reason he was here, though. The main reason, Derrick believed, was the team's hotshot quarterback, Aaron Hill. Coach Cameron thought so too.

"Get through to him, Anderson," Coach had told him last week. "Guts and talent aren't enough in this league. Never mind his reputation, Aaron Hill won't go to the next level until he plays with heart."

So maybe that was his primary job, the formerly great Derrick Anderson: Help Aaron Hill play with heart. When he prayed about the season, about what God wanted from him, he sensed it didn't have much to do with his own on-field contributions. Derrick was realistic about the coming schedule. He might not play a down all season. But he knew the secret to winning, and Coach was right. It had everything to do with the inside of a man, the life that happened off the field. Between Sundays. If the 49ers' starting quarterback would slow down enough to realize that, they might all win in the end.

The first fine layer of sweat broke out on his forehead and the small of his back. It was eighty degrees and breezy, the sort of late summer day that hinted of fall. Derrick kept his breathing even as he pushed himself. Four more laps and he could join the others.

He watched Aaron strut onto the field, then he shifted his attention straight ahead. Aaron was a nice guy, likeable. After seven seasons in the NFL, he was one of the most liked players in the league. The guy played through strained ligaments, back spasms, and concussions, and that made him a hero to his adoring public. As long as he could score a touchdown in a two-minute drill, the world loved him.

Off the field, Aaron was shallow and cavalier. He partied hard, though the press hadn't caught wind of the fact. A different stunning blonde or brunette waited for him after practice every week or so. He drove a Hummer and prided himself on being a slick dresser. All neat and put together, just like his reputation.

Derrick had a feeling Aaron had lost something deep along the way. No doubt, Aaron Hill was one of the reasons God had moved him to the 49ers.

"Hey, Anderson," Coach Chuck Cameron waved him over. "It's time."

"Okay." Derrick wiped his brow and jogged toward the others. The two-mile run was his own doing, a way of compensating for the years.

The sound of the guys drifted across the field, most of them talking about Friday night or laughing about something. As Derrick rounded the final curve, Coach Cameron blew his whistle and waited. The guys pulled up around him and silence fell over the team.

Derrick found a spot near the back, his stomach muscles pushing through his shirt from exertion.

One of the linebackers leaned toward him. "Show off."

"Yeah, you're jealous." He grinned and focused on Coach.

"Things are heating up." The coach paced a few steps. "I don't think I have to tell you all that's riding on this season." He tucked his clipboard against his side and studied them. "*Sports Illustrated* says ten teams have the chance to go all the way this year." He paused. "We're not one of them. The media thinks we're a quarterback, nothing else."

A disgruntled mumbling came from the group.

"Best offensive line in the league." Aaron Hill grinned and gave a nod to a few of his linemen. His support of his line was widely touted throughout the league. Aaron treated them to steak dinners and bought them iPods during the season.

Smart guy, Derrick thought. Without the line, Aaron would be like any other quarterback, scrambling for his life and winding up on his back half the time.

"So here it is." Coach Cameron's voice rang with sincerity. "We need to come together this year. Because the media's not God. *Sports Illustrated* isn't God. This year"—he walked along the front of the group, his eyes never leaving theirs—"I have a feeling. You know what I mean?"

The guys shifted, their attention fully on the coach.

"Let's get out there and prove some people wrong."

He didn't mention that his own job was on the line, but the intensity of his brief talk remained as practice began. Derrick lined up between Aaron and rookie quarterback Jay Ryder—a fourth-round draft pick out of Texas A&M. The three of them were taking snaps and firing consecutive short-pattern passes.

Aaron threw another one and grinned at Derrick. "I was waiting for Coach to say, 'Aaron Hill isn't God.'" He laughed. "Since he got all religious on us."

Derrick caught the snap and released it in a single fluid motion. "Well"—he kept his tone light—"you're not."

"Not what?" Aaron looked at him.

"God."

Jay Ryder grinned, but he didn't say anything. Jay was twenty-one, and he stayed quiet most of the time. Still figuring out his place on the team.

The center snapped the ball and hit Aaron in the chest. Frustrated, he snagged it off the ground and threw a bullet at the receiver. "I'm kidding, Anderson. Take a joke."

Derrick didn't push. Half the team was made up of people strong in faith, and Coach Cameron was one of them. His message wasn't meant to be humorous. Derrick spent enough time talking to the guy to know that much. Most likely, in his ongoing communication with the Lord, Coach had come to the realization once more that with God, all things were possible. All things.

Even a Super Bowl.

He and Aaron didn't talk again until after practice when they headed for their lockers. Derrick's was near the back, between Aaron's and Jay's. Coach made sure of that. Aaron took the lead down the aisle between the lockers. He'd been brilliant on the field today, probably spurred on by Derrick's comment.

Derrick kept pace with Jay. He was impressed with the young player. Four or five years and he would be a major contributing force in the league. "Good job today."

A smile lifted Jay's lips. "Thanks. My arm felt good."

They reached their places, and Aaron seemed to keep his back to them.

Derrick opened his locker and slipped off his cleats. As he did, his eyes fell on the photo that hung on the inside door of his space. A photo of his wife and him, and their four beautiful children.

"Your kids coming to practice next week?" Jay sat next to him and began working the laces on his shoes.

"They'll be here. Denae took them to Anaheim last week." He chuckled. "The two boys would rather be here than riding a rollercoaster. But she wants them to know more than the game."

"Wise woman." Jay slipped off his practice jersey. "So hey, I saw your name in the paper. What's that thing you did last night?"

Derrick pulled his shirt over his head and leaned on his locker. "Pizza party for some foster kids. The city's full of 'em."

Aaron turned and grinned at Jay. "Good old Derrick Anderson, saving the world one project at a time." He faced his locker again.

Jay raised his brow, as if to say maybe the comment was a little harsh. He pulled off his socks. "I did a report on you when I was in seventh grade. You did a lot of work with foster kids, even back then."

Derrick tried to focus. Aaron's reaction bugged him, but he kept his frustration to himself. The starting quarterback's cockiness covered up something deeper—that had to be the reason. He glanced at Jay and then at the photo of his family. "I learned something a long time ago." Derrick pulled his duffle bag from his locker and set it on the bench. The smell of sweat and ripe shoes was strong, the way it always was after practice. "Something that stayed with me."

"About foster kids?" Jay pulled his pads from his pants and hung them at the back of his locker.

"About life."

"Do tell us ..." Aaron turned around again. The frustration was gone, and in its place the easygoing smile known to sports fans around the country. "Oh, great and mighty one."

Derrick laughed to keep things light. At the same time, he remembered the kid's letter, the one the freckle-faced boy had given him last night at the youth center. He pulled it from his bag. If God wanted him to influence Aaron Hill, he'd have to get the guy to trust him. Easy for a rookie like Jay Ryder. Much more difficult for a proven player.

He cocked his head and stared at Aaron. "Who you are as a man, as a player, isn't about what happens out there on game day." He held up the envelope and then handed it to Aaron. "It's what you do between Sundays. That's what matters."

"Between Sundays." Jay drew out the words, as if they were hitting him in slow motion. "I like that."

Aaron took the letter. "What's this?"

"A kid gave it to me last night. Wanted me to give it to you."

Aaron gave the envelope another look and then tucked it along one side of his locker. "That's really how you spent your Friday night, Anderson? Having pizza with a bunch of kids?"

"And a whole roomful of foster parents."

Aaron whistled. "Doesn't get any better than that."

"You're doing it again this week, right? Didn't I read that?" Jay finished undressing and wrapped a towel around his waist.

"Every Friday or Thursday night throughout the preseason." Derrick hesitated. "Come with me this week. The kids'll love it."

"I was thinking that." Jay nodded, thoughtful. He looked like a taller version of Tiger Woods. Same lanky body, same easy smile. He would've been a hit with the ladies, but his family kept a tight circle around him. "Might help me connect more with the people of the city."

"Exactly." Derrick was almost ready for the showers too. "How 'bout you, Hill. You up for a Friday night at the youth center?"

Aaron chuckled, then he squinted and looked at the ceiling for a moment. "Let's see . . . Friday night." He raised his eyebrows at Derrick. "Booked solid. Sorry."

Jay slipped his bag back into the locker. "Why foster kids? I mean, the city's got sick kids too. And a bunch of other causes."

The reason didn't come up often. Most people never asked. Derrick tucked his towel around himself. "When I was young, my best friend was a guy named Mikey, a foster kid. He moved around, three or four homes, but he always stayed in the area." Derrick shut his locker. "'Cause of him."

"You stay in touch?" Jay leaned against his locker.

"No." Derrick felt the familiar pain, the one that never quite went away. "Mikey turned eighteen and started selling drugs. Got messed up with a gang. Two years later he was killed in a drive-by."

Jay groaned and stared at the rubber mat beneath his feet. After awhile he looked up. "Makes sense now."

"Hey, man," Aaron patted Derrick's shoulder. "I'm sorry. I didn't know."

"It was a long time ago." Derrick didn't want to talk about Mikey. "When I'm done with football, maybe I'll run for office. Get a bunch of programs in place so foster kids'll have some way to transition into real life."

They headed for the showers, and the conversation stalled. Even if Aaron made light of the idea, and despite the fact that his Friday night was booked, Derrick had seen something change in his teammate's eyes at the mention of Mikey. Whatever caused the difference in Aaron's expression, it was enough to give Derrick a glimmer of hope. The purpose God had in connecting him with Aaron Hill might not be something Derrick had to wonder about for weeks on end. Rather, it might be on the verge of showing itself.

For that reason, as he showered, he switched up his prayer for the starting quarterback. Rather than praying for an inroad to the guy's heart, he prayed for something else.

An open Friday night.

Four

Saturday night was a disaster, and Sunday was looking worse. Now on his day off, Aaron pulled into the parking lot at the 49ers facility in Santa Clara and climbed out of his Hummer. He never should've taken the girl up on her offer. She was gorgeous, but she wore a low-cut shirt and too much eye makeup. The trashy kind of girl he'd been good at staying away from.

Saturday night he got careless, and Sunday the story was on the front page of sports. He pulled a baseball cap low over his eyes and headed for the side door. The meeting today was between his agent and Coach Cameron. Not that Aaron had much to worry about.

His agent, Bill Bonds, had already briefed him earlier that morning.

"How bad is it?" Aaron was standing in the kitchen when the call came in. "What's the buzz?"

"No one's happy." His agent sighed. There was no hiding his frustration. "Cameron wants to bench you for the first preseason game. Teach you a lesson."

"Great." Aaron downed a glass of orange juice. "What about the front office?"

"They're against the idea. A little good publicity, a batch of stories off the subject, and they think everything'll be fine."

"The bar girl?" Aaron leaned against his kitchen counter. He could've had his pick from the women that night. A sigh squeezed through his clenched teeth. "Any news from her lawyer?"

"Not yet. I'm waiting for the call." Bill paused. "I'm pretty sure she'll drop charges, but it'll cost you, Aaron."

"That's fine. Whatever."

"Yeah, whatever." His agent gave a bitter laugh. "We'll talk about it at the meeting today, and listen …"

He waited.

"I've been looking out for you since you were a college kid, Hill. Image is everything. We can't afford this sort of thing."

"Yeah, well ... I met with my financial guy last week." He chuckled. "Pretty sure we can afford it."

"This isn't funny." Bill sounded tired. "Don't be late today, Hill. I mean it."

"Yeah, yeah. I'll be there."

His agent's tone put a cloud over the morning, one that stayed now as Aaron walked through the door, down the hall, and into the meeting room next to the cafeteria. He wasn't late, but he wasn't early either. Coach Cameron, two assistants, the offensive coordinator, and Bill were already seated around the table.

His agent took the lead. "Sit down."

"Listen." Aaron found the right sort of tone. He took the spot next to Bill and met the eyes of the coaches. "This whole thing's being taken out of context."

Coach Cameron's anger showed in the lines on his face. He stood and paced along a bank of windows overlooking the practice field. "A seventeen-year-old girl's giving out interviews like candy, telling the press you made out with her in the parking lot and tried to pressure her into having sex in the back of your Hummer." He stopped and stared at Aaron. "What exactly is being taken out of context?"

"Look," Aaron sighed. "She told me she was twenty-three. A girl wears that much eye shadow and anyone would believe her."

Coach's forehead creased with concern. "She said you forced your hands up her shirt and pushed her toward the back door of your car."

"Come on." Aaron tossed out a few weak chuckles, but stopped. No one else was laughing.

"Are you saying you didn't do those things?" Bill's tone was kinder now, gentler. He was working the situation for Aaron's benefit, the way he always worked it. No matter how Bill felt about Aaron's Saturday night, his agent wouldn't let the team know he was worried.

"Of course not." Aaron rocked back in his chair. "I kissed the girl, okay. I invited her back to the house. But forcing her?" he huffed. "Not bragging, guys, but I'm a gentleman with my dates." He tried a weak smile. "I don't have to force myself. Just doesn't happen."

Bill shot him a look, as if this maybe wasn't the time to talk up his off-field conquests.

Coach Cameron leaned against one of the windows. "You're amazing, Hill. Whole world thinks you're a hero, when you're nothing but a jerk."

"Listen." Bill was on his feet. "We didn't bring him in here to call him names. He was out having a little fun, and he's allowed that much." He returned slowly to his seat. "I'm expecting the girl to drop charges today."

"Four days before preseason?" The offensive coordinator shook his head. "I'd like to think my multimillion-dollar starting quarterback was home studying plays on the weekend. Not hitting up girls at the local bar."

Silence hung over the room. Coach Cameron finally drew a long breath and took his place at the table again. "The penalty holds. Derrick's starting at quarterback the first preseason game." He leveled a look at Aaron. "Maybe for the first two games."

"Look." Aaron felt a flash of anger rip through his gut. "That's ridiculous. I told you the girl's—"

Next to him, Bill Bond's cell phone rang. *Good*, Aaron thought. Maybe it was the girl's attorney.

Bill stood and excused himself. While he was gone, Coach Cameron talked about his plans for the season, his dreams. "We have no room for this kind of garbage, Hill. Not a minute of it." He tapped his fingers on the table. "You're not the only guy on this team." He gestured toward the window. "We got guys who'll get cut if things don't go well this year. Guys whose future depends on you. Ever think of that?"

Not even the slightest regret rattled around in Aaron's head. He shrugged, his tone light. "I didn't think I was on the clock."

"You need to start thinking." Coach sneered at him. "You're the quarterback of this team. You're always on the clock."

Before Aaron could think of another way to defend himself, his agent returned. Victory screamed from his expression. "Done!" He held up his cell phone as he took his place at the table. "She dropped the charges. Her official statement's going to say she must've misunderstood Aaron's intentions."

"What'd that cost you, Hill?" The offensive coordinator shot him a look.

"If you paid her off, the press'll find out." Coach Cameron glared at him.

The team had nothing to worry about. Bill had paid off women before. No one would ever find out. Besides, he really had thought the girl was older. She lied to him, trapped him. Now she had what she wanted. She was a snake, and Aaron should've seen through her. But it didn't matter now. The incident was behind him.

"Hey, listen." Aaron kept himself from smiling. This wasn't the time to act smug. He never meant to hurt the team. "I'm sorry, Coach. Really."

Bill looked surprised and somewhat relieved. He cleared his throat. "Exactly, gentlemen. Aaron meant nothing by this. Taking away his starting position at the beginning of the season won't be good for him or"—he looked straight at Coach Cameron—"for any of you."

"It'll be my decision." Coach's answer was quick. He stood, and the other three coaches followed suit. "We have another meeting. But we'll be watching." He narrowed his eyes. "I won't have a team marked by moral failure."

Aaron wanted to ask him whether the front office agreed on Coach Cameron's definition of morality. "Can I say something?"

"What?"

He could feel the warning look from his agent, but he didn't care. "I never asked to be defined by my moral character, only by my play on the field." He crossed his arms. "I don't want or deserve my reputation as a good guy." His voice filled with intensity. "The fans did that, not me."

"Oh, yeah?" Coach Cameron uttered a bitter laugh. "You're unbelievable, Hill." He walked to the door, stopped and looked back at Aaron one last time. "Rather than complain about your good reputation, maybe it's time you start earning it."

The coaches left the room and Aaron turned to his agent.

"Way to go." Bill raked his fingers through his hair. "You don't tell the head coach it isn't your fault people like you. Fan support is huge to the 49ers." Bill exhaled hard. "I spend my whole career investing in you, Hill. But you still don't get it, do you?" He stared hard at Aaron. "You shatter the image, and it'll all disappear. The fans, the endorsements, the autograph parties. All of it."

Aaron stared out the window at the stretch of grass beyond. An image, that's all he was. He knew it and Bill knew it. The coaches knew it. Maybe it would be easier if the fans knew it too. Derrick Anderson's words came back to him. *It's what you do between Sundays. That's what really matters.* That was fine for guys like Derrick Anderson, but Aaron had already had his chance at doing things right. Way back when Amy Briggs was still in his life. Since then, the only thing he wanted to do between game days was push himself harder in the weight room, faster on the field, always looking for the edge.

"Look"—Aaron turned to his agent—"I give everything I've got on that field. The 49ers aren't paying me to be nice."

"Yeah, well, maybe you'd like to take a look at this." He reached into his briefcase and pulled out a few pages stapled together. "AOL did a vote last night over a six-hour window." He moved the document close enough for Aaron to see. "They asked the public if the story about you and the teenage girl lowered their opinion of America's favorite quarterback."

His heart beat a little faster than before. "They did that?"

"Look at the results."

Aaron peered at the columns beneath the question. Sixty-three percent said the story had harmed the way they saw him. He winced. "Who verifies that garbage?"

"It doesn't matter." Bill flicked the paper. "Everyone who reads it takes it as truth, and in the process it becomes truth. Whether it's true or not."

"What's the second page?"

"Two faxes from your top sponsors. They're advising you to clean up your image or else."

Aaron flipped the first page and stared at the first fax. "They're threatening to cut me? Because of one story?"

"They can do that." Your sponsors are in the business to sell tennis shoes and sportswear. They make their money on a clean-cut image. The good kids, the athletes—they wear the stuff."

Aaron understood. He pictured himself sitting at the table with his offensive line Saturday night. The blonde vixen had lured him into the parking lot in no time. But who could've seen it leading to this? He sighed. "So what's next?"

"Damage control." He pushed the papers toward Aaron. "Keep that as an incentive."

"Meaning what, an autograph session after practice?"

"You're supposed to be doing that anyway." The stress showed in the shadows on Bill's face. "I was thinking more like this pizza thing Derrick Anderson is doing. Helping out with foster kids."

Aaron tightened the muscles in his jaw. Derrick Anderson. The coaching staff had run the acquisition by him before they hired him: "He'll be like a mentor, Aaron. Someone to help ground you a little." From the beginning Aaron didn't like the idea. Derrick was a legend. He would hardly go quietly into the night, so what place did he have on the 49ers? Aaron was the star quarterback of this franchise.

But the front office suits had their minds made up, and in the end Aaron had little choice except to make the best of it.

Aaron rocked back in his chair again. "So, go to the next pizza party with him? That's what you want?"

"It'd be easy. The team hosts the Bears Thursday night, so Friday'll be light practice. Spend the evening with a bunch of kids at a youth center, and people will think a whole lot more of you than they do today."

Hanging around a bunch of kids no one else wanted? He had nothing to offer kids like that. He could think of a dozen ways he'd rather spend a Friday night, but the letters from his sponsors were serious business. He didn't care about being good, but he cared about his sponsors. He could go with Derrick once, couldn't he? Put in an appearance.

Bill was moving ahead, talking about the logistics. "I've already asked Derrick. He says you can join him, no problem. Once you commit, I'll tip off the media. Tell 'em if they want to see the real Aaron Hill, they can catch him by surprise at the Mission Youth Center."

"Won't they see through that?" Aaron didn't like the idea, but there was no other way. If the stunt was going to work to improve his image, then the media had to capture it.

"This city loves you, friend." He gave a wary laugh. "Even now. Give them a reason to catch you doing something good and it'll be front-page news. I promise."

Aaron didn't need long to think about it. He had no choice. "Fine. But just once. If I need a charity, it'll be something less personal, raising money for a Little League park, something like that." He raised one eyebrow. "Kid charities are for the married guys, right? That's what you always told me, right?"

"That was in your first few years." The lines at the corners of Bill's eyes looked deeper. "To be honest, you'd be better off meeting a nice girl and settling down. You stay single much longer and people will peg you a playboy. I told you that last year, remember?"

Bill was probably right. He usually was. The agent had been with Aaron from the beginning, back when he was a sophomore in college. Bill couldn't legally sign Aaron until after college, but he hung around, handing out free advice and connecting Aaron with the best trainers and dieticians and financial planners. His UCLA coach warned him about Bill and anyone else too anxious to step in and help Aaron make decisions. But by the time he graduated from UCLA, Bill was more a father to him than his own dad.

Which was why, when Amy called and said she was pregnant, Aaron talked to Bill first.

Good thing. Bill did some checking and found out Amy was seeing other guys on the side. Aaron was shocked, stunned. If Bill hadn't had exact times and places where she'd been, Aaron wouldn't have believed it. He had loved Amy, and the news crushed him as nothing else ever had.

Bill apologized for bringing the truth to light, but Aaron didn't fault him. In fact, after losing Amy, the hint of doubt Aaron had harbored about Bill and his motives disappeared. Aaron moved into his pro career trusting Bill Bond completely. Everything Bill said made sense. And Bill had a lot to say—especially about Aaron's private life.

"You're better off single," Bill had always told him. "More marketable. A relationship will threaten your role as America's heartthrob." And always he would add, "Whatever you do, Hill, don't get someone pregnant. It'd be a death knell to your image."

His agent doled out advice almost daily, and always it was intended to help Aaron some way. Bill looked out for him, and when he had an idea— the way he often did—he talked about Aaron as if the two of them were a team. "We should think about that ..." or "We would never consider such an offer." That sort of thing.

Now Aaron watched as Bill made a few quick phone calls, the tips to the media he'd promised. Bill would lay down his life for Aaron, no question. If he thought Aaron needed to spend a Friday night with Derrick Anderson and a gym full of foster kids, so be it.

Aaron stood and motioned to Bill that he had things to do. Before he left, he needed to check his locker. He was missing a pair of running shoes, and he had a feeling they were mixed with the junk at the bottom of his space.

The locker room was empty, everyone else enjoying the day off. Aaron hurried down the long aisle to his spot and opened the door. As he rummaged around, he felt the envelope—the letter from the foster kid. He pushed it toward the back. No time for fan mail today. He wanted to spend an hour in his pool and get his Hummer cleaned up. He had a date tonight with a French bikini model, the sort of girl he could picture himself settling down with. For a few months, anyway. Or maybe forever. Which wouldn't be the worst thing. Because maybe settling down would do the one thing seven years and a string of women had never quite been able to do.

Make him forget about Amy Briggs.

FIVE

Megan had been up since just after four that morning, but she wasn't tired. Today was Monday, and she had a shift at the youth center that afternoon. These were the best days of the week, the days she felt closest to God. On occasion, she read her worn-out Bible, the one that used to belong to her grandmother. From what she could gather, Jesus wanted people to serve. More than that, maybe the entire reason people were created was to serve. So the world would get a better picture of Jesus, the way He had worked when He was on earth.

Megan had known church kids when she was in high school. Mostly the kind that spent Wednesday nights at youth group and Friday nights slamming back a six-pack of Budweiser. Popular kids from the right families, kids who had convinced their teachers and parents that being part of a church meant they were the good kids. They stayed away from Megan because she didn't have the right clothes or the right home life. Not one ever tried to be her friend.

No, Jesus wouldn't have hung out in stuffy wooden pews with mostly hypocrites, reciting an hour's worth of songs and prayers once every Sunday. He would've been at the youth center, shooting hoops with the kids who didn't have anyone.

She finished her paper route and put in her time at the diner. Then she hurried home and ran up two flights of stairs to her apartment. She had thirty minutes to be at the youth center, where Cory had gone after school, just enough time to grab a yogurt and an apple. She rushed through the door and when she finished eating, she made a quick cup of coffee, poured it into her travel mug, and changed out of her uniform.

Cory hadn't stopped talking about the pizza party, of course. When he was home, he checked the answering machine three times an hour in case he might've missed a call from Aaron Hill. Megan almost wished the guy would call. Then, for all time, Cory could put aside the fantasy that the quarterback was his father.

She tucked a loose strand of hair behind her ears and ran down the stairs. She was five minutes later than usual, and she wanted to make up the time. Which she would. She was used to making up time. Her jobs kept her running, and today was no exception. She hurried out onto the street, and five blocks later she zipped down the stairs and bought a ticket to Mission 24th Street. Some days she walked the whole way, but not this afternoon.

The kids expected her at a certain time. They counted on her.

Megan liked taking the BART — the Bay Area Rapid Transit system. It gave her a few minutes to think about the day and the grant proposal she was working on. She pulled it from her bag and studied what she'd written so far. It started with the scenario of a fictional foster boy, the year after his eighteenth birthday. In a short sequence of events, the boy graduates from high school and learns there is no longer room for him at his foster home. Not long afterward, he's stealing from the cash drawer at a convenience store and being locked up for theft. When they let him out, he connects with a drug dealer, running deals, collecting cash.

The story was compelling, and Megan had a suspicion that if she could get the proposal into the hands of the right people, the grant money might actually become available. Maybe a person didn't need to be highly educated or famous or wealthy to ask for government funding. Maybe they only needed passion.

She tucked the papers into her bag and surveyed the other passengers. At the back of the car were a mother and daughter, both of them hollow-eyed and silent. The girl was maybe ten or eleven, and she had her head on her mother's shoulder. Megan didn't want to stare, but for a moment she was looking at herself, just as she had at the youth center, the way she looked the few times she was reunited with her mother during her childhood. The brief flashes when she'd been granted the privilege of laying her head on her mother's shoulder. Anyone who'd seen Megan back then would've known from her eyes what she was thinking. How, if only she could freeze time, she would never, ever leave her mama's side again.

Megan looked away. The car was slowing, coming to her stop. She stood quickly and was the first one off. Whatever the story between the mother and daughter, Megan didn't have time to stick around and find out. The city was full of sad stories.

She ran lightly up the stairs and down the sidewalk toward the center. The sidewalk teemed with people, folks of every color, size, and shape. San Francisco was a melting pot of nationalities. The shops along the way told the story. A Korean thrift store, a Chinese dry cleaner, a Vietnamese grocer.

Megan pushed open the door to the center and glanced into the gymnasium. Four older kids were playing Ping-Pong, but most of the regulars weren't here yet. She set her bag under the desk in the office and found her whistle, the one she wore when she worked the pickup games.

On the way into the gym, she spotted a kid sitting on the floor in the hallway, leaning against the brick wall. His knees were drawn up, his head down, resting on his forearms. Megan looked closer and recognized him. He was a stocky black kid, loud and cocksure, a junior football player in high school. He'd been placed in a group home a few months ago — an event that triggered trouble for many foster kids. Last she heard, the boy was on academic probation, his place on the football team in jeopardy.

A trio of teenagers entered the building and grinned at her. Megan returned the smile and waited until they moved on into the gym. Then she headed down the hall until she reached the boy on the floor. "Rudy?"

He didn't look up. "Leave me alone."

Megan dropped slowly onto the floor in front of the boy. She sat cross-legged and made her voice softer, gentler. "Can't do that, Rudy. You know me."

A sigh slid through what sounded like clenched teeth. "Doesn't matter."

These were the same things she heard over and over again at the center. *Doesn't matter … leave me alone …* Kids who weren't coping, kids already jaded and betrayed by the system. The future was crashing in all around these kids. Of course it mattered or Rudy wouldn't be here.

Megan wasn't in a hurry. "Is it school?"

He was silent.

Details came back to her, a conversation she'd had with one of the other volunteer counselors. "You had a big math test Friday, right?"

"Yeah." He looked up, his eyes distant and defiant. Fear was there too, the way it was for most foster kids. But like the others, Rudy was good at hiding fear. He exaggerated a shrug. "Left my math book on the kitchen table and one of the kids took it. Couldn't study without a book."

Megan winced. "How'd you do?"

Rudy clenched his jaw. "Failed it." Another shrug. "Who cares, man? What's it matter?"

"A lot, Larry. You're going to college, remember?"

"For what?" He narrowed his eyes and shook his head. "Man, you talked to Toby lately? Got hisself a scholarship until Christmas break. Then what? School closes and he winds up in a mission, mixing with the homeless." Rudy shrugged again. "Didn't go back, 'cause what's the point? He wasn't staying in no homeless shelter all summer, you know?"

Megan felt her heart breaking. This was the exact scenario that needed addressing. Why wasn't a counselor at the college made aware of the situation for foster kids? What would it take to give them year-round housing through college? She stifled her frustration. "You can't give up, Rudy. Education's the only way out of here. You know that."

They talked a few more minutes, and Megan patted his shoulder. "Bring your math test Wednesday. You and I are going over it one problem at a time. I'll call your teacher so you can take it over."

He lifted his eyes, apathy and doubt meeting in his expression. "Then what?"

"Then we spend a few minutes every day going over it until the semester's over and you have a grade you're proud of."

Rudy looked at the floor for a few seconds. "I saw my picture the other day."

"Your picture?" A surge of hope pulsed through Megan's veins. He was listening to her, and that was progress.

"Yeah." He narrowed his eyes. "On a photolisting."

He might as well have slipped a knife between her ribs. The photolisting was part of the state's adoption website. Rudy was among hundreds of kids listed with a photo and a short bio. Kids who were a stone's throw from adulthood, still waiting to be adopted. She resisted her desire to tell him the photolisting was a good thing, that an adoption could happen. He had a better chance of winning the lottery. Instead, she sighed and put her hand on his big worn-out Nikes.

"They got it all fancy and everything." He spoke through clenched teeth. "Says Rudy Booker's a friendly young man with great athletic ability and much potential. Rudy's still hoping that you'll be his forever family." He threw his hands up. "What a lie, huh?"

There was no clearing a path through the jungle of disappointment Rudy was venturing toward. Instead, Megan took a quick breath and smiled. "You got me, Rudy. Me and your math book, which you're bringing Wednesday." She stood and reached her hand out to him.

For a few seconds he hesitated, but then he clasped her hand and pulled himself slowly to his feet. "Still don't know why."

"'Cause I said so." She wasn't nearly as tall as him, but that didn't matter. Rudy was a kid, and he, like so many of the teenage foster children who acted tough, really wanted a parent figure. Megan wasn't nearly old enough to be Rudy's mother, but the years had given her a wisdom that belied her age.

Rudy must've sensed that, because he gave her a reluctant grin. "Fine. But don't be surprised if I show up at your door with my suitcase someday."

"Any time, Rudy." She stopped and faced him. She was too young to adopt him, but she would never stand by and let him fall through the cracks. Not as long as there was a spot on her sofa. "I mean it."

This was the part of her job Megan liked most of all. Learning about the kids who were about to become a statistic, and doing whatever she could to show them a way to succeed. A way to survive.

After an hour of heated pickup ball, Megan retreated to the lunchroom. She needed to call a couple social workers, and the youth center had a phone in the small eating area. Communication between the adults who cared for foster kids was crucial.

An old TV sat on a rickety stand at the corner of the room, tuned in to ESPN. As Megan sat down, the story on the set changed and Aaron Hill's face filled the left half of the screen. A concerned-looking anchorman announced that charges initially pressed against San Francisco's star player for the 49ers were no longer an issue. "Early today, the teenager who first reported sexual harassment by Hill withdrew her complaint. A statement, issued through her attorney, said the girl was confident she misunderstood Hill, his actions, and his motives." The anchor looked down at his notes. "In other NFL news …"

The girl misunderstood him? Megan rolled her eyes and focused on the phone calls. She could only guess how much money Hill had paid for the misunderstanding to come to light. Stories like this about Aaron Hill were rare. Megan had only caught wind of an occasional tabloid headline where the quarterback had been seen at this bar or that party.

But the story wasn't a surprise.

Aaron Hill's arrogance shone through in every interview. He acted as if he were invincible, king of the world, an island. Rarely did he talk about his teammates or share the light with his supporting cast. He'd been careful with his reputation — or someone had carefully looked out for him. But that didn't change the guy's character. Megan was glad for Cory that Aaron Hill wasn't his father. The sooner Cory became convinced, the better.

As for the news, thanks to Mrs. Florentino, the story had slipped by without Cory noticing it. The woman down the hall had called Megan, concerned about the bad press surrounding Cory's hero. "I keep the paper tonight, yes?" she asked.

"Yes." Megan's heart warmed. The woman was beyond thoughtful. "You keep the paper. Thank you."

Megan finished her phone calls. One to a social worker about a teenage girl who'd come to the center last week with bruises on her arm. Megan had called the social worker the first time that same afternoon. Today the girl hadn't shown up, and Megan needed to talk to her social worker to hear the news.

"We moved her to a different foster home." The caseworker sounded encouraged. "Apparently she was sneaking out to meet her boyfriend, and last week they got into a fight. The guy's just a junior in high school, but already he has a history of abuse."

Megan was confused. "So they pulled her from her foster home?"

"No supervision. Something like this, we figure she needs a new environment." The social worker hesitated. "It wasn't a great match in the first place."

Megan wondered if she could add another sofa to her already crowded apartment. "Where is she today?"

"With a counselor. She's pretty upset."

The call ended with Megan more discouraged than ever. The girl gets abused and loses her foster family all in one week. Of course she was upset. Megan would make a point to pull her aside and talk to her when she returned to the center.

The second call was to Rudy Booker's social worker. Megan gave the man an update on the teenager and asked for the phone number of Rudy's school.

"I'll follow up on the math test." Megan found a pad of paper in her purse and jotted down the school's number. "I'm sure they'll let him take it again."

"Thank you." The man sighed. "I'll make a call too. But if you've got time to tutor him, that could make the difference."

"Yes." Megan looked out the door and into the adjacent gymnasium. Twenty-five kids were lined along the walls waiting for a turn on the court. "Sometimes the smallest things make the difference for these kids."

When she was finished, she hung up the phone and headed back to the gym. Cory met her in the hallway, his eyebrows raised high into his forehead. He still had his backpack slung over his shoulder.

"Any phone calls?" His eyes were so wide she could practically see the whites around them.

Megan wrapped her arm around his slim shoulders and pulled him close. "No."

Cory was antsy. He pulled back and searched her face. "Some kid told me Aaron Hill's in trouble with the police." Anger flashed in his eyes. "That's crazy, right?"

She wanted to be careful how she handled this one. Honesty was everything to kids like Cory. "The news said a girl accused Aaron of doing something wrong. But she changed her mind yesterday, so everything's okay."

Cory made a face. "Probably a Raider fan."

"Probably." Megan wanted to change the topic. "How was school?"

"I aced my spelling test." He stuck his chest out. "Mrs. West said she wouldn't be surprised if I'm the smartest boy in third grade."

"Of course." Megan's voice was ripe with teasing. "Look who's helping you with your homework."

"True." Cory hugged her again. "Hey, my bike got a flat tire. I walked it all the way up the last hill."

Megan thought about the money she didn't have. "I think there's a patch in one of the drawers in my office. Seems like someone donated a pack of patches a few months ago."

"So … not a new tire?" Cory didn't look disappointed, just matter-of-fact. As if he wanted to be sure about his options.

"Nope, buddy. No new tire this year."

"Okay." He skipped ahead of her a few feet and then turned around. "Let's fix it later. The guys want you to ref the next game."

Megan laughed. "Last time they told me I need glasses."

"That's only 'cause they love you." Cory gave her a silly grin. "But I love you more, know why?"

This was the best part of her day, no question. The teasing and laughter she shared with Cory. Now if only he would let go of his insistence that Aaron Hill was his father. That way she could adopt him and he'd never again have to wonder where he belonged.

She played with the bill on his baseball cap. "Why do you love me more?"

"Because"—his eyes twinkled—"you're going to take me to Derrick Anderson's pizza party again this week." He folded his hands, his eyes pleading with her. "Please, Megan?"

The organizers of last week's party had already talked to her, and like before, she had promised that both she and Cory would help with cleanup. "Tell you what?" She took hold of both Cory's hands. "Every time Derrick Anderson has a pizza party at the youth center, you and I will go. I promise."

"Wow!" Cory's eyes lit up. "You're the best ever! I mean it." He began turning in a circle, still holding her hands until they were both dizzy. Then he threw his fists in the air and danced around. "I can't believe it!"

Megan watched him, and her heart filled with love. Sometimes Cory seemed so old for his age, so worldly and wise. He was only eight, but on his bike he could navigate through the roughest parts of the city, getting himself to and from school every day, and to soccer practice and home again. The vehicle code suggested an independent bicyclist should be eight or in third grade, which Cory was. More than that, he was savvy to bicycle safety, more than most older kids.

Here, though, his face filled with hope and wonder, the truth was very clear. Cory was still just a young boy, a child. Weekly dinners with one of the 49ers was a dream come true.

After he settled down and they were on their way into the gymnasium, Megan stopped him. "One thing though …"

"What?" Cory was still buzzing with excitement. He bounced in place while he waited for her to continue.

"No more letters for Aaron Hill." She raised her eyebrows just a little. "Derrick Anderson's a good guy. He passed on your letter, I'm sure."

"But …" Cory's face fell, "Aaron hasn't called."

Megan wasn't sure how to say this, but it had to be said. If not now, then later. "Cory …" They were in the entryway into the gym, and she leaned against the doorway. The pickup game could wait. "What if Aaron isn't your dad? Remember, we talked about that."

A shocked look flashed in Cory's eyes. "But I told you … " His tone was filled with hurt. "My mom said it was true, and my mom never lied to me. Not ever."

Great. Megan steadied herself. *Any ideas, God? I'm fresh out here.*

Do not worry, daughter … every day has enough worry for itself.

The words seemed to come from somewhere deep inside her, but Megan had heard them before. They were from a Bible verse, something she'd read from one of the Gospels. She uttered a silent thanks to God. "You're right, Cory." She smiled at him. "Your mother would never lie." She put her arm around his shoulders again. "Let's not worry about it right now." The guys were picking teams on the other side of the gym. "We have a game to play."

For a few beats, Cory looked wary. As if he wanted to bring the subject up again. But Megan jogged with him over to the guys. The kids were a mix of ages and colors, both boys and girls. A few of the older kids had made sure the teams were fair, and for the next hour Megan did her best to officiate.

By the time the game was finished, Cory was himself again, but he didn't bring up Aaron Hill or the phone call that never came. Not that day or the next, or Saturday night when the 49ers played the Bears in the first preseason game. Aaron stayed on the field the entire first half until they were winning 21–0. Derrick played the second half and threw another three touchdowns.

Even then, Cory asked nothing about whether Aaron had called. Megan wasn't sure what to make of his silence. Most likely, he didn't want her to question the issue again. Whatever the reason, Cory believed with all his heart that his mother had told him Aaron Hill was his father. Even so, she hoped his silence on the issue might be a sign of something else. That no matter what he believed or even what his mother believed, the truth was clearer with every passing hour. Aaron Hill was a talented quarterback.

But he wasn't Cory's father.

SIX

Derrick felt better than he had in years.

The last game was proof he wasn't past his prime, and though the starting job would of course go to Aaron, Derrick stood ready to fill in whenever needed. The newspapers shouted loud about his efforts, calling San Francisco the only two-quarterback show in the NFL. For a time, it had looked like Derrick might even get the start for the game against the Bears. But in the end, the front office made the call. Aaron was the franchise. One shady news story wouldn't put him on the bench.

All that and this: Aaron Hill was sitting shotgun in his Ford F–150, ready to spend an evening at the youth center. When he first found out from Coach that Aaron wanted to come along, Derrick almost laughed out loud. The idea couldn't have been Aaron's. Miracles didn't happen that fast.

"It's the girl, right?" Derrick had raised a wary eyebrow at Coach Cameron.

The man massaged his temples and frowned. "He needs a little good PR."

"So the press'll be there?" Derrick bristled at the idea. "This isn't about us, Coach. You know that."

He put up his hand. "The media wants in on anything Aaron does. I can't believe they'll send a camera crew. But a reporter or two are bound to show up for a slice of pizza."

Derrick choked back any further complaints. This was what he'd prayed for, that Aaron Hill might have a Friday night free to visit with foster kids. Anything to help him see past his own reflection in the mirror. However it had come about, Derrick had a feeling his teammate was bound to make progress tonight. The kids had that effect on everyone they met.

"That's it, right?" Jay Ryder was in the backseat. He leaned forward and pointed straight ahead. "The big brick building?"

"That's it." Derrick pulled into the parking lot, found a spot near the back of the lot, and cut his engine. He looked at his teammates. "There'll be a lot of kids tonight." His voice held the slightest warning. "Be patient. Most of them haven't ever been to something like this."

Jay got it. His expression said so. He gave a firm nod and climbed out of the truck. Then he heaved the oversized duffle bag over his shoulder. "That's a lot of water bottles and bumper stickers."

"T-shirts too." Derrick grinned as he stepped out. "Kids love T-shirts."

Aaron looked uncomfortable as he fell in next to Derrick. He looked at his watch. "So, what's the story? These kids are wards of the court, or homeless ... or what?"

Derrick stopped and stared at his teammate. "You're serious?"

"'Course I'm serious." Aaron looked embarrassed and irritated all at once. "I've been in a football uniform since ninth grade, Derrick. What do I know about this?"

No matter how far Aaron had to go, he needed to start somewhere. Derrick steadied himself and took a slow breath. "Foster kids don't have permanent families. Most of the time they were taken from their biological parents because of drugs or abandonment or criminal activity."

"That's where foster parents come in." Aaron nodded as if this was the part he understood. "They take care of the kids until someone adopts them." He hesitated. "Right?"

Derrick jerked his thumb toward the big brick building. "Ain't nobody gonna adopt the kids in that youth center. They're too old and too jaded. They've been passed from one foster home to another. We got thousands of them right here in San Francisco."

"I studied that in college." Jay moved closer, so the three formed a loose huddle. "People want to adopt babies, not middle-school kids." He stuck his hands in his pockets. "Makes me wonder ... I never woulda got here without my parents' support."

"Exactly." Derrick frowned at Aaron. "You understand a little better now?"

The walls in Aaron's eyes became a little thicker. "It isn't my thing, but yeah. I understand."

Derrick paused, but only for a moment. Then he looked past Aaron and started walking again. "All right, gentlemen. Let's go love up on some kids."

They moved into the building and the buzz through the gym was instant. Derrick had brought along two other players! Jay Ryder and ... and

Aaron Hill! Derrick waved at the kids as he directed his teammates to the front of the room. They set up near each other, so the kids could form one line and visit with each of the players all at once.

Just as the first kids reached the front of the line, Derrick remembered the boy's letter. He was sitting next to Aaron, and he nudged him. "Hey, what'd you do with that letter?"

Aaron leaned closer and held his hand up to his ear. The room was loud with the sound of excited kids.

Derrick raised his voice just enough to be heard. "The letter I gave you last week—what'd you do with it?"

The blank look on Aaron's face told the story. "Letter?"

"From the boy." Derrick scanned the room, but in a sea of kids, the freckle-faced boy with the big eyes didn't stand out. "I gave you a letter from a boy I met last week."

Aaron's expression changed. "Oh, that." He hesitated. "It's still in my locker."

A frustrated sigh forced its way through Derrick's lips. "If I see the boy, I'll tell you. At least you can fake it."

Aaron looked bored. "Whatever."

The kids were forming more of a mob than a line, and volunteers were trying to straighten them out. With that, the director of the center announced the players had arrived—in case anyone had missed their entrance—and they'd be meeting kids and signing autographs for the next couple hours. Pizza would be there in just a few minutes, and after dinner there would be another drawing.

A pair of little girls, clearly sisters, stepped forward. "Hi." The voice of the taller one was barely audible over the roar of the group.

Derrick reached out and took her hand. "Hi, I'm Derrick Anderson. What's your name?"

"Susie." The girl held tighter to the hand of her sister. "We love the 49ers."

"Yeah." The smaller one beamed a smile at Derrick and then at Jay and Aaron. "You guys are the best."

The three signed photos for her the girls, and as they walked off, Jay leaned in toward Derrick and Aaron. "This is amazing. I love it already."

Derrick felt his heart soar. He kept scanning the line, looking for the freckle-faced boy, so Aaron wouldn't be caught off guard. All the while, he couldn't help but think that finally . . . finally he could feel God smiling down on him. Maybe the whole team really would get behind the idea of helping the foster kids in their city. No matter the deep pain of his past, Derrick had to believe God had a plan for his life.

And here, now, he could almost feel it taking shape.

Aaron was just getting the swing of interacting with the kids when he spotted her. Across the gym and a third of the way back, sitting by herself was a woman who took his breath. At first he looked away, focused his attention on the kids in front of him. After all, he was here because of his wandering eye for women. The last thing he needed was an infatuation over a foster kid volunteer.

But every few minutes, no matter how hard he tried, Aaron couldn't help but look. The woman had pale skin and striking features. Her dark hair shone in the light that still streamed through the side doors. All of that was nothing to the look in her eyes. She was talking to a thin black woman seated beside her, and all the while, her expression was strong and independent. He would never find someone like that in a bar or hanging around the player exit after a game.

She wasn't dressed flashy, and when she stood and went to the pizza line he got a better look. She wore jeans and a long-sleeved knit shirt, simple and subtle, but the strength and character she exuded stirred something inside him. Derrick had to elbow him to get his attention.

"Focus, will you?"

He stared at the woman once more. "Sorry."

Derrick followed his gaze and squinted. "That's her."

"Who?"

Jay was busy signing an autograph and chatting with a teenage boy, a football player. Derrick pointed to the woman. "Remember the kid with the letter? That's his mom."

"Oh." The feeling of disappointment was crazy. Of course she was married. A woman like that, someone would've fallen for her years ago. "So where's her husband?"

For the fifth time that night, Derrick gave him a look like he'd asked where to find a dress for next week's game. "Who said anything about a husband?"

Aaron ignored the comment and did his best to welcome the next child. A little boy, maybe four years old. "Hi, pal. How's it going?"

"Are you really Aaron Hill?" The tyke looked suspicious. "'Cause I thought you were taller. My foster dad says you're bigger than life."

A flash of pride swelled in Aaron's heart. He didn't want to be here, but the adoration wasn't a bad thing. "Tell him I said thanks, okay?"

He didn't want to connect with any of the kids, even the cute ones. Do the time and fix his image. That's all he wanted from tonight.

Aaron waited until the young boy had moved on to Jay. "You said she was the boy's mom. That must mean there's a dad, right?"

"Aaron, you're the dumbest quarterback I ever met." Derrick laughed under his breath. "She's his *foster* mom. I have no idea if she's married or not." A warning sounded in his tone. "I wouldn't worry about it. Get my drift?"

"I get it." Aaron held out his hand and shook the much smaller one of a quiet girl. He didn't like being reprimanded by Derrick Anderson. Guy was a do-gooder, worse than his reputation had it. He found a smile for the little girl. "Hi, I'm Aaron Hill …"

Even as he welcomed the child, he caught another glimpse of the woman. What was it about her? The combination of strength and beauty. He didn't want to take her into the parking lot and kiss her. He wanted to meet her. Somehow he had an unexplainable sense that just talking to her, standing in her presence, would be an honor.

The line of kids was still halfway across the building, and finally an hour into it, after a pair of reporters and a photographer had come and gone, Derrick nudged him. "There he is. Five kids back." He nodded toward a boy with a 49ers baseball cap and a face full of freckles. "He's the one who gave me the letter."

"Perfect." Aaron felt his heart skip a beat. Ridiculous, he thought. He was Aaron Hill, most well-known football player in the country. Why was he getting nervous over meeting a grade-school kid? Even as the question passed through his mind, he knew the answer. It wasn't the boy who made him nervous, but the dark-haired beauty watching the child from a distance. She hadn't looked his way once, not that he'd seen. So she probably had no use for football players. That only made her twice as attractive. And if he was ever going to meet her, it would be because of how he handled himself in the next few minutes.

With a boy whose personal letter he hadn't even bothered to read.

⤙

Cory could barely stand still. The night was going better than he ever dreamed. And now ... now he finally knew why Aaron Hill hadn't called him. He'd decided to come to the center and meet Cory in person! Of course! It was a much better idea than a phone call.

He'd been helping Megan, setting up the last row of tables at the back of the gym when Derrick and Jay Ryder and Aaron walked in.

"Look!" He wasn't the only kid to react to the sight of three 49ers quarterbacks entering the gym.

Megan looked up and something changed in her eyes. "Hmmm. Aaron Hill."

"He came for me!" Cory felt his arms and legs start to shake. "Why else would he come?" He pounded out a little rhythm on the table. "Can you believe it?"

A tired expression came over Megan's face. "Help me with the rest of the chairs, okay? Then you can get in line with everyone else."

Cory helped with the chairs. He could hardly stand waiting, but he did it anyway. Because what was his rush? Cory's heart slammed hard against his shirt, lots harder than last time. Finally, the tables and chairs were where they needed to be and Megan told him he could go. "But don't say anything about the letter." Her look said she meant serious business. "I mean it, Cory. If he says something, fine. But leave it to him."

Her last words were barely out before Cory raced to the back of the line. That's where he stayed, inching forward a little more every minute or so, until now. Now, when there were just four kids left in front of him before it was his turn. He tried to look casual and normal, like any other boy.

But his armpits were sweaty and his eyes were stuck on Aaron Hill and no one else. He hadn't noticed it on TV before, but he and Aaron had the same nose. The exact same one. And the hair too. Cory's was a little blonder, but still ... they both had blond hair. And so, of course his mother was right all this time. Not that he was mad at Megan for not believing it. What foster kid wouldn't want Aaron Hill to be his dad? It was just that in his case, it was true.

Otherwise, Aaron wouldn't have read his letter and come tonight.

Three more kids and then it was his turn. The kids in front of him moved up a little, but before Cory could take a step, two sixth-grade boys slammed into the spot. They turned and made a face at him. The bigger of the two got close to Cory's face. "Don't say anything, punk. Not if you wanna make it to the front of the line alive."

Cory pushed the kid. "No cuts, loser." He wasn't afraid of the boys. The director already said no cuts, and he'd waited long enough to meet Aaron Hill. But the big kid meant what he said, and when he got his balance back, he grabbed Cory by the shirt and threw him onto the ground.

Kids came running up yelling, "Fight … fight … fight."

Even now Cory had no fear. The kid sat on him, pinning his stomach to the ground, but Cory kicked at his back. Just then a bunch of volunteers came rushing up and someone grabbed the kid off.

"That's enough from you boys." The director snarled her words at the big kid and at Cory too. "You boys will go sit at the back of the gym. No player meetings for you."

As she finished talking, Megan hurried over and put her hand on the director's arm. "I saw what happened. If you don't mind."

The director gave her a mean face. "I show no favoritism, Megan Gunn. Your boy was part of the scuffle. He has to follow the rules same as anyone else."

"I saw it too." The voice was familiar.

Cory looked up and his mouth hung open. It was Aaron Hill. His father had left his seat up front and come to his rescue!

"Those bigger guys cut in front." Aaron looked at the older guys. He smiled, but his voice was serious. "You shouldn't pick on kids smaller than you. Didn't anyone teach you that?"

The boys looked stunned too. Cory wanted to laugh. They probably never figured they'd be getting a talking-to from Aaron Hill before the night was over. The director had no choice now. She took a step back and pointed the older kids to the back of the gym. When they were gone, she looked at Cory. "Next time someone upsets you, tell a volunteer."

Cory wanted to say that telling a volunteer would never have worked. Because he woulda had to get out of line to tell someone, and then he wouldn't get his place back. Even if he was right. But he had the sense this wasn't the time to say that. Instead, he gulped and gave a quick nod. "Yes, ma'am."

"Very well." The director smiled at Aaron. "Thank you for stepping in."

The kids who had been in front of Cory were talking with Derrick and Jay Ryder. Megan put her hand on Cory's back and looked at Aaron. "Thank you." She sounded very professional. Not fun like usual. "Cory's waited ... a long time to talk to you."

"I know." Aaron put his hand on Cory's shoulder. "Last week he sent me a letter through my teammate Derrick."

If Cory could've frozen time, if he could've blinked and made all of life stop right at this very point, he would've. Because all his life he wondered what it would be like to feel his dad's touch. And now ... with all the kids racing through the gym and grabbing slices of pizza, he finally knew. Suddenly he realized what Aaron had said and he gasped. "You mean, you read it? I knew it!" He grinned at Megan. "I knew that's why he was here."

Aaron laughed, but not the sort of laugh like when something was funny. He faced Cory and held out his hand. "I'm Aaron Hill, Cory. Nice to meet you. Officially."

Officially. Cory liked that. He shook the man's hand and again he felt the connection, the feeling only a father could give. He returned the shake. "Nice to meet you." He wasn't sure what to call him. Maybe it was a little soon for "Dad." "Aaron" didn't sound exactly right either. Because no one called a father by his first name, right? So he didn't use any name at all, and that felt like a good decision.

Then, before he could ask Aaron what he thought of the letter or whether all the stuff inside was a total surprise or how long he had loved Cory's mother, Aaron Hill did a funny thing. He turned to Megan and held out his hand again. "You must be Cory's foster mom."

She took his hand, but she took a step back at the same time. And she released his fingers right away. "Nice to meet you, Mr. Hill."

"Aaron." He smiled. "You can call me Aaron."

"Very well." She angled her head. "Kicker, right?"

Cory couldn't believe his ears. Megan knew every player at every position on the 49ers. She'd been a fan even before Cory was born, that's what she said. So how come she was acting like she didn't know? Just then she gave him a look that was fast and clear. Whatever she was doing, he wasn't allowed to ask her about it. Not here and now.

"Uh..." Aaron did another soft laugh. "Actually, I'm the quarterback."

"Oh, right." Megan nodded. "You back up Derrick Anderson, right?"

Cory watched the conversation through wide eyes.

Aaron opened his mouth, probably to explain that it was the other way around. Because he was the starter, not Derrick. Then he smiled and nodded, real slow like. "Okay ... yeah."

Neither of them was making sense. Cory tapped on Aaron's arm, real polite like. "You coulda called me. I gave you the number at the bottom of the letter."

For a few seconds, Aaron looked confused. Then he crouched down so he was more at Cory's level. "I figured I'd see you here." He held up his hands. "And now it all worked out."

It all worked out? The room started to spin and Cory's whole mind raced like the hundred-yard dash. So he read the letter and he believed every word? It all worked out, meaning he was here to claim his role as Cory's father? Was that what he was saying?

The line was just about finished, and the remaining kids were all around Derrick and Jay. Cory had Aaron all to himself, but just then, the director asked for quiet because she had to do the drawings.

Aaron held up his finger. "Just a minute. This is my part." He jogged over to the director, and one at a time he picked five names. Five lucky kids. But Cory's name wasn't one of them. When Aaron was done, he came back and looked right at Cory. "You didn't win, huh?"

"No." Cory didn't want to sound sad. No one liked a spoilsport. That's what Megan always said. "I'll win one of these days." He said that because it was the right thing to say. But inside, he was hoping Aaron would have a different idea. Because he was Cory's dad, after all.

Aaron smiled at Megan. "How 'bout you two come to the next game as my guests? We're home against the Raiders a week from tomorrow."

"The Raiders?" Now Cory was sure he must've died and gone to heaven. Three weeks ago if someone would've told him he'd be standing in the youth center getting invited to the 49ers game against the Raiders by none other than Aaron Hill, he wouldn't have believed it. Not for a minute. His throat was dry, and he tried to swallow. "We'd love to." He turned a quick look to Megan. "Right?"

Megan looked only mildly interested. "I'm off that day." She shifted her attention to Aaron. "Thank you, Mr. Hill. How should we get the tickets?"

Cory couldn't understand why Megan wasn't being nice to Aaron. Maybe it was because of the adoption thing. She couldn't adopt him unless Aaron said it was okay. But all that was too much to think about right now. All that mattered was Aaron, here, right here where he was always supposed to be! He'd read the letter and now he wanted Cory and Megan to go to a game as his guests!

Aaron found one of the raffle tickets and turned it over. "Give me your address. I'll send the package overnight. You'll have it by Monday."

Megan didn't look happy, but she gave him their address. "We'll do our best to make it, Mr. Hill. Your offer's very kind."

Cory waited for Aaron to correct her. He already asked Megan to call him Aaron. But he only smiled at her. "After the game maybe we can go out for burgers."

Her look got a little stronger. "All this because you read Cory's letter?"

He looked a little embarrassed. "I guess it really touched me."

"Yeah." She thought about that for a few seconds. "That's what I figured." She nodded at him the way she looked at the cat when he missed the litter box. Then she took a step back. As she did, she took hold of Cory's arm and gently led him away from Aaron. "Cory has to help with cleanup."

For an instant, Cory thought Aaron was going to offer to help too, but just then Derrick and Jay Ryder came up. Aaron seemed to realize he wasn't here by himself, and that Cory and Megan weren't the only people in the room.

"Time to go." Derrick patted Aaron on the back. Then he waved at Cory. "Good to see you again."

"Thanks." Cory smiled at him and then at Jay. "I'm Cory." He held out his hand. "Nice to meet you."

"You too." Jay shook his hand. "Fun night, huh?"

Cory's heart was still doing somersaults. "The best ever!"

Aaron was looking at Megan and there was something funny in his eyes. "I'll be seeing you." He held one hand up toward Cory. "High five?"

Even though Megan still had hold of his arm, Cory stretched and high-fived Aaron. "See you next Saturday."

"See you then." Aaron smiled at him, but once more he looked at Megan. "I'm looking forward to it."

She nodded, more at Derrick and Jay than at Aaron. Then she turned Cory around and walked him to the kitchen. Cory waited until they were behind the swinging door before he tugged on her sleeve. "Megan?"

She groaned and he heard the tiredness in her voice. "What?"

"Why'd you ask if he was the kicker?" Cory was worried about her. If she was having trouble remembering that detail, maybe something was wrong with her brain.

She looked a little angry at first, but then that look went away and her face was soft again. "I was just playing around." She leaned in and kissed Cory's cheek. "It's good for big shots to be humbled once in a while." Megan kept on toward the double sinks. There weren't many dishes; pizza wasn't that messy. A few cutters and the salad forks and bowls from the serving table. That was all.

Cory tagged along behind, but he was confused. Making Aaron feel humble didn't seem like a very nice thing for Megan to do. "So, are you, like, you know, mad at Aaron for some reason?"

"No." She rolled up her sleeves and turned on the water. Then she looked at him. "I have my doubts about him, okay? That's all."

"Why would you have doubts?" Cory took his place next to her at the sink. He scooped up a handful of forks and put them in a bowl of sudsy hot water. "Aaron read my letter, he came here to meet me. And now he wants us to go to the Raiders game as his guests."

"I know." She sounded tired again. "I'm sorry, Cory. You're happy, I know that. I don't want to spoil your night."

"Good." He swished the forks around in the water. His voice got a little quieter. "My mom prayed about this night all my life. Ever since I was born." He stopped swishing. "That's what she told me."

Megan smiled. "Then I guess God answered her prayers."

Cory stared at the soapy water. He liked the way that sounded, and even more, he liked how it felt inside him. Because that's exactly what had happened. Two years after she died, God answered the prayer that mattered most in his mother's whole life. Now he only hoped that wherever she was in heaven, his mother was watching.

Because Cory had a feeling the answers had only just begun.

SEVEN

He hadn't read the letter; Megan was sure of that much. The nerve of the guy to show up and lie to Cory, and for what reason? If she didn't know better, she'd think he was hitting on her, that the whole invitation was more about that. Whatever it was, the lie made Megan furious.

That Monday she made sure she left with enough time to walk the whole way to Bob's Diner. She needed the fresh air to clear her head. The conflict between her real thoughts about Aaron Hill and the sheer adoration Cory had assigned the guy was driving her crazy. When Cory was home, all she could do was smile and nod and agree that Aaron was the greatest man ever. Why else would he have come to the pizza party?

But Megan saw through the guy from the beginning. If Aaron had read Cory's letter, if he knew Cory thought that Aaron was his father, he wouldn't have made a casual appearance at a pizza party, talking about how Cory's letter had touched him. Rather, he'd be panicking. He would've either ripped up the letter and never given it another thought. Or he would've called and tried to clear up the whole mess. At the very least, he would've pulled Megan aside and explained how Cory's beliefs were mistaken. Instead, he said nothing about it, which could only mean one thing. He hadn't read the letter.

Megan dodged a group of people gathered outside a liquor store.

"Hey pretty lady," one of them called out.

Megan ignored the comment. The city didn't scare her. She delivered papers before dawn. She knew her way around every bad alley and gang territory. A couple of catcalls from a bunch of winos weren't going to make her skip a step.

So had Aaron actually been interested in her? The idea was ridiculous, but why else would he pick the two of them to be his guests? She slowed her pace. Guilt maybe. He might've been feeling badly about not reading Cory's letter. Still, the way he'd watched her all night made her suspicious. Then, when Cory had the run-in with the older kids, Aaron stepped up and seized the moment. Rescuing Cory from punishment and meeting her all at the same time.

Now Cory was absolutely certain that the invitation meant Aaron was claiming his role as Cory's father.

Megan had ten minutes and only two blocks left. She stared up between the buildings toward the blue sky beyond. *God, I don't get it. If Amy prayed about Cory meeting Aaron Hill, why didn't she tell me? Cory must have his facts wrong. He must. He was only six when Amy died.*

She kept to the outer edge of the sidewalk. Fewer pedestrians to veer around. *So we go to the game and then what? Should I pull Aaron aside and tell him the content of the letter? Or just let him stumble along until Cory says something?*

Her heart felt a wave of peace as she silently voiced her concerns to God. He was her Savior and her friend. He listened whenever she had things to work through. *Thanks for being there, God. I need Your help on this one. I can't stand by and watch Cory get hurt.*

There was no answer this time, no Scripture that came to mind. But a sense of God's bigness came over her. She would stay quiet and let the details play out at this week's game. God would take care of the details because He cared deeply for each child.

Including Cory Briggs.

Megan's work at the youth center that afternoon put her emotions on a rollercoaster. There was the success of helping Rudy Booker study for his math test retake, and knowing he was ready to ace it first thing tomorrow morning. Then came the breakdown by the bruised teenage girl, as she told Megan about the difficulty in transitioning to her new foster home.

"I don't want to be a boarder," she admitted, tears streaming down her cheeks. "I want someone to love me."

"God loves you, sweetheart. He has plans for you, even if they're hard to see right now." Megan whispered her response. If the legislators could see this, foster reform would be a cinch. Megan sighed. She pulled the girl into an embrace and let her cry.

On the way home, Cory was quieter than usual, and even now with dinner over and the dishes nearly done, Megan could feel a tension between them. Normally Cory would help with the cleanup, but he had homework. Megan didn't mind. She was still thinking about Aaron Hill and his motives.

She wasn't interested in Aaron Hill, no matter what he had in mind. In high school she'd dated a guy from a wealthy family, and in the end she'd walked away more jaded and independent than before. Society had drawn lines and Megan understood her place. Pro football players didn't date women on food stamps.

Not that it mattered. Megan had no interest in committing her heart to a quality guy, let alone a playboy like Aaron Hill. Even if he lived in Nob Hill.

Bottom line, on Saturday the delusions Cory was carrying around were going to come crashing down around him. Because Aaron Hill wasn't Cory's father, and she wasn't interested in dating him. So this Saturday would likely be the last time Aaron would invite the two of them to be his guests at a 49ers game.

She thought about her high-school romance again. Her life had never been normal, not in the way it was for other girls her age. Now she was twenty-five, and nothing scared her more than the idea of relying on someone else.

Even the right guy.

The dishes were finished, so Megan dried her hands. She wandered into Cory's room and found him sitting on the floor near his bed, working on math. He didn't look up as she approached, and Megan was worried. Maybe her skepticism was seeping through, troubling Cory more than she'd realized.

"Hey, buddy." She sat on the edge of his twin bed. "Whatcha doing?"

"Times tables. Fours and fives."

Oreo walked into the room, meowed, and came to Cory. "Good boy." Cory patted his black and gray face. "You're a good friend." The cat curled up on the other side of Cory.

Megan smiled at the picture they made together. She pointed to the math paper. "You can count by fives, right?" She put her hand on his head and softly twirled a piece of his hair.

"Five, ten, fifteen, twenty, twenty-five, thirty ..." Cory looked up at her. "Yeah, I can do that."

"Then you know your fives times tables. Five times three, count three fives. Five, ten, fifteen." She held up her hands and smiled. "See? Three times five is fifteen."

The corners of his lips lifted a little. "Hey, that's cool. I get it." He thought for a bit. "Six times five, count it six times. Five, ten, fifteen, twenty, twenty-five, thirty! Six times five is thirty."

"Right." She brought her hand back to her side. "You're a good boy, Cory. I'm happy for you. About the game this Saturday."

"Really?" He wrinkled his nose and looked at her. "You don't seem like it."

She slid down onto the floor beside him. "I'm sorry." She took hold of his hand. "I don't want you to get hurt, that's all."

"I won't get hurt. I can't." Cory smiled at her as if he were the caring parent, trying to comfort *her*. "Aaron asked us to be his guests so he could talk to us about what happens next."

Megan kept herself from any show of disbelief. "And what do you think will happen next?"

"Well, that's what I'm thinking about." He drew a small football on the corner of his math paper. "'Cause if he wants me to come live with him"—Cory looked up, his eyes glistening—"then what about you, Megan? You're all the family I have."

Never mind that the idea of Aaron Hill asking Cory to live with him would never happen. The dilemma was a real one for Cory. Megan squeezed his hands twice, their sign for "Love you." She kept her tone even. "Don't you think Aaron would know that? How I'm the only family you have?"

"Yeah, but ..." Cory bit his lip. "I always wanted my dad too. So I don't know what to do or who to live with. You know?"

Megan closed her eyes. *God, are You catching this?* She held her breath and then let it out slowly through her tight lips. All of a sudden she remembered the verse from the last time she didn't know how to answer Cory. She opened her eyes. "Remember how we talked about not worrying about anything more than we can handle in any one day?"

"Yeah." Cory didn't sound sure. "What does that mean for today?"

"Well..." Megan pulled Cory's math paper a little closer. "It means today we work on times tables. And Aaron Hill can wait till Saturday."

Cory nodded. He still had his hand in hers. "Can I tell you something, Megan?"

"What?" She felt her heart breaking over the child's angst.

"I love you."

Megan understood. This was his way of saying he was still worried about whatever might happen Saturday, but for her sake, he wouldn't talk about it right now. Not more than to simply let her know what was in his heart. "I love you too."

For now, that was all that mattered.

EIGHT

They were running forties when Derrick felt a snap in his right knee. Like a sudden wild fire, the pain exploded through his leg and up into his gut. He fell to the ground as a rush of legs passed him in a blur, and from somewhere near the middle of the field he heard a whistle.

"Stop. Everyone stop!" It was Coach Cameron.

No, God ... not now. Please ...

Coach was coming closer. He was a big guy, a former tackle, and he didn't so much run as waddle toward Derrick. At the same time, Jay Ryder was at Derrick's side, kneeling beside him. "What happened, man? What is it?"

"Nothing." Derrick grimaced and held his knee, gripping it, willing the pain to subside. Even so, he couldn't say the words, couldn't articulate that the worst possible scenario was playing out. His right knee already bore scars on both sides from those times when a surgeon put back together what a linebacker had dismantled.

"One more injury to that knee and you're done," the doctor had told him last time.

So this couldn't be it, not here at the beginning of his last season. He released his knee and sat upright. By then, Aaron Hill and a few other guys were making their way slowly back to him.

Coach Cameron reached him, huffing hard, his face creased with concern. "What happened, Anderson, talk to me."

"I ... I took a wrong step." He felt the sweat beading up on his forehead, felt the nausea that came with the worst injuries. But he wasn't giving in to it, not this time. He straightened his legs out in front of himself. "It's nothing." He ordered his lips to lift just enough for the slightest smile. "Really, Coach. I promise. Give me a few seconds."

Doubt flickered in the coach's eyes, but he gritted his teeth and took a step back. He waved at the others. "Keep running!"

Derrick leaned back on his hands and nodded to one of the trainers. "I'm fine, man. Really. Go on."

Aaron watched from his place in line, but when their eyes met, he looked away. Even in the midst of a series of pain waves that took his breath, Derrick felt his frustration rise. Aaron had kept his distance since the pizza party, and once Derrick overheard him talking to a receiver about some hot brunette he'd met at the event. If that's all he got from the outing, then where Aaron Hill was concerned, Derrick still had his work cut out for him.

Looking reluctant, Jay stood and joined Aaron. The two walked off, and Derrick stared at his right leg. *Come on, God … let me move it. Please.* He focused all his energy on the knee and then bent his leg and straightened it again. It hurt like crazy, but his ligaments weren't torn. The injury was nothing like the two others that had sent him to the hospital—one during his third year in the NFL, and the other on the eve of his ten-year anniversary in the league. He'd been playing seventeen years now. Seventeen years. He knew better than anyone what his body was capable of.

The late afternoon sun beat down on his shoulders, adding to the sick feeling in his stomach. *You can do this, Anderson. Get up.* He pulled his good leg underneath himself, and with all his weight on that foot, he stood. The blood pounded through his injured leg, a half second slower than the pounding in his heart. *Please, God…*

He looked across the practice field at the team. Everyone taking long swigs from their water bottles between their sprints. Off to one side, the coaches were gathered, talking, watching him. They'd paid a big chunk to get Derrick Anderson as their backup quarterback. So was this it? Was he through? Even from half a football field away, Derrick knew what they were saying.

Derrick still stood on just his left foot. The weight of his dangling right foot put pressure on his knee, as if his foot were being stretched away from his leg by some sort of mechanical vice grip. He rested his toes on the grass. How did it happen, anyway? They were running forty-yard dashes. The most basic drill in all of football.

The guys were starting their last set, so it was now or never. He was going to make his knee work, whatever the pain. The first few steps he stayed light on his right foot. The pain radiated out from his knee with any bit of weight, but it was a pain he could tolerate. Nothing was ripped or torn or broken.

Derrick was convinced. One foot in front of the other, he moved toward the team and took the last twenty yards at a jog. No wincing, no tears. Nothing but forward movement.

Coach Cameron met him first. He stared at Derrick's knee and then into his eyes. "You feel as good as you look?"

"I'm fine." He ran a few steps in place. The pain throbbed through his body, but he could tolerate pain. He was a pro football player. The only question was whether the knee would hold him up, and it was. It would.

"Okay..." Coach raised his voice. "But get it checked out today." He gave Derrick a final wary look, then turned his attention to the team. "Let's line up ... same groups."

Derrick's group was last, and he was glad for every minute of the break.

The quarterbacks ran in the same group with the kickers. They had four groups before it was their turn. Aaron came up beside him. "You okay?" His tone wasn't exactly friendly, but his interest seemed genuine.

"What's this? Aaron Hill gone soft?" Derrick laughed, and the release felt good. It was better than screaming.

"Never." He gave Derrick's shoulder a shove. "I want you at the top of your game, that's all." They were stepping up to the line, waiting for the whistle. Aaron winked at him. "Someone's got to push me."

The whistle blew and the group was off. The pain took Derrick's breath, but he could still run. He finished middle of the pack and then jogged off to the sidelines for a drink. His season was still intact. If he had to play the next four months with pain in his knee, he would do it. Because this was his last chance. God had brought him here for a dozen reasons—but none of them would take place if he was on crutches.

Practice was long that day, and even without the injury Derrick would've felt the drain of it. That's not what he was thinking about, though. For the past two weeks, with his family gone to Southern California, he'd come home from practice, sat in the hot tub for an hour, and then watched Sports Center while he stretched on the living room floor. Then he'd eat chicken and vegetables and hit the sack.

But not tonight.

⟶

Derrick pulled his Ford into the driveway of his hillside home. He'd been looking forward to this moment all day. His family had flown in during practice, and tonight he would see them for the first time in way too long. He babied his right leg as he swung his bag over his shoulder and headed for the front door. But before he could reach it, the screen swung open.

"Dad!" Larry, the oldest of his kids at almost sixteen, flew through the doorway, his arms outstretched.

Derrick braced himself and caught the boy in a full embrace. "Mmmm, you don't know how good this feels." He pulled back and put his hands on his son's shoulders. "Look at you! You're an inch taller!"

"Really?" Larry straightened himself. "Mom measured me. I'm almost six foot."

Before Derrick could respond, the door opened again. His thirteen-year-old twins, Lonnie and Libby, came bursting out at the same time. There were more hugs and joyful shouts as the kids celebrated the fact that they were all together again. As they headed into the house, Libby circled her arm around his waist. "I met a boy at our hotel, Daddy."

Derrick raised his eyebrows at her. "You're thirteen, young lady."

"Yeah, and the guy was seventeen." Larry rolled his eyes. "He barely noticed she was alive."

Relief eased his fears. He grinned at his daughter. "You trying to give me a heart attack, or what?"

Libby batted her eyelashes at him. "He was cute, that's all."

"Cute boys can wait." Derrick kissed the top of her head. "Till you're thirty-five or so."

"Daaaaddy." Libby giggled. She was straightening her hair now, and the little-girl look he so dearly loved had been replaced by a beauty that hinted at the way she would look as a woman. She stood on her tiptoes and whispered near his ear. "Mom can't wait to see you. She bought a new pair of pants just for you."

Butterflies danced around Derrick's heart, and he realized in the rush of emotions that his knee didn't hurt as bad as before. The pain would probably be gone in a few days. He caught a glimpse of blue sky as he walked into the house. *Thank You, God ... for all of this, and my knee too. Thank You.*

They walked straight to the kitchen, and there she was. Denae. The love of his life. She was tall and shapely, not one of those skinny women who usually made up the group of players' wives. Denae carried a little extra on her hips, but the curves only made her more beautiful. She wore a pair of black slacks that flared out at her ankles. The moment she saw him, her eyes lit up. "Derrick, baby ..." She had a dishtowel in her hands, and she tossed it on the counter.

"Denae ..." He caught her in his arms and held her close to his chest. "I missed you, honey. So bad."

She nuzzled against his neck. "That's too long, Derrick. The last few days I almost jumped on a plane and came home early."

He took a step back and surveyed her. "The pants are sexy."

"Just for you." She struck a pose, and the look in her eyes said more than her words. She took hold of his hands and pulled him close again. "Mmhmm. You're a sight, Derrick Anderson. I never get tired of looking at you."

"Mmmm." He rocked her gently one way and then the other. "Nothing was the same with you gone." He took a long sniff. "The house hasn't smelled this good since you left."

Denae flashed him a satisfied look. "The kids and I are making your favorite lasagna." She picked up the spatula from the counter and held it in the air. "Right, kids?"

"Homemade noodles and everything." Libby skittered past them and opened the oven door. The casserole inside looked like something from a magazine cover. "See, Daddy? Isn't it perfect?"

"It is!" He stretched out his arms and shifted his weight. A pain shot through his knee, but he ignored it. He looked behind him at Larry and Lonnie, and then at his girls. "C'mere you guys. You don't know how glad I am to see you."

The excitement created a buzz that stayed with them through dinner. The lasagna was the best he'd ever had. Or maybe it just tasted that way since it felt so right to have his family home again. Halfway through the meal, Denae asked about the milk, but Lonnie made a sheepish face. "Sorry, Mom. I left it in the kitchen."

"I'll get it." Derrick was used to helping out during the meal. If he was serving his family, he was loving them. His mama had taught him that, and she was right. But not until he pushed back his chair and tried to stand did he remember about his knee. He took a stutter step, and then settled into a more natural rhythm.

When he returned with the milk, Denae had one eyebrow raised. "Thank you, Derrick." Her look said she was on to him, on to the fact that he'd hurt himself.

Derrick smiled and did a light shake of his head, telling her not to worry, he was fine. The silent, subtle communication between them was something else he loved. How they knew each other as well as they knew themselves.

When the boys were finished with their third servings of lasagna, Larry pushed his chair back and faced Derrick. "We have two-a-days all this week. Can you believe it?"

Two-a-days. Derrick could remember when he was in high school and the team would hold practice twice a day for a week. He and his teammates thought it was such a big deal, working out that long. It always felt something like boot camp. And now his oldest son would have his first chance at the experience. He grinned at the boy. "You excited?"

"So excited, Dad. Coach says I'll be a starter on the freshman team, for sure." His eyes danced. "And if I tear it up, I might have a shot at varsity."

Derrick exchanged a high five with his son. "That's my boy."

"I prayed about it." His look grew more subdued. "If God wants me on the freshman team all year, that's fine. Wherever I can do the best for the team."

Emotion welled in Derrick's throat. That he was living his dream, still playing football after seventeen years in the NFL, that he had a family others only dreamed of having—all of that was enough to drop him to his knees each night in gratitude to God. But this ... the faith of his oldest son ... overwhelmed him. At a time when other kids were experimenting with dope and drinking, Larry was asking God to place him where he could do his best work for the team.

Derrick reached over and gave his son's knee a squeeze. "Keep that attitude, son. In the end, that's all that matters."

Larry shrugged, as if there couldn't possibly be any other way to think about life. "Like you always say, it's how we live our lives between Sundays that really matters." A mischievous look came over him. "Speaking of which, could me and Lonnie come to practice this week? When I'm home from two-a-days?"

"Please, Dad?" Lonnie had been quiet, wolfing down one piece of lasagna after another. The boy was going to be six-five if his appetite was any indication.

"Sure." Derrick shot a questioning look at his wife. "If it's okay with your mom?"

"It's fine." She waved her fork in the air in mock frustration. "Not like I have any say in the matter. I wanted them to play the piano, march in the band." She made a dramatic roll of her eyes. "But no ... not for my boys. Football and only football."

"And shopping?" Libby turned a hopeful smile at her mother. "Since school's almost here, and since the boys'll be busy?"

"You can roll your eyes at football," Derrick chuckled in the direction of his wife, "but you two have turned shopping into a full-contact sport." He winked at her. "I guess that makes us even."

The conversation continued, the good feelings of the homecoming coloring everything about the evening. Not until the children were out back, Libby on the phone to one of her girlfriends, and Lonnie and Larry tossing a football, did Derrick carry a load of dishes into the kitchen and find Denae watching him.

She put her hands on her hips. "How'd you hurt it?"

He stopped, his expression as innocent as he could make it. "Hurt what?"

"Your right knee." She motioned for him to come closer. "Come on, lift up the sweat pants. Let me see the swelling."

His shoulders slumped forward and a defeated chuckle sounded in his throat. "Good thing I don't have much to hide." He came to her and pulled up his pant leg. "You see right through me every time."

Denae stooped down. She touched her fingertips to the swelling on either side of his kneecap. "Derrick, look at that." She stood and stared straight at him. "How'd it happen?"

He tried to minimize the situation. "Simple sprints. Something popped, but I wasn't down more than a minute or so." He let his sweat pants fall back down again. "I'm fine."

"Fine." She tossed her hands in the air. "How many times have I heard that, Derrick." She mumbled something under her breath. "You need to have it checked."

"Baby, listen." His lighthearted attitude was gone. "I did. X-ray's fine." He needed her on his side if he was going to get through this season. He put his hand on her shoulder and looked deep, all the way to the center of her heart.

Something in her expression softened. "Okay." She worked her arms around his waist, and tenderly, with all the love the years had built between them, she kissed him. When she eased back, a shadow fell over her eyes. "Does it hurt?"

He could be honest with her. Slowly he nodded, never breaking eye contact. "Bad." He clenched his jaw, warding off the pain and disappointment at the same time. "But I can play on it, Denae. I know I can. God's gonna get me through this one last season."

She searched his heart, his soul. "You don't have to make good on the promise, baby." She pressed her face against his chest. "He would understand. You know he would."

A sea of sorrow welled inside him, but he swallowed it, held it at bay. "If I have anything to say about it ... I'll keep every word." He kissed her this time. "It's now or never."

The voices of their children outside drifted through the open kitchen window, mingling with the smell of late summer, hydrangea and honeysuckle. Derrick smiled, but he could feel his chin quiver. "You have to believe, baby."

She breathed in slow through her nose. "I do." Her eyes closed and she held him tight, clinging to him. "I believe with everything I am, Derrick."

For a long while, they stayed that way, swaying to the sounds of the children they loved so dearly. Sounds that wouldn't be around forever. Life had already given them proof of that much. When finally he took a step back, he grinned at her, finding the light and happy mood from earlier. "Now let's say we get some dishes done."

"No." Her eyes were still soft, still full of a love that knew no limits. "Go sit down and put your leg up. I'll bring you an ice pack."

He was about to protest, but her look stopped him. "All right." He blew her a kiss, and moved into their bedroom for a sweatshirt. That way he could sit out on the upstairs deck, the one that offered a panoramic view of the San Francisco Bay, and not feel too chilled.

As he walked into the room, his eyes fell on his family's picture, the one framed on the wall next to the closet, from six years ago.

Derrick slowed his steps, and as he reached the picture, he studied the faces. He and Denae, in love with all the world ahead of them. Their eyes told the story, really. Confident and full of joy. As if nothing in the world could dampen the happiness surrounding them. The relaxed look of untested people.

His eyes drifted down along the faces of his children. Nine-year-old Larry, straight and proud beside him, and the twins, just seven, standing in front of their mama. And in the middle, eyes bright with innocence, was five-year-old Lee.

Forever five.

With the softest touch, Derrick brushed his thumb along the image of Lee's arm, his face. "I miss you, son." His words were a pained whisper. He closed his eyes, and for a minute he was back again, back at the hospital holding his son's hand for the last time.

"You're gonna … win it all, Daddy! The … Super Bowl." His words were scratchy and strained, his eyes barely able to stay open.

This had been the running talk between him and Lee. Derrick had a Super Bowl ring for Larry and another for Lonnie. Now he needed one for Lee. Derrick couldn't see for the tears flooding his eyes. "Okay, little man. I'll win it all."

"For me." His breathing was labored, shallow and weak. "Win it … for me, Daddy. Like … we talked about."

"I will, baby. I promise."

"Daddy…" Lee's eyes opened once more, one final time. He looked like an angel, his eyes bright with childlike love. He patted Derrick's hand, soft and tender. "You're my best … friend."

The memory lifted and Derrick opened his eyes. That single promise had stayed with him every year, every spring training, and every summer camp. At the middle of every huddle, in the midst of every play, every game, he carried the promise in his heart. *Win it for me, Daddy.*

No one knew how hard he'd tried, but every year his teams had come up a few plays short, a few wins shy of the title. The well ran dry in Chicago, and this past February he and his agent talked about it.

"Maybe it's time to hang it up, Derrick. Go out standing tall." His agent was a good guy, one of the last in the business. Not once did he make a deal unless it was right for Derrick, whether it was good for the agency or not.

But all Derrick could see were Lee's eyes and the way he looked in the hospital bed that October day, an hour before he died. "No." He worked the muscles in his jaw and gave a strong shake of his head. "I wanna play. One more season." His look pleaded with his agent. "Find me the right team, man. I gotta win it all. One more time."

Derrick ran his thumb over the framed photo again. His agent had settled on the 49ers. The big game had eluded them long enough, he said. "You might be the missing factor, Derrick."

"How do you figure?" Derrick wasn't convinced about San Francisco. There were other teams more likely to win a Super Bowl — teams like Indianapolis or New England.

"Because ..." His agent smiled a knowing sort of smile. "You're a champion. You know how to be a champion." He wagged a finger in the air. "If you can teach that to Aaron Hill, the 49ers will be unstoppable."

Derrick took a step back from the photograph. He walked into his closet and grabbed the first sweatshirt on a stack halfway up a row of shelves. He slipped it on and went out through the patio slider on the far side of the room. The kids were still playing outside, grabbing at every last minute of sunlight. He sat down and gingerly lifted his right leg onto the footstool.

They'd won their first preseason game, but what would happen from here on? Especially if Aaron needed backup? As if in answer, Derrick's knee throbbed with every heartbeat. Here in this moment, futility breathed its hot breath on him. He could hardly picture winning a league game, let alone a Super Bowl. Doubts crowded him like so many cold shadows. He was a thirty-nine-year-old man with a bum knee. What could he possibly teach Aaron Hill about becoming a champion? And how — short of a miracle — could he keep his promise to Lee in this, his final season?

Derrick drank in a long gulp of fresh air and lifted his face to the sky. *I have nothing to offer, Lord. Nothing that'll make a difference this season. But You've got my little boy, Father. And You know the promise I made him.* He blinked back tears, just as a breeze drifted over him. It stung at his eyes, and he squinted. *I want to win it for him, Lord. So bad. So very bad.*

My son, when you are weak ... then I am strong.

Almost as if they were carried on the wind, the words spoke to his soul, calming him, assuring him. The verse was engraved on a wooden plaque that hung in the hallway near the boys' bedrooms. It was something he talked about with his kids often. How they shouldn't fear weakness, because only in the impossible moments could God truly show His power.

Suddenly he was overwhelmed with a sense of hope and direction, determination and courage. He wouldn't let an injury discourage him for all the games yet ahead. The season hadn't even officially begun. He sat up straighter in his chair. He would help his team, if it took everything he had. Somehow, he would help them, and in the end his efforts would make all the difference. He could feel it in his aching bones. God shone best in impossible moments, right?

Derrick ran his fingers gently over his right knee. It was one more thing the Lord wanted to teach him through the coming season. Learning how to be weak, so that God could be strong.

Because as moments went, the idea of an old man with a bum knee helping a team win the Super Bowl was about as impossible as it could get.

NINE

Cory watched out the window of their apartment, looking for the cab. Megan didn't want to take BART today. Sometimes it got too crowded on game days, and this was a big game—preseason or not. Every time San Francisco played the Raiders, it was a big game. So all week she'd been saving her tips, putting a little extra aside. That way they'd have money for a cab, which was really special.

Only here was the weird thing. Aaron didn't come to the pizza party last night. Cory got there early and so did Megan, and they waited. Because what was taking Aaron so long to talk about being a dad? He hadn't called, so all week Cory figured he'd see Aaron at the youth center. Derrick was there, Jay Ryder too. But no Aaron.

Cory waited his turn for Derrick. The lines were shorter every week, since kids were getting used to the idea of Derrick Anderson. When Cory was next, he stuck his hands in the pockets of his jeans and lifted one shoulder a few times. "Aaron didn't come?"

"No." Derrick looked sad at this. "He had other plans."

"Oh." Cory's eyes fell to the floor for a few seconds. When he looked up, he tried to sound hopeful. "Maybe he's getting ready for tomorrow."

"Tomorrow?"

"We're his guests for the Raiders game." The words felt good to say. "He read the letter I gave him. That's why." He didn't want to say too much.

Derrick patted Cory's arm. "Maybe that's it, then. Maybe he's getting ready."

"You're gonna win tomorrow, right?"

"Of course."

The conversation stayed with Cory all night and into this morning, but the part about Aaron didn't really make sense. What would he need to do to get ready? After the game they were going out for burgers. So why would that make him busy on a Friday night. He talked to Megan about it when they walked home, but just a little.

"He probably had a hot date." She laughed and took a few running steps ahead of him. "Come on, race you to the top of the hill."

Megan was always doing that, changing the subject when the subject was Aaron. Cory still wasn't sure why. She had to believe that Aaron was his father now. Otherwise, he never would've come to the youth center last week, and he wouldn't have invited them to be his guests. Her doubts made him mad, so he didn't bring up Aaron again last night.

"Cory? Any sign of the cab?" She was in the bathroom, doing something with her hair.

"Not yet." He planted his elbows on the windowsill and stared down the street in either direction as far as he could see. "You almost ready?"

"Almost."

Cory thought about wearing his Aaron Hill jersey, but he changed his mind at the last minute. First, he didn't want Megan saying anything about how he was trying too hard. And second, that was his special jersey. The one he slept in. He couldn't risk spilling mustard or Coke on it. Instead he wore the new 49ers T-shirt, the one he got in the drawing yesterday. That and his old faithful San Francisco baseball cap.

A yellow cab pulled up out front, and Cory jumped off the couch. "It's here. The cab's here!"

Megan stepped out of the bathroom, and for a minute Cory felt like he was seeing her for the first time. She wore a white shirt and jeans, but she had some of her hair pulled back. The rest was curlier than usual. Plus she had a little eye makeup on. At least it looked that way. "Wow." He whistled at her. "You look pretty."

"It's a big day for us." She took her bag from the table and held her hand out to him. "I've wanted to see a game in person forever. Just like you."

Cory took her hand and they hurried out the apartment and down the stairs, 'cause the elevator was still on the fritz. He couldn't help but think as they jogged out onto the street that maybe some of the reason why Megan looked pretty was because of Aaron. The way he'd looked at her that night a week ago at the pizza party.

But he said nothing. Instead, he took his seat, his heart pounding, and fastened his belt. The trip into the stadium was like the beginning of an adventure. He didn't want to miss a minute of it. They drove down a few streets and up a few more, and then they turned onto a freeway, and then another freeway, and finally they got off at a street right next to the water.

Cory checked the sign and it said Gilman Avenue, Monster Park. 'Cause that's what some people called it now, but not faithful fans like Megan and him. Candlestick. That's what it was, and that's what it would always be. The cab driver stayed on Gilman down toward the water and around the lower parking lots. Then he circled up and suddenly all the cars stopped. From every direction, cars were coming toward the stadium, hundreds of them. Maybe thousands even.

"Lots of traffic." Megan looked out her window. "Hard to believe all these people fit into that stadium."

The cab driver looked over his shoulder at her. "So right." He had dark brown skin and an accent. "That's why we need new stadium." He brushed his hand at the traffic. "Crazy people sit in traffic three hours for game."

Cory didn't mind the line of cars. The waiting gave him time to watch the people. Everywhere he looked, cars were parked in the lot on the other side of the big fence. Barbecues were set up along every aisle. Cory rolled his window down, and the smell of cooked burgers and hotdogs filled the cab.

"Tailgating." Megan leaned toward him and looked out his window. "People park early in the morning and eat their meals in the parking lot. It's called tailgating."

Cory stared at the people, at the celebrations they were having near one car after another. It was like a whole other world, the idea that people spent all day Sunday here. Back when his mom was alive, they spent Sunday at church. But Megan didn't like church that much. So they spent Sundays cleaning the apartment and getting ready for Monday.

Cory could definitely do this, spend all day at a 49ers game. The barbecue smell made his stomach growl. Megan told him they'd get hot dogs before kickoff and then, of course, they were having dinner with Aaron. Cory looked at the faces scattered across the forever parking lot. *And I'm the only one having dinner with Aaron Hill.* The thought made him feel good again. Aaron wouldn't have dinner with just any old kid from the youth center. It was on account of he was Aaron's son.

He tugged on his baseball cap and studied the sidewalk. Streams of people walked along both sides, heading for the gate. It was easy to tell who were the Raider fans and who were the 49ers. People wore jerseys and carried flags. They had black painted on their faces or red, and some of them had big hats with *Raiders* or *49ers* on them. When a car passed by, some of the fans would wave their flags and shout through colorful megaphones something not so nice about the Raiders or 49ers. 'Cause this was a serious game.

Aaron had sent a special pass for the parking lot, and Megan took it from the envelope.

"Here." She gave it to the cab driver. "This will get us up pretty close."

The man looked at it, and his eyebrows shot up. "You must know someone important, lady. This is VIP."

Cory wasn't sure what VIP meant. Maybe something about Very Inside Parking. The cab driver switched lanes, and in a little while, he pulled up to a gate with no one in line. He showed the pass to the man stationed there, and the man waved him into the parking lot where all the other people were having their barbecue tailgating. They drove slowly past one little party after another, until they reached a gigantic sign with the letter *A* on it.

The driver stopped. "Here you are, lady." He checked the red numbers on the box attached to his dashboard. "Eighteen dollars, fifty cents."

Megan made a slight face, like it was hard for her to pay that much money for a car ride. But she pulled out a twenty-dollar bill and handed it to the driver. "Keep the rest."

"Thank you." He took the bill and grinned. "Have very good time!"

Cory's eyes met the cab driver's in the rearview mirror. "Go 49ers!"

"Go team." The man waited until they were out, then he drove away.

Cory suddenly felt small. The crowd was all around him, and people were shouting and carrying drinks and food. A row of portable toilets stood close by, and Cory looked at Megan and made a face.

She nodded. "Me too."

They walked to a line of six people waiting for a turn, and that gave Cory more time to watch the people. A man was shouting something about wanting tickets, and a trailer was set up close to the bathrooms. Inside was every kind of 49ers shirt or hat or souvenir a person could ever want. And everyone was eating something or drinking something.

A boy and his dad walked past, both of them chewing on corndogs, and headed for the big gate marked *A*. At the same time, a helicopter flew overhead, and behind it was a sign flapping in the wind. The sign read, *Here's to Another Great Year! Go 49ers!*

The place was like 49ers heaven.

After they used the bathrooms, they got in another line, the one going through the big gate. The man taking tickets looked at Megan's and grinned. "Well, well … you've got the good seats!" He pointed up an escalator and told Megan to turn right at the top. "Box seats have a private elevator. The attendant will be just outside."

A private elevator? Cory's stomach did flip-flops inside him, and he was sort of out of breath. Like when he played soccer and it was the last minute of the game. He licked his lips and took Megan's hand.

"Amazing, isn't it?" She was watching everyone, just like he was.

"It's perfect. Everything about it."

The man in front of them wore a Raiders jersey. He turned around and noticed Cory's 49ers T-shirt. He had a big cup of something, probably beer. When he raised it in the air, a little bit sloshed out. "May the best team win."

Cory wanted to say that would be the 49ers, but he kept quiet. Megan told him some people took football very serious. So serious they might want to fight about their team. So Cory only nodded and smiled.

They reached the top of the escalator, and then after a little walk around to the right, they saw the private elevator.

"Should we get food first?" Cory stared at a food counter a few feet away. Lots of workers were busy handing out hot dogs and nachos and giant pretzels with creamy cheese. The people were loud all around them, so he raised his voice. "Huh, Megan, should we?"

"Not yet." She took his hand and walked him to the man standing outside the private elevator. "Let's find our seats first."

The private elevator took them to a much quieter walkway. It was all cement, and it went in a circle around the stadium. A woman in a red suit led them for a little walk and then pointed them to a small flight of stairs and a door. "That's Aaron Hill's box." She nodded to them. Then she went back to find the next people, probably.

Cory's heart was beating so hard he wondered if Megan could hear it. She led the way down the few stairs and opened the door. The box turned out to be a little empty room with three rows of seats. Maybe twelve or fourteen spots altogether. And across the front was all glass and a fantastic view of ...

"That's the field!" Cory jogged down the last few stairs and put his face up close against the thick glass. He checked around it. "Is there a way to open the window? So we can hear what's going on?"

Megan looked up and pointed. "They have speakers, so you can hear the announcer."

"Oh." Cory didn't want to look disappointed. This was Aaron's special spot, after all. But he wanted to be out there where the people were, where the action was. As close to the field as possible.

He dropped into the middle seat on the first row. "This is like a miracle, right Megan?"

"Pretty close." She laughed. And just then, two men came into the little room. They both had on fancy suits and ties, and when they spotted Cory and Megan, they stopped.

The shorter guy looked at Megan. "Hi." He made a strange face. "I'm Bill Bond, Aaron's agent." He nodded at the other guy. "This is Albert. He's Aaron's financial planner."

Cory didn't say so, but already he didn't like Mr. Bond. He sounded not altogether nice, and maybe a little suspicious. Like how did Megan and Cory get in there, anyway.

"Megan Gunn." She held out her hand and shook his. "Aaron invited me and my son to be his guests today."

"Oh." The man hesitated. After too long a pause, he smiled. "I see." He switched his attention to Cory. "And what's your name, young man?"

"Cory." He stood, because his mom taught him that was polite when someone new came into the room. "Nice to meet you."

"Yes." He looked back at Megan and frowned. "Nice to meet you too."

Megan took a few steps toward the door. "We were just going back up for a couple hot dogs." She smiled, but it wasn't in her eyes. "Would you gentlemen like something?"

"Uh ..." Mr. Bond glanced over his shoulder at a big counter at the back of the room. "Catering will bring us whatever we want." He did a curious laugh and looked strange at Megan. "That's always how it is in the box."

"Oh." Megan didn't look upset. "Well, Cory and I haven't ever been to a 49ers game. Let alone in box seats." She shrugged one shoulder. "Now we know."

Megan walked back to the first row, and at the same time, the two men sat down.

"I wanna be outside," Cory whispered. Only, because it was such a small little room, Mr. Bond heard him.

"You wanna be closer to the action, is that what I heard you say?" He walked down the couple steps and looked straight at Cory.

Cory gulped. Anything would be better than watching the game with this guy. "Yes, sir. But that's okay."

"Look." He took a pair of tickets from his pocket. "I've got fifteenth row, fifty-yard line. Saving 'em for a buddy of mine." He did a quick look back at the other guy. Then at Cory again. "How about you and your mom take these, and my buddy can sit up here with us?"

"Really?" Cory felt his heart beat hard again. Because that would be a perfect swap. He turned to Megan. "Can we?"

"Sure." Megan did a little eyebrow raise at the men. "I think that would be better anyway."

"Except," Cory remembered something. "What about after the game? We're supposed to meet Aaron here at the box."

"Hmmm." Mr. Bond looked uncomfortable, like he had a rock in his shoe or something. "I hadn't heard about that." He frowned in a way that was mean again. "I guess you should come back up after the game. I'm sure your name's on his list, if he invited you."

Cory couldn't wait to be out of the small room and back on the cement walkway toward the elevator. "What a creep!" he whispered to Megan when the guys closed the door to the room. "He didn't like us."

Megan laughed. "I don't think he was expecting us."

"Still …" Cory took long steps to keep up with her. "He didn't have to be rude."

"No. That's the way some people are when they're around someone famous. They start to think they're better than everyone else."

"That's stupid."

"Don't say stupid." She kept her eyes straight ahead, 'cause they were almost at the elevator. "It's not something your mother would want you to say. Me neither."

Megan was right. "Sorry. It's just"—he followed her into the elevator— "everyone's the same. So no one should think they're better."

When they were back with the crowds of people, Megan bought them each big, juicy hot dogs and giant cokes, and when they walked to their seats, Cory couldn't believe it! They were down so close to the field, he could see the looks on the faces of the 49ers. They were warming up on the field, and he could see if they looked frustrated or if they laughed about something. They were so close he felt like he was part of the team, practically.

He scanned the group, and then he pointed. "There he is." He shaded his eyes, because the baseball cap wasn't enough in this sun. "It's Aaron, Megan! Look!"

"I see him." She sounded calmer than him. But she was a grown-up, so that was okay.

For a minute, he stopped stone still on the steps and watched every move Aaron made. He wanted to jump around and wave until Aaron noticed him, but that probably wouldn't happen. 'Cause Aaron thought he was sitting up in the box.

"Come on, Cory. People are trying to get to their seats."

"Sorry." He followed Megan down one of the rows and they sat down. "Wow!" He pulled his baseball cap low and shaded his eyes again so he could look way up high to the glass windows of the box seats. "This is tons better than up there." He took a big breath. "You can breathe down here."

Megan smiled. "I agree."

Cory grinned. He liked Megan more all the time. Sometimes she was so much like his mom that he almost forgot she wasn't her.

The stadium was filling up, and Cory sat on the edge of his seat. He didn't want to miss a single thing, like the marching band, which was coming out onto the field.

Pretty soon the team jogged back to the bench and Aaron and Derrick Anderson moved close to the first row. They put some space between them and threw a pair of balls to a couple of receivers. "They're warming up!" Cory pointed at them. "Just like in high school."

"I see that." Megan asked to borrow the program of the woman sitting beside her. She began looking through it, as if she wasn't too concerned about the warm-up process.

Loud trumpets filled the stadium, and the marching band took the field. There were drummers and trumpeters and flute players and big horn-type things. Everyone stayed all together, one foot after another, just like on TV.

"It looks bigger in person, the whole band out there on the field." He had to shout so Megan could hear him. "See, don't you think it looks bigger?"

Megan finished looking at the program book, and she handed it back to the lady. "Yes," she leaned her head close to his. "It's all very big and loud. Much more than on TV."

The band stopped at the middle of the field, and then a big voice told them to stand for the national anthem. A heavy kid in a nice suit and tie came over to a platform and someone gave him a microphone. Cory could see all of it, just as it was happening. The boy didn't look that old, but he could sing like someone on *American Idol.* Cory put his hand over his heart, and he thought of his mom up in heaven watching this, and suddenly he felt tears in his eyes and he wasn't even sure why.

No, he did know why. 'Cause this was the happiest day in his whole life.

When the song was almost done, the most amazing thing happened. Streaking jet fighter planes zoomed over the stadium. They were so fast and loud, Cory's heart skipped a beat, and he gasped. "Wow!" He couldn't say it enough. When the planes passed and he could hear again, he felt his eyes get perfectly round and he looked at Megan. "Wow! Did you see that? Those were jet fighters. Probably keeping us safe for the game!"

Megan laughed a little, but the loud voice was talking again and Cory couldn't hear what she said. The coin toss happened, and San Francisco won. "They'll receive, I know they will." He bounced in his seat, and he was right. The 49ers would have the ball first!

Aaron was talking to Coach Cameron, nodding his head and looking very serious. After a few seconds, he turned and jogged out to the field where the rest of the offense was waiting for him. From the huddle he looked back at the coaches one more time, and it almost seemed like he was looking straight up at Cory.

Dad, Cory thought … *You're really my dad. Thank You, God, for hearing my mom's prayers all those times. I can't believe it's really happening.*

Aaron's first pass was a completion to one of the veteran receivers, the guy who was injured last year. "See!" Cory clapped his hand against Megan's knee. "I knew he'd be okay this year. I knew it!"

Six more plays, and on third and eight, Aaron threw a pass to the same receiver, right in the corner of the end zone. Cory was on his feet. "Touchdown!" He jumped around and high-fived Megan. "Touchdown, 49ers!"

Once the fans all settled back into their seats, Cory remembered his hot dog. It tasted better than any hot dog ever in his whole life, and by the time he finished it, Aaron had thrown a second touchdown pass. Just like their first preseason game, by halftime San Francisco was so far ahead, Coach Cameron took Aaron out of the game and put in Derrick Anderson. Cory was glad, because Derrick was a great player and a nice guy. Plus, how many teams had two quarterbacks who could win a game? Derrick kept things at a little slower pace, and in the end, the 49ers won 24 to 3. Like the man on the escalator said, the best team definitely won.

It took ten minutes to walk along with the crowd and find their way back to the elevator. This time they went up to the empty walkway, and when they reached the small room, there were four other guys with suits standing around talking. A TV set hung from the ceiling—something Cory hadn't noticed before.

"Let's stay out here," Megan came close so just Cory could hear her. "We might breathe a little better."

Cory giggled. Just then, one of the guys in the room stepped out and smiled at Megan. "You must be friends of Aaron's?"

"Yes." Megan looked uncomfortable, as if maybe they should've stayed down in the outside seats a while longer. "New friends."

Mr. Bond seemed to hear that part. He gave Megan a look, and then turned back to the men he was already talking to.

The friendly guy waved them into the box. "Come on, there's a tray of hot cookies in here."

Even with the hot dog and pop, Cory was still hungry. He raised his eyes at Megan, and she waited a few seconds. "Okay. Get a cookie, then come out here."

He skipped down the stairs, and the man was right. A tray of the biggest chocolate chip cookies ever was waiting right on the counter. They were still warm! He took two and a napkin, then he thought a minute and took a third. In case Megan wanted some. He was still getting the cookies balanced in his hands when someone walked up beside him.

He lifted his eyes and his breath caught in his throat. It was Mr. Bond, and he didn't look happy. "Hi." Cory tried a smile, but it didn't feel very strong.

"Hello." The man leaned against the counter and stared straight at Cory. "So, uh, how exactly do you know Aaron?"

"We met a few weeks ago." Cory was never afraid of anything, and right now he had to remind himself about that. He stood straighter and lifted his chin. "At the Mission Youth Center."

The man looked a little less mean at that information. "So, what … Aaron singled you out of all those kids and asked you to be his guest today? Is that it?"

Cory looked over his shoulder, but he couldn't see Megan. She was probably up the stairs on the empty cement sidewalk, waiting for him. He turned to the man again. "Not exactly." Megan didn't want him to talk about Aaron being his dad. But this guy was getting on his nerves. "I guess I was special to him."

Mr. Bond narrowed his eyes. "Why?"

"Because…" He licked his lower lip and took a step back. *Be brave, Cory, be brave.* He stuck out his chest. "Because I wrote him a letter and Derrick Anderson gave it to him."

"A fan letter?" The man looked very suspicious this time. Like when his teacher caught Zoe Walters cheating off Cory's paper in math last week. "You wrote him a fan letter, so he invited you to sit in his box?"

Cory needed air. He took a breath, but it didn't seem to help. There was only one way to get the guy off his back. He pulled the cookies to his chest. "I think it was more 'cause of what I told Aaron in the letter."

"What'd you tell him?" The other men were all talking to each other. No one even looked their way or tried to interrupt.

So Cory had no choice this time. He didn't blink. "I told him he was my dad."

Until that moment, Mr. Bond had a sort of tan type of face. But now his mouth opened up, and little by little his face turned gray. Like maybe he was going to pass out. "Listen, kid." He made his words small and tight and angry and threatening. "Don't ever say that again, you hear me? Aaron Hill has no children." He hissed the words, quiet so no one else could hear. "Don't ever tell a lie like that again, do you understand?"

That's when Cory realized something. He didn't need to stand here and explain himself to Mr. Bond. He knew the truth and so did his mother, and so did Aaron Hill. That's why they were his guests today. Instead of saying anything back, he took his cookies and the napkin, and marched past Mr. Bond and out the door. To the place beside Megan, where finally he could do what he hadn't been able to do once inside the small room.

He could breathe.

Ten

Megan was just about to give up on the idea that Aaron was ever going to meet them, when she heard commotion at the far end of the hall. Trailed by a few of his linemen, Aaron appeared, and she could tell by his expression that he was looking for them.

Cory spotted him at the same time, and he ran to meet him. "Great game!" He gave Aaron a side hug. Aaron gave Cory a quick glance, then did the same, but it didn't last long.

"Thanks." He was dressed in dark jeans and a neatly pressed light blue buttoned down shirt. He looked past Cory to Megan. Their eyes met and held for a long instant. "Megan ... Did you like the box?"

"Well ..."

They were closer now, and Megan crossed her arms. That's when she saw it. There was a striking resemblance between Aaron and Cory. She dismissed the idea. How could she keep the boy grounded if she allowed herself to fall into his fantasy? She smiled politely at Aaron. "Actually ... we took a couple tickets from your agent. Closer to the field."

"Perfect." He grinned at Cory. "I like the view better from down there too."

Three of the linemen stopped, curious looks on their faces. "Come on, Hill, introduce us." The biggest guy, a black man with a shiny bald head, grinned at her. "You keep all the pretty ones to yourself."

Cory was still stuck to Aaron's side, but now Aaron stepped away and put his hand on Megan's shoulder. "This is Megan Gunn. I met her at the youth center." Again he held her eyes.

"Hello." Megan made a subtle move away from Aaron, and he dropped his hand. She wasn't sure what to make of Aaron's attention. She smiled at the lineman and shook his hand. But at the same time she spotted Bill Bond, Aaron's agent. He was standing just outside Aaron's box, glaring at her, listening to every word. She focused on Aaron's teammate again. "Great game!"

"Thank you. If I'd known you were watching, I woulda been more nervous." He looked at Cory. "And who are you?"

Not now, God ... please. Make him keep it simple. She held her breath.

"I'm Cory." He bit his lip and nodded at Megan. "She's my mom."

They made small talk with the three linemen for a few minutes, and then Aaron took gentle hold of Megan's arm and led her toward the steps to his box. "Okay, guys. Enough. They're my guests."

She didn't like the way he had a hold of her, as if she were his property. But she didn't pull away, didn't want to make a scene. Aaron's teammates made a few more teasing remarks, and then bid goodbye to Megan and Cory. As they left, Aaron put his face near hers. "Now you get to meet the suits. It won't take more than a few minutes."

Megan wanted to say that she could pass. She'd already met two of them and she wasn't impressed. But making an issue out of the moment would only take longer. They spent the next five minutes mingling with the men in suits, and during that time she watched Bill Bond pull Aaron aside. Throughout their whispered conversation, Mr. Bond didn't look happy.

Whatever. If Aaron's agent didn't like him associating with people he'd met at the youth center, so be it. She held her head high and kept her attention on Cory, and whatever person was in front of her. Finally, Aaron broke free of the discussion with his agent, and he motioned to Megan. "Let's go."

She was more than ready. On the way out of the stadium, Aaron didn't act any differently. Whatever his agent had told him, he wasn't letting it change his plans for the evening. The three of them headed into the players' parking lot, and Aaron led them to a jet-black Hummer.

"Wow!" Cory ran ahead and then stopped a few feet shy of the vehicle. "Is this really yours?"

"Yep." Aaron pulled his keys from his pocket. He stopped and admired the vehicle. "It gets me around."

"I've never even been this close to a real Hummer!" Cory waited until Aaron opened the door. Then he climbed into the backseat.

Aaron led the way around to the passenger side. He stood a little too close to Megan. "So you had fun?"

"I did." She wasn't impressed by his chivalry, but as he held her door open she couldn't help but feel the slightest bit attracted. No wonder so many girls fell for him. She stepped into the car, and the smell of leather surrounded her.

On the way to the restaurant, Cory chattered on the whole time, breaking down the game one play at a time. Twice, Aaron looked at her and grinned.

"He's excited," she whispered.

"I know." He kept his eyes on the road. "It's fine. But later ... I hope there's time to get to know you better."

The comment dissolved her attraction. She'd been right; he was hitting on her. That's why the invitation to the game and dinner. He couldn't care less what Cory said, as long as he had the chance to get to know her.

Megan steeled herself. She'd make her lack of interest known as soon as she had the chance.

They drove to a diner not far from Nob Hill. Megan didn't have to ask if that's where Aaron lived. Anyone in the city knew that much. The restaurant was small, only four tables and a drive-thru window, but Aaron seemed to know the older couple who ran it. Megan hadn't thought about it before, but life as Aaron Hill wasn't as glamorous as it might seem. He probably ate at small family-run places like this so that he could finish a meal without being asked for an autograph.

Halfway through their burgers, a group of teenage boys came in and almost immediately, recognized Aaron. He spent the next ten minutes signing autographs and posing with one or two of them while the others snapped pictures with their cell phones.

When the boys had their food and were gone, Megan looked at him. "Is it like that often?"

A slight laugh came from him. "All the time." He gave her a look that said he didn't mind. "Goes with the territory."

They talked about the upcoming away game at Denver and the one after that in San Diego. Megan was waiting for him to ask about her personally, but he kept the conversation light. Maybe he already sensed her resistance.

"So." Cory sucked on his straw, slurping up a mouthful of chocolate shake. "Who stays at your house when you're on the road?"

Megan felt a wave of panic. Cory would only ask the question for one reason. He was fishing, doing the one thing she'd told him not to do. She shot him a look that ordered him not to take the conversation one step further.

"No one most of the time." Aaron picked at his french fries. "I have a housekeeper, and she has her own key. That's about it."

Cory must've caught her message, because he switched topics again, this time talking about Coach Cameron and how important the season was if he wanted to stay with the 49ers.

Megan didn't mind that the conversation centered mostly around Cory, but she wished the night were over. Where could it possibly lead?

When they finished eating, Aaron drove them back to their apartment. Megan didn't care if he saw how they lived. She was much too independent to worry what people thought of her or her low-income housing. She was doing the best she could.

"Wanna come up and see Oreo?" Cory's enthusiasm hadn't dimmed all night. "He's our cat. He's a 49ers fan too."

"Cory, I'm sure Mr. Hill has to get back home." She could sense Aaron next to her starting to protest. "Besides, we have to go over your spelling words." She turned to Aaron and held out her hand. "Thanks for a wonderful day. Cory enjoyed it very much."

"You can call me Aaron." He looked disappointed, and slightly dazed. He took her hand, but instead of shaking it, he held it. His eyes lifted to the apartment building outside and then back at her. "And yeah, if Cory has homework, then, sure. You better go."

Her heart reacted strangely to the feel of her hand in his, especially for so long. A part of her wanted to stay there beside him. But common sense had something to say about the situation, so she eased her fingers from him and uttered a nervous laugh. "Maybe we'll see you at the youth center."

"Hey, wait." He fumbled around the center console until he found a pen. Then he dug into another compartment and pulled out a pad of sticky notes. "Can I get your number? Maybe we can have dinner sometime?"

"You already have it!" Cory poked his head between the two front seats. "Remember? It's at the bottom of my letter."

Aaron's eyes showed his surprise. He hesitated for a second or two. "Of course." He cast a weak smile at Cory. "I almost forgot."

Cory put his arm around Aaron's shoulders. "This was the best day in my whole life. Thanks so much."

"You're welcome." Again Aaron's expression was slightly uncomfortable. As if he didn't quite know what to make of Cory's behavior. Cory slid across the seat and stepped out onto the sidewalk. Aaron turned a sheepish look toward Megan. "I really want to see you again."

Her, not Cory. A sudden anger consumed her. She lowered her chin and aimed her gaze straight at Aaron. "Well, then ... Mr. Hill ... I guess you might want to read his letter."

He did a short laugh. "Wait a minute ... I read it a few weeks ago. I already told him back when—"

She held up her hand. "Don't lie to me, Mr. Hill. And don't lie to that little boy." She kept her tone kind and gracious, but she could see her words were hitting him hard. "You can fool him, but you can't fool me. You haven't read his letter." She opened the door and gave him a final look. "I'm pretty sure we'll all know when you actually do." She stepped onto the ground. Her smile was the type reserved for annoying customers at Bob's Diner. "Thanks, again. Cory wasn't kidding. This was the best day of his life."

With that, she turned and took Cory's hand. They were through the apartment door and halfway up the stairs before Megan exhaled. She was right about Aaron Hill, and she couldn't believe it. He wasn't interested in Cory at all. For whatever reason, he'd taken a liking to her. Whether he was a banker or a pro football player, it didn't matter. The feeling wasn't mutual. Because for all his kindness and manners tonight, he'd broken Megan's cardinal rule. He'd lied to a child. And not just any child either. Because Cory never belonged to Aaron Hill, no matter what Amy had told the boy, and no matter how much they looked alike. He belonged to her.

The way he always would.

ELEVEN

Aaron barely paid attention to the road as he made his way from the Mission District north to his home in a gated area of Nob Hill. His heart and head were spinning in different directions, making him wonder at his sanity.

Megan Gunn had turned him down flat. She wasn't the least bit interested, and that was a first. For as long as Aaron could remember, girls had been easy for him. Women lined up to talk to him after games and practices, and in hotel lobbies across the country.

That's why Amy had been so special. She wasn't a groupie. Amy knew him in the deepest places of his soul, but since then he'd never let another woman get that close. There hadn't been any need, and besides, he never wanted to let anyone that close ever again.

Until now.

Megan wasn't glamorous or done up, the way the girls in his world were. She was too thin to be a cheerleader and her makeup would never stand out in a photo shoot. But her beauty stopped his heart each time he saw her. More than that, he was taken by her sheer determination and utter independence. The way she refused to call him Aaron, even.

He pulled into his driveway, parked his Hummer, and headed inside. Most game nights he dropped into his recliner and turned on ESPN. But not tonight. Tonight he needed quiet, so he could sort through the conversations from his time with Megan and Cory.

Mostly Megan. The boy was nice, but he was like any other kid. His constant chattering made it hard for Aaron to get to know Megan, hard for her to see who he really was. Still, until the very end of the evening, Aaron thought things were going great. Megan seemed relaxed and happy, like she was enjoying his company. Then at the end she pulled out the Mr. Hill thing.

And that's when the whole night crashed and burned.

He wanted her number, of course. How else could he set up a date or have a conversation without the kid interrupting the whole time? He'd planned from the moment he suited up before the game to ask her if he could call. Not that he was very good at getting numbers. They were usually given to him, unsolicited.

Not once when he tried to imagine how the evening would go had he thought that when he'd ask for her phone number, Cory would pipe in and say he'd written it on his letter. How could he have remembered the boy's statement about writing his phone number at the bottom of the letter? Or known that Megan would figure out the minute he asked her for it that he hadn't read the letter?

He groaned and let his head fall back against the recliner. Now that he thought about it, he vaguely remembered the kid saying something about a phone number back at the youth center. How could he be so stupid? The first time he'd lied to the kid about the letter, he'd made a mental note: next time he opened his locker, he'd dig around the bottom and find the envelope. Then he'd read it, so the next time he saw the boy he could look him in the eyes and talk about whatever he'd written.

After spending an evening with the kid, Aaron could pretty well write the letter himself. *Dear Aaron, you're my favorite player ... I've been watching you since I was two ... I've waited all my life to meet you ... I'm the biggest 49ers fan in the whole city,* etc., etc., etc.

The last part of the night hadn't worked out at all like he planned. He actually figured maybe he'd walk her and Cory up to their front door—or as it turned out—up to their apartment. He imagined Megan getting Cory off to bed, and the two of them sitting around her dining room table drinking coffee and getting to know each other. A kiss wasn't out of the question the way he first imagined it.

Frustration simmered in his belly. The boy would've loved it if Aaron came up with them. Megan had cut the possibility short. It was only nine o'clock when he dropped them off. And they had all day Sunday to get his homework done, but Aaron could hardly argue with her. Megan had her mind made up before they pulled up in front of her apartment.

He closed his eyes and imagined her home, her neighborhood. It was only a few blocks from the youth center, a neighborhood that was rough in the daytime. At night a single mother like Megan shouldn't even consider going outside. He'd read once in the *Chronicle* that the Mission District—the poorest in San Francisco—was also home to more kids per square block than any other in the city.

Kids like Cory.

He opened his eyes, stood, and wandered into the kitchen where he poured himself a glass of water and leaned against the dishwasher. The housekeeper must've started it before she left, because the door was still warm. He thought about Megan and Cory. They didn't have a car, clearly. Like so many people, they probably walked and took the BART everywhere. No telling how they'd made it to the game earlier that day.

He sighed. Maybe that's why he was taken with Megan Gunn. She was a fighter, a survivor. How else could she be a single mom to Cory and still keep food on the table?

He realized then that he hadn't once asked her what she did. As if somehow being a foster mother might be her only job. But that wasn't possible. Otherwise, they wouldn't have any sort of home at all. Money from the state for foster care paid only enough for a few trips to the grocery store. Derrick had told him that.

Suddenly he knew what he had to do. He took his cell phone from his pocket and found Derrick's number. Coach had made them swap numbers first day of spring training. Before he hit the Send button he stopped himself. He had nothing in common with Derrick Anderson. He had it bad for a pretty girl, that's all. The whole foster thing meant nothing to him.

He snapped his phone shut, but he could hear Coach Cameron's voice. "Hill, make sure you have Anderson's number. You never know when you might need advice from a champion."

At the time, he couldn't imagine himself ever picking up the phone and making that call.

And that was still how he felt even a few days later when practice was back in session. The confusion with Megan Gunn and the secret to understanding her might be something Derrick could help with. But Derrick was a smart guy. He'd know that Aaron wasn't interested in foster kids. He'd probably accuse Aaron of seeking another conquest. And Megan was more than that. At least Aaron thought she was more.

Practice was drawn out and Aaron found himself watching Derrick. No question, on the field he could learn from Derrick. The guy had already won more games than most quarterbacks win in a lifetime. But now, with the sting of Megan's words still echoing in his mind, a conversation with Derrick Anderson wasn't going to make him feel better. Because the guy wasn't only a champion on the field. He was a champion at life.

Something Aaron hadn't ever wanted to be.

⤙

Chuck Cameron stepped into his office and grabbed his water bottle. He walked to his window, the one overlooking the practice field. Whether this was his last season or not, he would always be grateful for his time in San Francisco. He couldn't hold it against the owners if they fired him this year. A team led by Aaron Hill should win the Super Bowl at least once in so many years of dominance. The temperature outside was cool, though the clouds overhead had broken up an hour ago. The break in the heat was nice. They'd gone through a lot today, and they had much more still to do tomorrow. If they were going to finish the preseason strong and make a serious run at the title, the team needed to be prepared.

And they would make a serious run. Management had left them no option.

He turned his back to the window and leaned on the sill. A week ago, he could almost feel their slim chances at a Super Bowl season dissolving like sand through his fingers. Aaron Hill was hanging out at bars, getting in trouble with girls, and distracting the team. But now ... well, now at least the media recognized a show of character in the team's franchise quarterback. Hill's Friday night stint at the Mission Youth Center was a good start. But that had more to do with Hill's pushy agent. If they were going to make a run at a championship, the changes in Aaron would have to be more than smoke and mirrors, more than an agent making a call to a few local reporters. No, he couldn't change Aaron Hill any more than he could will his team to win every game. But he could pray about both situations and let God bring the victories.

Chuck sighed, and a tired laugh slipped past his lips. The front office could fire him if they wanted. He wasn't going to change his ways now. No, he hadn't won the big game, but not every win could be notched on a playing field.

His precious niece Paige had reminded him of that just this morning. Chuck's kids were grown, but Paige, at eight years old, had taken a special liking to her uncle. Her mother — Chuck's sister — must've told the girl that this year was especially important for her Uncle Chuck. Whatever the reason, Paige had been calling him once a week. Just to say she was praying for him.

In the off-season, Chuck and his wife had spent time at his sister's house, so he had a chance to watch Paige. The girl had long blonde hair, blue eyes, and a heart of gold. When the good Lord talked about having the faith of a child, Chuck's guess was that he had Paige Rathbun in mind. The child was a ray of sunlight for her older sister, Katie, and her little brother, John. She sang in the church choir and prayed as easily as she breathed, and whether she knew a person or not, Paige's hellos were accompanied with a hug.

During Chuck's visit, Paige was instrumental in rescuing a golden retriever from an animal trap in the woods behind her family's home. Paige didn't see the dog as an inconvenience. "He's a gift from God," she said.

The same way Paige was a gift.

Chuck remembered the child's words from earlier today. "Sometimes God gives us hard things, don't you think so, Uncle Chuck?"

Chuck thought about Aaron Hill. "Yes, Paige. I think He does that sometimes."

"You know why?"

"Why?"

"Because He loves us enough to help us grow up."

Chuck let the words run through his mind again. He might lose his job this season, but he wouldn't lose his faith. Paige's phone calls always helped him remember that much.

As for Aaron, if he came out of the season a changed man, a man driven to make a difference in his community, and with even half the faith of Derrick Anderson, then Chuck would have the victory he'd been looking for. He grabbed his clipboard and flipped off the office lights. No matter what the outcome, he didn't need a trophy in the front office at the end of the season to prove he'd done his best with this group of athletes.

But it would be nice to have a job.

TWELVE

Aaron was headed toward his locker after practice when Jay Ryder caught up to him.

"I gotta tell you something." Jay's jersey was damp, his face streaked with sweat. He'd taken more snaps than usual today and spent a lot of time at the bottom of the pile. "I like that you're real, Hill. I can learn from you."

Aaron shifted his weight. He looked around to see if Jay's comment was some kind of a prank. "How's that?"

"The whole foster kid thing. I'm really into it, man. Just like you. Talked to my financial guy, and I might actually start a foundation, set up scholarships."

Aaron grabbed a water bottle from a passing trainer. He had no idea where his teammate was going with this. "Where do I come in?"

"I hate to say it"—he looked at the ground, a grin pulling at his lips— "I thought that first time you went to the youth center it was just a media stunt." His smile faded. "But I heard the coaches talking about you going again tonight, and I was impressed. Seriously, man."

Aaron twisted the cap off the water bottle. He'd considered going back—so he could see Megan again. Only he couldn't find the letter, the one from Cory. At least not near the top of the junk in his locker. And he could hardly face Megan without finally reading what the kid wrote. Not only that, but two voice mail messages from his agent and a comment from Coach Cameron had soured him on the idea of another visit to the youth center. Everyone wanted him to have this save-the-world image, but why? Wasn't it enough that he stayed out of trouble without turning into a bleeding heart? He wasn't Derrick Anderson. No one could push him to be something he wasn't.

Jay was looking hopeful, and Aaron wasn't sure what to say. He could go, couldn't he? Jay was counting on him, apparently, and if Megan was there, then maybe he could turn things around for the two of them.

"Yeah …" He took a long swig of water. "Wouldn't miss it. You, uh … you riding with Derrick?"

"Not tonight. Derrick wants to get right home afterward."

"I can drive. You live close." And like that, Aaron and Jay worked out the details.

A few hours later Aaron picked up his younger teammate and the two headed for the youth center. Jay was pensive from the beginning. "I mean, I think about my life and all. How good I've had it." He hung his elbow out the open window. "I'm only four years older than some of those kids. Four years."

Aaron wasn't in the mood for a talk on charity work, but he had no choice. Jay was a nice kid, and Aaron cared what the guy thought. They could be playing together for a long time still.

Jay stared out the windshield. "Four years ago if someone wished me luck and sent me out on my own, I never woulda made it. And that's what happens to these kids."

"Sad." Aaron switched lanes and picked up speed. Maybe he could find Megan and pull her aside, tell her she was right. He hadn't read the letter because he lost it. That might help.

Jay tapped his fingers on his thigh. "Makes me wanna do something, you know? Join up with Derrick and you and really make a difference. Change some laws." He shook his head. "Something."

"I know what you mean." Aaron checked the time on the clock radio. Five more minutes and they'd be there. He'd look for Megan first off.

"I keep thinking about what Derrick said. You know … how in the end people won't remember us by our wins and losses on game day, but for what we do between Sundays. It's true, isn't it?"

Aaron glanced at his rearview mirror. "Definitely."

Jay kept up the conversation until they were walking through the youth center's double doors. By then Aaron had tuned him out, tossing back a few single syllable answers to give Jay the sense of an attention span.

Sure enough, he spotted Megan as soon as he walked into the gym, and she saw him too. She looked his way, but then she turned her attention to another of the volunteers. About the same time, Cory spotted him. The boy lit up and ran toward him, and for the slightest moment, Aaron felt the pings of regret. The kid probably thought Aaron was there to see him.

"Aaron, you came!" Cory hugged him around the waist. "How was practice?"

"Good." He stared past the boy and watched Megan disappear through a door at the back of the gym. "How 'bout you?"

Cory's eyebrows sprang up. "You remembered? About my soccer?" He took off his baseball cap and ran his fingers through his hair. "Wow, yeah ... practice was great."

Aaron wasn't really listening. He found Cory's eyes again. "How's your foster mom?"

The kid's expression fell. "She's good. Really busy, that's all. I asked if we could go watch a practice, but she had to work."

Aaron had a dozen questions. Where did she work, and what were her hours, and how would she have taken Cory to the practice facility in Santa Clara in the first place. But he held back. Instead, he patted Cory on the head. "Gotta get up front with the guys." He motioned to the pizza table. "Bring me a few slices of pepperoni, okay?"

"Sure!" Cory took off as if getting pizza for Aaron was a timed event.

The first hour blended into the second, and the whole time Aaron kept his eyes on the far end of the room. Whatever Megan was doing in the back of the building, it was taking all her time. Surely, she had to have seen him, but she was making herself clear. She wasn't interested in talking to him.

He was frustrated, ready to leave with Jay, when Megan entered the gym with a dishrag in her hand. She tossed it on the first table and dried her hands on her jeans. Then for the first time that night, she looked directly at Aaron.

Cory was still hanging around, asking questions and getting a little annoying. He stood a few feet away from Aaron most of the night, waiting while Aaron talked to the other kids, and interjecting whenever he had the chance. Now, though, as Megan approached, he ran to her and joined her as she walked up.

Aaron wanted the kid to take a break, go to the restroom or something. But before he could say something, Megan put her hand on his shoulder. "Go see if they need more help in the kitchen, okay?"

"Okay." Cory looked ready to protest, but he set his jaw and jogged toward the back of the gym.

"He's a good boy." Aaron meant it. Even if the boy was a little too determined, he was considerate of Aaron's time with the other kids, and he was polite. "Best manners of any kid at the center."

The gym was almost empty. Megan kept a few feet between them and she crossed her arms. "His mother did a great job with him. She left big shoes when she died."

Jay was finishing up with the last few teenagers. As they left, he turned to Aaron and Megan. "I'm going to find the director, talk about some other ways I could help."

Aaron felt his heart rate quicken. With Cory and Jay gone, maybe he could finally figure out what was bugging Megan, why she'd kept her distance all night. He found her eyes, and tried to see past the walls there. "You were busy tonight."

"I was." She didn't break eye contact, and while her voice wasn't angry or bitter, it was definitely cool. "Did you read his letter?"

"I wanted to talk to you about that." He leaned against the wall and slid one foot up. "I can't find it. Should be in my locker, but maybe I dropped it that first day. Janitors might've found the envelope and tossed it."

"Well." Megan shrugged one shoulder. She smiled, but it didn't reach her eyes. "I guess that's your loss, then." She hesitated.

Aaron's mind raced for something to say. He wanted to salvage the moment, but their conversation was unraveling like a cheap sweater. "I'd still like to take you and Cory out again, if that's okay?"

"I'm sorry, Mr. Hill." She took a step back. "I don't see the point. But thank you for coming tonight. The kids loved it." With that, she nodded her goodbye, turned and walked across the gym to the back. She found her dishrag and began wiping down a table.

Aaron watched her, and his frustration mixed with anger. She made him feel like a socially inept schoolboy. Never mind that her face haunted him day and night, or that she was the first woman to actually turn him down. If she didn't want anything to do with him, so be it. He would leave the situation alone. But he would do one thing when he hit the practice facility Monday. He would take a few minutes and really dig through his locker. That way he could find Cory's letter and finally read it, the way he should've done from the beginning. And whether he ever used it or not, he would have the one thing he'd wanted for the past few weeks.

Megan Gunn's phone number.

⌐

Aaron ran out of time before practice, but now their final set of sprints was wrapping up. He finished the last of three runs and jogged toward the locker room. All day he'd felt uncomfortable, frustrated with himself. The weekend had been a total waste. First, the pizza party at the youth center, and then a loss to Denver on Saturday. If that wasn't enough, he'd spent Sunday evening at a party thrown by his agent, Bill Bond. The guests were a mix of financial planners, stock brokers, and real estate investors. That sort of thing.

"Glad to see you made another appearance at the youth center." His agent stayed by his side for most of the party. "You did your good deed for the weekend. Now you wouldn't want to be anyplace but here." He nodded at a group of guys across the room. "Big hitters, Hill, all of them. A couple of these real estate giants could turn five million into ten in a year."

Aaron grabbed a towel from the rack, flung it over his shoulders, and headed for his locker. He'd met every last one of the suits before the party was over. Because he always did what Bill said, and most people told him he was smart because of it. Bill was respected industry-wide, and whether his advice came on personal or financial matters, Aaron had always prospered because of it. But a dozen times through the night, he'd found himself wondering why it was so important that he turn five million into ten. And in just one year?

Last night the power guys at Bill's party droned on in one conversation after another, and Aaron barely caught any of it. He was too busy thinking about Megan Gunn and Cory, about the life they lived, and about Megan's determination to keep Aaron at bay.

There were women at the party too. Not the groupies he'd been known to hook up with, but sophisticated women, smart women. Daughters of senators and daughters of bankers. Women who handled the financial accounts of Fortune 500 companies. Aaron talked to ten of them, at least. But not one of them had a fraction of the passion he'd seen in the dark-haired foster mom. By the time he left the party, he was sure of just one thing.

If he could find the kid's letter, he was going to call her. After all, she hadn't really given him a chance.

Aaron's phone rang just as he reached his locker. He checked the caller ID and felt his irritation rise. What was it with his agent? The guy was calling every day lately. "Hey, Bill."

"Aaron, my man." His agent laughed. Bill was always laughing. "Did you see the paper?"

"The *Chronicle*?"

"Yep, the big dog. Front page sports." Another chuckle. "Looks like our publicity stunt worked."

Aaron leaned against the bank of lockers. Everything about Bill was getting on his nerves. Until this year, he worried that he wouldn't know what to do without Bill Bond, how to interact with the 49ers front office or the media, or even how to spend his money. But now—ever since Bill showed his disapproval of Megan at the Raiders game—the guy was bugging him. Aaron glanced at his teammates. A few feet away, Derrick and Jay had their lockers open too, but they were lost in conversation. Even so, Aaron didn't want to be heard. He dropped his voice. "What stunt?"

"The youth center. The 49ers beat writer picked up on it. Headline reads, 'Aaron Hill Shows His True Colors.' Story talks about how your image took a hit a week earlier, but days after the girl dropped charges against you, there you were, giving back to a bunch of foster kids. The fact that you were there this past Friday night, too, only makes you look more genuine." He snickered. "Almost sounds like it was your idea."

Aaron shielded his eyes. He took a big breath and held it for a few seconds. Then he puffed out his cheeks and exhaled slowly. "First of all, it wasn't a publicity stunt." His tone was seething, but he kept his voice low. "I went because I wanted to go."

Bill was silent for an extra beat. "This is Aaron Hill, quarterback of the 49ers, right?" He paused. "'Cause I thought I called Aaron Hill."

"Shut up." Aaron turned so his back was to Derrick and Jay. "Nobody makes me do something, got it? You suggested it, okay. But if I didn't want to go, I woulda stayed home."

"Okay." Bill drew the word out, like he was talking to a troubled child. "Point made. Either way"—his tone lightened halfway to where it had been before—"it worked. The paper loves you, the city loves you. Your fans love you." His laugh sounded defensive this time. "That's all I was trying to say. A little thanks might be nice."

"Do they know about the other night too?"

"You didn't tell me you were going. Otherwise I could've made a call."

"Do me a favor." Aaron evened out his tone. His agent was only looking out for him. "Tell me before you contact the press on my behalf, okay?"

Bill drew a loud breath. "All right, then. Good talking to you. Don't forget to call the real estate guy. He's waiting for you."

"Sure … fine." Aaron snapped the phone shut, and for a few seconds he stared at the floor, calming himself down. He hadn't thought about it before the Raiders game, but he was sick of being managed. He was going to be thirty this spring, and still he was like some sort of puppet. Whatever string Bill Bond pulled, Aaron jumped. With Megan that day at the park, Bill had lowered his voice and looked in her direction. "A foster mom, Hill? That the best you can do?"

Aaron hadn't wanted to get into it. "I met her at the youth center." He kept his voice light. "She and the boy have never been to a game."

Bill nodded, his distaste showing in his expression. "Well, then … one game should be enough, right?" He patted Aaron on the back. "Good deed done!"

His agent's message that day was unmistakable. Bill didn't want to see Aaron hanging around a woman he thought beneath him. Period.

Normally Aaron would've understood. Some women were bound to chase him for his money, but not Megan. And ever since the incident, Aaron's attitude toward his agent had soured some.

"Everything okay?" Derrick bumped him on the shoulder. Jay was gone, and they were the only two left in this section of lockers.

A weary smile tugged at his lips. "My agent … he's pushy."

"Bill Bond?" Derrick chuckled. "It took you this long to notice? Rumor back when you entered the league was that you didn't burp without asking permission from your agent."

"Great." He positioned himself in front of his locker. "I guess I never saw it before."

When Derrick was gone, Aaron hung his head against the frame of his locker. Was that really how people saw him? Putty in the hands of Bill Bond? And why hadn't anyone said something? The answer came to him as soon as the question hit his mind. He'd been nothing more than a college kid when Bill first came into his life. His own father wasn't interested in football. He traveled the globe as an international marketing director. His only advice when the media started hinting about a pro career for Aaron was this: Find a good agent.

Which was exactly what Aaron had done.

But lately he'd been wondering about more than the parties and publicity stunts. He wondered about Amy too. Amy had been everything to him before UCLA, before Bill broke the news that she was seeing other guys. But what proof had Bill really had? At the time, he remembered thinking he should ask. Because maybe Bill had pictures or a contact he could refer Aaron to. But he never did. He trusted Bill, and that trust parlayed into one of the biggest contracts and signing bonuses of his day.

The familiar locker room smells of sweat and rubber matting filled his senses. One year of football after another, and Bill had controlled his every step, something Aaron had always thought was a good thing. And maybe it was.

He closed his eyes and all he could see was Megan Gunn, her passionate determination, her eyes so deep he could fall into them. There probably wasn't a hundred extra dollars in Megan's bank account, but he had a sense she knew more about life than Bill and all his clients combined.

He opened his eyes and reached into the locker. The letter was in there somewhere, probably near the bottom. He moved his fingers past a few baseball caps and a pair of old socks, and then he felt it, the envelope. The one that had eluded him last week. He pulled it out and stared at it. Aaron's name was scrawled across the front in kid writing. It didn't matter that he could predict what it said. The letter came from the kid's heart. Here, in the silence of the locker room, he would read it with all the importance that had clearly gone into it.

He slid his thumb beneath the flap and gently pulled out the piece of paper from inside. It was folded four times, but once he opened it, Aaron could see the letter wasn't long. He leaned against the locker next to his and started at the top.

Dear Aaron Hill,

I've wanted to write this leter for a long time. Lots of days I started it and then I threw it away. Because how was I going to get it to you? But now I think maybe this will work. Derrick Anderson will be at the youth center Friday night, and he's your backup.

Aaron smiled. The kid definitely knew his 49ers football. He kept reading.

> *So Friday night I'm going to ask Derrick to give it to you. See, I have something really important to say. Because a long time ago my mom told me that you weren't just a nice football player. You're my dad. That's what she told me.*

Aaron scrunched up his face and read those last few lines again. What was this? A strange feeling spread through his chest. The kid actually thought he was his son? He felt like someone had punched him in the gut. No wonder Megan knew he hadn't read the letter. But did that mean she believed he was Cory's dad?

A sad laugh filled his throat and it became a groan. "Poor kid." He picked up where he left off.

> *My mom always prayed I could meet you, because a boy should have a father. Don't you think so? Anyway, now that you know, could you call me at my house? Thanks very much.*
>
> *Your friend, Cory*

Sure enough, at the bottom of the letter was a phone number scribbled larger than the rest of the words. Probably so Aaron wouldn't miss it.

He read the letter once more and stared at it a minute longer. He'd seen a lot of fan letters, but nothing like this. Where a kid got so caught up in adoration that he actually believed Aaron was his father. He took a long breath and thought about the conversation he needed to have with Megan. The boy wasn't his, obviously. He would start there. But he also needed to know what role Megan played in all this. As smart as Megan was, as clear-minded as she'd shown herself to be, he couldn't believe she would support Cory writing this type of letter.

That was probably why she was distant around him. She wanted to see how he'd react to the child's fantasy. Aaron added the phone number into his cell. Then he folded the letter, slipped it back into the envelope, and tucked it near the back of his locker. He felt a mix of sorrow and frustration over the boy's claim. Aaron didn't know Cory's past, other than the small bit Megan had shared the other night. That Cory's mother had been wonderful, and that she was dead.

He finished changing clothes, and then grabbed his duffle bag. If Megan thought the boy's letter was going to scare him off, she was wrong. The child didn't know any better. So he'd made a mistake? What if he did see Aaron Hill as his father ... or the father he never had? If Megan would see him again, Aaron would treat the boy the way he, himself, would want to be treated if he were in Cory's shoes. Not necessarily like a father. But like a friend.

Even so, he felt strangely uneasy. These were waters he hadn't navigated before, and maybe he'd be better off sharing the details with someone else first. Or maybe he just needed to hear Megan Gunn's voice again. He set his bag down, opened his phone, and pulled up Megan's number. But before he hit Send, he changed his mind. Instead, he pulled up Bill's number, and then—at the last second—he dialed the number of a guy he hadn't planned to call all season, let alone now.

Because no matter what he thought about his teammate, one thing was certain. Derrick Anderson was a straight shooter. He would listen and he would respond in truth, something Aaron wasn't sure he could get anywhere else.

And suddenly—where Megan and Cory were concerned—truth was something he desperately wanted.

THIRTEEN

Derrick was putting his ice pack back in the freezer when Denae padded into the kitchen in her bathrobe and slippers. Her smile lit up his heart.

"How did my man do in practice today?" She took a tea bag from a drawer and dropped it into the Starbucks mug from Houston. Derrick collected them for her when he was on the road.

"Held my own."

She looked at his knee and raised her eyebrow. "How's it feel?"

"Hurts. Bad." He felt the pain with every step as he came closer to her. "But I can play. No matter how much it hurts."

"Ah, baby ..." She took hold of the back of his neck and pulled him in for a kiss. "I wish you could see someone." She sidestepped him and filled her cup with boiling water from the hot tap near the sink. She turned and held the cup close to her middle.

"I will." He smiled. "After the season. For now ..." he chuckled, "nothing feels better than beating the Raiders."

"Except maybe beating the Seahawks." Her eyes sparkled, the way they did when she played with him.

"Seattle will be tough." He patted his thigh. "I might see a little more rest. As long as Aaron stays strong. And Coach wants Jay to take a few snaps."

"Never mind. God's got it all covered." She sipped her tea. "I already asked Him."

"Well..." He limped to the fridge and grabbed a string cheese. "Ask Him about Aaron Hill too. I think God's up to something big with that guy."

Before Derrick could finish his sentence, the phone rang. He was only a few feet away, and he forced himself not to favor his right leg. His strength had to carry him on and off the field. Otherwise, he wouldn't give his all when it was asked of him.

He picked up the receiver. The caller ID was blocked. "Hello?"

"Derrick?" The voice was familiar. "Aaron Hill. You got a minute?"

A chill ran down Derrick's arms. How weird was that? He asks his wife to pray for his teammate, and at the same instant the guy calls? He tried to focus. "Yeah, man. No problem. What's up?"

Derrick heard Aaron exhale, and with it came the certainty that something wasn't right. "You remember the woman at the youth center, the pretty one with dark hair?"

"The foster mother." Derrick lowered his brows. She was the one he'd invited to the Raiders game. What was Aaron doing thinking about a woman he'd met several weeks ago? At his pace, he should've moved on by now. "Her son gave you that letter."

"Right … her." He took a quick breath and rushed ahead. "I read it … I guess the kid thinks I'm his dad." He laughed, but it sounded forced. "How weird is that?"

Derrick braced himself against the counter. "Is it true?"

"Definitely not. Some sort of fantasy, I guess."

Aaron explained the main details, how he'd asked for her number. Only the boy had written the number at the bottom of the letter. "Megan knew I was lying. She saw right through me."

Since he'd joined the team, Derrick had been careful when he talked about his faith. For the most part, people wanted to see a sermon, not hear one. But if Aaron was asking for advice, Derrick was going to give it to him. He held his breath. "She's not the only one."

"What?"

"Who sees right through you. She's not the only one." He kept his tone easy, relaxed. "You've never talked about God, Hill. You ever give Him much thought?"

His teammate hesitated. "Not really. I mean"—he allowed a nervous laugh—"what's that got to do with Megan Gunn?"

"Everything. You start thinking about God, and I'll tell you what. You'll read letters from kid fans the first time around. Because you'd understand you don't play a down—on or off the field—without God letting you play it."

Aaron thought about that for a few seconds. "Yeah, well … anyway, this letter thing. I guess I'm not sure what to do next. I want her to think I made the right response."

"Sounds like this should be more about the boy than his foster mother." Derrick looked at his wife. He covered the phone and whispered, "Can I ask him over for dinner?"

Denae held her teacup up and gave a dramatic nod. "Get that boy over here. I'll tell him a thing or two."

Derrick nodded and uncovered the receiver. "Hey, Hill … we're barbecuing. Why don't you stop by for dinner? Maybe we can talk a little."

Aaron's hesitation lasted only a moment. "Tonight?"

"Sure, right now. We're a low-maintenance outfit. Just head on over."

"Okay … can I bring something?"

"Nah." Derrick reached out and patted his wife's lower back. "Denae's got it covered."

When the conversation ended, Derrick hung up the phone and looked at Denae. "Like I was saying, ask Him about Aaron Hill too."

"Just so you know … my stud husband"—she came to him and set her teacup on the counter—"I'm one step ahead of you."

"You've been praying for Aaron Hill?"

She smiled. "Since your agent first started talking about San Francisco."

Derrick kissed her on the forehead, and then on the lips. God had given him a start to this season he would remember always. Beating Oakland and then, against anything he might've imagined, the unreachable, unflappable Aaron Hill calls him for advice. That, more than anything else, was proof God was hearing their prayers.

And that maybe, He'd only begun handing out answers.

FOURTEEN

The doorbell rang just as Derrick was basting Denae's secret recipe barbe-cue sauce across a pan of raw chicken. He cupped his free hand around his mouth. "Somebody ... get the door!"

Denae was doing her face in the bathroom upstairs, but Larry and Lon-nie were in the other room in the middle of a mad NFL PlayStation game. This was the first time Aaron had been over to the house, the first time his kids would hang out with his teammate other than the quick hellos they'd exchanged at a few spring practices.

Larry sprinted past the kitchen and Derrick heard the door open, and then Aaron's voice. "Hi ... your home's beautiful."

"Thank you, sir." Larry's voice held a degree of awe. "My dad's in the kitchen."

"Using one of my other skills." Derrick's voice was ripe with teasing. "Which is more than I can say for you, my bachelor friend. All those Taco Bell wrappers in your locker!"

Larry and Lonnie headed out to the backyard, where Libby was curled up on the patio sofa doing her homework. Aaron entered the kitchen and came up alongside him. He held out his hands. "What, you took the chicken out of the package?" He waved his hand at Derrick and walked around the counter to the bar on the other side. "Even I can do that."

"No." Derrick tried to find a dignified look. "I've mastered the art of applying barbecue sauce." He dabbed the brush at the sides of one of the pieces. "Chicken has a certain amount of natural juice. You have to seal it in just so, especially if you want—"

"Don't listen to a word he says." Denae walked into the kitchen, came up behind Derrick, and took the basting brush from his hand. "Mmm-hmmm. Boy's been telling stories since the day we met." She snapped her fingers at him. "Don't you be taking no credit for my secret chicken, Derrick Anderson."

Derrick started to protest, but before he could say a word, Aaron shook his head, as if he were sorely disappointed in his teammate's duplicity. "I had a feeling." Aaron donned the innocent look of a choirboy. "You should've heard him. How he's been working over the stove all morning, and ever since he got back from practice. How he does all the cooking for the family."

"Thanks." Derrick feigned a defeated look. "The barbecue guy gets no respect."

Denae laughed, and as she finished basting the chicken, she smiled at Aaron. "I'm Denae Anderson. Welcome to our home."

"Thanks for having me." He winced. "Kinda last-minute."

"Don't go talking about last-minute. You come through the front door, that makes you family. No reservations needed."

"The invitation came at a good time."

Aaron sounded kind. A person meeting him for the first time could never have known he had a reputation for being a cocky braggart.

"I'm glad." She gave her husband a warning look. "Since *I've* been slaving in the kitchen all day."

Derrick held his hands out, palms down, and bowed to his wife. "Absolutely. Let the record show that all delectable meals made in this kitchen come from my lovely wife. I only do what I'm told. All of it under the fine direction of one of the best cooks in all of California."

A satisfied look crossed Denae's face, and she grinned at Derrick. "That's better." She took a potholder from the counter and opened the oven door. "The potatoes have another forty minutes." She waved the potholder at her husband. "Shoo … I got this! You and Aaron go out back with the kids."

Aaron stood and motioned to Derrick. "Let's take a look at that view of yours." He wandered toward the back door.

"I'm right behind you." Derrick put his arm around his wife's waist. "You're amazing, you know that?"

"My chicken, you mean?" She leaned up and brushed her lips against his. He felt the familiar desire, the feelings only she could ignite in him. "Not the chicken. Because you put Aaron at ease without even trying."

"God works best in comfortable places."

Derrick studied her. "You're something else." He kissed her this time, and then he headed for the back sliding door. "Let me know if you need anything."

"Just you, baby." Her smile warmed the whole house. "Just you."

Outside, Derrick stopped and watched the happenings in the backyard. Their home was centered on a two-acre square bluff overlooking the San Francisco Bay. Off to the right side was a half-court for basketball, complete with extra-high netting so no one had to chase a ball all the way down to the beach. The middle yard, the part that took off from the house toward the back landscaping, was plush, manicured grass. And on the left was a shop garage with a large patch of asphalt where over the years he expected to watch his kids play with remote control cars and bikes and skateboards. It was the sort of backyard any kid would love to have, and Derrick looked forward to hundreds of hours out here with his family.

"Come on, old man." Aaron held up a basketball in Derrick's direction. Then he passed it to Lonnie, who passed it to Larry. "Let's go two-on-two."

"Yeah, Daddy." Libby looked up from her homework. She had her legs curled up beneath her, and she wore an oversized USC sweatshirt. "I love when you play basketball."

Derrick made a funny face at his daughter. He felt like Bill Cosby. "You like when I play basketball?"

She giggled. "Football too. It's just you don't play basketball that much anymore."

"Well, young lady..." He walked past her toward the court. "I guess I'll have to change that."

Again she giggled, and the sound made his heart soar. He loved having a daughter, loved the way she adored him. She always said that one day she'd marry a man just like him. If she wanted him to play more basketball, he would. But there was no way he was playing two-on-two right now. He might be getting around without a limp, but the pain in his knee was still constant. He couldn't risk a worse injury in a pickup game.

For that matter, Aaron couldn't either.

He reached the court and moved just inside the fence. "Don't tell me your contract lets you play hoops during the season." Derrick raised his eyebrows at his teammate. "I know mine don't."

"Ah, come on." Aaron's grin proved he'd been caught. Of course, his contract forbid pickup games during the season. "You're just afraid."

Derrick pointed to himself and let his mouth hang open. "Me?" he mouthed the word. Then he wagged his finger in the air. "*Au contraire.*" He added a French accent for effect. "I don't need a pickup game to beat you at B-ball." He held his hands out and caught a pass from Larry. He was outside the three-point line, but he eyed the basket, launched the ball, and swished it.

"Nice, Dad." Lonnie grabbed the ball and passed it to Aaron.

Derrick tipped an invisible hat toward Aaron. "You got something to say about that?"

"Yeah. Step back." Aaron waved him out of the way. He took aim and shot an air ball, one that missed even the backboard by a foot.

"Oooh…" Derrick studied his teammate with an exaggerated look of concern. "Sorry, man. Did you think we were shooting left hand?"

"That's an *H*, and I don't mean for Hill." Lonnie ran after the ball and took a shot from the corner. When it swished, all four of them shouted their approval, and the game grew competitive quickly. Larry got the letters in HORSE first, and then Lonnie. Derrick and Aaron were neck and neck for the last five shots, until finally Derrick shot a basic free throw, underhanded.

"How's that from an old man."

Aaron shook his head and grabbed the ball off the ground. "Doesn't get any more old-school than that." He dribbled the ball to the free-throw line, set his feet apart, and swung the ball back between his legs and up toward the hoop. The ball ricocheted around the rim, bouncing three times before popping out to the side.

"Dad wins!" Lonnie raised both fists in the air. "Way to go, Dad."

"Good try." Larry patted Aaron on the back.

"Yeah," his grin showed his defeat. "Remind me to come over every week. I usually need to file taxes to get this sort of abuse."

The boys launched into a half-court game of one-on-one, and Derrick and Aaron walked across the yard and up a slope to the rock fence at the far end. They sat on it and stared at the ocean beyond.

Aaron narrowed his eyes. "You can see halfway to Hawaii."

"We love it." He looked over his shoulder at the boys. "I plan to watch the kids grow up in this yard."

A comfortable silence settled over them. In the distance, a jet flew over the bay. Derrick was grateful for the laughter and the game of HORSE. But that wasn't why Aaron wanted to talk to him. Something was changing just the slightest bit in his heart, Derrick could sense it. He found a softer tone with none of the teasing from earlier. "So … about the boy's letter."

"I still can't believe it." Aaron kept his eyes on the view. "Kid thinks I'm his dad. I mean, how crazy is that?"

Another possibility entered Derrick's mind. "It's not the pretty foster mom, is it? Trying to get money from you?"

"Hardly." Something softened in Aaron's eyes. "I think she's a little baffled by the boy's thoughts too. Her name's Megan, the foster mom. Maybe she's waiting to see how I'll handle it."

"That's heavy stuff."

"Yeah." His voice grew distant. "I don't know if it's meeting all those foster kids or what, but ... I don't know. I feel crummy lately." He pulled one leg up onto the rock wall and circled his knee with his arms. "And my agent's bugging me. Pushing more than usual."

"What about this Megan?"

Aaron started to say something and then stopped. A frustrated groan came from him and he shook his head. "She turned me down. She knew I lied about the kid's letter, about reading it."

"Hmmm. Not good."

"No. It's a bad time to feel like things aren't going right. I need to be at the top of my game, you know?"

"Either you or me." Derrick allowed a smile into his voice.

"Yeah. I guess." Aaron laughed, but it sounded tense. "You know how many girls I've been with, Derrick?"

"Lots." This wasn't the time for a funny line. Derrick's soul ached for the emptiness he was sensing in his teammate.

"A whole lot." He narrowed his eyes and looked deep at Derrick. Deeper than ever before. "But not one of them ever made me smile the way you smiled when Denae walked into the room."

"So maybe this is the year." Derrick patted Aaron's back. He stood and nodded at Aaron to follow him.

"The year?"

"Yeah." Derrick tossed him a smile over his shoulder. "The year you figure it out."

They went inside and took the tray of chicken out to the barbecue. Lonnie and Larry stayed nearby, getting pointers on the fine art of grilling chicken. When they were seated around the table, Derrick said the prayer.

"Father, we thank You for this food and the hands that prepared it. The female hands."

"Got that right," Denae muttered.

A few giggles sounded from around the table, and Derrick cleared his throat. "Seriously, God, we're grateful for all You've given us, and for the love You've blessed us with. We ask that Aaron would take a little bit of that love home with him tonight. In Jesus's name, amen."

Derrick wasn't sure, but he thought maybe Aaron was a little pensive after the prayer. If he was, he didn't stay that way for long. Dinner was a blur of one-liners and extra helpings and the sort of warmth that marked every day Derrick spent with his family. Throughout the meal, he would catch Aaron mid-bite, his fork in his hand, studying the kids and Denae and the way they interacted with each other.

God, You're touching his heart, aren't You? Right before my eyes. A shiver ran down Derrick's spine, and he tried to imagine what the Lord was doing in Aaron's life and how that process must've been directly connected to Derrick's decision to play for the 49ers. It was more than he could get his mind around.

After dinner, when the kids were busy with the dishes, Derrick and Aaron walked out to the upstairs balcony. From there, the view was breathtaking— especially with the setting sun.

"Man, how do you ever leave?" Aaron sat on one of the cushioned patio chairs.

Derrick took the one next to him. "The view?"

"All of it." He allowed a single laugh, one that expressed his amazement. "Your family's like something from a TV show. I didn't have a single meal like that one when I was a kid."

"We're blessed." Derrick used the word on purpose. Because luck had nothing to do with the evening Aaron had just shared in.

"I'd say so." Aaron leaned over and dug his elbows into his knees.

Just watching him made Derrick cringe. With great care, he lifted his right leg up and rested it on the footstool.

"You're a churchgoer, aren't you?" Aaron craned his neck and stared at him. "I mean, you talk about God, but it's more than talk for you, right?"

"It is." He felt a surge of joy. He'd prayed for this chance, this opportunity to help Aaron see that faith in Christ was the only way to tackle the emptiness. "My family and I go to a Vineyard church in the city. Meets Saturday night and Sunday mornings. Rockin' choir ... big potluck dinners. Lots of ways for the kids to stay involved." He nodded. "And preachin' right from the Good Book. Every week I learn something."

"What about when we're on the road?"

"During the season, I go when I can make it. But Denae's there with the kids. The stability's good for 'em."

Aaron squinted at the setting sun. "So you believe the whole story, God made the earth and sent His son, the crucifixion and resurrection. All of it?"

"I do." He pictured Lee, the way he'd looked that day in the hospital. "Even in the worst of times."

They were quiet, both of them focused on the sun as it dropped beneath the horizon, casting brilliant rays of light across the Pacific. In the glow of pinks and pale blues, Aaron turned to him once more. "Tell me about the family picture. What happened to the fourth kid?"

The pain in Derrick's knee was nothing to the sudden ache in his heart. He pressed his lips together. "You notice more than you let on."

"Sometimes."

Derrick sucked back a long breath. If telling the story about Lee would help Aaron understand faith, help him get a picture of what it was to truly believe, then he would tell it now. No matter how much it hurt. "It was seven years ago. October. My tenth season in the NFL."

Aaron shifted slightly in his chair, his attention completely on Derrick. The look on his face said he hadn't meant to bring up something too deep, too personal. "Hey, man, I didn't mean to pry."

"It's okay. Sometimes it's good to go back." Derrick steadied himself and the years rolled away. "I was boarding a plane in Dallas that Sunday night after a game against the Cowboys, when my phone rang. The flight attendant was saying something about shutting off our cell phones, but I took the call. Denae was on the other end, hysterical."

He could hear her still, the way her voice sounded frantic, desperate. "Derrick, it's Lee ... it's our baby, Derrick. Dear God, it's Lee ..."

All around him players were chatting about the game and positioning their airline pillows and buckling their seatbelts. But Derrick was trying to catch his breath. "Denae, baby, calm down." He placed his hand around his mouth so his teammates wouldn't hear him. "I can't understand you, baby. Talk to me."

"Someone ran the red, Derrick. Dear God, no." She let out a loud wail, one that echoed in his heart still today. "I need you, Derrick. Please. Dear God, not my baby. No!"

Derrick could feel his heartbeat double, and for a moment he considered tearing down the aisle and getting off the plane. But then he realized that would be crazy. He couldn't get to Denae any faster by leaving his seat. Instead he gripped the phone as tightly as he could. "Is there ... is there someone else around? Someone I can talk to?"

She was still weeping, but she must've heard him, because she handed the phone to a man with a calm, professional-sounding voice. "Hello, this is Doctor Lander. Is this Derrick Anderson?"

"It is." His heart slammed against his chest and panic choked him. "What happened?"

"I'm sorry, Mr. Anderson. There's been an accident. A speeding car ran a red light and broadsided your wife's van. We've checked out your wife and oldest three children. They're all fine."

Get to the point, Derrick wanted to scream. What about Lee? "Our ... youngest?"

"He took a severe blow to the head. He's in critical condition." The doctor's voice was heavy. "You need to get here as soon as possible."

No, God, please not Lee. Derrick closed his eyes and bent over his lap. He pictured Lee, jumping into his arms as he left for the airport the day before the game. "Daddy, I love you ..." *Please, God, not little Lee.* He found his voice. "I'm on my way. Please ... put my wife back on."

Denae was still sobbing when she came back on the phone. "Pray, Derrick. I can't ... I can't lose my baby."

The flight attendant could sense something was very wrong. She didn't ask him again about his phone, but the plane was moving. Derrick promised he would pray and then he hung up and turned off his cell. Nearly four hours later when they landed in Chicago, Derrick took a Town Car straight to the hospital.

The story was always difficult, but Derrick hadn't realized till now that there were tears on his cheeks. He swiped the backs of his hands across his face. "He was still conscious when I reached his room. The other kids were huddled on the floor against one wall, crying. Denae was standing by the bed, holding Lee's hand."

Derrick's breath caught in his throat, the way it always did when he allowed himself to go back to that horrific moment. His eyes fell on Lee, the way his head and face were swollen. At that point, Derrick didn't know his son's prognosis, but he didn't need a doctor to tell him the situation was grave. He hurried to the side of the bed and tenderly, carefully, he took hold of his son's other hand. "Baby ... Daddy's here."

Lee blinked slowly, the blink of heavy sedation. "Daddy?"

Sorrow flooded Derrick's heart and soul and he struggled to speak. "Jesus is with you, Lee. Everything's going to be okay." His words were as much for himself as they were for his son.

Across the bed, Denae met his eyes. Tears were streaming down her face and she shook her head. "It's not good," she mouthed. Then she squeezed her eyes shut, released Lee's hand, and turned so he wouldn't see her break down. After a minute, she motioned for Derrick to follow her.

An ocean breeze washed across his face and he looked at Aaron. His teammate was gripped by the story, stunned by it. Derrick sat up straighter in his chair. "The news was worse than I imagined." Derrick's voice was distant, lost back in that long ago fall. "You know, you figure he's talking, he's coherent. He must be okay." Derrick shook his head. "He wasn't."

Denae led him into the hall and she collapsed in his arms. "He's bleeding," her face twisted in a gut-wrenching sorrow capable only from a parent losing a child. She fought for her voice. "Doctor says he can't stop it. Blood's coming from too many areas."

For the first time that awful night, anger sliced through Derrick's grief. "So what? We're supposed to stand by and watch him die?" All his life Derrick had tackled adversity, as a high school player at a school where black kids were looked at with disdain by alumni, and at college when he had to battle for a starting position. He worked hard for his success, every touchdown pass, and dollar earned. Always Derrick believed a person had control over his destiny.

But not here, not in a hospital room.

The panic was back, and suddenly Derrick didn't want to debate Lee's prognosis in a cold, sterile hallway. He wanted to be in the room beside his boy, holding his hand. And that's what he did. He kissed Denae's tears and then returned to Lee's side.

The media touched on the story of Lee's death, but no one but Denae and the kids knew about the part that came next. Aaron Hill wasn't family. He wasn't even a close friend, not yet, anyway. But if he was the reason God moved Derrick to San Francisco, then he'd tell the story.

He massaged the muscles above his right knee. "We had one more conversation, me and Lee." His voice was choked with a hurt that was never far from the surface.

He reached the boy's side and took his hand again. "How're you doing, little man? You hanging in there?"

Lee squinted at him. "Daddy?" He clung tight to Derrick's fingers. "My head hurts."

"I know, baby. I'm sorry." He felt more helpless than ever in all his life. *God, no ... not Lee. Stop the bleeding, please.* "What can I do, baby?"

For a few seconds, Lee was quiet. Then his little boy smile lit up his swollen face. "Win ... a Super Bowl, Daddy! ... Okay?"

The statement was the strangest thing. Lee had only recently become aware of Derrick's status, the fact that he'd won two championships. A few weeks before the accident, Lee asked to see his rings, the rings he kept in a bedroom drawer. Derrick had showed him, and Lee had done his own figuring. One ring for Larry, one for Lonnie, so now all he needed to do was win one for Lee.

Derrick had asked him about Libby, but Lee wrinkled his nose. "Girls don't care about Super Bowl rings, Daddy. That's for boys."

And now, with his brain bleeding uncontrollably, his youngest son remembered.

Derrick bent over the hospital bed, and with his free hand, he ran his knuckles over the boy's swollen cheek. "A Super Bowl, baby? That's what you want?"

A tired little laugh breezed across his lips. "Yeah. You're gonna ... win it all, Daddy! The ... Super Bowl." His words were scratchy and strained, his eyes barely able to stay open.

Tears blurred his vision, but Derrick did the only thing he could do. He lifted his boy's hand to his face and tried to hold on, tried to will life and healing into him. Then in a rush of determination unlike any he'd ever felt before, he nodded. "Okay, little man. I'll win it all."

"For me." Lee's breathing was getting worse, shallow and weak. "Win it … for me, Daddy. Like … we talked about."

"I will, baby. I promise."

Derrick had heard about cases where a dying person had one last shining moment, the final flicker of a fading fire. For Lee, that moment happened then. His expression lit up once more. "Daddy …" his eyelids opened wider than before. He looked like an angel, his eyes bright with childlike love. He patted Derrick's hand, soft and tender. "You're … my best friend."

"You're mine too."

Denae was back on the other side, stroking Lee's arm, his legs. But no amount of love or prayers or willing him to be healed could change what was happening. Lee's eyes closed, and after a few minutes, his breathing grew slower and then finally stopped. And the bright ray of sunlight that had been their youngest son was snuffed out before he ever really had a chance to shine.

Derrick sniffed. The tears didn't embarrass him. If recalling Lee's death didn't make him cry, he'd be worried about the condition of his heart. He wiped at his face again. "I miss him."

For a long time, Aaron didn't say anything. He stared at the sky, at the fading pinks and lengthening shadows. When he finally put words to his thoughts, they were strained with confusion. "You still believe? Even after that?"

"More than ever." The determination in his voice was the same he'd felt that day in the hospital room. "I never coulda survived losing Lee without Jesus. Woulda died from sadness, man. No way." He pressed his fist to his chest. "In here, I believe with everything I have that Lee…" His voice broke. He took a few seconds to find control again. "Lee is with Jesus. Happy and whole, helping get things ready till we're all together again." He felt drained from telling the story. "What would I have if I didn't have that?"

They sat a long time in silence, and then Aaron thanked him. "I had no idea."

"Everyone has their struggle."

"Yeah."

Without another word, Aaron stood and shook Derrick's hand. Derrick followed him to the stairs and listened as Aaron moved down into the kitchen. He thanked Denae and told the kids goodbye, then let himself out the front door. With someone else, Derrick might've been worried about the abrupt exit. But this was Aaron Hill, and the exit could only mean one thing. The evening, the story, their family, had made an impact on the guy. So much that Derrick guessed Aaron didn't know what to do with his feelings.

When he was gone, Derrick went to his bedroom, to the photo that hung on the wall by the closet. God used all suffering to build character, right? Wasn't that what the Bible taught? Because losing Lee changed everything for Derrick.

After that, his faith could never be something passive, a pleasant outing to a friendly church service. Faith became everything, because heaven held one of his own. He was passionate about making sure his family all wound up together in heaven.

But here on earth, winning another Super Bowl ring was important too.

He kissed his thumb and pressed it next to Lee's precious little face, beaming at him from the photograph. Nights like this, he could still hear his son's last laugh, see his last smile. "It might happen, baby. This might be the year."

Either way, he was certain of one thing. Aaron Hill had listened to every word tonight, and if God was going to change him, the journey might just begin right here.

In the legacy of a little boy who never really had a chance to live.

FIFTEEN

Aaron drove without thinking, without processing even one bit of Derrick's story. He drove until he came to Baker's Beach, the stretch of rocky sand just west of the Golden Gate Bridge. It was almost nine o'clock, but a few couples still dotted the sand. Aaron didn't want to talk to anyone.

He walked away from the bridge, toward the part of the beach that drew fewer people. Feelings were building in him, weighing on his heart, but he couldn't think about them, not yet. He pushed himself. Long strides, his hands in his pockets. Only when he was far away from anyone else, did he walk toward a craggy boulder near the surf. He climbed to the top, drew his knees up, and sat facing the water, and finally ... finally he stopped.

He rested his arms on his knees and let his head fall against his fists. And there, for the first time Aaron could ever remember, he felt his eyes tear up. Anger and sorrow and guilt and helplessness welled up inside him. Strange and deep feelings for Derrick and the precious child in the family photo, and for Megan, who had dedicated her life to helping kids without families. And for Cory, who wanted a father so badly he was willing to make up the idea that Aaron might be his dad.

All of it mixed together in his heart until he could barely breathe for the sadness. He had always respected Derrick Anderson. Yes, when the 49ers brought him on board, Aaron had felt threatened. How could the franchise have room for two star quarterbacks? But from the beginning, Derrick had made it clear. He was there as much to mentor Aaron and Jay Ryder as he was to make any real contribution on the field.

The story Derrick told him tonight changed everything about how he saw the man. Aaron lifted his face and let the ocean breeze dry his eyes. He didn't cry; he wasn't sure he could cry. Even so, his heart ached for the thoughts weighing on him. He stared at the moon's reflection on the bay and tried to imagine what that night in the hospital room must've been like.

He'd never been a father, never cared for anyone as much as he cared about himself and his career. No one except Amy Briggs.

When Derrick told that story, Aaron felt like he was there, like it was his own son Derrick was talking about. The hurt somehow transferred deep into his heart, to a loss he'd never registered before tonight. The loss of a different child that maybe, just maybe, was his own. The one Amy had told him about his sophomore year at UCLA.

By then Bill Bond had already been saying how Amy was seeing other guys on the side, and how she was only sticking around for the money. When Bill heard about Amy's claim to be pregnant, he scoffed at the idea. "She's playing you, Hill. You're a star, and you're letting a girl play you. Come on, now."

Aaron even wondered if maybe his agent had talked to Amy, discouraged her from fighting for their relationship. Aaron had asked him, but Bill only dismissed his question. "You take care of the football," he would say whenever the subject came up, "and I'll take care of the riffraff. And there will always be riffraff." At the time, Bill's comments were comforting. Aaron couldn't trust Amy, but he could always count on his agent.

Every day, every year since then, he'd told himself the same thing. He couldn't have been the father. Amy was seeing other guys and maybe she wasn't even pregnant. He never saw proof, never saw her with a bulging middle. And he certainly never heard anything about the child.

A boat passed by, and from somewhere out on the water he could hear laughter. He waited until it faded, until only the lapping of the water against the shore remained. The smell of seawater filled his senses, and he hung his head again.

What if he was wrong? Aaron gritted his teeth. What if Amy had really been pregnant? What if she'd had a child, Aaron's child, and he'd spent all these years not knowing it?

How could he have turned her away, let her fall out of his life without even a hint at closure?

What was he thinking back then? He was a kid, a boy whose dream was unfolding faster than night traffic on the Ventura Freeway. Strangers waited for him every time he left a class or headed out to his car in the UCLA parking lot. Bill Bond was the one who stuck, the one who seemed like the friend and father he'd never had.

Bill thought Amy was bad for his career, so that settled it. Aaron gave her some lame words and a lot of cold shoulder, and after a blur of seasons, he signed a pro contract. By then, Amy was so far gone from his life, it was like she never existed at all.

But she had existed, and he'd wronged her.

Hearing Derrick's story tonight stirred his memory and his conscience and brought to light wrongs that had been eating at him since the last time he talked to Amy. Even if he hadn't acknowledged it until now.

He opened his eyes and Megan Gunn's face filled his heart. She was crazy for that little boy of hers, even if she was only his foster mother. In that way, she was the opposite of everything about him. When he'd heard about a fatherless child, when Amy had come to him with news of her pregnancy, he'd taken a quick door and disappeared from her life. When Megan heard about a child without a father, she stepped up and gave her whole life, everything she had. Her freedom and reputation, her dating life, her time and finances. All of it.

His face was dry, but the ache in his heart stayed. What sort of person was he, to let all these years pass without even calling Amy? If she really was seeing guys behind his back — however Bill Bond knew that — then no, they wouldn't have worked out. But he could've at least had a final conversation with her. He could've asked why he hadn't been enough for her.

Then, as if the events of the evening had crystallized his memories of Amy, he realized for the first time that something didn't ring true: Amy hadn't dated a single guy all of high school until the two of them went to his prom. Why would she have suddenly done any differently? He should've pressed his agent harder about his evidence, his proof that Amy was cheating.

A crazy thought hit him, and his gut tightened in a sick feeling. What if Bill had made up the whole story about Amy? He might've done it in a twisted attempt to protect Aaron, right? It was possible. Even now, nearly a decade later, the breakup didn't make sense.

He slid down off the boulder and walked to the water's edge. Amy was probably married with three kids and a wonderful life. Whatever had happened back when he was a sophomore in college, she was certainly over it by now. Over him.

He couldn't do anything about the past, but he could try to figure out his future. He needed to talk to Bill, get more details about whatever he'd found out about Amy. Bill didn't like Amy, and now he didn't like Megan. Maybe Aaron had spent enough time listening to his agent and not his heart.

He turned and began walking back to his car, his Hummer. Nothing felt right, not the way he carried himself or the way he looked at tomorrow. Something needed to change, but he wasn't sure exactly what. He pulled out his cell phone and punched in Derrick's phone number. His new friend answered on the first ring.

"Hey, man, you forget your doggie bag?" It was the Derrick he was more familiar with, the one with a ready one-liner.

Aaron didn't feel like smiling. He kept walking. "You doing that pizza party thing for the youth center again this week?"

"Yep." The teasing dropped from Derrick's tone.

"Can I go?" He was breathless, but not from the walk. "I'm serious, I can't explain it. Being with those kids ... it made me feel good."

"I don't know, Hill. No one at the center wants a media circus."

"No press. I didn't bring any last time. I won't even tell my agent."

Derrick was quiet for a beat. "Okay. The kids would like it."

"Good." A hint of relief sparked in his soul. "Thanks, man."

The drive home took longer than usual, Aaron's mind running through the details of everything he'd seen and felt that night. He needed to be stronger, needed to stand up to his agent a little more often. He couldn't go back and make things up to Amy. But he could spend next Friday night at the Mission Youth Center, working alongside a woman unlike any he'd ever met. And maybe this time he wouldn't try so hard to hit on her. It might be enough just to watch her, study her.

Maybe in the process, some of her strength would rub off on him.

Sixteen

Megan wasn't sure what to make of seeing Aaron Hill enter the youth center next to Derrick and Jay Ryder that Thursday night. But here he was, and something seemed different about him. Every time she stole a glance in his direction, he was locked in sincere conversation with a child, not just giving out an autograph and a practiced smile, but actually caring about them. At least it looked that way.

Megan grabbed a dishrag from a bucket of hot soapy water. She wrung it out and worked it over the food table. It was six-thirty and most of the kids had already eaten since the party started at five tonight. Megan lifted her eyes to the front of the room. It was Cory's turn to talk to Aaron.

Megan straightened, because this was her boy. He could catch her watching and that wouldn't be a problem. Without looking, she dropped the rag on the table and took a few steps forward. Cory was standing directly in front of Aaron, and Aaron had his hands on Cory's shoulders. Whatever the quarterback was saying, the atmosphere looked happy and upbeat. Which left only one explanation. The guy still hadn't read Cory's letter.

Megan sighed and returned to her cleaning. What would it take, five minutes? Could Aaron really care so little about the boy that he wouldn't give even that much time to read the letter of a young fan? She tucked a strand of hair behind her ears and took her anger out on the messy table. She was finishing the job when she heard Cory run up behind her.

"Megan, quick ..." He was breathless and excited.

She set the rag back in the bucket and turned to him. He needed to get home and work on his times tables. "Ready to go?"

"No." He came to a sudden stop and his expression fell. "Aaron wants to go to the park." Cory pointed toward the open gym door. "It's still light."

Megan hesitated. She didn't want Cory spending time with a guy who couldn't be bothered to read a kid's letter, but maybe the park was a good idea. That way she could pull Aaron aside and tell him what she thought of him. Megan nodded slowly. "Yes." She brushed her hands on her jeans and smiled at the boy. "Let's go to the park."

The line of kids was much shorter today, so Aaron had no trouble leaving early. He said a few words to Derrick and Jay, and then he looked at her and smiled. It wasn't the come-on smile he'd flashed at her the first time they met. Now there was depth and something else in his look. A bittersweet sadness. Whatever it was, Megan's heart reacted to it, and she chided herself. The next hour had to be about Cory, not about some misguided infatuation the guy had for her.

They met up at the door and he kept his eyes on her. "Thanks for doing this." He glanced at Cory. "I know it's a school night."

"That's okay." Cory placed himself between them. "I only have a little homework."

"You have your sevens." Megan gave him a teasing frown. "Let's not forget that."

"Right. My sevens." Cory managed to seem subdued for a moment before bursting into a big grin again. "Still, the sevens will always be there. Right, Megan?"

Despite the seriousness of what lay ahead—at least from her perspective—Cory's comment made her laugh. She put her hand on his shoulder as they walked. "You have a point."

They were passing the youth center parking lot when Aaron motioned to his Hummer. "Just a minute." He jogged over, opened the door, and snagged a football from the front seat. He smiled at Cory as he shut the door. "Wanna play catch?"

"Wow! Really?" Cory ran to him and held out his hands. Aaron tossed him the ball, and the two caught up with Megan again and headed up the street. Again Megan was baffled. No matter how she tried, she couldn't figure Aaron out. If he'd read the letter, then why was he taking them to the park? Why offer to play catch with the boy? If he hadn't read the letter, then his actions were all a well-put-together show, intended to impress her that he was someone he wasn't.

Megan redirected her thoughts. The sky was blue, the day warmer than usual. "Indian summer," the customers at Bob's Diner had called it earlier today. It was still warm enough that none of them needed a jacket. Cory kept the conversation going as they made the five-minute walk. "Derrick's pretty good." Cory squinted up at Aaron. He had the football tucked beneath his right arm.

"Derrick's very good." Aaron's tone held a level of respect that hadn't been there before. "He's teaching me a lot."

Megan listened, interested. The papers had hinted that Aaron had been frustrated when Derrick was acquired earlier this year. She let her eyes meet Aaron's. "Derrick could help the team this year."

"He could." No defensiveness rang in his tone. "No question. I'm glad we have him."

They reached the park and walked until they came to a large patch of grass. Aaron took the ball from Cory. "Okay ..." He drew his arm back, ready to throw. "Go long!"

Cory ran as fast and hard as he could, his eyes never leaving Aaron. "Ready!"

Aaron winged a perfect spiral straight into Cory's hands. "Nice catch." He jogged a little closer and held out his hands. Cory threw the ball back and Aaron chuckled. "You're pretty good, Cory."

"Thanks."

Megan felt guarded and jaded, and she wondered at her sanity for allowing this trip. Still, Cory would remember it as long as he lived, the chance to play catch with Aaron Hill in a city park. She moved to a nearby bench and sat down, mesmerized by the picture they made. Again, she noticed a resemblance between them. The same sandy blond hair, the same cheeks.

Ridiculous, isn't it, God ... why am I thinking that way? Cory isn't Aaron's son, so why sit here and get caught up in the fantasy? Just because they look so natural together? That's not a good reason, and I know it. So give me a clear mind, God. Please...

She filled her lungs and kept her focus. This wasn't about Cory, not a bit.

When ten minutes had passed, a boy from Cory's soccer team called to him from across the small park. The boy was with his dad and brothers, and he wanted Cory to join him on the climbing structure. The boys didn't seem to recognize Aaron through the long shadows and trees that marked the distance between them, and when Cory hesitated, Aaron tucked the ball under his arm. "Go ahead. I want to talk to Megan for a minute anyway."

Her heart skipped a beat. What could he want to talk to her about? Cory headed off to play with the kids, and Aaron ambled over to her. The bench wasn't long, and now she slid toward the side, giving him plenty of room. He sat down and caught his breath, his eyes still on Cory. "I like that kid."

"He likes you." Megan folded her hands. It took everything she had to keep her tone pleasant. "But I think he'd like you even more if you read his letter."

Aaron set the football down between them and leaned over his knees. "I read it." He was still watching Cory. "That's why I wanted to come here. So we could talk."

Megan gripped the edge of the bench. "You understand, right? Cory thinks you're his father."

Aaron looked at her. "You and I both know that isn't the case."

There it was. Never mind the resemblance, Aaron Hill was not Cory's father. "Of course." She hurt for Cory, for the disappointment ahead. "That little boy wants a dad so badly, he somehow created this ... this idea. And now he believes it."

"I know. I can tell." Aaron sat up straight and shifted so he could see her better. "I've never had this happen." His words were thoughtful, not rushed or nervous. "I figured you'd know best what should take place from here."

Megan tried to understand. She angled her face. "You don't owe him anything, Mr. Hill."

Her use of his last name hit its mark, but this time Aaron didn't correct her. Instead, his eyes danced with a teasing that made him seem warm and familiar. "I realize that ... Ms. Gunn." He paused. "But I like him. And I sort of like you too." He grimaced. "Though I'm not sure why, really."

The awkwardness of the moment and the emotions battling each other came together in a nervous laugh. She leaned back on the bench and turned her attention to Cory again. "I'm not sure either."

"Anyway ... Cory has to know the truth." His teasing faded. "I've learned a little about kids lately. Someone told me the other day that I shouldn't lie—not to kids or adults."

"True." Megan stifled a smile. "So Cory needs to know, and you're not sure how to tell him?"

"Or if I should tell him." He sighed. "Maybe it should come from you."

"Maybe." A pair of birds flew past and landed in a tree a short distance from the bench. The sounds of the boys on the play equipment made the atmosphere feel comfortable and familiar. "Actually, I've told him before. Lots of times."

A curious look came over Aaron. "So he's believed this for a while?"

"Since his mother died." Megan felt the familiar sorrow. "Two years ago, when Cory was six."

"Oh…" Aaron closed his eyes for a moment and groaned. "I wondered… about his background, what led him to the foster care system."

"His mother and I were friends. We worked together."

"Did she …" He sounded slightly uncertain. "Did she ever mention me?"

"No. Not once." Megan gave him a sad smile. "She was single as long as I knew her. Never dated. Spent every spare moment with Cory." Her attention shifted to the boy, still playing in the distance. "If she thought you were her son's father, she would've said something. I have to believe that."

Aaron was quiet, taking in the details of Cory's life.

"I want to adopt him, Mr. Hill. I'm all the boy has." She felt the futility of Cory's situation, deep in her heart. "The system won't let me make him my own until they get his father to sign off. He insists you're his father, so his social worker isn't ready to label him abandoned."

"Wow." He raised his eyebrows. "It's that serious, then."

"It is." Her tone lightened some. "That's why I knew you hadn't read his letter."

"Yeah." He winced. "I got that pretty much the minute I read it." He stretched his legs, linked his hands, and placed them behind his head. "How did you wind up with Cory?"

"His mother came down with pneumonia. She called me, but it was too late." She shrugged. "Cory had nowhere to go, no family, so he stayed with me during the funeral week, and that's when I realized it was up to me. I went through the training and became a foster mother."

For a few seconds Aaron said nothing. Then he looked at her and his eyes seemed to see deeper, past her heart and into her soul. "You must love him very much."

"I do." She felt the weight of her responsibility, the way she felt it often. "There're so many kids like Cory. Someone has to do something to help them."

They talked some about the system, and how younger children could get by okay. "But when no one steps up and adopts these kids, then what?"

She told him the statistics, how hard life was on the older teenage foster children and how they were often left to fend for themselves once they became adults. "Derrick told me at the last pizza party he's talking to Jay Ryder about the two of them starting a foundation. Derrick and Jay might testify before the state legislature and see about getting laws changed."

"I'm impressed." He sounded sincere. "I didn't know much about foster kids until a few weeks ago."

"And now a foster boy thinks you're his dad." Her smile was intended to show him empathy. This talk was good for her. He wasn't the bad guy she'd made him out to be. Deep inside he cared more than she gave him credit for, or at least he was starting to care.

"Cory deserves a dad." Aaron picked up the football and rolled it around in his fingers. "Every kid does."

They talked a few more minutes, and then Cory came sprinting over. Megan wanted to finish the conversation. "I'll tell him. It's okay."

"That'd probably be better."

Cory reached them, a smile stretched across his face. "Ready?"

"More catch?" Aaron stood and patted Cory on the back. "You bet."

For another fifteen minutes, they tossed the ball. Megan watched, and in the distant part of her heart, the part that still believed in happy endings, a sorrow took root. Because the moment Cory was having was all make-believe. Aaron Hill was a busy guy. Just because Cory had some strange delusion that Aaron was his father didn't obligate the quarterback to spend time with him. Megan hoped Cory was holding on to every moment of this magical afternoon. Because the odds of it happening again—now that the truth was out on the table—were next to nothing.

Aaron walked them back to the center and gave them a ride home. Again, he looked like he wanted to come up, maybe share coffee or more conversation. But he didn't ask. Cory told Aaron goodbye. "Let's play again sometime, okay?"

"Definitely." Aaron reached into the backseat across the console and gave Cory a hug before the boy stepped out onto the curb. Then he turned and faced Megan. "We're away this week and next."

"I know. Cory told me." Megan's mouth was dry. Why was she letting him have this effect on her? She wasn't a football groupie, and she didn't want to date him or anyone else. So why did he make her heart beat faster every time he looked into her eyes? "And no more pizza parties, right?"

"Not for now. Derrick said he might put something together mid-season on our bye week, but it'll be pretty busy." His eyes lit up. "After the season, though. Derrick and Jay are talking about making a regular event out of stopping by the center."

"That's right." Megan had heard the director talking about the possibility. Nothing was for sure yet. "Anyway, thanks for reading his letter." She looked intently at him, trying to figure him out. "I sort of thought we wouldn't see you again, once you knew what Cory thought about you."

"Why?" His smile was easy. "Little boys create fantasy worlds all the time. It's part of being a kid." The smile faded. "I don't want him hurt, that's all."

"I'll tell him. Maybe not tonight, but before the weekend."

Megan wasn't looking forward to the moment. Cory wouldn't believe her at first, but if she explained that she and Aaron had talked, then as sad and difficult as the truth would be for a while, the boy would have no choice but to believe it. She took a quick breath and reached for the door handle. "The good news is I can adopt him now. If he tells the social worker he doesn't know his dad, and since there's been no father in the picture all these years, the judge will clear him for adoption."

A depth shone in Aaron's eyes. "I don't envy you, having to tell him the truth."

"Yeah. I'll be doing a lot of talking to God this week."

For a moment, it looked like Aaron might ask about that, about God. But Cory was waiting on the sidewalk, and Megan had to get going. Aaron put both hands on the steering wheel. "Can I call you? After the road games?"

There was no reason for Megan to say yes. But before she could stop herself, she grinned at him. "I'm not sure why, Mr. Hill." She could feel her eyes sparkling. "But you can call. I can let you know how Cory took the news."

"Okay." He started to reach out, as if he might take her hand or touch her shoulder. Then he pulled back and smiled. "I enjoyed today, our talk. Learning about Cory and getting to know you better."

She smiled before she could stop herself. "Me too." Then, with her heart racing at triple time, she stepped out on the sidewalk, shut the door, and gave him a final wave.

On the way up the stairs, Cory tapped on her arm. "Hey . . ."

"What?" She stayed a step ahead of him, because if she moved fast enough, maybe she could outrun the strange emotions whirling in her heart, the feelings she was starting to have for Aaron Hill.

"You looked sorta happy in there, talking to Aaron." He was teasing her, using the voice kids use when they think two people like each other. "I think he has a crush on you, Megan."

"He doesn't." Her answer was quick. She reached the third floor and made a straight line for the apartment door. "He's just trying to be nice."

"Hmmm." Cory had to run every few steps to keep up. "I don't think so."

Once they were inside, Megan directed Cory to get his backpack. "Take your math papers. I'll be in your room in a minute."

He did as he was told. When she was alone, she fell against the door and closed her eyes. Her heart was still racing, still betraying her. She should've said something to stop the madness. She could've told him that, by the way, she wasn't interested, or she could've asked him not to call. Most of all, she could've avoided saying "Me too" when he told her he enjoyed their talk that day. But then that would've been going against her own beliefs, and that's what troubled her most.

Because lying wasn't right, no matter what.

SEVENTEEN

Aaron didn't call her after the road games, and he wasn't sure why. Mostly just that he had a lot to figure out about himself, and someone like Megan Gunn deserved a guy with his act together.

It was Monday night, first official game of the season, and the 49ers were hosting the Cardinals. Anticipation and energy were at an all-time high, and the entire team felt it. All week, sports announcers and media members had guessed about the game and about the coming season. Indianapolis would be strong again, and so would the Bears and the Patriots. Most talk shows liked San Francisco in tonight's game, because the team had buffed up its defense with the draft and traded well for a receiving team that would complement Aaron's abilities. But the team was still picked to place just third in their bracket. Sports media believed Aaron didn't have what it took to win the big game, and oddsmakers in Vegas had them a twenty-to-one shot to win the Super Bowl. The worst odds since Aaron had joined the team.

They were on the field, finishing warm-ups, and Aaron surveyed the stands. Cory would've loved it here tonight, but Aaron couldn't bring himself to invite the boy, to lead him or Megan into believing something that he wasn't sure he could carry through. Aaron wasn't worthy of a girl like Megan Gunn, so maybe it was best to take a step back. Besides, the boy had to know by now that Aaron wasn't his father. So a phone call to Megan or an invitation to the game could've come across as patronizing or charity. Still, Aaron wished they were there.

No matter his own shortcomings, he hadn't stopped thinking about either of them since he dropped them off at her apartment.

Aaron tried to clear his head, tried to focus on warm-ups, which were nearly finished. He took the snap from the center, danced back a few steps, and fired it at a passing receiver. This time, instead of the neat tight spiral he was known for, the ball soared past his teammate and landed ten yards on the other side of the guy.

"You with us, Hill?" Derrick was taking snaps a few feet away. "I mean, come on, you never call, never write. We have one dinner and you ditch me."

Aaron laughed. "I'm here. It's just my head."

"Yeah, well." Derrick stared at him, just as one of the coaches blew a whistle. "Game's starting in five minutes. Might be a good time to reattach it."

"Right." He slapped Derrick's helmet as they jogged back to the sidelines. "I'll do that."

They lost the coin toss, and Aaron was glad. He needed a few minutes to focus on the game. The hype and commotion was all a distant roar compared with the thoughts in his head. Every spare moment since his talk with Derrick, he'd been more and more aware of the life he'd been living. How many people had he used since he'd come into the league? The more he thought about it, the more the trail of his success as a player seemed paved with a stream of nameless, faceless girls, none of whom had meant anything to him.

And for the most part, he probably meant nothing to them. At least that's always what he'd told himself. The girls he hooked up with weren't the types to get broken hearts. They were the type that marked their night with him as another conquest, another line on their résumé. The sort of girls Bill Bond approved of—as long as none of them was underage—because they came and left in the shadows. Girls that didn't hurt his image as a bachelor.

"Keep your play toys in the closet, Hill," Bill would say, "and everything will work out fine for us."

But the more Aaron thought about foster kids and the statistics, how so many became street people, he had to wonder. Some of the women he'd used over the years were probably looking for a way to feel needed. Even for only a night. Did his agent ever think about that?

Aaron knew the answer, and the weight of his sin, his responsibility to those women, stayed on his shoulders like a lead blanket. Even here on the sidelines. Beneath the weight of it, he struggled to find the carefree, cocksure athlete he'd been before showing up that first night at the youth center.

Aaron focused on the unfolding game. The 49ers' defense held the Cardinals to three plays and a punt. Now it was his turn, whether he felt good about himself or not. He jogged over to Coach Cameron and listened for the plan.

"Hill, what's eating you?" Coach's eyes were dark with worry.

"Nothing." Aaron let his gaze fall to the ground. "Just some things I'm working through."

"Work it through later." Coach gave him a hard pat on the back. "I mean it, Hill. We need you a hundred percent tonight."

"Yes, Coach." Aaron steeled himself against the crud in his heart, the weight on his shoulders. Coach was right. This was their opening game. The team needed him. He ran out to the huddle and shot a look of intensity at his offense. "All right guys ... let's do this!"

He sounded convincing, but the drive stalled at the Arizona thirty-yard line. A field goal put them ahead by three, still no matter what he tried, Aaron couldn't engage his heart in the game. He'd played football since high school, and not once in all that time could he remember a game where he struggled to give his all. Until here, opening night. A game televised to the entire country.

The team battled Arizona all night, and Aaron threw an uncharacteristic three interceptions. Before the fourth quarter, Coach pulled him aside and threatened to put in Derrick or Jay. The talk was enough to give Aaron the push he needed, and in the final five minutes, he threw two touchdown passes, giving the 49ers a three-point victory. His performance was pathetic by any measure. He threw for just over a hundred yards and his touchdown to interception ratio was his worst in four years. But it was a win, and Aaron was grateful.

Media flooded the locker room after the game, but Aaron had nothing to say. What could he tell them? That he felt like a creep? That his self-centered past suddenly felt shallow and empty and the result left him with little desire to even play the game, let alone win it? All of America would think he'd lost his mind.

He found Coach Cameron and begged off from the post-game interview. "I'm not feeling good."

"Is that what you call it?" Coach's expression went from sarcastic to concerned. He pursed his lips and shook his head. "Don't worry about the press. I'll handle them. Get home and get some rest. The schedule won't get any easier."

Aaron stared at the ground. "I'm sorry." His eyes met his coach's. "I'll figure it out."

Coach held Aaron's look for a long moment. Then he nodded and headed off to face the press.

Aaron shuffled toward the showers, dizzy from the strange feelings plaguing him. After a game like tonight, it wasn't always smart to dodge the press. They expected the key players to show up after the game. His missing the interview would give them reason to speculate that something was wrong, that Aaron Hill was maybe fighting an illness or an injury. Two or three games like the one he'd played tonight and they'd start talking about whether he'd lost his edge, whether he should be replaced.

He undressed and stepped into the shower. The hot water felt good on his shoulders, but it didn't wash away the heaviness surrounding him. At some point, he needed to talk to his agent, have a sit-down with him, and get to the bottom of the situation with Amy — even if it had been years since her name had come up. Plus Bill had called a couple times in the past week, telling Aaron about a few A-list actresses and one country singer who had expressed interest in him.

"Say the word and I'll set it up, Hill." Bill sounded beyond excited at the prospect. "We could use a connection like that."

Aaron had made himself clear both times. "I'm not interested. I can find my own relationships."

Bill didn't act offended. He only chuckled, dismissing Aaron. "You'll come around. Guys like you need to mix with your own kind."

Aaron ended both calls before things got too strained. The conversation he needed to have with Bill wasn't one they could have with his agent chuckling on the other end of a phone line.

Aaron ran the bar of soap over his aching biceps and under his arms. If he didn't know better, he'd think the fog in his head was depression. Something he'd never even considered.

When he was dressed, he grabbed his bag and kept his head low. Derrick caught up with him just as he was heading out to the parking lot. "Hey, man ... talk to me."

"I'm okay."

"You're doing it again." Derrick put his hands on his hips. "You're lying to me."

"No." Aaron tried to find a smile. "I need some time, that's all." He appreciated his teammate more than the guy knew. But he needed to be alone now. Being in Derrick's presence only made him feel worse about himself. All he had to offer was glitz and looks and athletic ability. The deeper places — the places that shone brightest for Derrick Anderson and even for Jay Ryder — were for Aaron draped in cobwebs.

Derrick studied him. "All right, but I'm warning you, man."

Aaron waited. He wasn't quite able to look his friend in the eyes.

"I'm talking to God about you, Hill." He shook his head. "Mmm-hmmm, let me tell you, when someone starts talking to God about you, look out."

"Yeah?" He looked at Derrick.

"Oh, yeah. Changes start happening so you don't recognize yourself in the mirror." He took a step closer and gave Aaron the sort of hearty hug typical between athletes. "I'm here if you need me, man. Seriously."

He coughed and tried to find his voice. He wanted to thank his friend, but all he could manage was, "See ya." Then he hurried outside to his Hummer.

As he neared it, a slim blonde woman wearing a short dress and heels stepped out from behind one of the other player's cars.

She blocked his path and batted her eyes at him. "Hey, Aaron."

He vaguely recognized her. Once maybe a year or so ago they'd shared a night together, he was pretty sure. Now the thought of that, the way it was empty and meaningless, made him sick to his stomach. But the familiar temptation was there too. He stopped and shifted his bag a little higher onto his shoulder. For a few seconds he gritted his teeth, forcing himself to get control. He lifted his chin and averted his eyes. "Hey."

"It's been too long." She ran her finger down the length of his arm. "I'm free tonight … let's find somewhere quiet for dinner."

Aaron worked the muscles in his jaw. He'd used the blonde for his own selfish pleasure, and she wasn't even bothered by the fact. Not outwardly, anyway. And worse, his body was responding to her touch, reminding him of the pleasures that could lay ahead tonight if he were willing. He breathed in sharply through his nose and then looked straight in her eyes. "Look, I can't tonight." He broke eye contact and stared blankly at a point beyond her. "I'm busy."

The girl's face turned red, and she stumbled for something to say. Her expression grew softer, sexier. She took a step closer. "What I have in mind

… won't take all night, Aaron." She put her hand on his shoulder, her fingers working small delicate circles on his upper back. "You sure you're busy?"

The familiarity of the moment intensified the struggle. Aaron stared at his shoes and considered her offer, the way a night like those he had experienced so often before might ease his burden for a while. But then what? He pictured Megan, her determination to make life right for an orphaned boy, and he pressed his lips together.

In a rush, he pushed the young woman's hand off his shoulder and took a step back. "Go find some other football player." He snarled at her, the feelings of temptation quickly giving way to disgust. "I told you I'm busy."

Without another look at her, he walked past her to his Hummer.

"Aaron…" He could hear her walking toward him. "I'm sorry if I came on too strong … maybe we can just have coffee somewhere … maybe we—"

He climbed into the driver's seat and slammed the door before she could finish her sentence. He hated the girl for trying to make him give in, and he hated the fact that he'd slept with her before.

As he drove off, he realized something else. He hated his car. Everyone in the city knew he drove a Hummer, and at stoplights he was often recognized by other drivers. For what? So he could make it clear to the world he was Aaron Hill, that he had enough money to drive an expensive car? So he could feel bigger than life on the field and off?

The cell phone on his console vibrated and he punched a button.

"Hey, Hill … good game." Bill Bond's voice filled the car.

"It wasn't good, and you know it." Aaron gripped the wheel and picked up speed as he entered the freeway. "I've been in the league seven years, Bill. You don't need to blow smoke at me."

"So it wasn't our best showing." Bill's voice was upbeat as usual. "Got the whole season ahead, friend … not to worry!" He barely paused. "Speaking of which, I'm your best friend and you don't make it up to the box to say hello after the game? I mean, come on, Hill. I had three brokers I wanted you to meet."

"I didn't feel good." Aaron switched lanes and settled back into his seat. He needed a meeting with Bill, but he would let his agent do the talking first. "What's up?"

"Strategy." He dropped the friendly tone, and his voice took on an urgency. "This is a big year for you, Hill. Very big. Everyone in the business is whispering about it being time. You prove yourself now, or maybe you're not all America had you cracked up to be."

"Maybe I'm not."

Bill paused, and then he let loose another short burst of laughter. "Yeah, well, this isn't a joke, friend."

In college, and even in the years after signing his pro contract, Aaron had liked how Bill called him friend. The word seemed an accurate reflection of the relationship he shared with his agent, the way the guy looked out for him. Aaron usually felt comforted by the fact, reminded that Bill wasn't only interested in making money off him, but in caring for his career, his future. The way a friend would care.

Lately the word grated on Aaron's nerves. It felt cheap and forced and saccharin. Bill never asked how he was or how he might be feeling, why his game had struggled tonight, for instance. His calls were always about strategy and key meetings and endorsements. Things good for Bill's bottom line.

His agent was going on about a new plan, something he'd discussed with some marketing people at one of his big sports clothing sponsors. "Here's the deal…" Bill picked up speed as he went along, practically stumbling over his own words in his excitement over this new venture, whatever it was. "Okay, so at the meeting we all decided your image needs an update. The foster kid thing was nice short-term, but it's not enough."

Anger rose quickly in Aaron's gut. He was tempted to push the Off button, but strangely Bill's monologue fascinated him in a twisted sort of way. It was like looking in the mirror and seeing what he'd become, what he'd let himself become.

"So …" Bill was clearly winding up, "we all agreed it was time you got married."

"Married?" Aaron was so caught off guard he nearly rear-ended the car in front of him. He hit his brakes. "Are you kidding me? A marketing meeting can't decide my personal life."

"Of course not." His agent rushed ahead. "You'll pick the lucky lady. I mean, come on, Hill." He laughed. "You have some say, after all."

Aaron clenched his jaw and waited.

"Here's the reason. You've been single all these years and it's been a good thing. Good for your image. Boys and teenagers and college kids, all of them could relate to you. Best quarterback in the league, a fearless gunslinger admired by women around the country. Around the world!" His tone changed. "But you're almost thirty, my friend. Stay single after thirty and you lose some appeal. Guys have less ability to relate to you, understand?"

Aaron gritted his teeth. "That's garbage, Bill. No one makes a corporate decision to get married. I'm not even dating anyone."

"Good." He sounded beyond relieved. "As a side note, I did some checking at the Mission Youth Center on that woman you asked to the Raiders game. Megan Gunn."

Aaron couldn't remember giving Bill her name. But he wasn't surprised that his agent found out. He had a way of knowing whatever Aaron was involved in, something that even a year ago had brought Aaron comfort. Not anymore. He felt his anger double. "I don't believe this."

"She's not your type, friend. She's a single mother, of course. But more than that—her mother was a drug user, a street person. You probably don't know, but this ... this Megan has several jobs—none of them high paying. She dropped out of college and she apparently has no plans to complete her degree."

"So basically she's poor." Aaron's voice seethed with rage.

"Slow down, there. It's more than that. She's a single mother." He paused. "How would that look? Everyone who saw you together would wonder if maybe the kid was yours. Otherwise why would you spend so much time with him?" He whistled low. "An illegitimate kid, I'm telling you that would be bad, Hill. Very bad."

Aaron wanted to know about the rest of the marketing meeting. "So your little strategy session, who do you think I should marry? Did you figure that out?"

"Not exactly." He laughed again. "But I've been telling you about the A-listers, the actresses and the singer. I know you don't agree yet, but Hill, you have to think about it. There's some real potential there."

"Potential?" Aaron felt his face growing hot. More amazing than his agent's plan was the fact that he was serious. He truly thought he could plan Aaron's marriage at a marketing meeting.

"Starlets. That's the trend. Big name entertainers have their agents contact the agents of certain star football players. A meeting is set up and voila! Instant romance." Again, he barely stopped long enough to breathe. "The marketing gurus think a wedding with one of the top stars could raise your endorsement worth a million dollars a year or more. I mean, talk about your win-win situations. It'd be the top news for a month."

His anger became a sick feeling that hit with a vengeance. Aaron needed all his concentration to focus on the road. "So just flip through the tabloids and pick out a starlet?"

"No." Bill sounded hurt. "Nothing like that." His voice changed, as if this next part was top secret information. "The fact is, those inquiries I told you about, they're legit, Hill. A couple phone calls and the first meeting's a done deal."

That was it. He couldn't take another minute. "Look, Bill. I'm on the road. I'll call you back." He stabbed his finger at the Off button. Was his agent out of his mind? Or was this how Bill had always acted? His agent thought nothing of telling Aaron this was the year he should get married, that he might be worth another million or so if he did. Because he'd been making calls like this one since he first gained Aaron's trust.

A starlet? Aaron shook his head, his breath hissing out in disbelief as he replayed the conversation in his mind. A big wedding, something the newspapers and ESPN and the tabloids could all get excited about. Everyone but him. He leaned back in his seat and exhaled long and slow.

He didn't want to marry a movie star, someone more self-centered than he'd always been. If he were going to marry some day, he would choose someone different.

He thought about that for a moment. He'd never really explored his feelings before, but he suddenly realized he'd prefer a woman who couldn't care less that he was Aaron Hill, famous quarterback. He'd had enough of the shallow women he picked up in bars across the country. Women like the one he'd pushed away in the parking lot tonight. No, he wanted someone with depth. A woman with strength and determination and intellect. Perhaps a woman who understood the virtue of volunteer work and helping the less fortunate. Someone whose faith and honor shone from the depths of her heart. Who was willing to work three jobs so she could pay rent and keep food on the table. A woman with dark hair and fine features and unforgettable blue eyes.

The sort of woman he'd been avoiding every day for the past few weeks.

A woman named Megan Gunn.

Derrick and Denae prayed with their kids and went out on their upper deck to talk. It was late, and already they'd told the kids they could miss the first half of tomorrow's school day. That was their tradition whenever Derrick's team played a Monday night game.

It felt good to fall into the patio chair outside their bedroom slider. Derrick worked his fingers into the muscles above his right knee. "Long day."

"Definitely." She made a curious face. "Something's wrong with Aaron. Did you feel it tonight?"

He sighed and gripped the arms of his chair. "Baby, I think the whole country felt it."

"I was ready to walk down there and give Coach a piece of my mind." She huffed. "Keep my baby on the bench when the game's falling apart."

Derrick smiled. "Mighta helped."

She crossed her arms. "That Cardinal team isn't so great. You could've won the game with one hand tied behind your back."

"That's my baby." Derrick allowed a quiet bit of laughter. "Still my number one fan."

"No one loves you better." Her attitude still sounded in her voice. "I could barely sit there watching that young guy mess things up."

A softness filled Derrick's heart. "Aaron's got it bad, that's for sure."

Denae's tone lifted some. "So what's the problem? Do I need to talk to the boy?"

"No." Derrick stared out at the moon on the water. The bay was so beautiful. It was one more way he felt God's favor on him this season—even if winning the Super Bowl was a long shot. "Remember, baby, we talked about how God brought me here for a reason."

"I know." She still had some frustration in her expression. She brushed her hand in front of her. "So why does He park you on the bench through a nail-biter like tonight?"

His answer was slow in coming. "Because maybe He brought me here for Aaron Hill."

"Yeah. You've said that before." She sounded doubtful. "You really think that, baby?"

"I do. God's working in that young man." He made a fist and pressed it to his heart. "I can feel it deep inside."

"Could be indigestion after a game like that." She muttered the words under her breath. Then she turned and faced him. "Don't get me wrong, I like the guy. But tonight … he wasn't trying, baby. You'da done better."

"I don't know." Derrick leaned his elbow on the arm of the chair and stroked his chin. "This season's something special, Denae. It's like God's working out a bunch of miracles all at once." He turned to her. "Really."

She was quiet for a long time. Then she reached out and took his hand. "So maybe next time Coach'll put you in?"

Derrick smiled again. "Maybe even that."

Neither of them said anything about Derrick's promise to Lee, or the fact that this was his last season to make good on it. Winning a Super Bowl wasn't something a player could control by himself. It wasn't something a team could will, either. Every team in the NFL wanted a trophy at the end of the run. Besides, Denae was right—Aaron looked weak out there. He'd struggled bad against a team that figured to finish in the bottom half.

Maybe that's exactly the way God wanted tonight to go. Maybe it would get worse before things started moving full speed ahead. That way when they all stood around at the end of the season marveling at the victories on and off the field, they would know for certain they hadn't found their way there by hard work and determination.

But by God alone.

EIGHTEEN

Megan was making macaroni and cheese in a pot on the stove, and Cory was sitting at the kitchen table reading *Tom Sawyer* from the school library. The radio was tuned to a country station, and a song about miracles was playing. Megan hummed along, but even then, Cory's silence hurt.

Megan had told him the truth about Aaron, and since then, Cory had been much quieter, less excited and talkative. The furor over Aaron Hill's involvement in their lives had dropped off now that it had been three weeks since their outing to the park. Megan understood Cory's disappointment. But she wished there was a way to get through to him that the truth wasn't her fault.

The problem was he still believed the fantasy. Which was exactly what Megan had feared all along. She was beginning to wonder if maybe she'd taken the wrong approach with the news. Maybe Aaron should've been the one to set him down and explain that no, he wasn't Cory's father. That way, maybe Cory could hardly refute the fact.

She glanced at him, but he was lost in the book. He'd been reading more lately, books and not the newspaper. He still tuned in for the games, glued to every play — especially Monday night when Aaron pulled the game out in the last quarter. But Cory didn't talk about the 49ers as much as usual.

They'd been at the youth center late tonight, taking part in an informal tournament of three-on-three games. It was after seven, and she and Cory were both hungry. She stared into the pot and willed the water to boil.

"Megan?"

"Yes?" She looked up, careful to smile at the boy.

"Did Tom Sawyer have a dad?" He planted his elbow on the table and cocked his head.

The question took Megan's breath. *God, do You hear this child? How can I ever be enough for him when all he wants is a father?* She sighed, but not so loud that he could hear her. "I don't know, buddy. What do you think?"

"Well..." Cory looked back at the open book on the table. "He musta had a dad somewhere. Because everyone has a father." He lifted his eyes and met hers.

His point was well-taken in a biological sense. "That's true." She stirred the spoon through the water and noodles again. "But not every father knows how to be a dad. Sometimes they miss out on their child's entire life. A boy like Tom Sawyer might never have known his dad, not ever."

Cory furrowed his forehead and studied the book again. "I think Tom Sawyer had a dad. Maybe the author didn't write that chapter."

"Maybe." Megan stared at the noodles again, but this time her vision blurred. How could she adopt a boy who was so desperate for a daddy? She was still pondering the question when the phone rang. She set the spoon on the countertop and picked up the receiver. "Hello?"

"Ms. Gunn?" Aaron Hill's voice filled the line.

Megan's heart skipped a beat. Why was he calling now, after three weeks of silence? "Yes?"

"I'm parked out front." He sounded unsure of himself. "It being a Friday night and all ... I wondered if you and Cory would like dinner out at Pier 39?"

She stared at the packet of powdered cheese mix on the counter. Then she caught herself. It didn't matter how good dinner at the pier sounded. They didn't need Aaron's charity, and there could be no other reason why he was here. She turned her back on Cory. "Tell me why."

"Why what?"

"Why dinner? Why now?"

He exhaled and his frustration was evident. "Can you come down here, Megan. Please."

She hesitated, but then she felt herself giving in. He'd driven all the way out here. He deserved the chance to explain himself. "Just a minute." She hung up the phone, turned off the stove, and stared at Cory. "Be right back, okay?"

"Where're you going?" He'd been too lost in the book to figure out who was on the phone.

"Downstairs. I have to talk to someone."

"Okay." Cory didn't look interested. He focused on the book again. "Is dinner almost ready?"

"Almost." She slipped on her sandals, and as she hurried out the door and down the stairs, she ran her fingers through her hair. No matter how she'd reacted on the phone, it felt wonderful to hear his voice again. But what was she thinking? She reached the last few stairs and slowed her pace as she moved toward the door. She was as bad as Cory, fantasizing that Aaron Hill had changed into a gentleman, and more, that she could ever trust a guy like him with any piece of her heart.

More likely, the youth center had showed him a side of life he hadn't acknowledged before. Now he was focusing his attentions on Cory and her as a way of making up for times when he hadn't thought of those less fortunate than himself. In other words, he probably saw them as a charity case. She took a steadying breath. She would thank him profusely for coming and explain that they were getting along fine. They didn't need his favors.

She opened the door and scanned the street for his Hummer. It took a few seconds to realize he was right in front of her, in the driver's seat of a light gray pickup truck. It was newer, a full-size with rear doors and a long bed. But it had none of the sparkle of the Hummer. She wrinkled her eyebrows, curious, just as he stepped out and met her near the doorway of the apartment building.

He must've realized she was looking for his Hummer, because he nodded to the truck. "I traded it."

"Really?" Megan narrowed her eyes.

"Yeah." He kept a polite amount of distance between them. "I needed a change." His eyes met hers and held. "In a lot of areas."

Megan wasn't sure what to say in response, so she crossed her arms and looked down at the cement for a few beats.

"Now." His voice was soft. "You were saying?"

Something about his tone washed over her like a caress, and her cheeks suddenly felt hot. She was saying? She swallowed hard and tried to remember their conversation from a few minutes ago. But his nearness was unnerving, breaking down her defenses and leaving her unsure of even a single reason why she and Cory wouldn't have dinner out on the pier with him. She lifted her eyes. "You don't have to do this, Aaron." It was the first time she'd used his given name, the first time she hadn't been completely on her guard. Because there was no reason now. She wanted to be transparent before him. "I told him you're not his father."

Aaron slipped his hands into his jeans pockets. Pain shaded his expression. "How'd he take it?"

"He didn't." She laughed, but it held a hidden cry, a sound of defeat. "He told me he'll believe forever that you're his dad."

Aaron hesitated and then turned halfway around, his eyes raised to the sky. After a few seconds, he looked back at her. "That's so sad."

"I know." A chill hung in the air, and she crossed her arms more tightly. "That's what I mean. You don't owe us a night out." She lifted one shoulder. "You've done enough."

The muscles in his jaw flexed and he took a step back. He seemed to be searching for the words. Finally he came closer again, his eyes locked on hers. "Maybe this isn't about Cory. Maybe I just want to take you out to dinner."

"Why?" Again, she felt defeated. She uncrossed her arms, held up her hands, and let them fall to her side. "I'm not your type. You …" She looked into the air between them, as if the answers might be drifting by on the breeze. "You're a celebrity, Aaron." She thought about her life, her paper route and her shifts at Bob's Diner, and she uttered a sad laugh. "We couldn't possibly be more different."

"Except one thing." He reached out and touched her bare arm.

The feel of his fingers against her skin sent shockwaves through her body. A part of her couldn't understand why she was fighting him so hard, when all she wanted to do was feel his arms around her. Her teeth chattered and she bit down to still them. "What?"

He looked deep at her, and the tenderness in his eyes was as real as the air they were breathing. "I can't stop thinking about you." He made a light-hearted face. "Believe me, I've tried. Nothing works."

She wanted to say that she knew the feeling. Because as sensible as she was, as much as she prided herself on being intelligent and a realist, she saw his face everywhere she looked. Even when she wasn't watching the 49ers on TV. Instead she bit her lip. "I'm not ready, Aaron. I can be your friend, that's all."

Nothing in his expression changed, but the hint of a smile brightened his face. He let his hand fall back to his side. "I can handle that."

"So." She tilted her face, studying him, trying to figure him out. "Dinner at the pier?"

He nodded, and he looked up to the windows in the apartments above them. "Better go get Cory."

Megan giggled. She stepped back, and then turned and ran lightly through the door and up the stairs. She had questions about herself. Why was she agreeing to this night when it couldn't possibly lead anywhere, and how could she allow Cory to live out his fantasy by spending more time with Aaron? And when did Aaron become the sincere, genuine guy she'd just talked to down on the sidewalk? She silenced the questions as soon as they hit her. She had no answers, anyway. For now, maybe it didn't matter. She and Cory didn't have much, after all. And if this was the last time the two of them hung out with Aaron Hill, so be it. They'd at least have this: A night they would remember the rest of their lives.

⚊

Cory could hardly believe it.

Megan came rushing into the apartment and told him to get his shoes and his sweatshirt. They were having dinner with Aaron Hill. He took a minute to catch his breath over the idea, but then he closed his Tom Sawyer book and jumped up from the table. He wanted to say, "See, Megan, I told you so. Told you Aaron is my dad. 'Cause otherwise why would he come to take us for dinner?"

But he didn't say that. He only hurried with his shoes and his sweatshirt, and tried to make his heart stop pounding so hard. The strange thing was that Aaron hadn't said anything about the letter yet. Megan said he talked to her about it, and that he really wasn't Cory's dad.

Cory wasn't so sure he really said that, 'cause why wouldn't he just tell Cory and not Megan. Plus, if Aaron really didn't believe Cory was his son, then that only meant it was Cory's job to convince him. His mother hadn't lied to him, definitely not. She would look right straight in his eyes every time she told him, "Aaron Hill's your daddy, Cory. But it has to be our secret."

He remembered those words coming from her as much as he remembered her saying that Aaron had been her friend in high school and how Aaron was only her friend until he asked her to some dance when they were seniors. A prom or something. Aaron Hill was his dad. That's what she said. Megan always asked then why didn't his mother ever tell Megan? That was a good question. Why didn't she? That would've made everything much easier, 'cause then when she died, there wouldn't be any confusion.

But his mother hadn't expected to die. She got a cold and it went to her lungs and she died without making any plans about Cory's father. That's what happened. And so after Megan's talk with him about Aaron not being his dad, Cory pulled out his special box, the one with the things from his mom. He had some letters she wrote to him, about how much she loved him and how she would always be there for him. Because that's what she wanted, but God had other plans. That's what Megan said.

Also in the box were the newspaper articles, the ones about Aaron. There was one from when he was doing great at UCLA his junior year, and people were talking about him being a pro one day soon. His mom went to a different college. Junior college. But still, she and Aaron were boyfriend and girlfriend. And there were a couple articles from the next year when Aaron won a lot of games and he got drafted in the first round, third pick by San Francisco. After that, she had two in the box from his first couple years as a 49er. Then she stopped cutting out stories about him.

Pictures were in the box too. Pictures of Cory when he was little and when he was learning to walk, and one of him and his mom on the first day of kindergarten. But that was all, 'cause she died after that.

But in the box there was also a big yellow envelope, and inside were three envelopes with Aaron's name written across the front. Another one just said the word "PRIVATE." All three were sealed tight, the way his mother had left them. A long time ago she taught him that you don't open other people's mail. So, even though lots of times Cory was tempted, he never opened the letters. 'Cause they belonged to Aaron.

And that sent a wave of excitement through him, because now Aaron came back! And maybe tonight, or maybe very soon, he would give Aaron the letters and then that would clear up any confusion. He tied his shoes and grabbed his sweatshirt, and then they hurried out the door.

Because it wouldn't be nice to keep his dad waiting.

Nineteen

Aaron felt like a schoolboy. The sense of victory over convincing Megan to spend an evening with him rivaled the feeling he had after a playoff win. They drove out to Pier 39 and parked, with Cory chattering in the back about Monday's game.

"I never for minute thought you'd lose." He leaned forward and gripped the corner of Aaron's seat. "Not for a minute."

"I did." Aaron rolled his eyes and cast a quick look at Megan.

She put her fingers to her lips, covering a light laugh. "It didn't look good."

"It didn't feel good." He kept his tone easygoing, but only to cover up how he'd really felt that day. How he'd felt every hour since, until now. Later, if the night worked out the way he hoped, he'd have a chance to talk to Megan about the changes happening inside him. He had a feeling she'd understand.

Pier 39 was busy, but that worked in Aaron's favor. With so many people milling along the walkways, between the shops and restaurants and street performers, the crowd would help hide his identity. He wore a baseball cap and a jacket with a high collar. Most of the time he could get away with being in public if he dressed like this.

"You've been before, right?" Aaron walked beside Megan, with Cory on his other side.

"Not often." Her smile held a distance again, the caution that had marked her conversations with him since the beginning. "But yeah, once in a while."

"I've never been," Cory piped in.

They were hungry, but on the way to the restaurant, as they walked along the soft worn slats of wood, they passed the carousel. Cory slowed to a stop and watched it go round a few times. People of all ages sat atop the painted animals and benches, most of them laughing, enjoying the ride. Cory looked at Megan. "I thought merry-go-rounds were for little kids."

"Not this one." She put her arm around his shoulders. "See that." She pointed at the paintings that made up the perimeter of the attraction. "Look close. There's Coit Tower and the Golden Gate Bridge, Lombard Street and Alcatraz." She turned her attention to Aaron. "I read somewhere that this is the only carousel in the country with paintings of its home city."

"I didn't know that." Aaron had the sudden impulse to take her hand, but he resisted. She wasn't ready, that's what she'd said. She wanted a friend, and for now, that's what he would be.

"Wow ..." Cory took a step closer. "That's cool!"

That was all Aaron needed to hear. He saw a ticket booth a few feet away and he motioned to Megan that he'd be right back. As crowded as the place was, the carousel had no line, probably because it was the dinner hour. He bought three tickets and returned to Megan and Cory. "Everyone should ride once."

Cory wasn't about to act too excited. Aaron understood that. At almost nine, he already had a sense of machismo, especially in a crowd. He was a kid who understood the streets and navigated the Mission District on his bike, like he'd told Aaron the first time they met. But there was no mistaking the thrill in his eyes as they got in line and then as they boarded. They chose a trio of painted horses, and Megan climbed on the outside one. Aaron helped Cory onto the inside horse, and he took the middle.

While the carousel made its rounds, Aaron had the strangest thought. What if this was really his life, here between this endearing child and the woman who took his breath away? They were coming to a stop when a teenage boy in the crowd pointed at him. "Aaron Hill!" He looked around and then back again. "Hey, that's Aaron Hill!"

"Looks like we need a fast get-away." Megan climbed off her horse first. She whispered the words to Aaron. "Got a plan?"

"Be my date." He held his elbow out to her. Then as Cory jumped off his horse, Aaron took his hand. "Come on ... let's get out of here."

Megan looped her hand around his bicep, and they hurried off. A little family, with no idea why some kid was yelling at them from the crowd. They slipped between a couple shops and walked out toward the water, toward a walkway that took them to the west end of the pier. The evening was beautiful, the way mid-September always was, but the weather and the fading blue sky had nothing to do with the way he felt. Megan was still holding onto his arm. Aaron released Cory's hand and reached over to cover Megan's fingers with his own. If he had his way, she would never let go. "Thanks." He tried to smile at her, but he got lost in her eyes. "That doesn't happen all that often."

"I'm sure." Her look said she didn't believe him. But she didn't mind, either. She seemed to notice that she was holding onto him longer than necessary, longer than she should. She withdrew her hand and allowed a little extra space between them. "Where are we eating?"

"Yeah." Cory ran a few steps ahead, turned around and walked backward. The way he had a habit of doing. Before either Aaron or Megan could say anything, he backed straight into a wooden post. But he only laughed at himself and gave his back a quick brush-off. "Like I was saying, I'm so hungry I'm dizzy."

"We're almost there." Aaron's heart felt light and free, better than it had felt for weeks. He had no idea where his feelings might lead, especially when he hadn't dealt with his past. But he had to find a way to keep Megan from running out of his life. She was right about their differences. Still, other than his agent's control tactics, there were no rules saying a pro quarterback had to date certain people and avoid others.

Unless that wasn't the reason she was keeping her distance. Maybe she'd read about the teenager in the parking lot of the bar a month ago, or the ongoing tabloid talk that he was a serious bachelor, playing the field outside the stadium as much as he played it inside. The possibility was enough to bring the fog back around his mind and soul. He deserved his reputation. If she'd already made her mind up about him, then he wasn't sure what he could do.

They were at the west end of the pier now, and a crowd gathered off to one side. Even from where they stood, they could hear the barking of dozens of sea lions, perched on an outcropping of rock halfway between the pier and Forbes Island. The farther they walked out onto the pier, the more nervous Megan looked. She checked over her shoulder and stared at the length of the pier. "Is the restaurant up there?"

"No." He pointed out to a small island not far from the end of the pier. "It's out in the water."

"The island?" Megan turned her eyes to him. Her alarm showed in her eyes. "Aaron, I ... I can't."

"There's a restaurant out there? On that island?" Cory walked a little closer toward the crowd. "That's so cool! How do we get across?"

"A shuttle boat." Aaron had eaten there a number of times with his linemen. The restaurant had gourmet food, but more than that, it had an intimate atmosphere. He was much less likely to be recognized. "I know the owner."

"Great!" Cory ran toward the edge of the pier and grabbed onto the wooden railing. He pointed at the sea lions, then looked back at Megan.

Only a slight nod came from Megan. She anchored her feet and stared at the wooden slats beneath them. Her face looked pale, and she shook her head a few quick times. "I can't ... do it." She kept her voice low, as if she didn't want anyone else to hear.

"Why?" Was she sick, was that the problem? "It's the best food here."

"No, it's the ..." she gulped, "the boat. I'm afraid, seriously."

He considered laughing, but he had a strong sense she wasn't teasing. He put his hand on her shoulder. "Really? You're not kidding?"

"I'm not." She shivered a few times and cast wide eyes back at the water. "I'm scared to death of boats."

"How come?"

"I'm not sure." She bit her lip. "I can't swim, for one." She was being painfully honest, because the walls from earlier were down now. "And I saw a show once when I was a little girl, about a boat lost at sea without a captain."

He studied her, and he liked what he saw. In the strength that made up the woman before him, he'd found a chink, one small slight weakness. Cory was still over at the railing, whistling at the sea lions, mesmerized by them. Megan wanted Aaron to keep a certain distance, he was aware of that. But here, now, he only wanted to reassure her. He took a step closer, put his arm around her shoulders, and pulled her close. The hug was the same type he would give a sister, but it sent feelings through him so strong they made him dizzy.

"We'll go somewhere else." He swayed slightly with her. "I didn't know, okay?"

She nodded her head against his chest, and after half a minute she stepped back. "Sorry. I guess I don't think about it that often." Her cheeks were redder than before. "I don't understand it, to be honest. I can do a pa-per route in the dead of night, but I can't step onto a boat."

A paper route? In the city in the dark? Aaron felt a rush of adrenaline release through him. Megan was young and beautiful, hardly someone who should be out on the dark streets delivering papers. He hoped she was kid-ding, but he made a note to ask her about it over dinner. Again, he wanted to take her hand, but he only motioned toward Cory. "Let's take a look."

She followed him to the edge of the pier, but even there Megan seemed nervous. She gave Cory a thumbs-up when he said he'd like to dive off the pier and swim around with the sea lions all day. "Me too." She made a seasick face at Aaron. "Can't think of a better way to spend an afternoon."

Aaron laughed. "Come on, let's go eat." He touched the small of Megan's back and directed her and Cory toward a flight of stairs. "There's a place up here that's all windows." He looked at Cory. "You can watch the sea lions the whole time we eat."

Cory's eyes opened wide. "Wow! This is the best day ever."

They were the same words the boy had said after the Raiders game, and again Aaron knew without a doubt, the boy was telling the truth. Megan didn't say so, but the reason she hadn't been here often—the reason Cory had never been here—was because of money. It had to be. Something Aaron hadn't thought about since long before he signed his pro contract. But if his agent was right, if Megan worked three jobs, then certainly every dollar mat-tered.

They walked up the stairs and into the Sea Lion Café. The food wouldn't be what it would've been on Forbes Island, but that didn't matter. He was here with Megan and Cory. They could eat leather burgers and he'd have a good time. As they entered the restaurant, he leaned close to Megan. He needed her to help hide his identity. "Do the talking, okay?"

She seemed to understand and she took the lead. The hostess sat them next to the window, and Cory took the seat closest to the glass. "Wow, you can see forever from here."

Aaron looked at Megan across from him. Cory's statement suddenly took on a different meaning, and Aaron wanted to tell Megan he felt the same way. Just maybe he could see forever from here too. But he couldn't say so, not now.

They ordered fish and chips, and during dinner, with Cory distracted by the view, Aaron told Megan about his visit to Derrick's house. "He has it all." There was no mistaking the wistfulness in his voice. "His family is amazing."

"I've always liked him." She pulled her iced tea closer and fiddled with the straw. "He has a strong faith, from what I've read."

"He does. I wanna be just like him when I grow up." Aaron grinned and rested his forearms on the table. The noise in the restaurant was less than it had been, so he kept his voice low. "He doesn't make a big show of it, but it's there … in everything he does."

"I like that." She grinned at him. "I don't believe in church. But I talk to God all the time."

Aaron mulled over the strength of Megan's opinions. She didn't want a relationship and she didn't believe in church. Clearly, she struggled with trusting people, and that raised his sensitivity level. He drew an even breath. "Derrick says church isn't so bad. Sort of where it all happens — the teaching, the worship … the growth. But he calls it 'talking to God' too."

She stirred her straw through the ice cubes in her drink. "That's all it is. Just like you and I are talking right now."

"Hmmm." The idea of talking to God still felt intimidating, but it seemed less foreign all the time. "Derrick's talking to God about me a lot." He gave her a guilty look, one that made her laugh. "No question I need it."

Megan looked out the window for a few seconds and her eyes grew distant. "I saw a TV special on him once, how he's been through every set of emotions possible. The highest highs, and the lowest lows."

Aaron pictured the little boy in Derrick's family photo. "He lost a child six years ago."

Sadness colored her expression. "A car accident, wasn't it?"

"Yes." Aaron took a deep breath and he recounted the gist of Derrick's story. Then he told her about Derrick's promise to little Lee.

Megan looked worried. "You can promise a child a lot of things, but winning the Super Bowl?"

"It's a big order." Aaron leaned back in his chair. "He's pretty serious about it. He's committed to doing everything he needs to do." Aaron looked at his empty plate. "It's his last season."

She sipped her tea and lowered her eyebrows. "I didn't know that."

"He doesn't want a lot of fanfare."

A smile pulled at her lips. "That's fitting. For the sort of guy he seems to be."

They finished eating, and Cory wanted to go back to the edge of the pier, so he could get closer to the sea lions. They headed back down the stairs and closer to the water.

Aaron spotted a bench, one in a much less crowded area. He nodded toward it. "Want to sit there?"

"Sure." The shy look was back in her eyes. Which was better than the walls she'd had earlier.

The sun had set, and now in the dusk it was harder to make out the sea lions on the rocks off the pier. Cory didn't seem to mind. He took his place next to a boy his age, and they appeared to start up a conversation. Aaron sat down on the bench, leaving plenty of room for her. She joined him and gazed out at the water, toward the lighthouse on Forbes Island. She seemed intent about something, so he waited for her to talk first.

"Sorry about the boat thing." She gave him a side glance and then looked back out at the water. "It's ridiculous."

"Don't worry about it. Fear has a mind of its own."

"This one does." She worked her fingers into her hair and shook it out around her shoulders. "The air out here feels so good." She leaned against the armrest and met his eyes. "Next time I'm out here, I'm taking a boat ride. I hate limiting myself."

Aaron wasn't surprised. If he knew her as well as he was starting to, having any fears at all was probably a thorn in Megan's side. "Tell you what … I win the Super Bowl, and we'll take a boat ride around the bay."

"The whole bay?" She looked like a child, considering the idea of crossing a major street for the first time.

"The whole bay." He loved this, having fun with her this way. He raised his hands, feigning innocence. "That's what you want."

"It is." She didn't look too happy with herself. Then she raised an eyebrow at him. "Of course, you have to win the Super Bowl first."

"You have doubts?"

She angled her head from one side to the other. "Let's just say I wouldn't buy the boat tickets quite yet."

"Thanks." He put his hand up on the back of the bench and studied her profile. She was watching the water again, and he let the silence wash over them for half a minute. Then he asked the first question that came to mind. "What do you do when you're not at the youth center?"

For a split moment, it looked like she might put walls between them again, then she pulled one foot up on the bench, hugged her knee, and faced him. "Well…" Her eyes shone with a newfound trust. "I deliver the *Chronicle* before dawn, and then I go home and get Cory up and ready for school. After breakfast, he sets off on his bike, and I walk to my main job."

Shock hit him hard in the face, but he didn't flinch. Megan actually delivered newspapers before dawn every day. His heart softened, but he kept his tone even. "And your main job?"

"I'm a waitress at Bob's Diner." She said it the same way a quietly confident person would say they were a surgeon or a professor. Her eyes shone with pride and determination. "It's sort of like working as a counselor." She grinned. "We have a lot of regulars."

He didn't know Bob's Diner, but he could imagine a greasy spoon nestled between a dry cleaner's and a drugstore somewhere in the Mission District. And Megan, treating each day like another wonderful counseling session. He ordered himself not to feel sorry for her and instead grabbed at some sort of response. "You've worked there a while?"

"I have. That's where I met Cory's mother. We were coworkers for almost five years before she died."

"So you've been there seven." He smiled.

"Exactly." She looked out toward the water again. "I was a foster kid." Again, she had no shame in the fact. "Did I tell you that?"

"No." He wanted to say he wasn't surprised. That would explain a lot. Her independence and her resistance to relying on other people. Her compassion toward kids like Cory. "Was it hard? Growing up?"

"Sometimes. They moved me around a lot because they kept giving me back to my mom."

There was much Megan wasn't saying, but Aaron didn't want to pry, so he waited. They weren't in a rush. Cory was still busy talking with the kid beside him, and now that darkness had settled over the pier, there was an intimacy between them, a feeling he didn't want to push.

She stretched both legs out in front of her. "My mom loved me very much. I was lucky that way." She found his eyes again. "She had a terrible addiction."

Aaron could imagine what Bill Bond would say about Megan now. A single foster mother working three jobs and struggling with a broken past, a mother who was an addict. It made him want to put his arms around Megan and keep her safe, protect her so no other bad thing could ever harm her again. Protect her, even, from the judgment of his agent.

"The drugs and alcohol killed her in the end. By then I was a college sophomore. I dropped out of school to care for her." She smiled at him and her eyes told the story. She wasn't bitter, but the disappointment remained. "She died later that year."

He breathed in slowly through his nose, letting the story find its place in his heart. "I'm sorry."

"It's okay." She pulled one foot up onto the bench. "We were very close when she died. At peace with each other."

Aaron couldn't begin to grasp the sorrows that had made up Megan's life. He crossed his arms, unable to shake the way he hurt for her. "And your schooling?"

"I'll go back someday. Maybe."

"What were you studying?"

"I was still finishing the pre-reqs, but I knew I wanted a degree in sociology. That or psychology. I always figured I'd be a counselor or a social worker. Without some of my foster parents, I don't know where I'd be." She paused. "I guess I figured I'd use my degree to give something back to the system."

"You're doing that now. Without a degree."

"Thanks." Her eyes filled with kindness. "That's what I tell myself."

Again, Aaron had the urge to take her hand, or rub her shoulder. Connect with her some way so she would know how touched he was that she trusted him with her story. How sorry he was for her. The fact that his agent wouldn't approve of the amazing woman sitting beside him was proof that just maybe Aaron had put his trust in the wrong person. Thinking about the man's words now only filled Aaron with a simmering rage. He dismissed the thoughts. In this precious time, with Megan opening her heart to him, he wanted only to be available for her.

He stretched his arm along the back of the bench again, and as he did he inched a little closer. More to keep their conversation intimate than to gain any advantage with her. "Tell me about your paper route."

She giggled and sat up a little straighter. "It's not glamorous. I get up at four o'clock and walk a few blocks to the drop-off point. Lots of us get our papers there, but it's on the edge of my route." She did a dainty shrug. "I'm the only one without a car."

He silently struggled against the unfairness of Megan's life. She really didn't have a car? She and Cory had virtually nothing, a problem he could remedy in an afternoon. But the strangest part was Megan didn't seem like she needed anything. As if her simple life suited her just fine. "So ... you walk around handing out papers?"

"Exactly." She held her thin arms out and flexed. "It's better than going to the gym every morning."

As she brought her hands back to her sides, her arm brushed against his fingers. Maybe it was his imagination, but she seemed to notice it too. Because she looked down at the pier for a few seconds, and she swallowed. As if she was trying to pretend she wasn't feeling it, the unbelievable attraction between them.

"Anyway, yeah, I wear a bag stuffed with papers and I walk my route. Up and down about four blocks, and then I go home."

He could picture bums and crazy people lurking in the shadows as she passed by, beautiful and vulnerable. "You've ... you've never had a problem?"

She laughed. "I'm not afraid of street people. They leave you alone if you know where you're going. Even the gang members. I carry pepper spray, just in case." Another wave of easy laughter came over her. "One time I used it on a trashcan."

He gave her a crooked grin. "A very aggressive trashcan, I'm assuming."

"It seemed that way. I was tossing a paper and the can tumbled toward me. I thought I was being attacked, so I grabbed the spray and unloaded."

"And ..."

"A tabby cat ran out from behind the can, sneezing his head off." She gave a single understanding nod. "Last time I was ever attacked by a tabby cat."

"Or a trashcan."

She leaned over her knees, laughing at the memory. "I can only imagine what the wino across the street must've thought. He probably ran for the shadows for the next month whenever I came along."

"Crazy papergirl."

"Yep."

Aaron had a hundred things he still wanted to talk to her about. Her hopes and dreams and her goals for the foster care system. But Cory was walking back toward them. The crowd had thinned considerably, and only a few couples strolled along the edge of the pier. Even the sea lions had quieted.

Megan stood to greet the boy. "Ready to go, buddy?"

"Yeah. The sea lions are falling asleep."

They were walking back when Megan stopped and stared out at the ocean. "It's so big."

Cory stood beside her and shaded his eyes. "Someday I wanna sail around the world."

"I always wanted to do that when I was a kid." Aaron took the spot on Megan's other side, and at the same instant, they took hold of the wooden railing. As they did, their fingers touched. In half a second, Aaron made the decision not to move his hand. She must've done the same because she kept her hand where it was, slightly beneath his.

"It's beautiful." She was so close he could smell her subtle perfume. Their shoulders touched, and again she didn't move.

"Can we do this again next week?" Cory peered past Megan to Aaron. "This is the greatest place. Better than the park."

"That'd be fun." Aaron winked at the boy. "It's a lot better than sitting around an empty house by yourself." Which was what he'd been doing lately, ever since his first visit to the youth center. Actually, it was since he first saw Megan. He thought of only her and dreamed of spending an evening like this with only her. Their fingers were still touching, and instinctively Aaron looped his pinky finger around hers. She gave his the slightest squeeze, and the sensation made his head spin. She couldn't know how badly he wanted to take her in his arms and love her, protect her. But he couldn't rush her. If he did, she would fly from him like one of the seagulls at the end of the pier.

And that would be that.

Cory yawned and Megan gave Aaron a knowing look. For a moment, there was only the two of them, and Aaron could see the one thing he'd wanted to see all night. The fact that she felt the same way—if only for an instant. She released his finger and took a full breath. "All right, then … I guess we better get going."

They made it all the way to the truck without stopping this time, and Aaron held the door open for her and then for Cory. He was so glad he'd traded in the Hummer. The truck suited him much better now, the person he was somehow trying to become. When he dropped them off, Megan hesitated. Then she took his hand and held it for a couple heartbeats. "Thank you. For tonight."

Aaron had to use all his strength to keep from leaning close and kissing her. Instead, he held back and nodded. "Thanks for talking. I could've listened all night."

She smiled. "Next time we'll talk about you." She climbed out and waved one more time, and then she and Cory were gone. It occurred to him then that Cory hadn't said anything about being his son. The boy didn't believe the truth, and so Aaron had half expected him to bring the issue up during dinner. But Cory was well-mannered and quieter than usual most of the night.

Maybe next time they were together, Aaron would talk about the subject. And there would be a next time, Aaron was sure. Whenever that was, if Cory knew that Aaron was going to be his friend, it might not hurt so much that Aaron wasn't his dad. He grinned as he pulled his truck back into traffic and headed home. His heart was full, and he hadn't felt this good in a long time. Maybe ever. Whatever the season brought, through intense workouts and hard-fought competition, he would hold tight to the memory of this night.

And if he found the courage, he would ask God to help Megan feel for him what he felt for her.

However slow he needed to move from here.

TWENTY

Somewhere along the course of the night, Megan had lost her ability to stay distant. She had fewer reasons to dislike Aaron, now that he knew about Cory's fantasy and even so, he was still coming around. News accounts and *Sports Illustrated*, televised post-game interviews and gossip columns all showed Aaron being arrogant and indifferent. He was fearless on the field, yes, and he won often. But he never showed the sort of humility and compassion that made sports so compelling.

But tonight, he was someone entirely different. Walking beside her and listening to her, holding her when she let her crazy fear of boats stop him from taking her to a gourmet restaurant ... that guy intrigued her. And when he showed up at her apartment again the following Friday, she and Cory went with him back to the pier without hesitation.

They ate at the Sea Lion Café again, and Cory and Aaron had their picture taken in the arcade. Afterward Cory spotted the Turbo Ride. Megan didn't care for amusement park rides, so she wasn't sure she should attempt it, but Cory took the lead, bouncing and talking loudly about how he'd seen this on TV once and it was the best ride ever and how they had to all three ride it because the seats went straight across and Aaron could sit in the middle.

"What exactly is it?" Megan was relieved it had nothing to do with water. It was inside a building, after all.

"It's amazing!" Cory grinned. "That's what."

"Which one should we ride?" Aaron put his arm around Cory's shoulders and they stared at a sign listing the possible adventures.

"Extreme Log Ride!" Cory turned and high-fived Aaron. "That's gotta be the best!"

Megan hung back as Aaron and Cory moved up to the front of the line, ordering tickets. "Hey, guys ..."

The music from inside the Turbo Ride was so loud they didn't hear her. She moved to Aaron's side. "Not the Extreme Log Ride, okay?"

Cory giggled. He held up three tickets, each of which read, "Extreme Log Ride."

"Come on." Aaron was being pulled toward the entrance line by Cory. He waved for her to follow. "I'll keep you dry!"

She let her shoulders slump forward. "Fine." Her heart thudded in a strange off-beat pattern. *Ridiculous*, she told herself. *It's a simulator.* She caught up to them just as the double doors were opening. "I'll have you know"—she leaned close to Aaron, so Cory wouldn't hear her—"I'm scared to death."

"You said you wanted to get used to being on the water." Aaron touched his hand to the small of her back and let her go in front of him. Teasing colored his voice.

The theater was dark with only eight rows of eight seats. They chose the third row and Aaron took the middle, like Cory had planned. Megan buckled her seatbelt and wondered if everyone in the theater could hear her pounding heart. She gripped the arms of her seat, pursed her lips, and exhaled. It was only a movie with special effects. If it felt too crazy, she could close her eyes and she'd be fine. She took a steady breath, just as Cory leaned around Aaron.

"It's not real," he whispered. "You won't get wet."

"I know." Her returned whisper was marked with light sarcasm, and she caught Aaron grinning into his fist. "Thanks, Cory."

The lights faded to black and the screen came to life. Immediately the seats lurched forward and Megan swallowed a scream. "I'm not made for this sort of ride." She muttered the words, and as she did she felt Aaron's hand cover her own on the armrest.

He leaned close. "I won't let you drown." He breathed the words against her cheek. "It'll be okay."

Instantly they were on the water, sitting in a flimsy-looking log. At least it felt that way. The seats rocked gently in time with the rhythm of the water, as the log at first floated across calm waters toward what looked like a steep drop-off. Whatever lay ahead wasn't nearly as frightening with Aaron's hand over hers. Megan pressed herself toward the back of the chair. "Here we go ..."

The log reached the edge of the waterfall and the nose went straight out at first before gravity sucked it straight down. Megan's stomach dropped, and suddenly the feeling inside her wasn't silly amusement park nervousness. It was outright fear. Without thinking, she grabbed onto Aaron's arm and buried her face in his shoulder. *Breathe, Megan ... come on, breathe.*

Almost instinctively, Aaron put both arms around her and cradled her close to his chest. "I told you I wouldn't let you drown." His words were velvet against her face.

She peeked at the screen, and now the log had reached the bottom of the drop and was jerking and fighting its way through thick, frothy white rapids. The simulator jolted and jerked and bumped as they hit various rocks and pushed their way forward. But with Aaron's arms around her, the irrational fear that had seized her a few seconds ago eased. She turned back toward the screen. It was incredible. It truly felt like they were on the log, surrounded by angry water on every side.

Then the strangest thing happened. Megan was actually enjoying the ride. Safe in Aaron's arms, she didn't care if they hit a rock or dropped off another waterfall. Because her mind was only partly focused on the adventure on the screen. The greater adventure, the one happening in her heart, was all but consuming her. Here, her head against him, his arms around her, she could smell his cologne, feel his heartbeat and the rise and fall of his chest with every breath. The sensation was intoxicating, unlike anything Megan had ever known.

"Feeling better?" His words were like a soft caress, filling her senses.

"Much." She was grateful for the darkness, grateful he couldn't see the heat in her cheeks.

She wasn't sure how Aaron could have such an effect on her so quickly. No matter how she felt right now, the thought of falling for him was more terrifying than any boat ride. But no matter what common sense had to say, Megan was only certain of one thing.

She didn't want the log ride to end.

After another minute of rapids, their vessel survived and floated into still waters once more. Aaron released his tender hold on her, but again he covered her hand with his and gave it a single squeeze.

The lights lifted and Cory jumped from his seat. "That was so cool! See, Megan, no problem!"

Megan thought about the feelings tumbling around inside her, her attraction to Aaron and the senselessness of it. She smoothed her T-shirt and smiled at the child. "I'm not sure."

"I kept you from drowning." Aaron winked at her. They left the theater with Cory in the lead, and Aaron reached back and took her hand. Softly, he ran his thumb along her palm. Before they walked into daylight, he grinned at her. "Personally, I think we should ride it again."

She kicked lightly at his tennis shoe. "So you can see me scared to death."

For a moment, she thought he might turn around and pull her into his embrace. But he only hesitated, still looking over his shoulder. "Was it that bad?" His smile sounded in every word.

She held his eyes, knowing that whether or not she wanted them to be, her feelings were laid out for him to see. "No." She tightened her fingers around his hand, mesmerized by the feel of his skin against hers. "It wasn't."

They finished the night with ice cream, and Aaron maintained a comfortable distance between them. A couple times he suggested another go-round in the Turbo Ride might be smart, but his comment only allowed him to exchange a knowing smile with Megan.

As they licked their cones, Megan studied Cory. She was impressed with him, both tonight and last week when Aaron took them to the pier. The boy still believed Aaron was his father, but he hadn't mentioned the idea even once. She sensed the subject would come up eventually.

It happened on the ride back to their apartment. Cory leaned up between Aaron and Megan and gave a troubled sigh.

Aaron reached a red light and glanced back at Cory. He seemed to sense Cory was thinking about something other than sea lions and turbo rides. "So did you ace your spelling test?"

"One wrong." Cory sounded disappointed. "I hate getting one wrong."

"Me too." Aaron snuck a quick look at Megan. "All the other ones might be easy, but you miss out on that one that's most difficult, and it ruins everything. Because really that's the only one that matters."

"Right." Cory didn't look too deep into Aaron's statement.

Sitting next to him, Megan was trembling. Aaron's message was unmistakable, and it sent a warm, tingly feeling through her body. Was that really how he saw her? The one woman in his life who was difficult, the only one who mattered? She looked out the windshield and tried to imagine what might become of her if she actually let herself fall, if she trusted Aaron Hill with her heart. Cold terror ran through her veins, but it mixed with a warmth she'd never known any other time in her life, a warmth that only being with him could bring.

Cory was talking about school and his upcoming soccer game. "You can come if you want. I play tomorrow morning."

"Well…" Aaron thought for a minute. "We have another away game this weekend, so I'll leave early tomorrow." His eyes lit up. "But let's try for next Saturday."

They talked about Cory's game time and set a plan. Cory was still leaning forward, and again Megan could practically feel him thinking. "You know what else I've been doing?"

Aaron kept his eyes on the road. "What?"

"Going through the stuff my mom left for me. It's all in a box, so I can pull it out and look through it any time."

"That's good." Tenderness crept into Aaron's tone. "I'm sure the things in the box are very special."

"They are." Cory sounded more nervous with every few words. "She wrote some letters for you in there too. They have your name across the front, but I never opened them 'cause you don't open other people's mail." He was picking up speed. "So I can get 'em to you if you want, 'cause maybe you'd like to read what she wrote sometime. Plus she cut out articles of you in college and when you signed with the 49ers and—"

"Cory…" Megan looked at him. "That's enough."

The implied warning in her voice made his expression fall. "I was just saying…"

"Cory…" She mixed compassion with a no-nonsense tone that put an end to the conversation. She faced forward again, afraid to look at Aaron. Megan had heard from Cory once a long time ago about the letters, but she hadn't seen them. Just one more part of Cory's imagination where Aaron was concerned. Now though, she felt sorry for the boy. He knew he wasn't supposed to talk about this, but it must've been building inside him all night. Finally, she met Aaron's curious look, and she mouthed a silent apology.

Aaron looked in his rearview mirror. "Letters like that are a very important thing, aren't they, Cory?"

"Yes." His voice was small.

"Maybe you can show me sometime." His voice was relaxed, casual. It was clear he didn't believe anything in the letters was really written by Cory's mother specifically to him. But he must've wanted to validate Cory's feelings.

Megan's admiration for him doubled. When Amy died, when Megan made her decision to take Cory as her own, she knew the sacrifice she was making. Guys would have to like Cory if they were ever going to like her, which ruled out most of the men she would ever meet. Megan could still hear the determination in the voice of one business guy, a man she'd met at Bob's Diner: "You've got a kid …" He held up his hands like a traffic cop stopping traffic. "Never mind. Too much baggage."

Megan didn't care, really. She would've been fine if she remained single — for a year or a decade. Forever, if that's the way things worked out. That's what she'd always told herself. She'd made a good life for Cory and her, and that, combined with her friendship with God, was enough. No one to rely on, no one to let her down.

As Aaron dropped them off, he leaned over and hugged her, holding on a little longer than necessary. He drew back and looked deep into her eyes. "When can I see you again?"

"Aaron … I don't know." She couldn't think straight, couldn't imagine a way to answer him without diving into waters she couldn't escape. Her mind was dizzy with his nearness, and she couldn't catch her breath. Everything inside her screamed for the chance to kiss him, to get lost in his embrace without thought or reason interfering. Instead, she thanked him for the night, and her eyes held his as she climbed out and headed inside with Cory. Only then did she exhale.

By the time she fell into bed that night, she realized something about herself. Maybe she didn't want to be single, after all. Because more than air, she wanted Aaron Hill beside her again, protecting her from a simulated log ride, their arms touching.

She rolled over in bed and willed herself to fall asleep. Her paper route was in five hours, and she wasn't thinking straight. No need wasting sleep over Aaron Hill, no matter how she'd felt in his arms, no matter how her heart soared when she was with him. Everything Aaron did was newsworthy and public — the sort of life Megan never wanted for herself. Aaron Hill falling for a papergirl? That sort of thing simply didn't happen. Even if she could stand the thought of letting herself fall.

A sigh came from her soul and filled the quiet room. These past few Fridays were just a chance at friendship, and Aaron, a person who was breezing through their lives at a time when she and Cory needed the diversion. But no matter how she tried to convince herself that her feelings for Aaron couldn't possibly amount to anything, she came up short. It was too late to question whether she was falling for Aaron Hill. She'd fallen. Totally and completely. Whatever became of the situation, she would hold tight to the memory of today. The conversation, the laughter, the sunset.

And the thrill of a log ride that would stay with her forever.

Cory was glad Megan wasn't too mad at him. She tucked him in and told him it wasn't good to break the rules, but she understood why he did it.

"He's a very nice man," she told him. "But he's not your dad, Cory. You have to believe that."

This wasn't the time to tell Megan, even politely, that she was wrong. So he nodded and set his picture of him and Aaron from Pier 39 on the windowsill next to his bed. When he had it balanced just right, Megan prayed with him, and she asked God to work out all the questions that didn't have answers. Cory wasn't sure what that meant, but it had to do with Aaron. He knew that much.

When Megan was gone and the door to his room was closed, he crept off his bottom bunk and turned on the flashlight by his bed. 'Cause the main light might shine through the door and Megan would know he was up. He moved really quiet and aimed the flashlight under his bed toward his box of special things. Then he pulled it out and shone the light straight inside.

There had to be a clue, right? When he read mystery books, there was always a clue. And since Megan didn't believe him and even Aaron didn't believe him, he had to find something. He pointed the light at one of the envelopes with Aaron's name on it. What would be the best thing, the best way to prove he was telling the truth? He bit hard on his lip and thought for a minute. A picture, of course. A photo of his mom and Aaron together. But he only had a handful of pictures and they were of him or his mom and him. That's all.

He sifted around and found the envelope marked with only the word "PRIVATE." His fingers felt it on the top and the bottom, and then he picked it up. It was lumpier than the other envelopes, so it might have something other than a letter inside. Something that might be a clue.

All this time Cory always figured this letter was for Aaron too. But it didn't say Aaron's name, actually. Private didn't mean only Aaron could open it. His heart jumped around a little more than before. Private only meant his mom didn't want lots of people passing it around and making it public. Yeah, that's right. Because in English they studied opposites and public was the opposite of private. So if he didn't make whatever was in the envelope public, he would still be obeying his mom's wishes.

Cory held his breath and suddenly he was convinced. He blew the air out of his lungs and ripped a small rip down the side of the envelope, which wasn't easy since he had the flashlight in one hand. Carefully he shook the envelope and out came just one thing. A picture. Cory's heart beat like a loud drum and he could hardly hear himself think. He picked up the photo with his left hand and aimed the light at it with the other. He did a long gasp, so long he had to press his lips together so Megan wouldn't hear him in the next room. This was the clue he'd been looking for, a clue he would save for just the right moment.

The picture was of a teenage girl and a guy in sort of a slow dance kind of pose. They were dressed in nice clothes next to some flowers, and beneath it in gold letters were the words, "Prom, 1995." And the people in the picture were his mom and a guy who looked almost the same all these years later. A guy who matched with the newspaper clippings in his special box, and so Cory had no doubts at all.

The guy was Aaron Hill.

TWENTY-ONE

Derrick took his seat on the private jet preparing to fly the 49ers home to San Francisco, and he hung his head. He was as dazed as the rest of the guys, trying to fathom how they'd lost two straight road games to mediocre teams. He clenched his jaw and willed himself back in time, back to that first Monday night when they had one win and unlimited potential.

He leaned his head against the cool window. What had gone wrong? How could they be 1–2 now, with the season in a tailspin just three weeks in? Derrick had no answers for himself, no more answers than Coach Cameron had for the media. But one thing was certain. Derrick had underestimated how it would feel standing on the sidelines, helpless to make a difference. The competitor inside him knew without a doubt he could've won those games. Instead, he and Jay Ryder had been forced to watch while Aaron and the rest of the team imploded.

Aaron was trudging up the aisle, one of the last on the plane, his expression set. Derrick lifted his head and watched his teammate, studying him. Aaron had been open and genuine at the dinner Denae cooked after practice a month ago. Derrick felt certain God was going to use the season to build a bond between them, to give Derrick the chance to mentor Aaron, if not on the field, then certainly off it. But since then, Aaron had been distant with everyone on the team — even Derrick.

The empty window seats were gone by the time Aaron reached Derrick's row. He said nothing, but he stopped and tossed his bag into the overhead bin. Then he took the aisle seat, leaving one between them. He buckled his belt, closed his eyes, and leaned his head back.

People could sit wherever they wanted on the flight home. The fact that Aaron chose to sit by him was a sign; it had to be. No matter how he acted or how little he said, Aaron needed advice, strength. Derrick looked out the window at the ground crew, busy tossing bags into the belly of the plane. *Okay, God ... things don't look too good. But Aaron's here.* He felt a ray of hope. *Give me the words. Please, God … it's third and long. I'm counting on You.*

Derrick waited until the plane was in the air, and by then it looked like Aaron was asleep. A few minutes into the flight they hit sharp turbulence, and Aaron blinked his eyes open. He pulled a magazine from the seat in front of him and flipped through it. Derrick watched him, and he could feel God with him, feel His Holy Spirit giving him the words and tone and timing to finally say something to his teammate that might really matter.

"Lookin' for the answers?" Derrick stared at Aaron, his voice not quite teasing.

Aaron looked slightly confused at first, but then he shifted his attention from Derrick back to the magazine. With an exaggerated breath, he closed the magazine and slipped it back in the seat pocket. "I'm beginning to wonder." He mumbled the words, and he avoided looking at Derrick again.

"Beginning to wonder what?"

"If there are any answers."

Derrick had a feeling he wasn't just talking about the losses. "My daddy once told me you can't play football with a head full a' trouble. You gotta pick your battles and play 'em out one at a time." Derrick kept his words slow and easy. "Daddy was a wise man."

"Yeah." He hesitated for a few seconds, then he turned his eyes to Derrick. "The woman at the youth center, remember her?"

"Megan, right?"

"Right." Aaron's heavy heart left fine lines around his eyes and mouth. "I'm falling for her, man. In a big way."

Derrick let that sink in, and nodded slowly. "I can see that. Guy finds a great girl and all of a sudden he walks around the locker room frowning and slouching and making a beeline for the showers." The sarcasm helped keep the moment light. "Makes good sense."

"It's not her." He gazed into nothingness. "She thinks I'm someone else."

"Hmmm." Derrick tapped his knee. "You mean like Jay Ryder? 'Cause if she thinks you're Jay Ryder, girl needs glasses. Jay's a black man, Hill, and that ain't right if you're out there all walking around and stuff, letting her think she's got a chance with a guy like Jay Ryder."

Aaron didn't want to laugh, that much was obvious. But he could only pinch his lips together for a few seconds before a low chuckle slipped. He shook his head. "I'm serious, man." He took a long breath and his half smile faded. "She thinks I'm a gentleman. But until I met her, I wasn't even close. And that's what's not right. It's like…" He stared at the controls above their seats and adjusted the airflow. "It's like I have to fix the broken parts of me before I can move forward with her. You know?"

"Truth is, I usually charge for this kind of thing, but"—Derrick leaned against the window—"I happen to have a little time on my hands. How much broken are we talking about?"

Aaron ran his fingers through his hair. "A lot of broken." He closed his eyes for half a minute, and when he opened them his expression grew distant. "Her name was Amy, first girl I ever loved. Only girl until … well, until recently."

The story started slowly, sputtering from one detail to another in a way that wasn't chronological or compelling. But what Derrick learned from it was enough to give him the widest window yet into Aaron Hill's soul. His teammate talked about Amy and her pregnancy and how his agent had steered him away from her.

The sum of it was similar to what Aaron had talked about that night after dinner. The fact that he'd been with more women than he could remember. Always under dark and shady circumstances, always with a different blonde or brunette whose name he would forget a day later.

"Not to be rude"—Derrick raised one eyebrow—"but that's a lot of risk." He whistled low. "You ever get yourself checked?"

"Lots of times." Aaron sighed. "I'm careful. I learned how to play the game early on."

"Rules change all the time in that game." He looked at Aaron significantly, with a dramatic shake of his head. "People losing every which way every time you turn around. I mean, all those touchdowns you've thrown, that's one thing. But if you're still passing your blood tests, I'd say you're luckier than most people think." He made a wry face. "Seriously, man."

"Anyway…" Aaron was quick to move past the gritty details. "I'm finished with that. Just thinking about the things I've done … it makes me sick. I feel empty and terrible." He pressed his hand to his chest. "Like my insides are filled with rotten potatoes."

Derrick made a face. "No wonder you head for the showers so fast."

"Exactly." Aaron wasn't laughing. "It's affecting my game. I can feel it."

Suddenly Derrick knew it was time. "Remember I told you … maybe this is the year you'll figure it out?"

"Yeah." Aaron stared at him. "You're right. I'm figuring it out, but the truth's only making me feel worse, so now what?"

"That, my friend, is the right question." Derrick's smile was genuine, the teasing from earlier entirely gone. "Everyone has a load of garbage from their past." He touched his fingertips to the place above his heart. "Sits in here, twisting and hurting and stinking up a man's life until nothing's right."

Aaron was gripped. He didn't blink or breathe, even.

"Here's the secret." He pointed at Aaron. "Only God can take the garbage out, man. Only God."

Tears shone in Aaron's eyes, and he blinked, steadying himself. "I know all about God." A sad laugh sounded low in Aaron's throat. "Believe me, God doesn't owe me any favors. So how am I supposed to get Him to take away the garbage?"

"That's easy." Derrick's gaze was intent, and he prayed silently his words would pierce the fog of guilt and confusion surrounding his friend. Then he smiled. "You ask Him." He tossed his hands. "That's it, Hill. You take yourself to a quiet place where you can think and you tell Him about all your garbage. Then you ask Him to get rid of it. And when it's gone, you ask Him to fill in all the empty, cleaned out places."

A nervousness came into Aaron's eyes. "But that's like, I don't know, talking to God. You have to know what you're doing for that."

"You don't have to know nothing at all." Derrick rested his forearm on the seat in front of him. His tone was lighter now, because he could sense Aaron pulling away. "Know why?"

Aaron looked at him.

"Because it isn't about how good you are, Hill. You and me, we'd fail that test first thing." He smiled, as if this next part was a secret. "It's about how good *God* is. And when you figure that out, everything else will line up the way it's supposed to."

They were quiet for a while, and Aaron asked a few questions about the short patterns, the ones that were giving him fits so far this season. After that, Aaron closed his eyes and in a little while he was sleeping. Derrick stared out the window and realized how drained he felt. He wanted, this season more than any other in all his life, wanted to win and keep winning.

But after tonight, something else would drive him to push harder, sending him early to practice on a knee that burned with every step, encouraging him to be a positive voice for his teammates even when everyone else was down. Because there was something he wanted even more than a Super Bowl ring this season, and that … that thing was suddenly very possible.

He wanted Aaron Hill to find healing in Christ.

TWENTY-TWO

Megan took her spot in the bleachers and pulled her wool coat tight around her shoulders. Across the park, four games were getting started under a thick layer of clouds, and Megan felt the chill to her core. The temperatures that day would reach the seventies — typical for September — but Cory's ten-thirty soccer games felt colder every week.

Cory was warming up with his team, looking every minute or so toward the parking lot. This was the game Aaron had said he could attend, and Megan expected he'd show up, which was bound to be awkward. She looked out across the field, but all she could see was the article in the *Chronicle*, the one that hit Monday, just a few days after their last night at the pier.

Between her paper route and her shift at the diner that day, she read the sports section. Partly because she wanted to know what Aaron was doing, how he was doing. But also because she wanted proof that he was who he seemed to be when they were together. And until last Monday, she was becoming convinced. Maybe the rumors about him before were only that. Maybe he hadn't been the sort of playboy the press hinted at all the years he'd been in the NFL.

But last Monday, buried in a compilation of sports briefs, was Aaron's name, and it caught her attention. The story was just a few lines, but it was under a small headline that read, "Playboy Aaron Hill Has His Eyes on the Stars." Megan didn't want to move beyond the headline, didn't want her image of Aaron shattered. But she had no choice. She slid the newspaper closer and consumed the next few lines. Basically, the story said various A-list actresses had inquired about Aaron, and that Aaron was very interested in one of them. His agent was putting together plans for a first meeting. Details, the story promised, would be pending.

Megan had sat down, unable to draw a full breath as the news hit her. She read the story again, and a third time. He was interested in an A-list actress? So the whole time he'd been acting interested in her at the pier, he'd only been waiting for a call from the actress? She folded the paper and pushed it to the other side of the table. She'd been a fool for letting herself fall for him in the first place.

He called her on Wednesday, but she let it go to her answering machine. She had nothing to say to him, not if he was only playing her the whole time. She and Cory would be just fine without him in their lives; in fact, they'd be better. Safer. Megan turned slightly to ward off the wind. Cory wouldn't talk about his reasons, but he was more insistent than ever that Aaron was his father. Of course he would feel that way. Their two Friday nights at Pier 39 had made even Megan feel like they were a family. What was an eight-year-old boy supposed to make of the situation?

Monday's article stayed with Megan all week, convincing her that the next time she saw Aaron, she would have no choice but to break things off. He called again yesterday, but she didn't pick up. She couldn't. For Cory's sake, and for her own. No matter how attracted he was or how he seemed to feel about her, his people were busy connecting him with some actress. Which was a better fit for Aaron, anyway. Still, he didn't have to lead her on, not her or Cory.

Now she would protect the two of them from getting more involved. She lifted her eyes to the clouds overhead. *God, this won't be easy. You've always given me strength whenever I need it.* She breathed in slowly through her nose. *Well, I need it more than ever.*

Daughter, I am here … I will never leave you or forsake you.

The verse that breezed through Megan's soul was one of her favorites. It was the Scripture that convinced her she could be single forever, if that's what God had for her. Because even single she was never alone, not for a minute or an hour. Not even in the darkest times. God was with her. He would never leave her or forsake her.

Peace came over her, and the chill in her bones eased. A pickup truck like Aaron's pulled into the parking lot, and a man with Aaron's build climbed out. As he walked across the far field, Megan had no doubts. He'd come to the game, just like he promised, and he was looking for them, trying to figure out which field Cory was playing on.

She stood and waved, and he spotted her immediately. He broke into an easy jog as Megan sat back on the bleacher. She shifted her attention to Cory, and sure enough, the boy had spotted Aaron, probably at the same time Megan did. He was waving and jumping, his whole face taken up by his smile. He even took a few running steps toward Aaron, before he seemed to realize he was in the middle of a warm-up drill.

Aaron reached her, and his eyes danced the way they had the last time they were together. "Hi." He took the spot beside her, slipped his arm around her shoulders, and gave her a quick hug. "Did I miss anything?"

"Not yet." She smiled because she wasn't angry. He'd made her no promises, after all. But she could feel the walls in her eyes. "His team's warming up."

"Good." He rubbed his hands together. He wore a sweatshirt and sweatpants. "It's colder than I thought."

She looked up. "It'll warm up when the fog breaks."

He hesitated and she could feel him look at her. As if he understood something had changed between them. "Everything okay?"

"Fine." Another smile. Then she turned her gaze to the field. "I love watching Cory play soccer." She kept her tone light because she didn't want to give her feelings away, not completely. This wasn't the place to cut ties with him. That could come later. For now, it was more important that they focus on the game.

Aaron's body language showed his concern, but he must've realized there was nothing he could do. Not if Megan wasn't willing to talk about whatever was going on. So instead, he cupped his hands around his mouth and shouted. "Let's go, Cory ... Make it happen!"

Then, and throughout the game, as Cory scored first one goal to tie the game, and then a second to win it with a minute left, Megan savored the feel of Aaron beside her. For just one more hour, it felt good to believe they might've had a chance, that maybe he really had feelings only for her. And it felt good to have a man cheering for Cory, something the boy had never experienced.

When the game ended, Megan felt herself being pulled back into reality. She congratulated Cory, and Aaron did the same.

"Thanks for coming!" Cory's cheeks were red and the joy in his eyes knew no limit. He slipped his arm around Aaron's waist as they walked toward the parking lot. "Wanna get lunch and take it to the park?"

"Sure." Aaron cast her a questioning look.

"Sounds good." She averted her eyes, but only so she'd stay strong. She'd already made up her mind about what would happen after today. Now she had to act on her decision.

They picked up subs from a deli and made their way back to the same park, a few blocks from the youth center. They sat at a sturdy picnic table, and while they ate their sandwiches, Cory talked about the game and how his teammates passed better than ever before, and how a few of the guys knew it was Aaron Hill cheering for him, and how one guy even asked for Cory's autograph because of it.

Megan barely ate her lunch. Her stomach was in knots, and now she had no doubt Aaron had picked up on the fact that something was wrong. When they were finished eating, Megan put her hand on Cory's shoulder. "Hey, buddy, could you do me a favor?"

"Sure." He grinned.

A flash of pain ripped through Megan's heart, because maybe Cory would not look as happy as he did right now for a very long time. She steeled herself against the hurt of what lay ahead. "Could you go play on the equipment for a little while? I need to talk to Aaron alone."

Cory's smile dropped off some, but not in a way that showed he was truly worried. He looked at Aaron and then back at her. "Sure. I wanna get on the swings, anyway." His smile was back in full force. "I'm trying to set a personal best on how far I can jump."

Megan could feel Aaron watching her and sensed that he wasn't willing to make another minute of small talk. She forced a smile for Cory. "After that amazing soccer game, today's probably the day to do it."

"Yeah." He climbed off the picnic bench and took a step back. "Thanks." He started his familiar backward running, and he waved at her and Aaron. "See you in a little bit." Then he turned around and sped off to the swings.

They were sitting across from each other, and for a few minutes, neither said anything. Already the air between them was dramatically different. Awkward and strained. Aaron broke the silence first. "Did I miss something?"

She sighed and turned her eyes to him. "I've been thinking …"

"Oh." He hesitated, and then a nervous laugh sounded from him. "Why does that seem like a bad thing?"

"Because …" She hated this. If only she could slide over to his side of the table and cling to him the way she had during the Turbo Ride. This part of the adventure was even more frightening than going over a waterfall. She searched his eyes. "It could never work, Aaron. Me and you."

His expression froze, and for a few seconds he only stared at her. "You're kidding, right?" He let loose a single, bitter laugh. "I'm gone for a week and everything changes?"

She wasn't sure she wanted to get into the gritty details, but she had no choice. She couldn't let him wonder why her feelings had changed. She lifted her chin and breathed in long and slow. As she exhaled, she faced him again. "I read Monday's paper."

Aaron blinked, as if he were still waiting for her to make sense. "Okay …" He laughed, but it sounded tense and desperate. "We lose a couple games and you're ready to give up on me?"

She hesitated. "You know what I mean. The piece about you and the Hollywood actress."

He couldn't have looked more surprised if she'd suddenly started speaking Japanese. "What piece?"

Megan's head began to spin. She gripped the edge of the bench with both hands and stared at him. He had to know about it, right? The truth behind the story, if not the article itself. Her mouth felt dry as she tried to find the words. "The article about you and some actress being interested in each other." She met his eyes straight on. "Your agent's working to set up a first meeting."

For a few seconds, Aaron looked stunned, too shocked to move or speak. Then his face grew red and anger blazed in his eyes. He stood and turned his back to her, and he walked to the nearest oak tree. He clenched his fist and drew it back like he was going to send it deep into the tree trunk. At the last second, he stopped himself and then released a few controlled hits against his other palm. Every muscle in his body looked tight with rage.

He walked a few steps to the side, stopped and took two more steps in another direction. He was the picture of pent-up fury and Megan couldn't understand. Didn't he think she'd find out, that she'd see it in the *Chronicle*? Even if he didn't know about the article, he had to understand that the media would find such a story sensational.

Aaron finally relaxed his hands and stared up through the trees at the still foggy sky. He groaned, and after a little while, he turned and faced her. Fifteen yards separated them, but from where Megan sat, she could see the turmoil in his eyes. He came to her slowly, and as he reached the bench he narrowed his eyes, looking at her more intently than ever. "I had nothing to do with that article, Megan. You have to believe me."

Confusion swelled inside her. She wanted to believe him, but his words didn't make sense. "You didn't know about it?"

"No." He dropped back to the edge of the bench, still facing her. "My agent must've called it in. That's all I can figure."

His agent. Megan shifted her eyes away from him and onto the ground near her feet. The same agent who showed such disdain when she and Cory showed up for the Raiders game during the preseason. If he was Aaron's agent, he was in constant contact with Aaron, constantly working deals for him. The article meant the guy either had no knowledge of Aaron's feelings for Megan, or he disapproved of them. A sad weariness came over her as she found his eyes again. "There has to be some truth to it, Aaron."

Anger changed his expression. "There is." The muscles in his jaw flexed. "My agent *wants* me to date a Hollywood actress. Thinks it'll be good for my image. Which is something I'll be talking to him about when I'm done here." He seemed to catch the fact that he was talking too loud. He lowered his tone, his eyes pleading with her. "But I don't want that kind of setup. I never authorized him to run the story."

Megan studied him, the sincerity in his eyes. Slowly, gradually, she felt herself changing her mind about the incident. So maybe he didn't want to date an actress, and maybe his agent was responsible for tipping the paper about the story. "Still…" Her voice was softer than before, more vulnerable. "He's your agent. He knows you better than I do. He must."

Aaron's breathing came faster, in short bursts. He shook his head slowly, clearly warring with his emotions. Finally, he shrugged his shoulders and looked hard at her. "He doesn't know me at all. Not who I am today … who I want to be."

His statement rolled around in her heart, but in the end, the answers came from her soul. She reached across the table and put her hand over his. "We're too different, Aaron. Can't you see it?" Her heart thudded against her chest, because she hated this, hated breaking away from him. But God had allowed her to see the article for a reason, to warn her. "Look … you're a nice guy, Aaron. A different guy than I had you figured to be." Her voice mixed with the sorrow inside her. "I had a great time." She turned her attention toward the distant swing set, and Cory, pushing himself as high as he could go. "Cory had a great time too."

"And that's bad?" Aaron was deeply upset, his voice told that much. He pulled away from her touch and stood, his back to her again. "It's just like I thought."

Her heartbeat came harder, faster. "What?"

He put his hands on his hips and stared into the sky. The fog was clearing, and he seemed to find a blue patch. For a long while, he only gave an occasional shake of his head, a few sounds of disbelief. When he finally turned to her, he met her eyes straight on. "It's my past, right? You can't see around it, and you know what?" He put one foot up on the bench where he'd been sitting. He leaned over it, his eyes intense. "I can't see around it either."

Aaron had never gone into detail about his past, but he must've figured she knew, that his public persona hadn't escaped her. "It doesn't matter, Aaron. I don't want to fight." She stood and walked around to his side of the table. She sat on the table and set her feet on the bench. "You've been a good friend, but ..." She felt a rush of tears, and she hesitated until she had control. "It has to end sometime. I'm just saying it might as well be now. Before it gets harder for either of us. For Cory."

He let his shoulders fall forward, and he turned and sat next to her on the table. Their knees touched, but only for half a second. Aaron seemed intent on keeping some distance between them. "I knew this could be difficult, Megan." His anger was gone, and in its place was a sorrow so strong it hurt to look in his eyes. "But I didn't think it was impossible."

She held her hand out to him, and for a moment, he hesitated. Then, reluctantly almost, with both hands he took hold of her fingers. She couldn't fight her tears much longer. "I'm sorry. I think we better go."

At first it looked like he might argue again, try to convince her that she was wrong and that he'd never let go of her hands no matter what she thought. But then defeat came over him like a wet blanket, changing his expression and his posture, and in that single change, Megan could sense it was over. Because deep inside, he must've realized that she was right.

"Okay." He brought her hands to his lips, and he kissed her fingers. "I'll take you home."

The kiss burned through her, because it wasn't the kiss she had longed for just a week ago. And because it was goodbye, no question.

She went to get Cory, and like every other time they'd been together, Aaron dropped them off at their apartment. Cory must've sensed something was wrong, but he didn't ask a lot of questions. When it came time to get out of the truck, Aaron parked and gave Cory a hug. But by then she was already waiting for Cory near the front door of the building. No sense dragging out the inevitable.

She waved a quick goodbye, because she couldn't speak, and she waited until she hit the stairs inside the building before she let herself break. The whole way up, she navigated with the stair rail, because she couldn't see for the tears.

"What's wrong?" Cory trudged along beside her, his voice somber. "Did something happen?"

How was she supposed to explain the situation to Cory? Better to let the passing of time tell the story. She sniffed. "I'm just ... sad. That's all."

He didn't ask again, and when she reached the apartment, she set her bag down. "I need a nap, okay, buddy?" Tears were still filling her eyes, but she was holding back on the sobs.

"Okay." He kicked his foot a little. "I'll take a shower."

With that, Megan went into her room and locked the door behind her. She didn't make it to the bed before the sobs washed over her. Wave after wave after wave of disappointment and hurt and regret. She'd actually let herself believe that it was possible, that the famous 49ers quarterback might sweep her off her feet and give her the love and the life she never dared dream about. And look where it had gotten her.

She squeezed her eyes shut and willed herself to feel God's presence. He was here, just as He promised. Always. Never forsaking her. It took everything she had, but finally as the sobs slowed she could sense Him in the room with her. Her God and Father ... her Friend. And good thing. Because with God she could survive this, the pain of saying goodbye to Aaron Hill.

Even if she was never the same again.

TWENTY-THREE

Aaron had Bill on the phone a minute after he pulled away from Megan's apartment.

"Hill, my friend ... I was just thinking about you and how we need to get dinner at Morton's one of these—"

"Shut up, Bill." Aaron's tone was sharp and mean. He didn't care. "Tell me about the article. The one in the *Chronicle*."

Bill uttered an indignant chuckle. "What about it? I got another one coming out in a few weeks. Reporters are crazy for this stuff, man. I mean, we're talking celebrities, Hill. You're in the big time now. There with the other young guns fresh off the draft."

His rage made it hard for him to focus. "Another article? Bill, I never authorized the first one."

"Right, so thank me." His laugh became more of a huff. "I mean, someone has to look out for your image. Leave it to you, and you'll drag in some single mother on welfare."

"Wait!" Aaron seethed, his blood running hot through his veins. He pulled his truck over and slammed it into park. "You don't know the first thing about Megan Gunn, so leave her out of this." He planned to meet his agent in person, but now Aaron was glad a phone line separated them. Otherwise, he might've knocked the guy senseless. "Stick to the subject, Bill. The article." He raised his voice. "You called the *Chronicle* and told them a bunch of lies?"

"Listen." Bill's voice held some attitude now. "I've been doing that since you were a sophomore at UCLA." Bill allowed a momentary burst of anger. "I don't have to run everything by you, Hill. You got enough to do on the field. That's why you hired me, right? To handle your contracts and your connections and your image." He paused, his disgust obvious. "You're welcome."

Bill went on about how a little appreciation would be nice since he basically spent all day and every night thinking up ways to help Aaron have an edge in the public eye and with other endorsement companies who might be —

"Bill!" Aaron gritted his teeth. "What's the next article say?"

His agent hesitated. "Same thing. You're interested in one of Hollywood's young elite. Just enough to keep you on the cutting edge."

Aaron clenched his teeth and gripped the steering wheel with both hands. "Call the paper, Bill." His voice was calmer now, almost frighteningly so. "If the article runs this week, I'll sue you. I swear I will." He lifted his head and stared straight ahead. But all he could see was Megan, the hurt in her eyes. "Are you listening, Bill?"

"I am, but you've got this whole thing wrong, friend, this is the best —"

"Stop." He wanted to ask about Amy, about the tricks Bill must've pulled back then. But this wasn't the time. He needed to focus on the season. That conversation, and his decision about whether Bill would remain his agent after a stunt like this, could wait until he hung up his cleats — hopefully, well after the New Year.

Aaron sat up straighter and every word dripped in cool venom. "Pull the article, Bill. Or my attorney'll have an official notice on your desk next week and we'll be through. Understand?"

"Listen, call me later." He sounded frantic. "I'll pull the article. Come on, Hill, don't get crazy on me. I'm your friend, the guy who made you what you —"

Aaron hung up. He'd expected that after he told off Bill he'd feel better about the situation. At least his agent would know not to manipulate the media on his behalf ever again, and that should have brought some sense of satisfaction. But as Aaron pulled back onto the highway, he didn't feel even a little better. Because, amidst the trash piling up in his heart, was one more piece he didn't know how to deal with. The fact that somehow, without meaning to, he'd done the one thing he couldn't forgive himself for doing.

He'd lost a dark-haired, blue-eyed girl whose soul was as clean as his was full of filth, a girl who would take with her a piece of his heart.

Even if they never spoke again.

⸺

Cory sat in his room, staring at the things in his special box. Something had gone very wrong, but he wasn't sure what. He went over the events of the day again and again. The soccer game was a winner, and the lunch was good. But sometime when he was on the swings Megan and Aaron musta had a fight. Sometimes that happened when people had questions, and Megan definitely had questions. Why did Cory still think Aaron was his dad? And Aaron probably had questions too. Why was Cory holding onto something that wasn't even true? Those sorts of questions.

So now, he couldn't sit back and wait on his clue any longer.

He pulled his backpack to him and took out a piece of paper. Then he wrote Aaron another letter. This one was shorter than the first one. He folded it, and then he tucked the photo of his mom and Aaron inside. He would have to get an envelope later, because they were in the kitchen, and he was supposed to be taking a shower.

No matter what happened, even if Megan was mad at him, the next time he saw Aaron he would give him the letter and the picture. Then maybe whatever was wrong between Megan and Aaron would clear up, because that's what happened when people had proof. Cory smiled, even though he didn't feel like it. 'Cause when Aaron looked at that picture, that would be that.

And there wouldn't be any questions at all.

—

The season went from bad to worse. Derrick had no choice but to stand by and watch as the team won just eight games over the next thirteen weeks. He and Denae prayed about the team and the season, the pressure on Coach Cameron, and the struggles in Aaron Hill's head. In the end, they had to agree with the headlines in the *Chronicle*. The 49ers wild card berth in the playoffs was nothing short of a miracle. Even more, they had to admit, along with everyone in the sports world, that a team with a 9–7 record had the same chance as snow in Phoenix.

Which was where the Super Bowl was being held.

According to the announcers on ESPN, San Francisco would be knocked out in the first round. Derrick figured most of his teammates felt the same way, including Aaron Hill.

But no matter what Derrick tried, Aaron wouldn't say more than a few words. The demons that haunted him earlier in the season had apparently gotten meaner, because without question it was Aaron's worst regular season performance ever. He threw more interceptions than touchdowns and battled speculation from the press after every game. Internally, there was talk of replacing him with Derrick or Jay, but now that they'd made the playoffs, the front office didn't want to rock the boat. Replacing Aaron would be a major news story. It would take the focus off the playoffs and place it squarely on the conflicts San Francisco was facing.

With each passing week, Derrick worked harder to control his anger at his teammate. This was Derrick's last season. His last chance. Aaron knew it and still he couldn't get his head in the action.

The wild card game took place on a cold, cloudy afternoon at Soldier Field against the defending NFC champion Bears. During warm-ups, heaters were set up along the sidelines and a temperature gauge showed below freezing conditions. Snow was in the forecast. Derrick tried not to feel the frustration from the season as the team huddled together in the locker room around Coach Cameron.

"You guys know as well as I do ... only God could have brought us here. Not once all year did we play to our potential." He managed to sound intense and positive, something even he had struggled with during recent chalk talks. "But now that we're here, I don't care what the media says." His voice built with the sort of passion that simmered deep inside Derrick, even after all the ways the 49ers had struggled. Coach looked around the room, singling guys out, staring them down. "Now that we're here, we have as much a chance as anyone else. Three wins." He held up three fingers, his gaze intense. "Three wins and we're there, suiting up in Phoenix for the big game."

Coach didn't mention the unlikelihood that they'd win those three games. ESPN had been spouting the statistics all week. Since the wild card system began in 1970, only eight wild card teams had advanced to the Super Bowl. Of those, only four had won the title. Coach seemed to read his thoughts. "I don't care what the statistics say." He pointed at Aaron Hill and then two of the team's top receivers, and their leading running back. "This team has what it takes." He paused. "Now go out and win that ball game."

By kickoff, a ten mile-an-hour wind had started up, sending bitter cold along the sidelines. The 49ers were first on offense, but Aaron led a stuttering drive that stalled around the fifty. A punt put the Bears back deep into their own territory, and on San Francisco's next possession, Aaron chipped away a few yards at a time before he handed off for the first score.

Derrick paced the sidelines, trying to stay warm. *Thank you, God ... come on, help us out...*

But the victory on the field was short-lived, and by halftime Chicago had a ten-point lead. Aaron was one of the first players into the locker room, and Derrick caught up with him next to his locker. He slammed his palm against the metal door and glared at his teammate. "Talk to me, man! What's happening out there?"

Aaron braced himself against his locker and hung his head. "Nothing's clicking."

"Yeah, starting with you." He leaned closer and brought his voice down to a low hiss. "You were supposed to talk to God about the garbage, remember?"

He shook his head, his response tortured. "There's more now."

Derrick clenched his teeth and slammed his hand on the locker again. He did a half turn and then spun around and faced Aaron. "That's your fault." The anger inside him surged to the surface. "This team needs you, Hill. Today. This afternoon. I don't care if you got a mountain of garbage in that cold heart of yours. Just play your game."

For a few seconds, Aaron said nothing. Then in a rush he slammed shut his locker and stormed off. Derrick didn't feel bad. They didn't have a chance if Aaron didn't rise to the occasion. If he wasn't going to talk to God, so be it. Either way, he had a responsibility to the team.

Coach said basically the same thing before they went out for the second half. And this time, the Aaron Hill who took the field was the fighter, the warrior. He threw a touchdown pass three minutes into the third quarter, and then again in the fourth, as the sky broke open and released a blinding burst of snow onto the field.

"There it is." Derrick's knee throbbed in the freezing cold, but he didn't care. They could do this, they could win it despite everything. He found Aaron on the sidelines after the score and slapped him hard on his helmet. "Come on, Hill ... make it happen."

Aaron didn't say anything, but his expression told the story. Whether it was Derrick's talk or a switch that flipped inside his brain, Aaron wore his game face now. The snow continued, and with five minutes to play, Chicago kicked a field goal. By then the lines on the field were all but impossible to see, and the officials called a timeout so they could clear the snow off the yard markers. Derrick could hardly watch from his place next to Coach Cameron. *Please, God ... keep Aaron focused ...*

The last few minutes of play were an icy battle. Aaron struggled to move the ball, but a few close first downs and another touchdown pass tied the game. A beautiful kick in the waning seconds, and the 49ers squeaked by with a one-point win.

The atmosphere in the locker room after the game could hardly be called celebratory. Guys were exhausted, mentally and physically. The idea of taking on the Seahawks next week seemed daunting. But as Coach pointed out, they still had life. And at this point, anyone with life had a chance.

At O'Hare International Airport, Derrick boarded the private 737 and looked for an empty row near the back. He had business to do, so he didn't want to talk to anyone. But as he passed Aaron, whose eyes were closed, he stopped. Then he bent close to his teammate. "Hill ..."

Aaron blinked his eyes open, and for a moment they only looked at each other.

"Talk to God, man. I'm serious." He straightened again. "No one can do it for you."

With that he kept walking. There wasn't anything else to say, really. In light of all they'd been through to get here, and all that lay ahead, if Aaron didn't figure out how to break free, they might as well hang up their cleats now. Telling Aaron what to do would never be enough. It hadn't worked once all season. That was the business he had to do. So, for the next four hours Derrick talked to God almost constantly, begging Him that someway, somehow, Aaron would cry out for help. And in doing so, a miracle would happen.

The miracle he'd come to San Francisco to see.

TWENTY-FOUR

Aaron ached all over from the Chicago game. He'd been sacked four times—not once because of his linemen falling down on the job. He alone was the problem. He didn't need Derrick to tell him. He was so distracted, so burdened by whatever it was, that he could barely focus. Even in the middle of a play.

He slept in late Tuesday, and when he climbed out of bed, everything hurt. Now he was supposed to get right back into shape and battle it all over again on Saturday. Just five days. He staggered into the kitchen and by the time he'd had breakfast and unpacked his bags, it was two o'clock when he reported to the 49ers training facility.

The trainers were waiting for him. He alternated between sitting in hot water and ice, and then they worked him through a series of stretches—all designed to keep him loose. His body, anyway. But through every minute of it, he could hear Derrick's voice in his head. Since Megan backed out of his life three weeks into the season, the garbage inside him had only gotten heavier. Some days he was sure the burden would do more than affect his game. It might strangle the life from him.

He told himself he could handle it, he could work through it. If Megan didn't want anything to do with him, fine. He could get along without her, same way he'd done before he met her. He had offers, and if he wanted to, he could have a warm body in bed next to him tonight.

Only he didn't want to. Not with Megan's eyes and heart still consuming him.

Now as he finished up at the training facility, he had the strongest desire to run, to get into his truck, pick a direction, and drive until sunup. Even then he couldn't outrun himself. He started to head home, but he drove past his exit and didn't pull off until he reached Pier 39 and a parking place at the back of the lot. He rolled down his window and stared at the carrousel in the distance.

How had things gotten so bad? Aaron couldn't find an answer, and when he set back out on the road he thought about going to Derrick's house. But he knew what Derrick would say. So instead, he drove back home and wandered around his house. Therapy had taken the edge off the aches, and good thing. Aaron wouldn't take pain meds. He'd seen too many players get addicted, popping pills between downs. His second year with the 49ers a player he'd hung out with at the Pro Bowl died in his sleep after a three-year battle with pain pills. The guy was thirty-one years old. No, when the pain got that bad, Aaron wouldn't look for a prescription. He'd simply call it a day.

But his trainers couldn't do anything to touch the pain inside him. So maybe the end of his career was coming, after all. If he couldn't get his head in the game, he had no right being on the field, no matter what Bill Bond said.

Aaron walked into his backyard and sat in the chair overlooking the pool. His agent still called every few days.

"I pulled the article, so come on, man. What's wrong? Talk to me, friend … we need a dinner out, a chance to relax."

Aaron always cut him off before he could get going. "I'll figure it out." That was his answer to everyone. Everyone but Derrick. Aaron stared at the gray sky and tried to feel something. But his mind, his soul, all of him felt stone cold, and finally—around eight o'clock when darkness lay thick over his home and his heart, he climbed into his truck and headed for Baker's Beach, the same place he'd gone before, back when it first occurred to him that Derrick might be in his life for a reason.

He parked and climbed out. The air was damp and cold, which wouldn't be good for his aching shoulder. He grabbed his leather jacket from the driver's seat, slipped it on, and zipped it up to his chin. Then he buried his hands in his pockets and started walking. This time the beach was completely empty, which suited him. He turned left, like before, and walked to the big rock.

Somehow he had a sense that here, in the cold black of night, it might finally happen, he might finally find the courage to talk to God. He walked hard and fast, breathing deep, stirring something new and uncertain in his blood. When he reached the rock, he climbed up and found the flat section at the top. Then he drew up his knees and stared out at the shiny black water. No moon pierced the sky tonight, no sign of stars. In the far distance, the soft hum of traffic on the bridge mixed with the hushed sounds of a nearly still surf. Here, there was no last-minute wildcard win, no playoff game five days out. No world watching and waiting for him to fail. He was alone.

Just him and God.

Because after all his running and trying to figure his pain out on his own, it had come to this. Him and God. He stared into the emptiness and thought about the Creator, the all-knowing Savior, the One he'd been running from. His parents never talked about faith or belief. Small wonder. They lived for their jobs, creating a void in Aaron when it came to relationships of any kind — God included. But his high school coach had been a Christian. It wasn't something the man talked about much, but after hours, when Coach gave him a ride home, he would drop him off and say, "Keep your eyes on Jesus, Hill."

As long as he played for Coach, Aaron never really knew what that meant. But his junior year he went with a group of teammates to a church summer camp. The things he heard from the speaker that week floored him. Jesus was alive? His Spirit was moving among them? He had died on the cross for their sins, for Aaron Hill's sins? Night after night that camp week, kids came forward after the speaker finished — some of them weeping. And the counselors talked about how many students were giving their lives to Christ.

Aaron came close. The last night when the speaker was talking about the emptiness inside, and how every one of them had a hole in their hearts that only Jesus could fill, when he told them Jesus was calling them, and that only someone very foolish would fight the pull of Jesus Christ, Aaron felt himself start to get up. Then he looked a few feet over and spotted some of his teammates. Weakness wasn't tolerated among the guys, not for a minute. Whether the teammates had come forward for Jesus at some point, Aaron didn't know. But in that moment he couldn't admit his emptiness and he couldn't admit the hole in his heart.

He didn't come home from camp a Christian, but he came home a believer. Jesus was Mighty God, Wonderful Counselor, Prince of Peace. He had no doubts. But every day since then he came to believe something else. That the holy God of the universe couldn't possibly want anything to do with Aaron Hill. After all, he'd had a chance to make a commitment to Jesus before, and he'd failed. What would God want with him after that?

The wind off the water was cold, and Aaron slid one leg down along the craggy, cool rock. His thoughts about God only grew worse as time went on, as he walked away from Amy and began believing he was something special, someone famous. For years it wasn't so much that he felt ashamed before God. He simply didn't think about Him because there was no need. Between him and Bill, life was going along just fine without God.

All that changed with Megan Gunn.

The junk in his heart, the emptiness, the guilt and regret—all of it had been there before that fateful day at the youth center. He thought about her, about the way she'd caught his attention and taken his breath from the beginning. It wasn't just her beauty that shone a spotlight on the ugliness inside him. Rather, it was something in her eyes, an innocence and kindness that stood brightly in contrast. That's when the trouble started. After getting to know Megan, he saw himself differently, felt differently. As if every awful, mindless, self-centered thing he'd ever done was suddenly and painfully clear.

He hung his head and tried to find a warm bit of air for his lungs. When he looked up, he stared past the Golden Gate Bridge to the waters beyond, to Alcatraz Island.

He'd always been struck by the ghost of the prison, the way the captives must've felt knowing there was no way out. He wondered about the futility of being a prisoner in a place like Alcatraz. But here, tonight, he didn't have to wonder because he knew. He was just like them. Trapped in a prison of his own guilt and humanity with no way out.

Derrick's words filtered through his heart, his soul. *Maybe this is the year ... talk to God, man ... He's the only one who can take out the garbage.* He stared down at the rock beneath him, and like a volcano building steam, every wrong thing he'd ever done, every empty hour came to mind, filling him, torturing him, until finally ... finally he slid off the rock and fell to his knees.

"God! I can't bear it!" He shouted the words and the darkness around him swallowed them without an echo. He couldn't catch his breath, couldn't hold his body up under the weight of his own guilt. "I've done it all wrong, God. All of it." And then, his sides heaving, he silently recounted everything he could remember. Every time he'd ever used a woman, and every promise he'd casually broken. Every selfish decision and careless attitude toward people less fortunate than him. The cockiness and arrogance, his judgmental spirit. Even the way he'd pushed the blonde woman aside in the parking lot that night earlier in the season. Callous and careless, as if only he mattered. One by one by one, he laid the burdens of his heart flat before God until the array of trash stretched out before him was staggering, overwhelming.

Dampness from the sand soaked through his jeans, but he didn't care. He bent over his thighs, his head hung low. "Take it, God ... take it from me. I can't live another hour with the guilt. It's strangling me."

And then he remembered things spoken by the speaker, the one from the final day at church camp his junior year of high school. Things he'd blocked out until here, now.

Jesus died for your sins ... He was God in the flesh ... He could've commanded a hundred thousand angels and His rescue would've been certain... He went to the cross for you, and you alone. The speaker's voice had filled the lodge, and now the memory was alive again. *If you were the only person in all the world, He would've gone to the cross anyway. Your sin sent Him there ... yours, and yours alone. He loved you that much.*

Aaron felt the full extent of his choices, his years of selfish living. And finally, gratefully, tears erupted from the smoldering mountain of his sin. His tears became deep sobs, deep and tortuous and silent until he understood clearly what he needed to do. He straightened, standing on his knees, and raised his hands to the starless sky. "I'm sorry, God. I'm sorry!" His sobs rang out in the winter air. He could do this, he could talk to the Creator of the Universe. "Forgive me. Take my life and set me free!"

A gust of wind washed over him and he fell silent, awestruck. After a long while, when his tears were dry and his hands were down again at his sides, he realized something. He actually felt different. Something wonderful and alive was happening inside him. The heaviness was gone, and in its place, he felt new and light and whole and healed. The prison bars were broken and he would never, ever be captive again.

He had God in his heart, and he would hold onto Him forever. He would ask Derrick about going to church because he wanted a place where he could learn and grow and connect with people who had found this hope ages ago. He breathed deep, and joy he'd never known filled his lungs and flowed into his veins. Until this moment, the season had been a drain, a burden. But now, all his days stretched out before him like an amazing adventure, one he would live for God. Whether Megan joined him or whether he never found another woman like her, he would be complete, whole.

Slowly, carefully, he rose to his feet. His knees were cold and wet and aching, but he barely noticed. For the first time in his life, the holiness of God consumed him, taking his breath, showing him he was nothing next to Jesus Christ. Nothing and everything. Because the place that had only an hour ago been filled with a mountain of trash, was clean and full once again. Full with the power of God now and forevermore. All because of what Jesus had showed him here on a cold stretch of winter beach. Aaron smiled to himself as he turned and headed back for his truck. Only one thing could make this night any better.

A call to Derrick Anderson.

The phone rang in Derrick's house late Monday night, just as he and Denae were getting into bed. Denae gave him a look, and Derrick shrugged. He picked up the receiver and stretched his legs out across the layers of sheets. "Hello?"

"I did it." The voice on the other end released a few bursts of happy, carefree laughter. "I did it, man. I really did it."

He recognized the voice. "Aaron?"

"I drove out to the beach and I talked to God. Just like you said." He laughed again. "I can't believe it, man. I never felt this good in my whole life."

Derrick motioned to his wife and pointed to the phone. "He did it," he mouthed. He could feel his grin filling his face. "Aaron talked to God!"

"What? Are you too shocked to speak?" Aaron sounded five years younger. "You shoulda told me to do this months ago."

"Now wait a minute ..."

"I'm kidding you, man. I called to thank you." The laughter in his voice dropped off and he was silent for several seconds. "You saved my life, Anderson. I couldn't have waited another day."

"You know what I think ..." Derrick's voice choked with emotion. "I think the Seahawks better watch out."

As it turned out, Derrick might as well have been a prophet. Led by a changed Aaron Hill, the 49ers swept into Seattle and dominated the Seahawks in the Divisional Playoff game that Saturday. They started strong and never quit, and when they notched a 24–3 victory, Derrick was less surprised than anyone. Because Aaron had been a talented quarterback before. But now he was a talented quarterback operating by the power of God.

And nothing on heaven or earth could come against that.

TWENTY-FIVE

Megan's volunteer shift at the youth center Monday night was more wearying than usual. One of the older foster teens, a sixteen-year-old boy, had been picked up for selling drugs. When the details came from the director that afternoon, the story made more sense. The boy had been through three foster homes since school started in September, and now—because of bad behavior—he was facing expulsion from school.

The story was sad, because the people close to the boy had seen the train barreling toward the cliff. With no stability, no one to believe in him, and no future, the boy had gone the way of the street, found his place among drug dealers always looking for the newer, younger guys to do their dirty work.

Back at the apartment, she finished washing the frying pan, dried it, and put it away. Oreo walked into the kitchen and rubbed against her ankles. "I know … time for your milk."

Cory was watching Sports Center, mesmerized by the dramatic retelling of the showing by the 49ers against Seattle. Megan tried not to watch, but when she heard his name, she stopped and leaned her elbows on the counter. If she'd had her way, she would've stayed away from sports all season. It had been too hard to watch, knowing that Aaron was struggling so badly.

Once in a while, she even wondered if maybe she had something to do with his terrible season. Certainly, he hadn't connected with any movie stars, at least not that the *Chronicle* had picked up on. Whatever details were pending never came, except in the tabloids. When she was at the market, she'd see a small headline about Aaron Hill finding solace with this actress or that one. But there were no photos, and the reputable news and sports agencies only talked about his game.

It had been more than three months since she told him goodbye, long enough that she should've been over him. They only spent a few days together, after all. Even still, she thought about him constantly, when she did her paper route early in the morning and when she fell into bed at the end of the day. Part of it was Cory. Never mind that Aaron wasn't Cory's father, Cory held to his beliefs. As far as the boy was concerned, Aaron was his dad and his hero all at the same time, and he talked often about missing Aaron and hoping for another night at the pier. Whenever the 49ers were on TV or when there was a story in the *Chronicle* that Mrs. Florentino brought over, the boy was consumed.

And so Megan had kept tabs on Aaron Hill without wanting to.

The image on the TV screen changed and Aaron's face appeared. Cory was sitting a few feet away, cross-legged on the floor, his head blocking part of the picture. The TV wasn't very big to begin with, but with Cory in the way, Megan could only make out half of the image. She sighed and moved into the next room so she could see better. As she came closer, Megan froze in place.

His eyes were different. Even from last week, when his interview after the Bears game had been short and terse. Yes, she was sure of it. Something about his eyes and his expression was different now. Almost like through the sweat and grime he was glowing from the inside out. She took a step closer. "Turn it up, Cory. Please."

He looked over his shoulder at her and smiled. "Yeah, listen to this. I already heard it three times, but listen."

The volume came up and Aaron's voice filled her home, her heart. "I can't take the credit ... it was a team victory."

The announcer was next. "You can say that, but three touchdowns for more than four hundred yards with no interceptions? Did you ever think you'd come out against the Seahawks and have your best game of the season?"

Aaron smiled and there it was again ... a clarity and vulnerability in his eyes that she'd never seen before. He laughed like a high-school kid without a worry in the world. "Yeah, I guess I sort of did." His eyes shone. "Something happened this week. I guess it made all the difference."

There was a knock at the door, and Cory jumped up. "Mrs. Florentino's bringing us some chocolate cake." He darted past her. "She promised."

"Okay." Megan remained unmoved, glued to the interview. The announcer didn't look like he knew what to make of Aaron's statement. "You wanna let us in on the secret?"

"Yeah." Aaron grinned. "I took Derrick Anderson's advice."

Cory opened the door and before he could say anything, a voice sang out. "Cory! You grew an inch since I saw you last!"

Megan felt the blood drain from her face. The voice was the same one coming from the television. She turned quickly in case her mind was playing tricks on her, but there he was. Aaron Hill, standing in her doorway, looking past Cory straight at her. Now, in person, she could see the change in his eyes more clearly. Adrenaline raced through her, and she took a moment to feel her feet on the floor. When she did, when her lungs were working again, she took a step closer, her eyes locked on his. "I have a question."

He looked deep at her, past the lonely months to the place that had made the decision to say goodbye. "What's your question?"

"What did Derrick Anderson tell you to do?"

Cory seemed to remember something important. He gasped and raced into his room. Megan was ten feet from him now, and Aaron closed the gap, moving toward her until they could hear each other breathing. A crooked smile lifted his lips and he shrugged one shoulder. "He told me … to talk to God."

A knowing came over her and she grinned at him. "So that's it."

"What?"

"Your eyes." She made a half turn toward the TV and then back to Aaron. "You were just on Sports Center, and I could see it. Something was different." A light laugh tickled her throat. "Now I understand."

He wore a tan-colored coat, and he reached inside his pocket and pulled out a thick envelope. "Here."

She wasn't sure what to say. He might've figured out how to talk to God, but that didn't mean they'd found common ground or that she should open up her heart to him again. The reasons that existed before still existed today. But the only words she could say were the ones she felt most deeply. "I can't believe you're here."

His grin softened. "I sat outside for half an hour trying to get up the guts."

Her heart melted. She looked at the envelope still in his hand. "What is it?"

"Open it up." He handed it to her. At the same time, Cory came into the room with an envelope of his own.

Megan stared at the boy, and then at Aaron. Whatever was going on, she was completely in the dark. She took the envelope from Aaron, opened it, and as she pulled out the contents, as she sorted through the documents and realized the extent of his gift, she brought her fingers to her mouth.

"What?" Cory raced to her side and peered up at the papers in her hands.

"Tickets." Her eyes found Aaron's. "To the conference championships in New Orleans."

Cory raised his fist in the air and jumped in a full circle. But then he stopped and cocked his head. "How'll we get there?"

"It's all here." She didn't blink, didn't break contact with Aaron. "Plane tickets and a hotel room. Everything."

"A car will meet you at the airport and take you to the hotel, and then to the game." He took a step back, his expression humble. "It's all taken care of."

She handed the tickets to Cory, and stared at him. "Why, Aaron? After so long?"

"To thank you." He still wouldn't take his eyes off her. "For helping me see what I'd become."

"Wow!" Cory held the tickets out. "We're going to the NFC championships!"

Megan was speechless, but more because Aaron was really here, standing in her apartment giving them an opportunity like they'd never had all their lives. She heard what he'd said, but she wasn't sure she understood it. "For helping you see?"

"I'll tell you later." He laughed. "I won't keep you." He took another step back toward the door. "I just wanted to make sure you'd be there."

She hesitated, the reality still sinking in. "We will."

"How will we meet up with you?" Cory ran to Aaron and took hold of his arm. "There'll be so many people."

Aaron thought about that. "Let's have a sign." He hesitated. "I know … when they put the cameras on me, I'll do this." He held up his first two fingers and did a little wave. "That'll mean I'm looking for you."

"Okay!" Cory clapped his hands. "Perfect!" He was still for a second. "But will we see you?"

"Probably not." His smile dropped off some. "We'll get right on a plane after the game. But I'll know you're up there."

"Oh." Some of Cory's excitement dimmed, but not for long. "We're going to New Orleans!"

Megan wasn't sure what to say. "Thank you, Aaron."

He put his hand on the door. Clearly, he wasn't going to hug her or push her in any way. Even if a part of her wanted him to. He looked deep at her again. "I want to talk later, when the season's done."

"Okay." She could hardly wait.

Aaron was telling Cory goodbye when he gasped. "I almost forgot!" He held out his envelope to Aaron. "This is for you. I need you to read it."

Easy laughter came from Aaron and Megan at the same time. They swapped a look, and then Aaron took the envelope. "I will. As soon as I get to the car."

"Good!" Cory hugged him. "Talk to you soon."

Aaron mouthed a gentle goodbye in her direction and raised his hand. She did the same, and then he was gone. It took a minute for Megan's shock to wear off, and when it did, she remembered Cory's envelope. He was back in his room. "Cory, come here."

He darted out and looked at her. "Yes?"

"What was in the envelope?"

"Proof."

She gave him a curious look. "Proof of what?"

"That Aaron's my dad." He said the words calmly, matter-of-fact. "I found a picture of my mom and him at a dance. I wanted him to have it."

A chill ran down Megan's arms. "Don't joke with me, Cory. I mean it."

"I'm serious." He looked hurt. "I found it a few months ago, but I didn't want to show it to anyone but Aaron. Because he's the only one who has to know the truth."

The surprises from the night were beginning to add up. Megan sat down at the kitchen table and put her head in her hands. She was suddenly breathless, the possibility only beginning to make its way through her mind. Even then, it was too big to get her head around all at once. If Cory had a photo of his mother and Aaron, then ... then could it be that all this time he'd been right? That what she'd thought was a fantasy was the truth all along? And how could it be true when Amy had never once mentioned that Aaron was Cory's dad, or even that he might be.

She felt dizzy and giddy and like she was dreaming all at the same time. Whatever was happening—between Aaron's change of heart and Cory's proof—there really was only one explanation.

God was up to something bigger than all of them.

TWENTY-SIX

As he walked down the stairs of her apartment and headed for his truck, Aaron felt God's presence stronger than at any time since his night at the beach. He'd done what he'd come to do. Megan had the tickets, and now she and Cory could have a weekend like nothing they'd ever had before. And in a few weeks, Aaron would tell her what his comment meant, how God had used her to open his eyes to all of life. Real life.

He stepped into his truck, but before he turned the key, he opened Cory's envelope. He'd learned his lesson about lying to kids, or anyone else. The rest of his life he wanted to live out the change in his heart. This was one small way he could make that start. Inside the envelope were two others, both with his name written across the front. Aaron narrowed his eyes, confused. The writing was cursive, definitely not Cory's. Third in the package was a piece of folded paper. He opened it and a wallet-sized photo fell on his lap. Before he picked it up, he read the words on the page.

"Dear Aaron, I figered you needed proof. So here it is. Tell me if you believe me now. Love, Cory."

A strange sensation came over him, and without drawing a breath, he picked up the photo from his lap and turned it over. He stared at it, not believing his eyes. It couldn't be … it couldn't … Slowly, certainly, the bottom fell away and he began to freefall. This wasn't happening.

The people in the photograph were he and Amy Briggs.

His Amy.

His heartbeat doubled and a layer of sweat broke out across his forehead. Amy Briggs was Cory's mother? He'd talked about her with Megan, but never once had either of them mentioned her name. Megan had always been intentionally vague, rarely even calling Aaron by his first name. There would've been no reason to ask about Cory's last name. Until now, Aaron hadn't even thought about the fact that the boy didn't share Megan's name.

The whole foster kid thing was too new to him. If Amy was Cory's mother, then ...

But the truth was ... the truth was as clear as the picture in front of him. Cory was his son! His very own! He drew a sharp breath and wondered if he might explode from the shock ... the shattering realization and the joy bursting inside him. Cory was his son? He looked at the photo again. Cory was his son! Amy had been pregnant with Aaron's child, just like she'd told him all those years ago. So, Cory had to be his son.

His emotions shifted. What had he put the boy through? All these months Cory had stood by his story, that he was Aaron's son. Period. And the whole time — for years in Megan's case — nobody had believed him. Aaron Hill, the father of a foster kid? A kid whose mother never even mentioned the idea? He and Megan both chalked it up to the boy's overactive imagination and his deep desire for a dad.

Aaron groaned out loud. His heart broke for the boy who wanted his dad so badly he would never, ever give up. What must he have been thinking when Aaron made so light of his insistence? And all those recent times when he'd thought about Amy, how he'd never given her a proper goodbye and how he'd turned his back when she'd come to him, pregnant...

And then another reality hit him, devastating him.

Amy was dead.

The girl he still thought about, the one he figured was married and living a wonderful life with some other guy, had in reality raised Cory by herself in a poverty-stricken environment, and then she'd died of pneumonia two years ago. The blow tore at him, stirring fresh debris into the gutters and alleyways of his heart. Amy had lived poor and alone, working at a diner while he signed his contract for millions of dollars and moved on without her. He hung his head and pictured her, the girl he'd loved so much back in his early college days. His Amy was gone. She'd died without his ever making things right.

He remembered the envelopes, the ones with his name written in cursive. His stomach churned as he sat up straighter and picked up the first of the two. There was no time to waste. The boy in the third-floor apartment was his son, and he didn't want another ten minutes to pass without going back up and making things right. He opened the envelope and held the paper tenderly, as if it still contained a little piece of Amy.

Dear Aaron,

He stopped and closed his eyes. Her voice, her face, all of it was there in front of him again. "Amy … why didn't I see it?"

There were no answers; there might never be. He opened his eyes and started over again.

Dear Aaron,

Yesterday our son was born. The experience was more miraculous than anything in my life, and I only wish you'd been there to see for yourself. He's beautiful, Aaron. I named him Cory Joseph Briggs. The first time I held him I saw you in his face. He has your eyes and your cheekbones. I can practically see the strapping boy and athlete he'll become.

I know you're going through a lot of changes. I'm not even sure how I'll get this letter to you. You must know about your agent, how he called me and told me to stay away from you. He threatened legal action if I contacted you again …

What? Aaron's heart skidded into a strange rhythm. Bill had contacted Amy? Threatened her? Heat filled his face and pulsed through his body. He reached for the buttons on his phone, but then stopped himself. He would deal with Bill, but not yet. From this day on Cory would come first.

He drew a jagged breath and found his place again.

… but somehow I must find you. Especially now. Either that or I'll wait forever for you to come back, to find Cory and me. Because I've asked God to get your attention, to touch your heart and help you remember who you used to be. Before your world went crazy.

This time Aaron set the letter down on his lap. Tears blurred his eyes, and he blinked so he could see again. That's exactly what had happened. Directed and fed by his agent, Aaron's world had gone crazy and he'd allowed every minute of it. He lifted the letter and kept reading.

Don't feel bad, but my mom gave me a few weeks to get out. She was very upset about the baby, which I can understand. I just wish she would help me. But either way Cory and I will be fine. I'll get a job and an apartment and I'll pray for the day when you come back. I promise

you, Aaron, as long as I live I'll wait for you. Wherever you go, I'll go.
So that when you're ready to find me, I won't be far away. I love you,
Aaron.

Amy

The air left his lungs and he let his head fall back against the seat. So
that was why she moved to San Francisco, the reason she and Megan wound
up at the same diner. Amy had moved here because she was following him,
waiting for him. He pressed his fists to his eyes and swallowed a series of
sobs. How could he have missed out on this, on her?

With all his remaining strength, he picked up the other envelope and
opened it. Cory was waiting. He needed to get through this so that he would
have all the information available when he went for the first time to his boy,
his son. He studied the letter, and the date. It was written first, before the one
talking about Cory's birth. He began to read.

Dear Aaron,

You're acting different these days, and I don't know what's hap-
pening. Maybe it's your agent, pulling you away from me, into a new
and glamorous future. Or maybe it's something worse.

I know what my mother would say. Now that I've given you what
you want, you're finished with me. My friends tell me you're seeing
other girls, but I can't believe that. Not after the promises you made
to me a week ago. I can't believe you'd listen to your agent over me,
so I can only think of one reason why you would turn away from me,
Aaron.

What I'm about to tell you, I've never told anyone else. I never
will. Three nights ago, I was at Pierce College walking back to my car
when a man grabbed me and pulled me into the bushes. I won't go
into detail, but I want you to know the truth. He raped me. He wore
a mask and he only said a few words. When it was over, he left me on
the ground and he ran away. By the time I pulled myself together and
reached my car, I didn't have the strength to go to the police. I was
ashamed and sick inside. When morning came, I knew I could never
tell the police or anyone else. I had no way of identifying the guy, noth-
ing at all. He was tall and he was white. That's about it.

Aaron had to stop. He was furious and sick to his stomach. Amy had been raped? Was she serious? And where had he been, out to dinner with Bill Bond? Believing suddenly that everyone—even Amy—was hanging around to share in his money and power and fame? He clenched his fists. Amy had been attacked, and he hadn't so much as been a crying shoulder for her.

Aaron willed himself to draw a breath, and he realized how amazing the timing was. Because if he'd gotten this news before his talk with God, it might've sent him over the edge. It was difficult enough now. He didn't want to read another word, but he lifted the paper, anyway.

I have to tell you about what happened to me, because I'm afraid that somehow you know. Not that anyone would've told you. But maybe you know instinctively. Maybe the last time we talked you sensed something different in my voice. And maybe that's why you're acting different. That's why I have to be honest. I want no secrets between us, Aaron. I've never been with anyone but you. If I have my way, I never will again. Not until the day you marry me. Okay ... now you know. Because I believe you, Aaron. That someday you'll come back and marry me. I love you.

Amy

His hands shook as he folded both letters and placed them carefully back in their envelopes. He knew without a doubt that Amy had kept her promise. She was that type of girl, no matter what lies Bill Bond had told about her. If he was right, then she had died loving him, waiting for him. The truth was bigger than all his other poor choices combined. Aaron trembled as he gripped the steering wheel. His breaths came shallow and fast, and he felt a layer of sweat bead up across his forehead. How could he be such a creep, believing Bill Bond over his precious Amy? Had the glare of fame and fortune been that blinding? The truth was unbearable, and he grew sick to his stomach.

But then ... gradually, a greater truth dawned on him.

He didn't have to carry this sort of pain anymore. First, because Amy was safe now. In heaven with Jesus. And second, because he could ask God to take away his guilt.

Lord, I messed up so bad. I didn't watch my little boy grow up, and I lost the chance to tell his mother how much I loved her, how wrong I was. No matter what my agent said. Forgive me, God ... please forgive me. I can't bear the guilt otherwise.

It took a while, but an otherworldly peace came over him. A peace that was not without deep sadness. An urgency built in him, then, and he grabbed the small photograph, rushed out of his truck and back upstairs to the sparse apartment Megan shared with Cory. He knocked on the door and when Megan answered it, he launched into an explanation.

"He's telling the truth ..."

She searched his face, trembling. "He told me. Is it ... is it really possible?'

"Look at this." He handed the photo to Megan. "Amy was my first love. I was ... I was going to marry her." He could've cried, but his excitement had the upper hand. "What's his last name?"

"Briggs." Megan's words were fast and anxious. She was as blown away by the turn of events as Aaron was. "Cory Briggs."

The reality was still sinking in. "He's my son, Megan ... he really is." There would be much to talk about later, notes to compare. But for now all that mattered was—"Cory!"

The boy came running up to the door. His smile held none of the drama and intensity both Aaron and Megan were feeling. He simply looked into Aaron's eyes. "Do you believe me now?"

Something amazing and marvelous was happening in Aaron's heart. He stepped past Megan, touching her hand without looking at her. Then he dropped to his knees for the second time that week, and he held out his arms. "Cory ..." Happy tears choked his voice, but he didn't care.

The boy hesitated for only a second, then he ran the few steps that separated them and landed hard in an embrace that was eight years coming. "So..." Cory sounded small, still not quite sure. "You're my dad, right?"

"Yes." Aaron held him to his chest, stroking his small back and rocking him. Something inside him told him to be careful. Tests would be needed before he could know for sure. But he and Megan would take care of that right away. Not that he needed tests. They would be merely a formality. Cory really did look just like him, something he hadn't seen before today.

Aaron squeezed his eyes shut. "I'm sorry ..." He pressed his son's face to his heart and managed the most precious words he'd ever said. "I'm your dad, Cory. I never knew until today."

They hugged for a long time, and Aaron stayed and tucked him in when it was bedtime. Aaron rubbed Cory's back for a minute or two. He'd missed so much, but tonight was the first of many times when he would be with his son before he went to sleep.

He and Megan would work out details of a paternity test in the morning. Aaron would look into it. When he left, he hugged Megan and his feelings for her came back in a rush. "Can I ask you something?"

"Anything."

"Did Amy … as long as you knew her, did she have someone special, a boyfriend?" The question made things somewhat awkward between them, but Aaron needed to know.

"No one." Megan's answer was quick and heartfelt. "She never even dated. Said she didn't have time because Cory needed her."

Aaron reacted physically to the news, hunching slightly and struggling for his next breath. Everything Amy had told him in the letters was true. She had waited for him until her dying day. Aaron took Megan's hand and held it for a beat. "I have a lot to think through."

Her eyes danced. "I can't believe it."

"Me neither." There was something else he was only now realizing. Megan wanted to adopt Cory. She'd told him so. But now that Aaron had found him, he couldn't possibly let him go. The fairytale ending was obvious, but so far, Megan hadn't wanted to think of him that way, as someone she'd date. They had much to work through.

For now, it was enough that they parted with smiles and promises to talk tomorrow. He walked slowly back to his car, playing over the night's events. They were so far beyond unbelievable, even he couldn't quite grasp his new reality. But the sad truth about Amy was what stayed with him most as he drove home. He would always regret the decisions he made surrounding his breakup with Amy. And he needed to have a much overdue conversation with his agent. But there was something he could do now, while there was still time. He glanced at the photo once more. He might not have gotten the chance to tell Amy he was sorry.

But he could spend the rest of his days loving their little boy.

TWENTY-SEVEN

More than 70,000 fans packed the newly renovated Superdome for the NFC championships the third Sunday in January, but Derrick's attention was on just one person. His teammate, Aaron Hill. The pageantry of the contest caused the pregame to be drawn out an additional half hour — more time to focus on the task ahead.

Before the coin toss, Derrick found Aaron on the sidelines and grabbed his arm. "You play with the power of God today, understand?"

"No other way." Aaron's eyes held a fire Derrick hadn't seen since he joined the team.

Derrick slapped Aaron's helmet and then walked down the line, yelling encouragement at players and groups of players. "This is it, boys ... this is our day!" He stopped at Jay Ryder and spoke a few inches from his face. "Whether you play a down or not, you're a winner, Ryder, you understand me?"

Jay nodded, but he wasn't quite focused, his feet antsy. The team's two punters were questionable, and Coach had told them Jay might have to step in. Jay, who hadn't punted in a game since high school. Derrick slapped Jay's shoulder a few times as the announcer's voice echoed through the building, driving the fans into a frenzy.

"You hearing me, Ryder?" Derrick shouted above the roar of the crowd. "You're a winner, man. You get the whole between Sundays thing." He gripped the back of Jay's helmet and met him straight on. "When the season's over we're gonna change some lives, but right now ... right now we're taking no prisoners!"

This time Jay's eyes were clear and intense. He nodded and then he smacked Derrick on the arm. "I'm ready ... ready, man. Let's get it!"

Already they had made history. No wild card team since 1989 had even made it to the NFC championship game. But here they were. Derrick moved closer to the field and watched as his team won the coin toss and elected to receive. They would have the chance to draw first blood. Derrick bounced on his toes. His knee hurt but not as much as before. If Aaron needed him, he'd be ready. His eyes moved up to the seats of the packed stadium, to the vast sections of red and the handmade cardboard signs that said, "49ers Faithful" and "We Believe!" and "It's Our Turn!"

The Superdome rocked with noise, roaring with the excitement. The marching band competed with the announcer, and TV cameras were everywhere. Derrick eyed the roof of the structure. This was the first time he'd been here since the stadium reopened after Hurricane Katrina. He smiled. The city had done a great job on the storied building, improving it in record time so that it stood as a beacon of hope and determination to all who passed by. The city would rise again. The way the 49ers might win today and also rise again. And with the changes in Aaron...

Be with him, God ... guide his hands.

Derrick stretched his arms one at a time, and then rattled off twenty high-knees. The nervous energy and noise in the building was infectious, and up and down the sideline Derrick could tell his teammates felt the same way. Antsy, anxious, ready to get the show on the road. The San Francisco offense was on the field ready for their leader. A few more seconds with Coach Cameron and Aaron jogged to the middle of the huddle. Even the way he carried himself was different than earlier in the season. The story was on all the sports news shows, the change in Aaron Hill and how it couldn't have happened at a better time for the 49ers.

Derrick grinned in the direction of his friend. If his sense about the game was right, the sports anchors would have more to talk about after today. "Come on, Hill ... take it to 'em!" He shouted the words as loud as he could, not that Aaron could hear him. In the Superdome, noise had nowhere to go. Aaron would have an almost impossible time calling plays today. But that was okay too. Coach Cameron had worked on hand signals all week, not just with Aaron but with the entire team.

Aaron took the first snap, danced around the pocket for what seemed like forever, and then fired an eighteen-yard bullet to one of the rookie receivers. Derrick jumped along the sidelines, high-fiving his teammates and smacking shoulder pads. They could do this ... he could feel it. He stopped and bent over his knees watching as the next play started. Aaron handed off and the rusher dodged two tacklers for a five-yard gain. Derrick paced a few steps in either direction, clapping his hands, hard and intense. "Keep it going, boys … keep it going!"

The drive didn't stall once. From the New Orleans twelve-yard line, Aaron took the snap and tossed a floater into the end zone. The receiver had no one near him, and he reeled it in for a touchdown. San Francisco 7, Saints 0, and only two minutes had fallen off the clock. But the Saints weren't about to be outdone. They'd gone most of the history of the franchise without playoff success. They battled back, nicking away at the yardage and using up seven minutes to notch a twenty-four-yard field goal.

During the Saints' drive, Aaron came up to Derrick and grinned. "I feel great, man. I can see the field, every player." He shook his head, amazed. "I just wish I would've listened to you sooner."

"Yeah, ya dummy." He smacked Aaron's shoulder pads. "That'll teach you."

A TV timeout, and then Aaron and the offense were back on the field. Aaron threw beautiful passes and with first and nine, goal to go, he took the snap and watched his pocket collapse, watched the Saints defense move into the end zone to cover the receivers, and suddenly the only thing in front of him was green. Without the slightest hesitation, he tucked the ball to his side and ran toward the goal line.

At the same time, the star linebacker for New Orleans realized what was happening. He ran to stop Aaron, and at the last minute the linebacker left his feet and grabbed at the quarterback. In the process, their two helmets made a sickening crash, and Aaron fell limp into the end zone. The officials had their hands raised straight in the air, signaling the touchdown. But already Coach Cameron was waddling out onto the field, his face stricken.

A hush fell over the crowd, and people rose to their feet. Derrick wanted to run out, too, but he couldn't. Coaches needed to assess injuries first and then — if the player was down for several minutes — other players might be allowed out to offer encouragement or to pray. Derrick moved along the sideline as far as he could, so he was parallel with his friend. Aaron was motionless, Derrick could see that better now. His legs were sprawled out just the way they'd been when he first collapsed.

"Get up, man … get up!" he shouted, his voice tight with fear. He'd seen hits like this before, and once in a while a guy never got up again. A shudder ran through him, and he shouted again. "Get up, Hill!"

The linebacker was already up, his hands on his hips, head hung, pacing dizzy circles a few feet from where Aaron lay. One of the New Orleans coaches ran out to meet him, and the two walked off the field to the Saints' sidelines.

On the JumboTron screens, the network was showing the replay in slow motion. Derrick didn't want to look, but he had to, had to see how serious the hit was. At the point of impact, Aaron's head reacted violently, snapping sharply back. As the replay ran, a horrifying gasp came from the crowd. Derrick's eyes darted back to his teammate on the field. "Get up, man!"

But Aaron still hadn't moved. Coach Cameron was surrounded by other coaches and a host of trainers, and now Coach waved frantically at the paramedics on the opposite sideline. His message was unmistakable. Get here. Fast. The paramedics pushed a stretcher between them as they jogged out to the place where Aaron lay. One of them had his arm tucked around a backboard and a brace.

God, please … not Aaron. Wake him up, God … this can't be happening!

Aaron had told him earlier that he'd invited Megan, the woman from the youth center, and Cory, the boy. There was more to the story, Aaron told him. They'd have to talk about it later. Now Derrick looked into the stands, wondering where they were, knowing they were also praying for Aaron.

Finally, after several minutes, the paramedics lifted Aaron and strapped him to a backboard. Carefully, they lifted him onto the stretcher and as they did, Aaron moved his feet. As if he wanted to get the message out to everyone in the stadium, he flexed his toes and then pulled his knees up.

Derrick bent halfway over and exhaled. "Thank you, God." The hit hadn't done permanent damage to his spine, that much was obvious now. Derrick straightened again, just as Aaron raised one thumb into the air. Slowly at first, the shocked fans began to clap and cheer, and over the next few seconds their show of support for Aaron grew into a thunderous roar. Aaron Hill might be down, but he wasn't out.

Only then, as they wheeled Aaron toward the tunnel, did Derrick snap back to reality. They still had a little more than three quarters to play, and Aaron was out! Derrick was so worried about his friend that he hadn't remembered until just now that suddenly he was the quarterback, the one the entire team would be looking to.

Derrick sucked in a quick breath and jogged in place for a few seconds. He was ready. Never mind the pain in his knee, he'd been playing on it all season. And back home in San Francisco, Denae and the kids would be pulling for him, cheering him on, covering him in prayer.

He was stretching his arms again when Coach Cameron yelled for him.

The game was in progress, the Saints offense on the field, but it was stalling fast. The 49ers' defense was fired up, determined to pay back New Orleans for its debilitating blow to their quarterback. Derrick jogged closer. "Coach?" Derrick could see desperation in the man's eyes. Even getting this far, if the 49ers lost today, Coach Cameron's job in San Francisco was likely over.

As they stood facing each other, their eyes locked, Coach Cameron's fear turned to sheer determination. "Warm up, Anderson."

"Yes, Coach."

Derrick grabbed a couple of receivers and a ball and moved to a clearing on the sidelines. On the field, the Saints punted and the network called a TV timeout. Derrick ran his tongue over his lower lip. This was his moment, the one he'd come to San Francisco to play. He had time for just six warm-up throws and a few words with Coach before he ran out onto the field.

He expected to see wide eyes in the huddle, and that's exactly what he found. But it wasn't the big-eyed look of fear and uncertainty. The offensive line, the receivers, the tailbacks … all of them were intent on victory for one reason — they trusted Derrick Anderson. Most of them were young enough that they'd probably grown up watching him play on TV. If Aaron Hill was out, Derrick could lead them. There wasn't a San Francisco player on the field who didn't believe that.

Derrick took the snap and straightened in the pocket. Whatever pain his knee had felt all season, faded in the rush of the moment. He was playing the game, his game! He had a chance to make good on a promise he'd made six years ago, and nothing … nothing was going to stand in his way. He dominated through the second quarter, but three drives fell short of a score. The Saints, having collected themselves, rallied for ten points, giving San Francisco just a four-point lead going into halftime.

Derrick wasn't worried. He'd found his rhythm. After more than a quarter on the field, he could see the weaknesses in the Saints defense. The long ball was open, and after halftime, Derrick planned to connect on a handful of dramatic passes. He jogged toward the tunnel and into the locker room, where the team was given a report on Aaron. He had a concussion, and he'd been taken to the hospital for tests.

A murmur ran through the players huddled around Coach Cameron, and the coach raised his hand. "Listen, he's okay. I talked to him before he left. The tests are only for precaution. I've been contacted by hospital personnel, guys. He may be out for the season, but he'll be back here in the locker room before the game ends."

Relief came over Derrick like a burst of sunshine. *Thank you, God … You're beyond merciful.* Derrick could picture Aaron, hurrying the technicians up, wanting the tests to be finished so he could get back to his team. When he did, Derrick wanted the victory well within hand.

He ran out onto the field for the second half feeling as good as he'd ever felt. God was carrying him, holding his knee together for this, his last season. With that in mind, he tore into the third quarter and had an easy time in the fourth, despite a couple touchdowns by the Saints. As time ran out, Jay Ryder was called onto the field where he booted a forty-eight-yard punt that put the ball on the one-yard line. Half the team embraced him as he ran back to the sidelines, and moments later the 49ers won the game and the NFC championship, 32–25. Derrick looped his arm around Jay's neck, and he raised the ball to the stands with one hand and pointed to God in heaven with the other. All around him, the San Francisco crowd went crazy. Never mind the 9–7 regular season. The 49ers were in the Super Bowl, and the miracle Derrick had believed would happen was on the brink of coming true.

He was almost to the locker when he spotted Megan and Cory pressed against a rope, amidst a mob of fans. The two were probably the only San Francisco fans not celebrating.

"Derrick!" Cory shouted to him. "We need to see Aaron. Please… the security people won't let us in."

Derrick looked from the child to the woman. Aaron would've wanted to see them more than anyone else. He pursed his lips and took the lead. He spoke to the gatekeepers, and Megan and Cory were given temporary passes and allowed to cross the line. Derrick gave Megan a reassuring smile. "Follow me."

When he'd cleared them through another few security points and into a room where they could see Aaron, Derrick saw Coach Cameron signal him. "Be ready, Anderson! A hundred reporters want a piece of you."

Derrick nodded. "How's Hill?"

"Groggy. His head hurts, but he's propped up in the locker room. Doctors say he'll be fine."

Derrick pictured the hit again, the way it rocked Aaron and knocked him unconscious. "Wicked hit, man." He met the coach's eyes. "God was with him."

Coach Cameron smiled. "He was with you too."

A smile started at the corners of Derrick's lips and ran all the way through him. "Tell the press I'll be there in a minute."

He jogged to his locker, acknowledging the congratulations along the way. He didn't need anything, but he wanted a moment alone before the crazy aftermath began, before speculation started and the media began reminding fans every hour that the odds were vastly against San Francisco for the big game in two weeks.

Before any of that, he needed this. He opened his locker, braced himself against it, and hung his head. *God Almighty, today ... today was for You. And it was from You.* He wiped the sweat off his forehead and brushed it on his damp jersey. He'd given everything he had out there, and even now the ache in his knee was only a distant throb. He breathed hard, worn out from the exertion. *So, I wondered if You could do me a favor, God?* Tears stung his eyes and mixed with the sweat on his face. *Could You tell my little boy ... his daddy's trying to keep his promise? Please, God ... and kiss his face, okay? Because if he were here, that's what I would do. And You're a better Dad than I could ever hope to be.*

He sniffed and grabbed a towel from inside his locker. He scrunched it in a ball and pressed it to his face, drying the tears and grime and sweat. *Oh, and also ...* He dragged the towel across his cheeks and tossed it back in the locker. *Tell Lee one more game. Just one more game.* As he slammed the locker door shut, he willed himself to find control again. *Thanks, God.*

With that, he walked through the locker room to the waiting press, where for the next half hour he did something that came as natural to him as suiting up for a game. He hung with the reporters, fielding questions and smiling and giving entertaining answers, careful to give all credit for the unlikely win to God alone.

Where it would always belong.

Megan's stomach had been in knots since Aaron took the hit, but even then, she couldn't let her fear show. Not with Cory sitting beside her. The only reason she hadn't tried to come down to the locker room sooner was because the announcer had given occasional updates on Aaron's condition. He had a concussion, he'd been taken to the hospital, his tests were negative, and now he was back at the stadium in the locker room. The last update said he was expected to make a full recovery, but his prognosis for the Super Bowl was uncertain.

With each announcement, Megan felt her fears ease, but still she wanted to see for herself. Even then, without Derrick, they never would've gotten through to see Aaron. Now, though, they waited in a room across the hall from the lockers. Ten minutes passed, and then the door opened and Aaron's agent poked his head through. He stared at Megan and then at Cory and his expression changed from confused to irritated. "What are you doing here?"

Megan steeled herself against the man's disapproval. "Aaron invited us."

Next to her, Cory started to say something, but Megan put her arm around his slim shoulders and gave him a squeeze. Cory took the hint and grew silent.

Bill sneered at her. "Fans aren't allowed behind security lines."

Cory took a step forward, his voice defiant. "Derrick let us through. We want to see Aaron."

The agent steadied his gaze straight at Megan. "Aaron doesn't have time for charity work during the season. I'll speak to him about this disruption." He held her eyes for a moment longer, then he was gone.

Megan realized she'd been holding her breath. She exhaled hard and turned to Cory. "Thank you."

Cory's eyes blazed. "That guy's mean."

"Yes, he is. But no one can know about you and Aaron until it's time, okay?"

"Okay." Cory looked dejected, but not for long.

Before Megan could say anything else, a man with a shirt marked "trainer" wheeled Aaron into the room. The wheelchair must've frightened Cory at first, because he hesitated, staying close to Megan. But his joy at seeing Aaron sitting up, his eyes open, must've won out because Cory ran to Aaron's side and gently touched his arm. "Are you okay?"

"I'm fine." His eyes were only half open, his voice groggy. But he smiled at Cory and then winced as he shifted his attention to Megan. "Do you need a ride home?"

Megan blinked. A ride home? She looked at the trainer, and the guy mouthed the word, "concussion." Megan nodded, but her stomach churned with renewed fear. She pictured him on the field, unmoving, unconscious. At the time, she couldn't draw a breath, couldn't move or speak for all the horrible scenarios playing in her head. He could've been paralyzed, or if his neck had broken in the exact wrong spot, he could've died without ever getting up. By the end of the game, the announcer made it sound like Aaron was doing so well he was probably joking around with the trainers in the locker room.

The truth was far from that. Aaron rested his head in his hand and massaged his temples. Cory stood beside him, rubbing small gentle circles into his back. "I prayed for you."

Aaron's face twisted in pain. "Me too." He tried to focus on Cory. "I prayed on the beach."

Worry filled Cory's eyes, and Megan gave him a calming look. "It's okay. He'll be all right." But at the same time she shot another frantic look at the trainer.

The guy moved around Aaron and came close to Megan, so close Cory couldn't hear what he was saying. "He'll hurt for a while. He's dizzy and he can't see clear. It'll take some time."

"Shouldn't he be in the hospital?" She was shocked that medical professionals had seen Aaron's condition and released him.

"He has no bleeding in the brain; the tests were clear. The emergency room doctor wanted to hold him overnight for observation, but the team doctor promised someone would stay with him for a couple days. Make sure he doesn't develop any new symptoms." The trainer glanced at Aaron, and then back at Megan. "He's on pain meds too. So he's a little loopy."

Megan swallowed hard. "Okay." Her knees trembled, and her hands shook so bad she could barely tuck her hair behind her ears. "I shouldn't worry, then?"

"No." The trainer's tone was reassuring. "This happens in football."

Great, Megan wanted to say. But instead she moved past the trainer to Aaron's other side. She put her hand on his shoulder and stooped down so her face was near his. "We're here, Aaron. You're going to be okay."

He squinted at her, and then he stretched his arm out. "Megan ... take my hand."

A surge of hope welled inside her. He knew who she was! *God, let him be okay. Please* ... She reached out and gently took hold of his fingers. They were much larger than hers, but his touch was as gentle as the breeze off the bay. "You're in the Super Bowl! Can you believe it?"

He looked like a person trapped in a room with too much noise. He made a face and stared at his knees. When the pain or whatever had passed, he bunched up his eyes and stared at her, as if he were trying to see through thick fog. He brought her fingers to his lips and kissed them. The way he'd done at the park that day. "You're so beautiful, Megan."

The trainer nodded at her, and stepped toward the door. "I'll be out here when you need me."

"Thank you." Megan wanted this time alone with Aaron, though she had no idea where it would lead. She didn't belong here, the woman linked with the team's star quarterback. Aaron's agent was right. That role was reserved for the elite and famous, the actresses hinted about in the *Chronicle.* Which was something she wanted to ask him about, whether anything had come from his agent's efforts. But Aaron had only stepped back into their lives a few days ago. And now...

She looked at Cory. He was glued to every word, every move Aaron made. "You'll be fine by tomorrow." The boy looked at her and nodded, probably trying to convince himself. "Right, Megan? He'll be fine tomorrow?"

"He will." She wasn't sure, but it was the only answer for now. They stayed a few minutes longer, and all the while Megan could hardly think, hardly breathe for the feel of his hand against hers. She prided herself on being smart, on knowing when a situation wasn't good for her. But here, when all the signs told her to run, she was stretching out the moment as long as she could.

When she went to leave, she put her arm gingerly around Aaron's shoulders and gave him a side hug. "We'll talk when we're back home, okay?"

For a few seconds he didn't look like he knew what to make of that. Then he dropped his voice to a whisper, his eyes clearer than they'd been since he came into the room. "I love you."

Megan's breath caught in her throat, and she took a step back. "We'll ... we'll talk, okay?"

He held her eyes for a second or two, and then he let his head fall into his hand again. Megan shifted her attention to Cory, but he was bent over, tying his shoes. Megan was almost certain he hadn't heard Aaron's statement. If he did, he was bound to have questions.

They were out of the stadium and in the Town Car on the way back to the hotel when Cory grinned at her. "You should marry Aaron."

Megan's heartbeat quickened, but she kept her composure. "I'm not marrying anyone." It was the safest answer she could give. If she wanted to keep what was important to her, if she wanted to protect herself from getting hurt, then she'd stay in her apartment with Cory and their cat, Oreo, and nothing about her life would ever change.

Cory frowned at her. "But you should. Then everything would be perfect." His features relaxed. "You and Aaron could get married, and then I'd have a mom and a dad! And we could eat dinner at Pier 39 every Friday night!" He paused. "Plus he loves you, Megan." His tone took on the familiar sing-song sound. "I heard him tell you."

She brushed off the possibility. "He didn't know what he was saying." Despite her alarm and the flush in her cheeks, Megan felt for the child. In his world, the answers really were that simple. She stared out the window and tried to think of something to add that would put the idea to rest, a sensible response.

But she had none to give, and a knowing came over her. The ride ahead was going to be difficult for her. Difficult and painful. Because Aaron didn't want to marry her, not if he was thinking clearly. But one day soon he would want to bring Cory home. The boy was Aaron's son, Megan had no doubt. The resemblance between them was uncanny now that she knew the truth. Where would that leave her? Especially when all she could hear were his whispered words of love, words that had touched the most private places in her heart.

Whether he knew what he was saying or not.

TWENTY-EIGHT

Aaron sat in the lobby of the clinic a few miles from Cardinals Stadium and closed his eyes. The injury had happened more than a week ago, but his head still hurt and that worried his doctors. Even so, he was getting a little better every day. The double vision was gone, and his short-term memory was almost back to normal. The day before the flight, the doctor had cleared him for certain tasks—driving and light workouts.

He was doubtful for Sunday's game against the Chargers, but Coach wasn't sharing that with the press. Aaron was in his hotel room last night when he heard the coach interviewed on a special edition of Sports Center. "Aaron Hill's making a very fast recovery. The coaching staff expects him to be the starting quarterback this Sunday."

Aaron had stared at the TV screen, confused. Three doctors had weighed in with their opinion earlier that day. Only one of them thought he had even the slightest chance of playing in the big game. But then, Coach was praying for him. Coach and Megan and Cory and everyone in Derrick's family. If he kept improving, anything was possible. For now, though, the game was not the first thing on his mind.

He leaned his forearms on his knees and clasped his hands. There was no reason to be nervous. He'd set up this meeting a week ago, arranged to take the blood test here in Phoenix—so they wouldn't have to wait longer than necessary. Cory was his son, he had no doubt. But in case the issue ever was called into question, Aaron wanted the paperwork. When it was finished, he would frame it and set it where he would never forget, never go a single day without appreciating the gift he'd been given in finding his son.

A nurse stepped into the waiting area and smiled. "Mr. Hill?"

The clinic was known for its high-end clients, and for its ability to be discreet, even keeping the information from his agent if necessary. Bill Bond had no idea his star client was about to take a paternity test. The news would've pushed him over the edge for sure. Bill was in town for the game, but Aaron had kept their time together to a minimum. His agent was upset by the presence of Megan and Cory at the conference championship in New Orleans. Just yesterday, Aaron met Bill in a private meeting room at the hotel to discuss offers for more endorsements. When the short meeting ended, Bill shook his head, clearly disappointed. "You're giving people the wrong impression, bringing that woman and her son to the game." Bill paused. "When the season's over, we need to talk, friend."

"Yeah." Aaron hadn't wanted to get into it, but he could agree on that much. "We definitely need to talk."

Now Aaron followed the nurse into a small room, and with little fanfare, she swabbed his arm and asked him if he was aware that the test was for a DNA paternity match, and he confirmed the fact. If she knew who he was, she didn't say so, and as she drew a vial of his blood, she didn't make small talk. When she was done, she slipped a small bandage across the needle mark and went about her business.

Aaron appreciated her silence. He couldn't risk having news of this visit in the press, not this week or ever. A minute later, when the nurse had labeled the vial and filled out a piece of paperwork, she gave him another polite smile. "That's all, Mr. Hill. The sample will be sent to the lab, and when the other one comes in, a test will be performed to see if there's a match. You'll be notified of the private results by courier." She checked her notes. "If things go the way they're set up, you should have results in a week. Next Wednesday."

Aaron thanked her. As he left he pictured Megan, who was taking Cory into a clinic in San Francisco this same afternoon. He didn't know if the boy was afraid of needles, but for a strong moment he wished he were there beside him. It wasn't Cory's fault Aaron had walked away from the boy's mother. But at least some of the blame belonged to Bill Bond. Bill, who had made Megan feel uncomfortable, and who had threatened Amy, warning her to stay away from Aaron at all costs.

On the drive back to the hotel, his frustration and anger toward his agent grew to a boiling point. For weeks he'd been putting off the talk he wanted to have with Bill, all because he wanted to stay focused on the season. Because he didn't want a news story about him and his agent to take anything away from the team and its run at the title.

What did it matter now? Aaron wasn't likely to see a minute on the field, and the press was in such a frenzy about the pending game, they wouldn't run a story about Aaron's agent until a week after the contest. At the earliest. He waited until he was back in his hotel room before he took a long breath and pulled his cell phone from his pocket. It was time to do what he should've done months ago. Years ago. He opened his phone and uttered a bitter sigh. His agent was one of his top speed dial choices—not a friend or a wife or any family members. The others were all reserved for business contacts. Aaron's heart felt heavy at the realization and what it said about his life until now.

His agent picked up almost immediately. "Hill, my friend." His laugh sounded phony and forced. "It's about time. I was beginning to think you'd forgotten about me. How 'bout dinner tonight down the street?"

Aaron had wasted too much time for small talk. "Where are you?"

"Uh…" Bill hesitated, "all right, we'll forget the niceties." He kept his tone upbeat. Whatever Aaron wanted, Aaron got. "I'm in the lobby with a few financial guys. You can join us, in fact I was hoping you'd—"

"Get up here, Bill. Now." Aaron kept his tone even, otherwise his head would hurt too much. "You know my room number."

Bill dropped his voice a notch. "Everything okay?"

"No." Aaron massaged his temples. "Just get up here."

"Okay." He paused, his voice suddenly nervous. "Give me five."

The call ended and Aaron's head pounded from the pain. In less than five minutes there was a knock at the door. Aaron let his agent in, and he led the way to the living room of his suite. They sat facing each other. Bill sat deep against the corner of one sofa, and Aaron balanced on the edge of the other. He dug his elbows into his knees and fired an intense look straight at his agent.

Before he could talk, Bill started in. "Hey, how's your head, by the way? I meant to ask, but you were, you know"—he tried a short laugh, but it didn't quite work out. He waved his hand around—"distracted by whatever this is." He grabbed a quick gulp of air. "You still in pain or what?"

"I'm fine." Aaron kept the intensity in his stare. "I have a question."

Bill ran his tongue along his lower lip. "Okay." His throat sounded dry. "Shoot."

He didn't hesitate. "How'd you know Amy Briggs was cheating on me?"

Bill blinked and went stone still. His look said he was maybe worried about Aaron's sanity. "Amy Briggs?"

"Yeah, remember her? Girl I was dating back when I was a sophomore in college?"

"Amy … hmmm." Another laugh. "You've dated a lot of girls, Hill. You gotta give me more than that."

"Think hard, Bill." Aaron could see in his agent's eyes the guy was lying. "I knew her from high school. She lived in the Valley." He pictured her, the gentle way she had about herself. Her kind eyes and loyalty. "She was my girl when you and I met. She and I talked on the phone a lot." Sarcasm crept into his tone. "You told me it wasn't good for my image to be so serious about a girl, remember? You wanted me to think about football and my classes. Period. Because image was everything."

"It worked, didn't it?" Bill rarely took a tone with Aaron, but now his voice mixed defensive frustration and arrogance. He straightened and leaned a little closer. "You checked your bank account lately?"

Aaron felt like he'd been punched. Had he really traded whatever he might've had with Amy for a bigger bank account? The comment cut Aaron to the depths of his soul. "That's all you ever cared about, isn't it? The bottom line." His headache pounded, and he willed the pain to ease. "Tell me about Amy, Bill. I want an answer. You told me she was seeing other guys behind my back, and I want to know. What was your proof?"

After a long beat, Bill huffed his indignation. "Come on, Hill. I wasn't exactly a detective. Girls like that, the needy ones. They're with a different guy every weekend. You were too young to see it." He stroked his chin, nervous-like. His chuckle said he could hardly believe he was having this conversation. "What's it matter? You got what you wanted."

Aaron's head spun, and the edges of the picture Bill made began to blur. He closed his eyes and pressed his free hand to his brow. "So you're saying … you had no proof on Amy?"

"Okay, so it was a feeling." For the first time since he'd entered the hotel room, Bill sounded truly nervous. He tried to lighten his tone. "I remember the girl. She was trash next to you, Hill. You couldn't see it, so I had to see it for you."

Aaron wanted to throw up. He'd walked away from Amy because he was young and jealous of other guys. And because Bill knew that, he knew what buttons to push, what to say to make Aaron break up with her. And all of it had been nothing more than a feeling? He wanted to throw the guy out of his room, but he wasn't finished. "Amy wrote me a letter."

Bill looked doubtful, and Aaron had to use every ounce of his restraint not to fly across the coffee table separating them and pummel his agent. Aaron opened his mouth to tell Bill that he didn't have to worry about Amy any longer, because Amy was dead. But he caught himself. He didn't want to give his agent even the slightest chance to feign sorrow. He breathed in through gritted teeth. "She told me you threatened her." His words were slower now, each one fired at their target. "You told her she wasn't to contact me. Sound familiar?"

His agent's face was paler than before. He squirmed and shifted his position. "Of course I told her that. You were about to be famous, Hill. Someone had to protect you."

Aaron had all the information he needed. He stood, his head thudding with every heartbeat, and he stared down at Bill. The man he'd relied on and looked to, the one who had controlled the puppet strings of his life for so many years, looked suddenly small and pitiful. "You can go now, Bill. We're finished."

Bill didn't make a move to leave. His brief laugh made him sound dazed. "What're you saying?"

Aaron thought about Amy again, and he clenched his fists. "You're fired, Bill. We're through."

"Look, we can talk about this." Bill inched to the edge of the sofa. "You're not thinking straight, Hill. It's the concussion."

"You're right." Aaron took a step back and pointed to the door. "If I were thinking straight, I would've done this months ago."

Bill had no choice but to stand. "Hill, look, we can figure all this out when we get home. You and I can sit down and crunch numbers. I can show you the difference I've made being in charge of your endorsements and your image and the media connections and—"

Aaron closed the gap between them and grabbed Bill by the arm. Not hard enough to leave a bruise, but hard enough to get the guy's attention. "You're fired, Bill. End of discussion." He led Bill to the door. "My attorney will have paperwork on your desk tomorrow morning officially severing our ties."

Bill started to speak, as if he might list his accomplishments one more time. But instead he jerked his arm free and moved to the door. "You're sick, Hill. When you come to your senses, call me." He left and slammed the door behind him.

Aaron stared at the door for a few seconds until he was sure Bill was gone. Then slowly he went back to the bed and lay down. After a few minutes, the pain in his head let up. Before he could truly relax, he found Derrick's number in his phone and he hit the Send button. Derrick picked up after several rings.

"Okay, Hill, I'm a busy guy; just give it to me straight." There was a smile in his teammate's voice. "Press says you're the man. You ready to play?"

"Sure." Aaron grinned. "I was gonna ask you the same thing."

He chuckled. "The answer's yes. Now if we can just make it past the media circus."

"Yeah, well, I'm dealing with another kind of circus. Which is why I called." He massaged his eyebrows again. "Can you give me the number of your agent?"

Derrick paused. "Sure." He rattled it off by heart, and the teasing in his tone fell away. "Time for a change?"

"You have no idea. Bill Bond's controlled my life long enough."

"Yeah, well … guy is a genius, but he has the worst reputation in the whole league."

He thought about Amy, and his heart hurt. "I'm always the last to find out." He didn't want to go into details now. He could catch Derrick up later, after the game. They talked about the week's schedule and about Aaron's headaches. After the call, Aaron stared out the window and willed the pain that was returning to his temples to go away. On the list of things he needed to do—now that he was a father—he'd taken care of the first one. Next, more than anything, he wanted to see Megan. The last time they were together, his head was fuzzy and he couldn't think straight, but when they wheeled him into that small room in New Orleans and she and Cory were there, he wanted to take her in his arms and ask her to be his. Forever. The feeling had stayed with him ever since.

His past was an issue, certainly. And there was Bill's publicity stunt about the nonexistent young actress. He rolled onto his side. He couldn't blame her if she didn't think their worlds would mix, if she didn't want to take a chance on him. But whether she did or not, he wanted to be a father to Cory. The fact that Megan wanted to adopt him complicated things. So lately, Aaron had been asking God for another kind of miracle. That someday there might be room in Megan's heart for more than hurting people and foster kids.

But for him too.

TWENTY-NINE

Their light practice was over and Derrick was getting his things from the locker room when he got the word. Coach Cameron wanted to talk to him. He shoved his bag back into his space and returned to the front of the room, where the offices were. Derrick's knee was feeling better, but the official word coming from the 49ers was that Aaron would start on game day. Which was fine with Derrick. He'd done the job when his team needed him, and that's all that mattered.

That and his promise to Lee.

He reached the office door and went inside. "Coach?"

Coach Cameron looked troubled. "One of the doctors treating Hill just gave me his report for tomorrow. He doesn't want him to play."

"I thought ..."

"We were guessing." He sighed. "The reporters were like a pack of wolves this week. And if Aaron wasn't playing, we didn't exactly want San Diego knowing." He picked up a report on his desk. "Jay Ryder's our starting punter at this point." There were bags under his eyes. "Bottom line, Anderson, we need you. More than you know."

A surge of adrenaline hit him. "I'm starting?"

"Starting and finishing." Coach's smile hid the stress he must've been feeling. The front office still wanted all or nothing from the coach, according to the press. "You can do it, Anderson. You can. You've done it before. If you want my thoughts, it's a coin toss on which of you I'd rather have leading the team tomorrow."

Derrick listened, not sure what to say. This was it, his chance to win it all one last time. Not just as a bystander, but as the guy making the plays. Win or lose, the results would rest squarely on his shoulders. He gathered himself and stood a little taller. "I'm ready, Coach."

"The way I figure it, none of us should be here anyway." He stood and slipped his hands into his pockets. "As long as God's smiling down on us, there's no reason for Him to stop tomorrow."

Derrick grinned. "Exactly."

The meeting lasted a few more minutes while Coach went over a few slight changes in the game plan. When Derrick shut the office door behind him, he steeled his mind against any of the hype and hoopla of the past few weeks. All that mattered was tomorrow and the job he had to do.

A job he wanted to do just one more time.

When Derrick woke up Sunday morning, he smiled. God was with him, and He would be with the team that day. Not that God cared about winning, so much. But in getting them here, God had opened doors that should've been bolted shut. Derrick had the feeling He wasn't finished just yet.

The morning routine was familiar, but that didn't ease the nervous energy coursing through him. As he and Aaron suited up, they were quiet, each lost in their thoughts about the game. Before they circled around Coach Cameron, Aaron faced him.

"Waited my whole life to be here, man." His smile didn't hide his disappointment. "Dreamed about it since I was a kid. But right now ... right now I only want you to go out there and win it for your boy." He smacked Derrick's shoulder. "I mean it. Do your magic, Anderson. This is your day."

Derrick stared at the concrete floor and rubbed the back of his neck. When he looked up, his eyes found the photo of his family at the back of his locker door. The one that always stayed with him, the last one ever taken of Lee. Derrick felt his chin quiver, but he steadied himself. His emotions were high, filling his senses, driving him to play at a level he'd never found before. After seventeen years in the league, this was his last game. The very last. He turned his attention to Aaron. "Thanks. I'll remember that."

The pregame talk was what Derrick would've expected. Coach Cameron kept his words brief and full of punch. "I've been asked a hundred times this week what this season has taught me, and every time I say the same thing. It's taught me the importance of faith." He locked eyes with Aaron and then one player after another down the line. "Faith in a Creator with whom all things are possible ... and faith in our ability to come together as a team. Faith that no one ... no one can write our story except us."

In the end, his voice rang with passion. "Believe, men! Believe you can win this game." He raised his fist in the air, his face etched in determination. "Let's go get us a Super Bowl trophy!"

Derrick felt better than he had all season as he jogged down the tunnel and took the field. The new stadium's retractable roof was open and the roar of the crowd echoed in the cooling desert air. Derrick tuned out the sound—all of it. This was his game. When the 49ers won the toss, he took the field, and on the first drive he threw an eighty-two yard touchdown bomb to give San Francisco a 7–0 lead.

The game stayed close into the second quarter, and with fifteen seconds to go in the first half, the 49ers were up by three. Derrick was driving the offense, looking for at least a field goal before time ran out. With the team well into Chargers territory, the play was a fake handoff and a down-and-out pattern to the left side of the field. The ball was hiked and Derrick faked left and then planted his right leg for the pass.

As he did, a sickening snap shot through his knee and he crumpled to the field. The pain was immediate and blinding hot, and for the first few seconds all Derrick could do was try to breathe. *No, God ... not now! Please ...* He didn't need a doctor to tell him what had just happened. The ligament in his knee, the one that had been strained all season, was shot. Ripped apart. He rocked his head one way and then the other, his face twisted up. A scream built inside of him, but he swallowed it, pursing his lips, and forcing himself to exhale. *No! This couldn't be happening.*

Coaches were running out to him now and he had the sudden urge to get up. Never mind what he'd felt in his knee or the pain burning through him. If he could get up, he could play again. He sat and tried to move his right leg, tried to pull it up beneath him. But even the slightest movement tripled his pain and made spots dance in front of his eyes. He couldn't pass out. He had to stay strong, had to figure out a way.

"Anderson, don't move it." The trainer was at his side now, just ahead of the coaches. "I saw it happen. It's not good."

Derrick squeezed his eyes shut, because he didn't want to hear it. This couldn't be all there was. When he pictured himself taking his last snap ever, he saw it as a touchdown pass or a beautiful completion. He hadn't played nearly two decades to have it all end like this. But as the trainer carefully positioned his leg, and as he called for help, Derrick shut those thoughts from his mind. Only one thought mattered.

His little boy.

He couldn't give up, not when the game was half over. Maybe they could give him a brace or a shot of cortisone, anything to numb the pain so he could run again—just for thirty minutes more. But it was too late. He couldn't move his leg, and the pain was turning his insides into knots.

A cart was driven up by someone on the training staff, and a couple of them helped him into the back. As they did, every person in University of Phoenix Stadium rose to their feet. Chargers fans and 49ers Faithful alike sent up a round of applause that filled the air and washed over him. The rumors had come out in the weeks before the Super Bowl. After this game, Derrick Anderson was calling it quits. Here, then, the fans understood what they were watching.

This was their last time to show him how they felt about him. Their chance to tell him goodbye.

Derrick blinked back tears, and as the cart drove off for the tunnel, he raised both hands and waved to them. He had loved every minute playing quarterback in the NFL. He'd heard the cheers so many times, the sound of their applause was like meeting up with an old friend. But this was the last time he would hear it. Suddenly, the pain in his leg was dimmed by an even greater pain. The pain of knowing that the final lines in this chapter of his life had been written. Somewhere in the stands, Denae and the kids had to know too.

It was over.

The cart pulled into the area adjacent to the trainers' station and Derrick started praying. Not for his knee. That could come later. But for whoever was about to take his place.

Because right now, the entire season rested on the shoulders of that one guy.

⸺

Aaron knew the moment Derrick went down. The rest of the game was his. He was standing next to Jay Ryder, the third-string quarterback, and the two exchanged a look. "Coach wants me to punt. But I can do both, Hill. I can do it."

"No." Aaron clenched his jaw and patted Jay on the shoulder. "This one's mine."

Jay was a competitor and he would've done his best. But he hadn't taken a snap in a game all year. Besides, they needed him at punter. Jay grabbed him by the shoulders. "Okay, then. Win it, man. Finish it up."

Aaron nodded. There was no hurry. When Derrick was taken off the field, the 49ers let the clock run out on the next play. On the way into the locker room, Aaron jogged up alongside Coach Cameron. "I'm ready. Put me in."

Coach gave him a wary look. "The doctor ..."

"I know my own body." They reached the tunnel and Aaron stopped and faced his coach. "I'll be careful."

He hesitated. "Let's talk about it with the trainers."

In the end, there wasn't much discussion. Aaron was clear thinking and adamant. He could take the field and he could lead the team. When the decision was made, Aaron hurried from the office and into the training room. Derrick was there, laid out on a table, one arm raised over his head and covering his eyes. Aaron went to his side. "Anderson."

Derrick lowered his arm and their eyes met. Derrick's were red and watery, and his chin quivered. For a few seconds neither of them said anything. "I'm sorry, man. I wanted to finish it." He dug his elbow into the padded table and held up his hand. "You're in, aren't you?"

Aaron reached out and clasped Derrick's hand around his thumb. "Yeah." He swallowed, struggling. "Sorry about your knee." He didn't say that he was sorry about his career ending this way. That much was as evident as the tears brimming in both their eyes.

Derrick set his jaw and gave a sharp shake of his head. "Don't be sorry. Get out there and win it for my boy."

For the first time since Derrick fell to the ground, Aaron smiled. "For yours ... and for mine."

The trainers were out of the room now, and Derrick's brow became a series of deep wrinkles. "Yours?" He managed a nervous laugh. "You're still loopy, Hill." He nodded toward the door. "Go tell Coach to put Jay in."

"I'm serious." Aaron grinned. His mind was incredibly clear, actually. He pictured Cory and Megan, somewhere in the stadium witnessing the drama play out. "I have a son, Anderson." He looked at the clock. The team needed him on the field. "I'll tell you about it later. Just trust me. I've got more reason to win this thing than you know."

With that he gave Derrick's hand one more squeeze. "Talk to God for me, man."

"The whole time."

When Aaron took the field, the Chargers had scored and were up by four. On the first snap, Aaron got the ball, took three backward running steps deep into the pocket, and looked at his options. But as his eyes darted from one receiver to another, the ground seemed to tilt and his vision blurred. The rush of dizziness made him feel sick to his stomach, and he could see the linebacker barreling down on him. He released the pass just before the sack, but before he hit the ground he saw the ball fall far short of his man.

He shook off the hit, but he was slow getting to his feet. His teammates were coming together in the next huddle when San Francisco called a time-out. Coach was pacing the sidelines as Aaron reached him.

"No more passing. You're not ready." His voice was gruff, but his eyes were marked with fear. Another concussion at this point could leave permanent damage. Everyone knew that. "We're going to a running game." He barked a few orders at one of the halfbacks and two of the running backs.

Aaron couldn't argue. If that last pass was the best he could do, they had no choice but to switch up their game. But as the third quarter wore down, San Diego scored again, and at the start of the fourth, the 49ers trailed by eleven. During the TV timeout between quarters, Aaron pulled off by himself. It wasn't working, the revised strategy. He needed help and he needed it fast.

Then suddenly it hit him. The idea of praying was still so new to him, he hadn't realized something. Derrick was praying for him, but Aaron hadn't prayed for himself. So he sat on the edge of the bench, dropped his head into his hands, and cried out to God the same way he had at Baker's Beach.

I don't deserve this, God. I don't deserve anything from You. Aaron concentrated on finishing the prayer. *I can't play the rest of this game without You, God. I'm not asking for a win, just that You'd clear my head. Take away the dizziness. Let me see the field like never before.* The words settled deep into Aaron's soul. A strange peace and a knowing came over him. He'd done what he could do. Now he needed to play his game.

It didn't happen all at once, but with third and eight on their own forty-yard line, Aaron called an audible. Long pass to the end zone. A few of the players raised an eyebrow, but they didn't argue. Based on the third quarter, San Diego was probably lulled into thinking Aaron wasn't going to do anything more tricky than a quick dump pass. But this time when he stepped back in the pocket, he saw with a clarity that could've only come from God. His receiver was all alone, streaking down the field, and Aaron hit him with a pass that rivaled any he'd ever thrown. The touchdown closed the gap to four, and the networks called another timeout.

"Hill!" Coach Cameron's face was beet red. He stormed over to meet Aaron as he jogged off the field. "What're you doing? I told you no passes."

"Something happened." Aaron put his hands on his hips and tried to catch his breath. "I can see clear now. I promise, Coach."

"I don't want you sacked, you understand? No blows to your head."

"My line's holding. It was my fault before." Aaron gripped his coach's shoulder. "I asked God for vision, and He gave it to me. We have to play our game."

Coach looked like he was about to pass out from the stress, but he nodded. "Okay. Go with your gut. If it's there, if you feel it — call it."

The Chargers opened the fourth quarter with a touchdown, giving San Diego an eleven-point edge. Aaron felt himself narrowing in on what was needed, on the job ahead. With six minutes left, he used a couple audible passes to take San Francisco quickly into Charger territory. A running play for a touchdown meant the 49ers still had a chance.

San Diego wasted three minutes on short runs for little yardage. Their punt put San Francisco on the four-yard line. One more chance ... they had one more chance. Aaron's head throbbed from the intensity and exertion of the game. He had to hold on, had to find a way to dig deep for one more drive.

"Okay, Hill." Coach shouted at him above the roar from the crowd. "Less than two minutes and ninety-six yards to go. If anyone can do it, you can!"

Before he took the field, Aaron imagined Megan sitting in the stands. Megan who got up every morning before dawn to deliver papers on foot through the streets of San Francisco, and who walked miles each day to her job waiting tables.

God, if You would give me half the determination of that woman, I know I can do this. Help me find it ... please, God.

A verse came to mind, something Megan had told him about during a phone call a few days ago. It was from the book of Isaiah. *Those who hope in the LORD will renew their strength. They will run and not grow weary, they will walk and not be faint.*

That was it! He would take the field with all the determination Megan had shown him, with the experience of mastering the two-minute drill season after season. But he would do it by waiting on the Lord. He sucked in a full breath as he ran out to the huddle. He still felt weary and faint, but God would have the final say over whatever happened in the next few minutes.

A field goal wouldn't be enough, so everyone in the stadium knew Aaron was looking toward the end zone, and only the end zone. From the first snap, he followed Coach Cameron's game plan. A short run, a breakaway for seven yards, another short pattern. Gradually, in what felt like painful slow motion, the team trudged up the field while the seconds fell away. Aaron could feel himself running on some power other than his own. Even still he wasn't sure if he could pass. The dizziness was back, and he couldn't hurt the team. The risk was too great.

Finally, they inched into the red zone, the last twenty yards leading up to the goal line. Another few runs, a short pitch pass, and they were first and ten at the twelve with forty-six seconds to go. The next three running plays fell short, netting only a yard or two each.

Aaron huddled the team and glanced at the clock. Five seconds to go, fourth-and-two. There was no point going for the first down — time would run out in the process and the game would be over. It was a touchdown or nothing. A TV timeout bought them a breather. Aaron looked at his team, and he knew what he had to do. San Diego had to be expecting a pass, no matter how exhausted Aaron looked or seemed. With the eyes of his teammates locked on him, Aaron took the risk of his career. "Quarterback keeper." He felt the intensity in his stare. An intensity borne from the determination he'd witnessed in a woman he would long for all the days of his life.

Again, the guys didn't react. Never mind that this was how Aaron had been hurt in New Orleans. It was the last play the Chargers would be expecting, and for that reason, it had a chance. "We need just four yards." He shouted his encouragement. "We can do this! Come on guys, hold the line."

His teammates nodded, gave a single clap, and lined up for the play. Aaron felt his knees shake as he dropped back with the ball and faked like he was going to pass left, and then right. Then as the slimmest window opened in front of him, he took off. One yard, and then two ... and Aaron could see what was happening. His line was rising to the challenge, covering him, holding off the swarming defense like never before.

Aaron kept pumping his feet, running, pushing for the end zone. Three yards ... and then suddenly, he was across the goal line without being touched by a single Charger. The officials raised their hands and seventy-three thousand people were on their feet, screaming and cheering and hugging each other, crazed by what they had just witnessed. Aaron still had the ball tucked beneath his arm. They'd done it; they'd won the Super Bowl. As his teammates circled him, hitting him on the back and shoulders and lifting him in their arms, he pressed his hand to his helmet and let the tears come.

Because somewhere in heaven, a little boy named Lee was dancing with the angels and grinning down at his daddy. And in the trainer's room in the depths of the stadium, Derrick Anderson was grinning too. Because no matter who made the winning score, Derrick had done something a father was supposed to do.

He'd kept his promise.

Megan and Cory were exhausted and thrilled. They'd laughed and cried and hugged each other and everyone in Derrick's family during those first wild moments as the 49ers won the Super Bowl. Cory had been beside himself. "He did it, Megan!" he shouted over the chaos around them. "They won it all!"

The celebration had lasted long after the score and after the final seconds ticked off the clock. First, they'd waited as Coach Cameron accepted the Vince Lombardi Trophy, the one handed out each year to the winner of the Super Bowl, and now they watched while Aaron was awarded Most Valuable Player.

Someone handed him the microphone, and a teammate slapped a Super Bowl Champions baseball cap on his head. Aaron grinned, his face ten stories high on the JumboTron screen. "First I wanna thank God Almighty ... not so much for the win"—he looked at the trophy and chuckled—"though the win's pretty great. But I wanna thank Him for opening my eyes." He spoke another minute, thanking the fans and his teammates and the coaches. Then he put his hand on the smaller MVP award and raised the Super Bowl Trophy high in the air. "This one's for Lee."

Megan felt the slightest confusion. Then she remembered the conversation she'd had with Aaron early in the season, before their falling out. Lee was Derrick Anderson's son who had been killed in a car accident. Her eyes welled with tears again and her heart swelled with compassion for the man on the podium. A man who seemed at times like two different people—the one the world knew, and the one she alone had connected with.

Aaron was about to step down from the platform when it happened. He faced the crowd and looked in their general direction, then with his first two fingers, he waved. Megan brought her fingers to her lips.

"There it is!" Cory jumped as high as he could, pumping his fist in the air. He tapped the man next to him, shouting to be heard. "That was for us, did you see that? Aaron Hill waved like that just for us."

The man—decked in red and gold—gave him a mildly disapproving look and then returned to cheering for the 49ers. Cory didn't care. He turned to Megan and hugged her, and then he waved at the screen—as if Aaron could see them. The sounds around her—still loud and full—faded as Megan, too, set her attention on the big screen. As he waved once more with their secret signal, two things hit her. First, he was Cory's father and that wasn't going to change. It wouldn't happen overnight, but he would want Cory to live with him.

And second, maybe he really was in love with her.

As the celebration wound down and she and Cory finally arrived back at the hotel, Megan called the airlines and switched their flight to one leaving in a few hours. Though Aaron had hoped to meet up with them, she knew that would be impossible. He would be bombarded with TV and print interviews, and after all that, he would want to be with the team.

Aaron needed his space. Besides, she didn't want Cory around a horde of media, not with the DNA test results pending. Cory didn't really understand the reason for the blood test. She'd told him it was necessary and that it had to do with matching his blood with Aaron's.

"We don't need a test." Cory had been upset in the waiting room of the clinic, thinking he was being doubted again.

"I know, buddy. You look just like him." She patted his knee. "But the test might help other people believe."

But now, if it became public knowledge somehow, the scrutiny would be unbearable.

Megan waited until they were about to board their late-night flight before she texted Aaron. *Congratulations! We went home early, but we'll talk to you when you get home. Thanks for everything…*

Once she sent the message, she turned off her phone and rested her head against the window of the plane. Cory was tired, and he closed his eyes as soon as he was belted in beside her. The flight was full of fans headed home, most of them deliriously happy with the team's fifth championship. Megan watched them, and then turned her attention to the slight boy in blue jeans beside her. The DNA results would come this week. And so, while for every other 49ers fan the adventure had come to a wonderful, miraculous ending, the same couldn't be said for Cory. Whatever the test results, his adventure was hardly over. It had just begun.

She smiled to herself and once more she could feel Aaron's arms around her, his eyes melting into her own. She stared at the seat in front of her and allowed herself to imagine. Because if she could learn to trust Aaron Hill, maybe the adventure ahead wouldn't just be true for Cory.

But for both of them.

Thirty

Aaron paced from the kitchen to the front door of his house and back again. It was Wednesday and the results would arrive any time, that's what he'd been told. A courier service was supposed to bring by the sealed envelope just after three o'clock. He stared at the clock on the microwave: 3:10.

He took a glass from the cupboard and filled it with cool water. His headache was fading, but it wasn't entirely gone. He downed the glass and gazed out the window at his backyard. He wasn't worried about the results, but they mattered. Because once they were in hand, he knew what he wanted to do. What he had to do.

Even with the tension of waiting, he felt fantastic. He'd had time to think things through. During the media circus and yesterday's parade down the fan-lined streets of downtown San Francisco, he couldn't have been clearer about what he wanted next in his life.

Very simply, he was in love with Megan Gunn. Once he had the results, he had the rest of the afternoon and evening all planned out. Not just what he wanted to tell her, but where he wanted to take her. After all, he'd kept his part of the deal by winning the Super Bowl.

There was the rumble of an engine from the front of the house, and Aaron caught his breath. He spun around and darted to the front door. A yellow delivery truck was pulling into his driveway, heading up to the front door. Aaron watched it park, his heart pounding, every breath just the slightest drink of air. This was it … In a minute he'd know for sure that Cory was his son and then he could get on with the rest of his life.

He opened the door, signed for the package, thanked the driver, and shut the door behind him. His palms were sweaty as he clutched the cardboard mailer. He swallowed hard against his dry throat, and a lightheaded feeling came over him. Dazed and dizzy, he wandered into the kitchen and dropped onto the first barstool. He pulled the tab at the top of the envelope and then he stopped.

The blood rushed from his face and his stomach dropped. He set the cardboard container down and stared at it. Cory was his son; he could see it the moment he looked at the prom picture. Amy hadn't loved anyone but him all her life. That's what she'd told him in her letters, and Megan had verified the fact. Amy hadn't been with anyone but him…

But then, slowly, like an unavoidable car wreck happening right before his eyes, a possibility hit him. Amy had been raped. A week after she'd given in and slept with Aaron, she'd been attacked on the Pierce College campus. It was a detail he hadn't acknowledged over the past couple weeks, because it was too hard to accept. Somehow, it seemed his fault that she'd been alone that night, walking to her car. That if he'd been more supportive, more available, maybe she would've already been home, talking with him on the phone rather than working late at the library.

The idea was crazy, of course, and Aaron knew that in reality he couldn't have helped her that night. Either way, there was no point holding onto the truth that his special girl had been viciously attacked. Until now. He grabbed the slightest breath and considered the possible results that lay in the envelope. What if the precious boy who looked like him and longed for him had been fathered by a cowardly rapist? His heart pounded and his stomach twisted in knots. If that were the case, how could he ever tell the child the truth without destroying him? The boy would go from being the son of an NFL quarterback, to being the son of a twisted and depraved criminal. Aaron shuddered. He pictured Cory, the way the news would feel like a lie at first, impossible. If the results went that way, no matter how involved Aaron stayed in his life, eventually Cory would understand the reality of his situation. He would be the son of a rapist.

Anger choked Aaron, and his breathing came uneven and fast. He should've been there all along. If he wouldn't have turned her away, he would've been by her side when Cory was born and there never would've been a question, never a paternity test. He would've married Amy. He looked around at the luxury surrounding him, the granite counters and travertine tile floors. They would've lived here in this house, raising their son, and Amy would still be alive.

He picked up the cardboard mailer one more time. Slowly, like the first light at the crack of daybreak, an understanding dawned in his heart. The results were confidential, and he alone had received a copy. Weeks ago, he ordered the test and paid for it, and at the time, he figured Megan didn't need a copy. He would tell her the results as soon as he could see for himself, because of course Cory was his son.

Only what if that wasn't how it played out?

He stood and gripped the package, and he headed down the hall and into his office. With each step, he felt his fear lifting, dissipating, because he knew what he was going to do. He walked through the double doors of his office and toward the corner. There on the counter was a machine he used only once a month—when he had statements he didn't need, statements he didn't want anyone finding, to protect himself from identity theft, credit card theft.

Now, with a sense of right that consumed him and breathed new life into him, he took the contents from the mailer, and without looking at them, he stacked the two pages back-side up, neatly one on top of the other. Then he lifted them to the top of the machine and watched them dissolve through the mechanical teeth of the shredder.

And like that, it was over. He was Cory Briggs's father.

No matter what the test results said.

—

He found them at the youth center, where he'd known he would find them. He parked his truck, and already he heard the sound of a basketball pounding the old parquet floor. He strode through the entryway, on a mission like none other in his life. When he reached the gym, he leaned on the doorframe and watched them for a minute. Megan wore a sweatshirt and jeans and she had a whistle around her neck. She was officiating a pickup game that seemed to have no rules, and few boundaries.

After a minute or so, she spotted him. She'd been about to blow the whistle, but now she let it drop back into place. "Timeout," she shouted. Her voice echoed in the big old building. "Everyone, take five."

Cory noticed him then, but Megan stopped him from running over. She said something to him, and he nodded. But as he headed for the drinking fountain he grinned and waved at Aaron.

A lump formed in his throat as he waved back. Cory hadn't wanted the test in the first place. Aaron never should've pushed the point, but none of that mattered now.

Megan's eyes looked worried, and Aaron understood. She must've been more concerned about the results than she let on. She could vouch for Amy's lonely single life in the years she lived in San Francisco. But she hadn't known Amy back when Cory was conceived. A week ago, over a phone call, Megan had admitted that she was afraid for Cory. Afraid that he'd never recover if the results showed Aaron wasn't his dad.

Aaron stood straight and grinned. No worries now.

Megan reached him, her face slightly pale, lips parted. She searched his eyes. "You … you got the results?"

"I didn't need them." He wrapped his arms around Megan and held her, loving her. "He's my son, Megan. He's my boy."

"So … so the results didn't come?"

He wanted to lie to her, tell her that he'd read them and everything was just as he'd suspected. That Cory was his son, no question. But he was through lying. He put his hands gently on her shoulders and searched her heart, willing her to understand. "I didn't open them. I shredded them."

"But—"

He held a finger to her lips and dropped his voice to a tender whisper. "I don't need test results, Megan. Cory's my son." He turned his gaze to the boy. "He looks just like me."

She started to cry and she pressed her face against his shoulder. "Thank you … for not looking." Relief mixed with the emotion in her voice. "I wanted … I wanted him to be your son … so badly, Aaron. So badly."

"He is … it's okay." He stroked her back, and he had the sense something else was on her heart. That she wasn't entirely happy about the news. He eased away enough to see her eyes. "What else, Megan? What're you thinking?"

"I don't know." She looked down, and the color came back in her cheeks. "I love him too."

He wanted to tell her not to worry, that between the three of them, there was enough love to go around. But Cory was racing up to them. Aaron released Megan and turned to the boy. His boy. He held out his hands and swept him up in a hug that lasted a long time. When Cory was back on his feet, Aaron stooped down so they were eye level. "Remember the blood test?"

Cory looked confused for half a second. Aaron and Megan hadn't told him that the results were coming in today. He still didn't understand the significance of the test, other than its ability to match the two of them, once and for all. A worried look flashed in Cory's eyes. "I remember."

"We didn't need it after all." Aaron grinned. He kept his voice low, because the other kids weren't too far away. "You're my son, Cory ... just like you always thought."

Cory hesitated, and then he pumped his fists low at his waist. "Yes! I knew it! This is the best news in the whole world!"

For the slightest instant, Aaron imagined how differently this scene might've played out. He swallowed the possibility, stood, and exchanged a high-five with Cory. The boy peered over his shoulder and grinned at Megan, as if to say — in the most polite way — that he had certainly told her so. He'd told both of them. Then he flung his arms around Aaron's neck. "So what're we gonna do now?"

"That's why I'm here." He smiled at Megan. "I was thinking dinner at Pier 39."

"The Sea Lion Café?" Cory's eyes lit up. "That's a great idea!"

"Well," Aaron chuckled. "Not the café." He kicked the toe of his shoe lightly against hers. "Forbes Island. Because one of us made good on our deal. And now it's time for the other one to step up to the plate."

Megan raised her hands in mock surrender. "You're right."

"Cool!" Cory held up his pointer finger. "One sec ... I have to get my things."

When they were alone again, Megan's expression turned shy. "It's going to be a wild ride, isn't it?"

"It could be." He took hold of her hands and the feel of her fingers against his own melted his heart. "But ... we'd be crazy to miss it."

Megan smiled and her eyes danced. Because she clearly knew they weren't talking about the ferry ride over to Forbes Island, a trip that would last only a few minutes.

But about a ride that from tonight just might last forever.

THIRTY-ONE

M egan's heartbeat was anything but normal as Aaron helped her into the small cruise ship. Cory helped them decide that it would be better to eat at the Sea Lion Café where they had the best fish and chips in the world, and then take a boat ride around the bay. One that lasted an hour long.

As it turned out, most of the bay cruise lines were closed until April. The one that was open had a sunset cruise at five o'clock, so they saved dinner for afterward. The sun was splashing a waterfall of diamonds across the water as they boarded the three-story ship, and Megan fought hard against her fears. She wanted to conquer them, and that helped. They moved inside on the main deck and sat at a booth near the back along a row of windows. Megan gripped the tabletop and Cory giggled at her.

"We won't sink, Megan. Really." He kneeled on the seat so he could see out the window. "I always wanted to sail on the ocean at night."

"Oh yeah." She blew at a wisp of her hair and slumped against the back of her seat. "Me too. Always."

"Plus, if you think about it, you're not really afraid of the boat, right?"

"I always thought I was."

"Yeah, but without the boat you'd have to swim back."

"He has a point." Aaron took the spot on the bench beside her.

"Right." Cory giggled again. "So that means you're afraid of water. Only you drink water all the time, Megan. So you're not even afraid of that." He held up his hands as if he'd solved her problem.

Aaron hung his head and tried to hide his quiet laughter. He wore a UCLA baseball cap pulled low over his brow, because he'd told her he didn't want to be recognized. Not tonight. Not that there was much of a chance that would happen. The cruise was nearly empty, and most of the passengers appeared to be from a group of Russian-speaking foreigners.

Aaron picked up a brochure on the table and studied it. "Hmmm." His eyes shone as he looked at her. "Sunset's at 5:43."

"Great. So seventeen minutes of sailing under dark skies." Megan leaned her head back against the cool glass. "I might need help."

Under the table, Aaron reached for her hand. Always, he'd held her hand like a friend might, the way a father held the hand of his child. But this time, he worked his fingers slowly between hers and his eyes found the most anxious places in her heart. "I'll stay beside you the whole way."

"I won't." Cory grinned. He bounced a few times and pointed to the front of the deck. Where the bow of the boat came to a point, the ship was solid glass. Pillows had been placed on a carpeted area there, inviting guests to enjoy the cruise from a comfortable, secluded spot.

"Can I sit up there once we get moving?"

"Sure. You can go up there now if you want." Aaron settled against the back of the seat so that his shoulders were touching Megan's. "As long as we can see you, it's fine."

"Really?" Cory's eyes lit up. He was so full of life, so appreciative of the things he'd never had a chance to do before. "Okay"—he pointed again—"I'll be right there. You can watch me."

Megan tried to think of something to say, but she was completely consumed with the look in Aaron's eyes, the sensation of his fingers between hers. She forced herself to breathe out. "He's right, don't you think?"

Aaron hesitated. "About sitting at the bow?"

"About not sinking." She gave him a weak smile. "I can't believe I'm doing this."

For a moment, he looked concerned for her. "You don't have to." He glanced at the loading area. The doors were still open. "We can get off."

"No." Her answer was quick. Classical music clicked on just then and filled the boat with soothing sounds. With Aaron strong beside her, his fingers between hers, her fears were already easing. "I want to do this. You're with me, that makes me feel better."

"Right." He grinned. "That way, I can help you if we sink."

"Thanks." She allowed herself to melt into his arm a little more. "I might have to close my eyes."

"You better not." He ran his thumb along her hand. "You'll miss the sunset." Something in his eyes told her he wanted to say more, but he seemed to be holding back.

The engines moved into high gear, and one of the crew shut and locked the door. Whether she wanted to or not, there was no turning back now. As the thought crossed her mind, she wondered if that was true not only for the hour cruise, but for her and Aaron as well. There was no mistaking the look in his eyes, the gentle way he spoke to her, or the way he held her hand. He had feelings for her, and now that he was convinced he was Cory's father, a casual dating relationship would never work.

Because Cory belonged to both of them.

They would either need to move ahead as friends and nothing more, or they needed to consider jumping in. Otherwise, Cory would be confused, and that wasn't fair. He'd had enough confusion in his life already. She rested her head on his shoulder and stared out the window. She pictured the scene from earlier: Super Bowl MVP Aaron Hill walking into the Mission Youth Center and whisking them off for a cruise?

A part of her kept wondering when the director was going to yell cut.

"I never get tired of looking at the bay." His voice held a quiet joy. "Especially this time of night."

"It's beautiful." Megan sat up straighter and realized they were near a mostly glass door, one which led to a small deck that apparently wrapped around the main cabin. With so many windows, they could go outside and still have a clear view of Cory. Also, it was the only door that led out to the deck. So if Cory went outside, he'd have to come this way.

Aaron must've noticed at the same time, because he nodded toward the door. "Let's stand out there. Until we get too cold."

A shiver ran down her arms, but it had nothing to do with a chill in the air. The inside was plenty warm. No matter how tempting the idea, standing on the deck with Aaron seemed dangerous in a host of ways. Still, when he stood, she stood with him. Two other kids—a boy and a girl— were sitting by Cory now. They were dark skinned, from India maybe, and probably on vacation. Most locals would be home getting ready for school in the morning.

They slipped outside and Aaron paused. "Are you okay?"

She breathed in sharply through her nose and studied the water—so close she could feel the spray from the wake. In her imagination, this would be the most terrifying moment of all, standing outside on the deck of a boat, feeling the sway of the waves beneath her feet, knowing the water was only a few feet away. But something about the moment felt fresh and invigorating in a way she hadn't expected. "I am." She sounded as surprised as she felt.

There was a wooden bench down a little ways, and near it two heaters, warming the area for nights like this. Aaron led her to it. They sat and he slipped his arm around her. For a long time he said nothing. They were facing west off the rear of the boat, and the feel of the sun on their faces and the rhythm of the ocean was enough. But after a while he whispered near her ear. "Do you trust me, Megan?"

Her heart skipped a beat. She didn't want to seem nervous or startled, but she had to wonder. She turned slightly so she could see his eyes, and there, without a doubt, lay the answer. "You're not talking about the boat."

"No." He moved his hand off her shoulder and brought it to the side of her face. "I missed you ... not seeing you."

She wanted to talk, but she couldn't catch her breath. If he was going to kiss her, she wouldn't stop him. Whatever that said about her. "Aaron ..."

With his hand still sheltering her face, guarding against even Cory seeing what he was about to do, he leaned in closer and lightly touched his lips to hers. The kiss started slowly, marked by innocence and uncertainty. But it ignited a smoldering fire for both of them, because instead of coming up for air, the kiss grew deeper, slow and passionate.

When they drew away, there was breathless desire in both their expressions. Megan allowed herself to get lost in his eyes, swept away by the moment. "I can say one thing." She brushed her nose against his and he pulled her into his embrace. She kept her voice low and near his ear. "You made me forget the boat."

He nuzzled his face against hers. "You need the boat, remember?" He kissed her again, smoother, slower still. "I made you forget the water."

"Mmmm." She kissed him this time. "Whatever." She felt herself falling, getting lost in his embrace and his touch. And suddenly she wanted to know why ... why they were doing this and what it meant and what about the actresses that waited in the wings. She slid a few inches from him and searched his face. Her cheeks were hot, and suddenly the heaters were overkill. The occasional cold breeze from the ocean felt good. "What ... " She held her hair to keep it from blocking her view of him. "What're we doing, Aaron?" She looked over her shoulder at Cory, still sitting facing the windows at the other end of the boat. Then her eyes found his again. "What's happening?"

She hadn't wanted to be catty or jealous. It had never been any of her business until now. She gripped the bench seat. *God, give me the words . . .* "What about the actress?"

At first he looked baffled by her question, but then his expression changed and sorrow darkened his eyes. "That was my agent. I told you." He ran his thumb along her cheekbone. "I fired him last week."

Megan's heartbeat jumped around again, and this time it had nothing to do with the boat or the water. With Bill Bond out of Aaron's life, the future was that much more possible. "Really?"

"I don't want an actress, Megan." He worked his fingertips up into her hair, and the sadness in his eyes grew stronger. "That's why you stopped seeing me . . . right?"

"It is. I didn't want to keep you from someone . . . someone more your type." She should feel guilty for dismissing him so quickly that day at the park. She'd missed him every day since. But she couldn't, not when she was consumed with joy here beside him. Those days were gone. She brought her hand to his face, his rugged jawline. "I'm glad you don't want an actress."

The sun was setting, sinking into the water, and the reflection on the bay was stunning. Together they went in and checked on Cory, chatting with him and his new friends for a few minutes. When they went back outside, the sun had dropped below the horizon, and the sky was washed in pink. They found their places and kissed again, and then Aaron stood and looked down at her, smiling. She watched him, wondering. Maybe he was too cold and he wanted to go in where it was—

Slowly, Aaron dropped to one knee and held his hands out to her.

She started to shiver, but she took his fingers. What was he doing, and why did it feel like it was all happening in slow motion? "Aaron . . ."

"I love you, Megan Gunn." His words mixed with the sound of the wind and water, but they were clear and thought out. "I love the way you know who you are and how you don't need material wealth to be happy, and I love your dedication." He wasn't in a hurry. "I love your passion for foster kids, for changing the system." His eyes shone a little brighter. "I even talked to Derrick and Jay Ryder about putting something together to present to the governor . . . or to Congress. You could help us."

She held his hands a little tighter. His words spoke deeply to her because they proved that ages ago she had become more than a conquest. He didn't love her for her looks or because she was needy. She realized even now with Aaron declaring his love to her, she looked more like a college co-ed than the sort of woman the public would expect to see with a celebrity quarterback.

He wasn't finished. "I love everything about you, and maybe most of all, I love that you're my son's mother."

She felt her eyes begin to dance. She wanted to hug him, to let him know that she believed him and trusted him and that she didn't ever want him to leave. But she needed to hear him out. So she only gave him a slight grin. "*Foster* mother."

A dampness filled his eyes, but he never broke contact with hers. He reached into his pocket and pulled out a small velvet box. "Not if you marry me."

She brought her fingers to her lips and her soft gasp died on the wind. The air was getting colder, but she wasn't shivering like before. She was too shocked.

He opened the box, and a stunning solitaire diamond ring lay neatly inside. It wasn't overly large, but simple and understated. Like her. "Marry me ... be a family with Cory and me. Please, Megan."

She looked from the ring back to him, and there were tears in both their eyes. *God, is this really happening?*

My daughter, I know the plans I have for you ... to give you hope and a future ...

The verse spoke tenderly to her soul. It was one that hung on the wall in the youth center. Megan believed the promise with all her heart, but a long time ago she'd come to believe that God might not mean good plans here, on earth. Maybe the good plans were more like heaven, and that was great too. A hope and a future didn't have to mean the same exact plans a person might dream for themselves.

Aaron was watching her, waiting. He laughed, his eyes wide with a nervousness that was uncommon for him. "If ... if you need more time you can get back to me."

She stood and he did the same, facing her. Through her tears, she felt herself surrounded by a feeling she'd never known before, a feeling she'd run from whenever she thought it might be catching her. Especially where Aaron was concerned. But now, in the waning light, with the cruise ship making its way back to the dock, she framed his face with her hands and looked deep into his eyes, to the places of his heart and soul that she understood now belonged only to her. "Yes, Aaron Hill. I'll marry you and be a family with you." She tilted her head back and her laughter rang out in the air. She was crying as hard as she was laughing.

He caught her hand and he shook as he slid the ring onto her finger. It fit perfectly. "It's gorgeous."

"It reminded me of you that way." He eased his arms around her waist. "You're beautiful, Megan." He brushed his cheek against hers. "I about died when you stopped seeing me. I couldn't quit thinking about you."

"Me too." She leaned up and kissed him the way she'd wanted to earlier. Not sitting side by side, but like this, wrapped in his embrace. When they drew back, she smiled and it became a full-hearted laugh. "I can't believe this."

He caught the back of her head and brought her close to him again. His lips touched hers once more and he breathed against her. "Believe it. I'm never letting you go. Not again."

Just then Cory came running out. "I made a new friend from India and his name's—" He came to a sudden stop and seemed to notice the way Megan and Aaron were standing, face-to-face, their arms around each other. He giggled. "What's going on out here?"

"Well…" Megan turned so they were both facing Cory. She kept her arm around Aaron's waist, and he kept his around her. They exchanged a quick look, and then Megan showed her ring to the boy. "Aaron asked me to marry him."

"What!" Cory hadn't ever looked so surprised. "Really?" He turned to Aaron. "You did that?"

"I did." Aaron put his hand on Cory's shoulder. "I figured since I'm already your dad, and since she's your mom, it seemed only right that we should get married." He winked at her. "Because she's pretty terrific and because that way you can be with both of us at the same time."

Cory sucked in a fast breath, his eyes wide with excitement and thrill and shock. "Like a family!"

"Yes, son." Aaron looked like he savored the chance to say the word. "Like a family."

That's when so much about the day and the night came together for Megan. *I'm not afraid anymore, God. I'm here on a boat and I'm not afraid.*

Ah, my daughter, there is no fear in love. But perfect love drives out fear...

This time she almost had to sit down, so she clung more tightly to Aaron. Because God had rarely spoken so clearly to her. His quiet whispers reminded her of a verse she'd read after telling Aaron goodbye back in September. Perfect love drives out fear. She pressed in close to Aaron, and when the boat docked, the three of them walked off holding hands.

Megan wasn't afraid of boats anymore, at least not if she was with Aaron. And she wasn't afraid about how she would share Cory. She wasn't afraid to love, and she wasn't afraid to trust. As they headed for the Sea Lion Café, the reason was as clear as the night sky above them. She wasn't afraid anymore because the unfamiliar feeling that had come over her when she was with Aaron on the back deck of the boat wasn't passion or nervousness or uncertainty.

It was love, a love strong enough to drive away any sort of fear. A love only God could've given her.

Deep, profound ... and perfect.

⇀

Derrick was watching a Bill Cosby rerun in the TV room, with Denae and the kids gathered around him. They'd spent more time together than usual this week, catching up on the stories Derrick had from the Super Bowl.

Already he and Denae had planned a trip to Chicago, to the cemetery where Lee was buried. Derrick was on crutches, but he wanted to make the trip anyway. He and Denae would bring a photograph and tape it to the edge of the boy's tombstone.

The photo wouldn't be of the ring he'd just won, because that ring would take months to come in, so he'd take a photo of one of his other Super Bowl rings. That way he didn't have to wait.

Lee wasn't really in the ground at that faraway Chicago cemetery. But the baby he'd cradled and held, the one he'd swung up onto his shoulders—that body was in the grave. And so if he had to go to a place to make good on his promise, he would go to the cemetery.

On the television, Cosby said something funny about chocolate cake, and the rest of the family burst out laughing.

"Daddy," Libby whined at him. "You're not paying attention."

"Sorry, baby." He let the images in his mind fade. "I was drifting."

Derrick had his knee in a full brace, elevated. Surgery was coming at the end of the week, but the doctor had said the ligament tear was clean. A full recovery was possible. He wasn't too worried about it. As long as he could play catch with his kids and keep up with the boys when he coached. The episode was just ending at 8:30 when the phone rang. He picked it up from the arm table next to the sofa. "Hello?"

"Anderson … what are you doing?" There was the sound of wind or waves in the background.

"Hill … is that you?"

"It is." Aaron laughed. "What are you doing?"

"Watching Cosby. What else?"

"No you're not!" The familiar teasing rang in Aaron's tone. "Without me?"

"Just this once." Derrick chuckled. "That why you called? To ask me what I was doing?"

"No, something even more important." The noise in the background made it hard to hear. "I asked Megan to marry me, and you won't believe it! She said yes!"

Even with the noise, Derrick heard that. He leaned his head back against the couch and felt his friend's happiness to the core of his being. "I'm proud of you, man. First you talk to God, and now to Megan. We'll be talking to the president before you know it. Fixing things for those foster kids. You and me and Jay."

"And Megan. She's in too." He chuckled. "Hey, Anderson … be my best man, will you?"

"I already am. That's why you won the MVP, 'cause you finally started listening to me."

Derrick teased so he wouldn't let his emotions get the upper hand. There would be time for that later, when he pondered all the season had wrought. For now, he wanted to celebrate with his friend. "But sure, Hill. I'll say yes and make it official."

They laughed some more and the call ended half a minute later. Aaron had to go. He was finishing up dinner with Megan and Cory, bonding with his new family.

"Tell me that wasn't Aaron Hill?" Denae sat beside him. She kept her voice low so the kids could hear the beginning of the next episode of Cosby.

"Yeah, baby." He grinned at his wife, at the woman who had stood by him and prayed with him not only for the season, but for Aaron as well. "Talking about getting married and asking me to be the best man. Can you believe it?"

She'd looked like she was listening to Derrick's side of the conversation, and now her eyes shone. "Now, don't that just beat all?"

By then they both knew the story of the boy, and how he was the son of Aaron's high school girlfriend. The miracles of the past season were so much more complex than either of them could've dreamed. They'd won the Super Bowl, yes, and Coach Cameron was offered a five-year extension on his contract. But more than any of that, Derrick had made a friend. One he'd get the chance to tease and pick on and hang around with not just here in San Francisco, but for all eternity.

And that, by far, was the greatest miracle of all.

Epilogue

Cory looked at himself in the mirror and straightened his tie. It didn't look right, but that was okay. His dad would fix it for him before the wedding started. He lifted his chin and grinned at himself. He was the ring bearer, and that was a great job for a wedding. It wasn't too hard and there wasn't a lot of stuff to remember.

"Mom! Should I put my shoes on now?" He still smiled when he called her Mom. It sounded funny and good, but he was getting more used to it. Not that she would ever take the place of his first mom. But his first mom was in heaven, and Megan was here. He had a lot of years left to need a mom, so he was glad. Plus, he loved Megan.

"Yes, Cory," she called to him from her room. "We leave in five minutes. Definitely put your shoes on."

Megan was wearing regular clothes to Derrick's church that morning. The place had something called a bridal room, so Megan was getting dressed nice there. Which was good, because Cory didn't think her big white dress would fit in the Town Car.

They met near the door and Megan was practically glowing. Cory lifted his eyebrows. "Wow ... you look beautiful."

"Thanks." She smiled and adjusted her veil. Megan already had a girl over to the apartment that morning who curled her hair more perfect than ever before, and then she attached the veil. Now whenever Megan turned her head, the veil flew along behind her. It made her look like an angel.

Which Derrick said she was when they were together last Sunday at church. Megan had changed her mind about church, because she and Cory's dad and Derrick had a talk, and now everyone understood. Church was someplace where they could all come together and figure things out.

Sort of like a team huddle.

Once they reached the Andersons' church, everything happened fast. His dad found him and helped him straighten his tie. And they talked a little while about this being a day they would never forget. Cory knew that was true for him maybe most of all. Lots of people got married, but how many foster kids wound up with a mom and a dad all in one day?

The wedding started right on time, and the church was full of people. Lots of guys from the 49ers and people from the youth center too. When Cory reached the front, he stood next to his dad, and his dad put his arm around Cory's shoulders. Then they waited and special music started.

And nice and slow-like, here came Megan. She definitely looked like an angel now, and the whole crowd of people stood up and watched her walk down the aisle. Derrick was beside her, 'cause Megan didn't have a dad, and no dad ever showed up in her life the way Cory's dad did. So Derrick did the job.

Cory watched it all—the walking part and the part where Derrick let Megan go. He watched the part where his mom and dad said words to each other, promises about health and time and standing by each other forever.

Finally they said the "I do" part, which was the best part of all. Because his dad had said that after that, him and Megan were married for good. Sort of the happily ever after part. As that happened, as his mom and dad and him became an official family, Cory thought of something he hadn't before. It made his eyes sting, and he had to wipe away a little wetness on his cheeks.

'Cause his first mom had prayed so hard for Cory to find his dad. But Cory wasn't sure if his mom would've wanted Megan to marry his dad. That was something his first mom had wanted to do, Cory was pretty sure. That's why the tears were on his face. But all of a sudden he could see his mother again, see her the way she'd looked before she got sick, the way she must look now—in heaven—smiling and laughing and loving him with all her heart. And what he saw made him happier than he'd been all day.

Because somewhere up in heaven, his first mom wasn't sad at all. She was smiling. The way he and his new family all were.

The gushy kiss came next, and a whole lot of pictures. On the ride to the reception, Cory thought about the next week. He was staying with Derrick's family while his parents went on a honeymoon to Hawaii. A week wasn't very long, and it was good for his dad to have some time alone with Megan. Cory already had her for the last two years, so it was okay for his dad to have some time with her.

Plus, he liked Derrick's family, and Derrick best of all. Cory and his mom and dad spent a lot of time visiting at Derrick's house because it was the off-season. April. And that meant his dad had just short workouts each day until summer camp. Last week, Derrick talked some more with Cory's dad and Megan about church. He told them church is just a bunch of people who know they messed up. Also, it was easy to feel close to God at church. Sometimes that feeling could carry over on the other days, which would help. And Cory's dad said he understood, because life didn't happen only at church.

It happened between Sundays.

A NOTE FROM KAREN

Dear Reader Friends,

What an adventure, writing a book set in the NFL! All my experience as a former sports writer came rushing back as I tried my best to set this story in the very real world of professional football, while creating characters that were completely fictional. Lots of details—you may have noticed—were accurate: the names and locations of teams and stadiums, the schedule as it relates to this football season, and some of the rituals that go along with the game.

On the journey to writing this novel, I enjoyed getting to know San Francisco 49ers quarterback Alex Smith. We first met, many of you know, when our family attended a game in San Francisco as Alex's guests. We visited with his parents—Pam and Doug, and his fantastic sisters and brother. All of them, we learned, were excited not just about what Alex does on the field, but off the field. Between Sundays. His passion for helping foster kids sparked in me the idea to write *Between Sundays*, and he graciously agreed to help me have an inside look at the NFL and the positive things some players do with their time away from the game. Alex has an amazing family, a family full of love and hope and wisdom and guidance.

That's where this story really hit me, the importance of having a family. It was something Megan Gunn understood—whether it was just her and Cory forever or whether God helped her drop the walls around her heart so she could love someone like Aaron Hill. At our house, we see the benefit of family every single day. We laugh and love and listen to each other, and when disagreements come up, we talk about how right here—around the dinner table—are the best friends of all. The people who will love us no matter what. But the truth is, sometimes we can't love even our families until we let God clean out the garbage in our own hearts.

I'll let you in on a secret. At first I was going to have the test results show that Aaron wasn't really Cory's biological father. He was going to shred the results and keep the truth a secret forever. But my editors and I agreed that the new Aaron wouldn't have wanted to keep something like that a secret. Just so you know, in the process of changing this part of the story, I decided something else. Aaron really was, in fact, Cory's dad. There. Now you don't have to wonder.

I pray that as you read this book, you saw a little of what Megan saw about foster kids, a little of what Aaron saw about God's grace. And a little of what Derrick understood about miracles and the importance of keeping a promise—whenever possible. Life really is about how we live it between Sundays. I know I'll remember that a little more carefully after writing this book.

As always, please stop by my website at www.KarenKingsbury.com and leave me a comment on my guestbook. I love to hear your thoughts, and I'd especially like to know how this story touched your heart. At my website, you can also leave photos of your military loved ones so that people around the world can pray for them. In addition, you can leave a prayer request, or stop by and pray for the needs of others. Finally, pass this book on to someone you know, someone who hasn't read one of my books. As you do, enter my ongoing Share-A-Book contest. Winners are picked every spring. Details are on my website.

I pray that God holds you and yours close, and that you'll feel His touch a little more in the days to come. Until next time ...

In His light and love,
Karen Kingsbury

Reader Study Guide

1. How did fame and sudden wealth at a young age change Aaron Hill? Was it his fault or the fault of his agent, Bill Bond? Explain.

2. In what ways were Megan Gunn and Amy Briggs alike? Talk about their similarities and their differences.

3. Where did Megan find the strength to take on responsibility for Cory after Amy's death? Discuss Megan's faith through most of this novel.

4. Cory had a firm belief that Aaron was his father. Compare Cory's adamant belief to something a child in your world believes.

5. Discuss what it means to have a child's faith.

6. What do you know about the foster care system? Talk about your experience with this system.

7. Did you learn anything about the plight of foster children? How can you be part of the solution for these kids?

8. Bill Bond was a manipulative man. What motivated him to control Aaron Hill? Discuss our nation's fascination with celebrity.

9. Derrick was a strong presence of faith in *Between Sundays*. Talk about Derrick's faith, and how it impacted the people around him.

10. What tragedy did Derrick carry with him? How did it affect his faith?

11. How has tragedy affected your faith? Is it possible to have difficult times and still believe in God? Talk about this.

12. Talk about Derrick's marriage to Denae. What were signs that their marriage was a deep and wonderful one?

13. How important is humor to a successful relationship—friendship or marriage?

14. One of the people Derrick affected was young quarterback Jay Ryder. How important is it that people of faith also act as mentors for those around them? Give an example from your life.

15. Megan Gunn had a difficult time trusting people. Why do you think that was?

16. Have you ever had a hard time trusting someone? How did you resolve that situation?

17. Aaron wished for a chance to apologize to Amy. When he learned of her death, he knew it was too late. Are there people you need to apologize to? What is stopping you?

18. How would you define wealth? During most of the story, who was richer—Megan or Aaron? Explain your answer.

19. What did you think of Aaron's decision to shred the DNA test results? Explain why the role of mom or dad can't always be defined through a biological connection. Give examples.

20. Aaron Hill asked God to clear his heart of the garbage that had piled up. Talk about a time when you or someone you know reached that point with God.

Even Now
Karen Kingsbury

Sometimes hope for the future is found in the ashes of yesterday.

A young woman seeking answers to her heart's deepest questions. A man and woman separated by lies and years of separation...who have never forgotten each other.

With hallmark tenderness and power, Karen Kingsbury weaves a tapestry of lives, losses, love, and faith—and the miracle of resurrection.

Unabridged Audio CD: 0-310-25404-3
Softcover: 0-310-24753-5

Ever After
Karen Kingsbury

2007 Christian Book of the Year

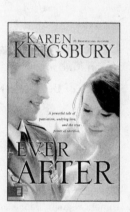

Two couples torn apart—one by war between countries, and one by a war within.

In this moving sequel to *Even Now*, Emily Anderson, now twenty, meets the man who changes everything for her: Army reservist Justin Baker. Their tender relationship, founded on a mutual faith in God and nurtured by their trust and love for each other, proves to be a shining inspiration to everyone they know, especially Emily's reunited birth parents.

But Lauren and Shane still struggle to move past their opposing beliefs about war, politics, and faith. When tragedy strikes, can they set aside their opposing views so that love—God's love—might win, no matter how great the odds?

Unabridged Audio CD: 0-310-25405-1
Softcover: 0-310-24756-X

Pick up a copy today at your favorite bookstore!

ZONDERVAN®
.com

One Tuesday Morning
Karen Kingsbury

The last thing Jake Bryan knew was the roar of the World Trade Center collapsing on top of him and his fellow firefighters. The man in the hospital bed remembers nothing. Not rushing with his teammates up the stairway of the south tower to help trapped victims. Not being blasted from the building. And not the woman sitting by his bedside who says she is his wife.

Jamie Bryan will do anything to help her beloved husband regain his memory. But that means helping Jake rediscover the one thing Jamie has never shared with him: his deep faith in God.

Softcover: 0-310-24752-7

Beyond Tuesday Morning
Karen Kingsbury

Winner of the Silver Medallion Book Award

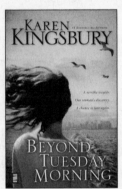

Determined to find meaning in her grief three years after the terrorist attacks on New York City, FDNY widow Jamie Bryan pours her life into volunteer work at a small memorial chapel across from where the Twin Towers once stood. There, unsure and feeling somehow guilty, Jamie opens herself to the possibility of love again.

But, in the face of a staggering revelation, only the persistence of a tenacious man, the questions from Jamie's curious young daughter, and the words from her dead husband's journal can move Jamie beyond one Tuesday morning ... toward life.

Softcover: 0-310-25771-9

Pick up a copy today at your favorite bookstore!

Let's Go on a Mommy Date
#1 Bestselling Author
Karen Kingsbury

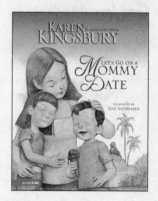

So, what is a Mommy Date?

This playful, rhyming story describes some of the best—the zoo, circus, park, animal farm, or movie theatre. But in the end, spending time together is what a mommy date is all about—whether it's a fun outing or simply snuggling down to read about such adventures together!

Jacketed Hardcover: 0-310-71214-9

Don't Sit on the Sidelines
Get Involved!

Did you know our society spends billions of dollars on foster children, only to abandon these kids when they're on the verge of becoming adults? It's like dropping the ball at the goal line.

Within two years of leaving the foster care system:
- 50% of foster teens end up unemployed
- One-third require public assistance
- Nearly one-third become homeless
- 25% become incarcerated
- Less than one in 10 attend college
- And only one in 100 actually graduate

Source: Children's Law Center of Los Angeles

At the Alex Smith Foundation, we don't believe in sitting along the sidelines, watching foster children fail. Our mission is to help foster teens transition to become successful adults.

The Guardian Scholars program is a comprehensive program for foster youth who will experience significant hardships in their efforts to gain a college education. These youth are forced to make difficult transitions into adulthood, often without traditional family support. By providing five-year scholarships, year-round housing and extensive individual guidance and support, the Guardian Scholars program provides the opportunity for individuals to change their lives, realize true independence, and reach their full potential. The foundation provides opportunity for high school sophomores and juniors to experience post-secondary education and encourage students to apply newly learned skills in local community-based organizations.

Your contributions can help.

For more information contact the foundation at:
619.980.3469 or online at www.AlexSmithFoundation.org

The Alex Smith Foundation

FORWARD PROGRESS FOR FOSTER TEENS IN TRANSITION

Three ways to keep up on your favorite Zondervan books and authors

Sign up for our *Fiction E-Newsletter*. Every month you'll receive sample excerpts from our books, sneak peeks at upcoming books, and chances to win free books autographed by the author.

You can also sign up for our *Breakfast Club*. Every morning in your email, you'll receive a five-minute snippet from a fiction or nonfiction book. A new book will be featured each week, and by the end of the week you will have sampled two to three chapters of the book.

Zondervan *Author Tracker* is the best way to be notified whenever your favorite Zondervan authors write new books, go on tour, or want to tell you about what's happening in their lives.

Visit *www.zondervan.com* and sign up today!

About the Author

KAREN KINGSBURY is America's favorite inspirational novelist with six million books in print. Her Life-Changing Fiction™ has produced multiple bestsellers including *Even Now*, *One Tuesday Morning*, *Beyond Tuesday Morning*, and the popular Redemption series. Her most recent release, *Ever After*, was named the 2007 Christian Book of the Year. She lives in Washington state with her husband, Don, and their six children.